D0334009

THE BISCUIT
FACTORY GIRLS

Elsie Mason

ORION

An Orion paperback

First published in Great Britain in 2020 by Orion Fiction
This paperback edition published in 2020
by Orion Fiction,
an imprint of The Orion Publishing Group Ltd,
Carmelite House, 50 Victoria Embankment
London EC4Y 0DZ

An Hachette UK company

1 3 5 7 9 10 8 6 4 2

Copyright © Paul Magrs 2020

The moral right of Paul Magrs to be identified as the author
of this work has been asserted in accordance with
the Copyright, Designs and Patents Act 1988.

All rights reserved. No part of this publication may be
reproduced, stored in a retrieval system, or transmitted,
in any form or by any means, electronic, mechanical,
photocopying, recording or otherwise, without the prior
permission of the copyright owner.

All the characters in this book are fictitious,
and any resemblance to actual persons, living
or dead, is purely coincidental.

A CIP catalogue record for this book
is available from the British Library.

ISBN (Mass Market Paperback) 978 1 4091 9646 4

Typeset by Born Group
Printed and bound in Great Britain by Clays Ltd, Elcograf S.p.A.

www.orionbooks.co.uk

For my mother, Joy, and my grandmother,
Gladys. With all my love.

Chapter One

Two days married and they were at war already.

Tom was in his uniform beside her. Irene was used to the scratchy feel of it as they sat pressed close to each other on the train. He had his cap in his hands. Their bags were stowed on the racks above them and they sat together quietly as the train rattled on.

The newly-weds were heading north and they weren't talking to each other.

Irene watched the others who shared their compartment. She liked the way they looked at her handsome husband. They nodded respectfully, taking note of his rank. They looked at her, too. Who was she? They were obviously a couple. The smart airman and his new bride. They hadn't said a word to each other for an hour.

When, for a few minutes, they had the carriage to themselves, Tom spoke up. 'I still think it's stupid, that's all.'

'Stupid!' she gasped.

'It's dangerous. It stands to reason that it's more dangerous to be living on Tyneside than in the wilds of Norfolk. You'd be much better off staying with your own family.'

Irene pursed her lips. 'I'm not going back and living there with my lot. I'm a married woman now. I've had enough of living at home. I'm sick of them all.'

'You'll not say that after you've lived with my family for a few days,' he promised.

'I can't go back and live in our village,' she insisted. 'I belong with you.'

'I won't even be there!' he said, getting exasperated now. 'In another three days I'll be back in Lincoln. I'll be back at the airbase. I won't even be at my mam's house for very long.'

Irene was dead-set. There was no way she was going back to Hunworth, her tiny village in Norfolk. She'd had eighteen years there already. All her life so far. Nothing ever happened there. They barely had electricity. It was like being back in the times of Queen Victoria.

'You've told me so much about your family and your town. I want to see South Shields for myself!'

He'd filled her head with pictures of the seaside and the ice cream parlour and beautiful Marine Park with the bandstand where there were dances on summer nights. He made his home town sound marvellous. Life down by the docks where his family lived seemed hectic and bustling. Irene felt like it was time that she lived somewhere busy, and saw a bit of life for herself.

'You won't like it,' he said sternly. 'I wish you'd listen to me. My family . . . well. They're a funny lot. And they're all crammed into this tiny little house on Frederick Street.'

'I'm used to living with a big family.' Irene had six sisters and they'd shared a room together all their lives. It was the claustrophobia of her own sisters and her overbearing ma that she was running away from. Anywhere would seem like a palace compared with her family's cottage on the village green. Even a cramped terraced house by the docks.

But her new husband thought she was being foolish. He sat there looking cross as their carriage filled up with new passengers, and they were forced to be quiet again. They weren't about

2

to have a row in front of strangers. Irene felt herself going redder and redder with pent-up emotion. She was dying to yell at him, and make her feelings plain.

Three months since they had first met, at a dance for airmen and Land Girls, and they hadn't had a cross word yet. Not until now. Not until the slow train journey north. Now all the tensions were coming out. She cast a sideways glance at Tom and he was staring straight ahead. He looked just as handsome as he always did, but wasn't there a stubborn look about him? A truculent expression in his round face that she hadn't noticed before?

Irene sighed. Well, he could complain all he wanted. They were travelling north now. She was going to meet all his family and she was going to live with them. She was one of them now, and they were just going to have to lump it.

She pulled her cardigan over her short-sleeved dress. Her going-away clothes were brand new. They were special and unfamiliar. She hadn't had anything new for almost a year. This was an occasion and she felt proud of wearing the dress. It was all warm, autumnal colours. Amber and red. It was from the fancy shop in Holt. She winced at the expense and all the coupons it took.

Then the noise of the engine was changing and the wheels underneath were shrieking. The other passengers were stirring, reaching for bags. Tom nodded at her, without smiling. 'York station,' he said. 'We change here.'

She took down her own bags, and refused to let him help her. They clambered down onto the steamy, noisy platform and the crowd felt overwhelming. She drew closer to Tom as he elbowed his way through the mass of people. Irene really wished they hadn't rowed. He was the last person she wanted to be arguing with. He only had a short few days of honeymoon leave and it felt like they were wasting precious hours.

In amongst the kerfuffle and steam and shouting and all the people shoving about on the platform with their cases and bags suddenly Tom was standing stock still. He was frozen for a moment on the busy platform like he was having a seizure.

Irene followed his stare and she saw the newspaperman with heaps of the evening edition. Headlines emblazoned on his boards. She could hardly make sense of the words. Tom was darting forward to grab him and ask what was going on. He was practically shaking the little man until his teeth rattled in his head.

The truth was soon told.

Tyneside had been bombed. The Luftwaffe had come out of nowhere, seizing their chance. Last night they had roared over the North Sea and into the mouth of the Tyne. They had raged and stormed over the docks, raining destruction on the heads of all who lived there. Many, many were dead.

'They say the docks are hardest hit,' Tom told her. 'And the streets closest to the shipyards. That's what Jerry was after. Putting the shipbuilding out of action. And now they've done it. Last night and in the early hours of this morning. They reckon that whole streets are still in flames . . .'

'Oh, God,' Irene said. 'What about your street, Tom? What about the street where your family live?'

He was scanning down the columns of print and all the words were blurring. 'It doesn't say exactly where's been hit. They don't have all the details . . .'

Irene bit her lip and grasped hold of his arm. 'I'm sure they're all right . . .' How stupid and futile her words sounded, though.

He lashed out. 'And that's where you want to live! Right where they're dropping bloody bombs.' He folded up the paper savagely and picked up his bags again. 'There might not even be a house for you to move into now. They might all have been blown sky-high!'

She gasped at his callousness. 'Eeeh, don't say that . . .'

'We don't know though, do we?' he burst out. 'We don't know what's happened to them!'

Then he was off, pushing through the crowd to their next platform and their connecting train. Feeling hopeless, there was nothing Irene could do but follow him.

Now they were on another train, rushing through the night. Pushing through the Vale of Yorkshire and the hills of County Durham. Everyone aboard had heard the news about Tyneside and a weight of dread lay on them all. The whispers were rushing through the carriages.

Dark fields went rolling by beyond the windows. The lights were low for the blackout and Irene was having awful misgivings. Here she was on her way to a place she'd never been, with a man she'd only known for three months and who she'd been married to for less than a week. She'd insisted she wanted to move north, and she'd even caused a row between them over the whole business. And now this. The whole town up in flames, probably. She felt foolish and selfish, and he was so worried about his family right now that she couldn't even find a way to say she was sorry.

She was further away from home than she'd ever been in all her eighteen years. She was rushing towards a place she'd only heard of in his stories. And now she was hearing it was a place of fire and death and terror. What on earth was she rushing into?

Then Tom surprised her. He squeezed her hand so tightly she could feel the little bones inside clicking. He was trying to reassure her. Even though he must be eaten up inside, and worried sick about his beloved ma and his three brothers and everyone else who lived on Frederick Street, he was still thinking about Irene. He was concerned about how his new young bride must feel. For that, she loved him even more than ever.

But still she berated herself – secretly – for being the kind of girl who dashed into things.

Look how deep she had got herself.

Coming all this way. It was all her idea.

Irene had no one to blame but herself.

All of a sudden they were arriving in the north.

Irene wanted to protest and say, 'Wait . . . what? Already?'

Even though the journey had been immense and it had seemed to fill up days with its arduous rhythm, now she didn't feel at all prepared. But Tom was on his feet and fetching down their cases from the overhead racks. He moved with the smooth, strong ease of someone used to drill, to routine.

He explained to her that they would have to cross Newcastle station and catch yet another, smaller train. 'But it's not a long trip. Just to South Shields. Just to the coast.'

So there was another leg to the journey. They weren't quite there yet. When they crossed the great iron bridge that spanned the Tyne, Tom touched the blind covering the window and it rolled up with a snap and she gasped at the view.

The river was dark and ominous. She caught an impression of a vast sky and a body of slow, dark water. There were tall buildings massed in huddles by the docks. She had trouble making sense of it, because night had fallen and everything was shrouded for the blackout. Of course, only last night this place was under bombardment by the Luftwaffe. It was a place that had been visited by a ghastly spectre.

Tom's face was still tight with fear. It was even worse now that he could actually see the Tyne and know that he was so close to home and finding out what had become of his people. He was urging this rattletrap train to go faster and faster, bearing them over the tall bridge and then into the vaulted station. He was urging them on and dragging their cases impatiently into the small corridor that ran the length of the train. He wanted to be first off and he wanted all the terrible news as fast as he could get it.

Irene followed him to wait in the side passage as the train approached Newcastle. Her own limbs felt heavy with dread.

The platforms of Newcastle and the carriages of the smaller train they boarded to carry them to the coast were full of whispers and then panicky shouts as the news filtered through.

It was such a clear night. Not a scrap of cloud and the moon was high and bright. Of course, that made it a dangerous night.

The bombers were back. They had come back for a second night over Tyneside.

Tom grasped Irene's hand as the train trundled along. The sky flared with hot orange and purple streaks. Flashes came two, three, four times in quick succession. The noise came rolling a few seconds after, drowning out even the screeching of the engines.

'Where are they? Where's it happening?' voices were crying out in the train as the lights flickered and dimmed. It made for a hellish journey through the night.

Irene knew better than to shout and scream, even when the sky lit up like daylight and dark spiky silhouettes could be seen on the horizon. She knew better than to make a fuss and to be a burden to Tom. He was already in bits, sitting helplessly as the train moved with agonizing slowness. Irene could hardly believe the trains were still running . . .

When they pulled into the smaller station and the many doors were flung open, there was no mistaking the screeching of the sirens. Wardens and guards were hurrying up and down the platform, taking charge and directing new arrivals to the shelters. Tom wriggled free of the crowd and demanded to know: 'Where are they bombing? Where's been hit?'

The helmeted figure of the ARP warden frowned at him, but took note of his uniform and answered quickly and civilly. 'It's the docks. It's the Sixteen Streets by the docks. They've come for another go at the shipyards and the streets left standing from last night . . . Hey! You're going the wrong way! You're supposed to head for the shelters, man! Same as everyone else!'

But Tom wasn't taking heed, and neither was Irene. Clutching all their bags and belongings they pelted out of the dark station and into the street. 'It's not far to home,' he muttered frantically. 'I'm sorry, pet. I'm putting you in awful bloody danger. We should be going where that fella told us. But I can't hang around. Not now I'm here. This is my home and my family's just a few streets away. I-I have to know they're all right . . .'

The wailing dipped for a moment of rare quiet, as if the sirens had lost their voices. From somewhere far above there came the endless, horrible droning of engines. It was the most hideous noise Irene had ever heard. But even when the sky started flashing in great, liquid eruptions of gold and white, she didn't take her eyes from Tom's. 'You were right. And I'll follow you there.'

Their short journey through the dark streets of South Shields was truly appalling. The noise was infernal and the brief flashes of light were impossibly bright, scarring their retinas, and sending them staggering through the fallen rubble and the detritus left strewn on the roads. There were still other stragglers out in public, dashing for the shelters as the bombs dropped somewhere nearer to the coast. 'I think . . . I think they're attacking further up the town tonight,' Tom shouted at Irene over the noise of distant blasts.

But that wasn't to say those planes couldn't turn round for another go. Any one of them, she knew, could pirouette on a whim and come streaking back to these dense streets in this corner of town. Now the roads were clearing Tom and Irene would be hectic, jerky silhouettes, weighed down by their worldly goods. They'd be easy pickings for the eager eye and trigger finger of a Nazi pilot.

I can't actually stand this, Irene thought, as she struggled to keep up with him. They'd just arrived and it was like the whole place was having its guts kicked out. There was the mephitic stench of a burst gas main and gouts of filthy water flowing over her shoes. Screams of people in distress, several streets away, sawed at her nerves.

And all at once the noise faded. The lightshow drained away and a chilly darkness descended over the town.

The welcome howl of the all-clear was sounding.

She sobbed with relief and staggered in the road. She almost fell down on her knees where she was standing.

All these streets looked the same to her. It was a bit of a rabbit warren down by the docks, she was discovering. She'd never seen so many homes crammed together in such profusion: endless rows of red-bricked houses in long streets running down to the dockyards and the stone arches of the railroads.

There was noise and confusion and still-smouldering fires. Crowds were gathered around ruins and blackened heaps of rubble that had clearly only recently been people's homes. As they hurried through the streets Tom was grim-faced and silent, observing the devastation all about them. Fires were still raging and survivors were being hauled from the wreckage. Bystanders were gazing at these hideous monuments in disbelief. To Irene the gaps in the terraces looked like teeth that had been punched in. She shook her head to clear it of images of violence, but it was hopeless. The smoke made her eyes stream. It was just like a chimney had fallen in, coating everything in soot, making her eyes and nostrils burn.

'The bastards,' was all that Tom would say. She had never heard him swear before and now she felt prissy for being shocked that he kept repeating this word.

It was all because of the shipbuilding, she knew. From the train she had been able to see the half-built hulls and the vast bulks of boats docked by the mouth of the Tyne. They seemed impossibly huge and impregnable, and yet they were all very vulnerable from the air. Of course they would be a natural target for the enemy. But the ships and the docks and the work that went on there were what fed the people who lived in this town. All this endless work and heavy industry filled these terraced houses with workers. It was a huge concentration of lives lived cheek by jowl. It boggled Irene's country-girl mind to imagine how many people lived in these few square miles. Their proximity to the violence and danger of recent days and nights made her feel hollow and sick inside.

Those Nazi planes just had to thunder inland from the North Sea and drop their bombs willy-nilly, knowing that, wherever they fell, hundreds of lives would be lost in an instant. These little houses would be the first thing they would have seen as they flew inland. What satisfaction could it have given them to reduce these homes to dust and flame? And to return for a second night, blasting more of the same into cinders?

Irene wondered whether the town had spotlights to pick out the danger? Were there anti-aircraft guns on the cliff tops? Had the town been able to defend itself at all? Or had they been caught out too suddenly? How could anyone live here, knowing that this could happen night after night, forever perhaps, until there was nothing of their home town left? How could the survivors even go on, waiting for the inevitable devastation?

Tom apologised, looking harrowed and frightened himself. 'Do you see now? You shouldn't be here, pet. You didn't have to come and be in the middle of all this . . .'

But she shook her head. 'No, come on. It doesn't matter. I'm here because I wanted to be. I was the one insisting, wasn't I? Let's find your family. Let's get indoors . . .'

'We're almost there,' he promised, and led the way, hurrying ahead.

It shocked Irene at first because she didn't understand what he was doing; why he had suddenly dropped the bags he was carrying, and even his good overcoat, into the roadside. Then he was off, dashing at full pelt. 'T-Tom . . .?'

They had just rounded the corner and Irene was in something of a daze.

This was Frederick Street. She could see the sign at the corner now. This was where they had been heading. It was Tom's home, where his family had been living for decades. Three whole households down this street held relatives of his. He was home and that's why he'd thrown down his belongings on the dirty, rainy, sooty ground and started to run like a mad person, away from his wife.

Oh, thank God, Irene thought. She offered up a brief prayer to the deity whose existence she had never really questioned until quite recently. Thank God this street looked like it was all in one piece. There was no greasy pall of smoke hanging over these rooftops. There were no crowds of shabby, silent people clustered around a shelled-out building. There were no pitiful doll's-house interiors suddenly exposed to public view. Frederick Street had escaped untouched.

Irene craned her neck anxiously as she made her way down the road. She was struggling, trying to carry Tom's luggage as well as her own. She realised that she had lost track of him, he'd hared off so quickly. Which door were they heading towards? A bleak feeling of suddenly finding herself lost in this strange place rose up in her. What if he'd vanished forever and forgotten all about his new wife? What if this whole thing had been some hideous kind of cruel trick?

She fought down the ridiculous panic. This wasn't about her. Yes, she felt displaced and frightened and had little idea what the immediate future held for her, but at least she was fit and well and safe. Unlike the poor souls of this place, the dead and the injured and terrified of South Shields. The survivors who lived here must be out of their minds with fear. The German bombers seemed to have gone for the night. But the same had been true last night, presumably, when the all-clear had come. But still the bombers had returned. Would every night be like this? They'd all be going to bed wondering if they'd still be here in the morning.

The shipyards seemed relatively untouched, compared with the surrounding streets. The cranes and hulks were all still standing, berthed in the harbour. So didn't that mean the Jerries would come back again and again, every night until the whole lot was blasted to smithereens?

What have I let myself in for? Irene wondered as she shambled along. Oh, Tom. Why was I so insistent? Why did I cause that row between us? What kind of hellish place have I demanded that you bring me to?

Just at that moment she heard his voice. He was calling her name. His voice was cracked and harsh. It sounded like he'd been crying, like he was overcome by emotion. When he appeared again, stumbling back up Frederick Street to help her with the luggage, his face was wet and bright with tears. She had never seen him cry before and the strangeness and novelty of it were the first things that struck her.

'They're a-alive, Irene,' he gabbled at her, looking jubilant. His joy seemed so oddly misplaced here, in the middle of this ruined town. 'Everything's all right. No injuries, even. No one missing. We're all OK. We escaped.'

He hugged her hard and the air was crushed out of her lungs so she couldn't even say anything or join in with his happy, relieved laughter.

But for how long? she was thinking. How long can any of us be safe in a place like this?

'Come on, love,' he urged her, picking up all their bags effortlessly and dragging her along. 'Come and meet everyone.'

The thought of meeting them was terrifying. But she knew she had to put a brave foot forward. This was what she had asked for. This was what she had said she wanted.

Irene fixed a smile firmly on her face and stepped towards her new home and her new family in the north.

Chapter Two

Now here she was in South Shields, with her eardrums ringing from the bombs and a whole lot of new people to meet.

As soon as she set foot in the back parlour, where all the family were gathered that night, Irene felt bewildered and besieged by names and rowdy greetings. It was too much to take in, and all those faces crowding in made her feel panicky. She felt Tom's hand on her back and that was reassuring, but he was just as loud and excited as the rest of his family. It was a reunion and they were hugging each other and crying out and bursting into tears.

Irene felt like a giant amongst them. The ceilings of this terraced house were low and the room was chockablock with heavy old furniture. Everything was bedecked with lace doilies and bits of china and plate. How many people were crammed into this room? At least twenty, it seemed like: brothers, aunties, uncles, cousins, sisters-in-law. Irene felt like she was twice the size of all of them. It was like being Alice in Wonderland, caught up in that crazy race with all the screeching birds.

'But why aren't you all in the shelters, you silly buggers?' Tom was shouting at them.

They squawked with laughter, hugging him, kissing him and yelling back: 'But you were coming home! We had to stay here! Your ma wouldn't go to the shelter! We had to wait for you! There's a party tonight for you coming home, our Tom!'

Irene felt dazzled by the bomb blasts and noise and was longing to sit down, and now she felt besieged by all this familial fuss.

It didn't help when she caught a glimpse of Lucky, the little cat who belonged to the house. Curious and undaunted as ever, Lucky jumped up on the table and pushed his queer, pink face towards the newcomer. Irene took one look at him and screamed out loud.

Lucky was entirely hairless.

The reaction was instantaneous. The cat panicked and flew off the table with a sizzling hiss. Everyone whirled about in alarm and Irene stood there, looking foolish and abashed.

'That thing!' she gasped. 'What was it?!'

Good-natured laughter filled the parlour. She frowned, feeling even more idiotic. Even Tom was chuckling at her. 'It was only Lucky. It's me mam's little cat. You needn't be scared of a creature like that! What's he gonna do to you?'

Irene bridled. 'I didn't know what it was. It's a horrid, pale, bald thing!'

More laughter erupted and suddenly Irene realised she was face to face with the most important person in the room. The crowd of relations had parted like the Red Sea to reveal a very small, seated woman.

She was in a cardigan pinned at the neck with a cameo brooch and her hair was iron grey, combed up into a bun. Her face was craggy and timeless and full of wisdom. Right now it was glaring up at Irene.

'This is my ma, Ada,' Tom said, pushing his wife forward and Irene felt like she was coming face to face with old Queen Victoria. She gulped. Yes, that was exactly how the old lady was behaving. Like an imperious matriarch, surveying Irene as if she was a prospective new subject, or an ambassador from a distant land. Somewhere primitive that Ma Ada's armies were in the process of colonising and taming.

Irene was determined not to be cowed. 'Hello, there,' she said, in a voice that surprised her with its strength. Even to her own ears she sounded foreign and strange. The room was filled with people talking in that jolly-sounding, sing-song accent that Tom had. A silence dropped over the place as the old lady studied Irene.

'Mam . . . this is me wife,' said Tom.

Ma Ada's eyes widened and it seemed that she stopped breathing for a very long time. Everyone in that room was hanging on her next utterance.

Irene's heart sped up and she looked at Tom. Surely this wasn't how he was breaking the news of his nuptials to his ma? No, he must have written to her. He'd sent her a telegraph, hadn't he? Irene remembered now. There was no way this was a fresh revelation to old Mrs Farley. She was acting up, that's what it was. Irene wasn't fooled by her bit of theatre.

'So,' said old Ma Ada. 'This is how you see fit to thank your poor old mam, is it, our Tommy? After I've dragged you and your three brothers up and made fine fellas out of you? Off you go to war in some benighted, godforsaken place out in the sticks and there you find . . . someone . . . some stranger's daughter . . . and you go and marry her in a rush behind your ma's back? Is that any way for a decent son to carry on?'

Tommy stammered. 'Mam, I . . . I . . .'

Irene stared at him. It was like he was turning into a little lad, regressing before her very eyes and losing all resolve.

His ma thundered on, never budging from her throne-like armchair. 'And all the while, as you're courting and clarting about and getting yourself involved in the lives of complete strangers, we're here at home, getting ourselves blown to smithereens. Do you even know what's been going on up here, lad? Do you know how lucky you are that this house is even standing and that there's anyone even here to greet you and this . . . new person tonight?'

Everyone in that room had their eyes fixed on Ma Ada. For a moment it felt like she was enjoying herself. She was torturing her beloved son just to get a rise out of him. But now, as she spoke about the bombing and the horrible events of the past couple of days, her voice cracked. Suddenly her expression was haggard and bleak. This was real emotion she was letting out. All the pent-up fear was flooding out and she couldn't stop it. She sobbed loudly and covered her face with both gnarled hands.

The hairless cat, Lucky, seemed to sense her distress. He leapt from his hiding place on top of the dresser into her lap. She stroked his pink skin and this seemed to pacify her.

Tom said, 'Oh, Mam. I do know a bit about what's been going on here. I raced up as fast as I could. I had to see you . . . I had to see the lot of you . . . to make sure you were all right . . .' He looked round at all the faces, so familiar to him, all of them anguished, happy, tired, relieved. To Irene they were still a confusing blur.

Tom's mam brought her feelings back under control. 'You're here now and that's good. I'm glad of that. I've got all my chicks under one roof. My whole brood. But how long for, eh? How long before you have to go back?'

He looked bleak at the very thought of turning round and repeating that journey south. All the way back down to Lincoln and Grantham and the airfield. Back to the skies over the Channel and into combat. Three days and by then it would seem like all of this was just a dream interlude.

Tom shook his head: everything he cared most about, everything good in the whole world, was here in this crowded little room. This parlour was the heart of his whole family, his entire childhood and upbringing. And now Irene was here, too. She was in the very bosom of his family.

For good or bad, she was staying here. It wasn't necessarily the way he would have chosen it, but she was in the care of his boisterous, rowdy family now. All his precious souls were together, for safety, while he went back to war.

'Irene will still be here with you,' Tom told his ma and the rest of his family. 'She belongs with you now. She's the woman I love. And she wants to be here with you all.'

The old ma and all the rest of them stared at the interloper. Irene smiled as warmly as she could. She felt brave. She felt curiously undaunted. She felt like someone they would want as a part of their family. Ma Ada was regarding her with suspicion. Some of the other faces were beaming back at her, seemingly friendly. She was determined to win them all over. That's all there was to it.

'I hope you don't mind,' she told her new ma-in-law, and brothers and sisters-in-law, as they all stared at her. 'But I want to do my bit. While this war's going on, and Tom and all the other lads are fighting, I wanted to come here, where I can do more to play my part than I could down in Norfolk. So, I hope that's all right with you all.'

They carried on staring at her, as if they weren't expecting her to say her own piece.

'Aye, well, then,' said Ma Ada. 'You're welcome, lass. But mind, you will have to help out, and you will have to work. Everyone here in this house has to pull their own weight.'

'She's a good worker,' Tom said. 'You won't have to worry about that.'

His ma nodded very regally and pursed her lips.

Irene thought: I will manage it. I'll make this lot accept me. I'm going to make myself belong to this whole bewildering family. She stood up and jutted out her chin.

'You're going to love her,' said Tom. 'I promise you.'

Who were these people that Irene had to get used to?

After the initial welcome, and then the all-clear sounding in the streets, most of the company melted away, back to their own houses on Frederick Street. Soon there were only the actual inhabitants of Number Thirteen left behind, though there were still enough of them.

'Don't worry about remembering everyone's names straight away,' Tom smiled at her. 'All that lot were my aunties and uncles and a bunch of nosey-parker neighbours.'

The ones she had to concentrate on memorising were Tom's brothers and their wives. His two older brothers were married, and his youngest was still a kid. There was Tony, who was in Navy uniform, and on a short leave home. He was broader and taller and quieter than Tom, and he was married to Beryl, who was dark and chatty. It was Beryl who took charge, once the welcoming committee had dispersed, and went to put the kettle on. Now that the air raid was over, out came the family's best china.

Then there was Tom's next brother, Robert, also in his early thirties. He was a tubby bloke with sandy, sparse hair; warm and friendly in contrast to Tony's reserve. Irene learnt that he was the pot man at the little pub – the Robin Hood – at the end of their street. He gabbled away quite happily until his wife, Megan, interrupted him. 'She doesn't need to hear your whole life story, Bob. Not yet.' The blonde-haired, rather glamorous girl nodded brusquely at Irene. 'I'm Megan, your other sister-in-law.' Her green eyes studied Irene shrewdly and Irene felt self-conscious, shaking hands with her.

And then there was Sam. He was twenty and fair-haired and grinning. He bounced around the crowded room like a puppy and hugged his brother Tom and then Irene impulsively.

'I'm the youngest,' he told them. 'I'm the only one round here who's not an old fogey.'

'Hey!' Tom warned him, laughing.

'Look at these muscles, Tom!' Sam said, rolling up his shirt sleeves and flexing madly. 'Look at this!' He was laughing as he showed off. 'This is me working down the docks, this. Fetching and carrying! It's doing me good, look!'

Old Ma Ada shook her head and tutted. 'Have you heard this, Tom? He went and got himself a labouring job. The brightest one of all my bairns, and now he's a navvy.'

'There's nothing wrong with that,' Tom said. 'We all have to do our bit somehow.'

Beryl returned with the tea tray and set it down on the table. 'That we do, Tom. You're right. And we're all dead proud of you, doing what you do. Our pilot! You're our hero!'

'Ah, get away with you,' Tom grinned, abashed, as they made a fuss of him. Irene watched on indulgently, glad to see him smiling and looking so happy with his family. She could hardly believe it was only an hour ago they'd been struggling through the horror of the South Shields streets, completely unsure what they'd see when they got here. But all was well. The family was all together and safe, for now at least.

Beryl poured the tea and opened a tin of biscuits. They smelt deliciously buttery to Irene, who suddenly realised she was starving. It was late evening and they'd had no dinner or anything today. Of course, mundane things like eating had been swept aside in all the upheaval and drama. All it took was a few broken custard creams to make her stomach rumble loudly.

'Eeeh, you and your broken biscuits,' Tom chuckled, reaching into the tin.

'Wight's best broken biscuits!' Beryl said, pushing them under Irene's nose. 'It's where I work, Irene. Megan does, too.

I'm trying to get a job on the ships, though. I want to learn welding.'

'Welding!' gasped Irene, through a mouthful of custard cream.

'Aye, I want to learn something they'd never have let me learn before there was a war on. I want to do something more useful than packing biscuits into tins . . .'

Megan spoke up: 'Hey, lady. The biscuit factory is important, too. You know that. The biscuits we bake and pack up, they go all over the world. They go to troops the whole world over. That's important, too.'

'These are patriotic custard creams!' Ma Ada smiled, munching happily.

'I just want to learn more, and do more,' said Beryl. 'That's all. Of course there's nothing wrong with Wight's biscuit factory. It's a grand place, with a great long tradition.' She beamed at Irene. 'And we've got you a job, hinny. If you want it. There's a job waiting for you at Wight's, if you're staying here for good, like Tom says. They're recruiting new workers all the time.'

'Oh!' said Irene. 'Well, I hadn't really thought yet . . .'

Ma Ada spoke up again: 'That's a really good idea, that. Then you'll be going to work with Megan and Beryl each day. Your two new sisters. They can keep a good, protective eye on you. She'll be all right, Tom, with these two looking out for her.'

Suddenly Irene felt somewhat trapped, wedged between her two new sisters, holding a cup and saucer, unable to speak with a mouth full of biscuit.

Tom was smiling gently. 'If she insists on staying here with you lot, then I suppose she could do much worse than working at Wight's. It's a decent place to work.'

'Something gentle, like packing or lining the boxes,' Megan said thoughtfully. 'Not the bake house. It's so hot in there, and so smoky. She'd probably pass out. She looks a bit delicate and pale to me, Tom.'

Delicate and pale! Irene swallowed her biscuit painfully and shook her head. 'There's nothing delicate about me! I was a Land Girl when I met your brother-in-law. I was up at dawn in the fields. And I've worked all my life, I'll have you know . . .'

Tom patted her shoulder. 'It's all right. It's just Megan pulling your leg, love. That's just her way.'

'Oh,' said Irene, and the others laughed. She looked at the glamorous, blonde Megan and saw a flash of scorn in her eyes.

Then Sam was saying, 'Well! Are all your bags in the hall then? We should get them upstairs, shouldn't we? I'll help! You two must be worn out, after all your travels.'

It was true. Irene felt a huge wave of tiredness go through her. She still hadn't even sat down yet. The only one in the parlour with a seat was old Ma Ada.

'You're in your old room, Tom,' his ma told him. 'Right up in the attic for the newly-weds.'

'Best room in the house,' Beryl nudged Irene, and smiled at her.

'Aye,' Megan said. 'Best of everything for the favourite son, eh?' There was something slightly sour in her tone.

Then, as Sam started hurrying about, flexing those muscles he was so proud of, Bob announced he had to be back at the Robin Hood to check on things after the raid. 'I'll come with you for last orders,' Tony said. 'We'll leave the women to get this lot settled in, eh?'

Irene noticed the way Bob looked at his older brother in his sailor uniform. There was hero worship in his eyes. There was something about Bob that she couldn't put her finger on. Was he a bit slower than the others, she wondered? It seemed an awful thing to think about someone. Certainly though, he was one of the friendliest of all the Farleys she had met tonight. The others had all looked at her appraisingly, weighing her up carefully, and coming to conclusions. Bob had just hugged her. He hugged her again as he left for the pub, saying: 'I'm glad I've got a new sister, hinny!'

Ma Ada shook her head, once he and his brother had gone. 'These lads of mine,' she tutted. 'Four of them! Four!' Then she glared at Irene. 'When are you thinking of starting a family then, Irene?'

'Erm . . .' Irene flushed crimson.

'Mam, man, for God's sake!' Tom barked out laughing. 'Let the lass get in the front door, will you?'

'I just speak my mind,' said Ma Ada, pursing her lips. 'I like to know what people's plans are.' She gave Irene a long, hard look, up and down. 'I'm very protective of my boys and my family, and I like to know absolutely everything that's going on.'

Irene gulped and was relieved when Sam took her elbow and led her back to the hall, so they could carry the bags up to the attic and the room that was to be hers.

The room was chilly, but it was clean and tidy. The double bed was an old brass one, and it had freshly aired sheets on. There was a large wooden wardrobe, but by the time Irene and Tom made it upstairs it was too late to go unpacking their things. They both felt exhausted.

A single small window looked out over the rooftops of the narrow houses. Beyond them could be seen the chimneys and the cranes of the docks, silhouetted against the open skies. The shipyards looked terribly conspicuous in the night, even with no lights anywhere. The moon was bright enough to expose the town in its vulnerability.

Plumes of dark smoke were still rising up as ruins burned, here and there across the town. Tom joined her at the window as she stood there, shivering at it all.

'Do you see now how dangerous it is here?' he asked her gently. 'Do you see why I got so cross and worried before?'

She nodded. 'It's terrifying, you're right.' But Irene looked at him steadfastly. 'Your whole family is going through it. They're all facing these dangers here together. And I want to be part of that family, Tom. I'm here now.'

He kissed her and clasped her in his arms. 'All right. I see how stubborn you are, Irene Farley. I can see we're going to have loads of these disagreements in the years to come . . .'

'I hope not,' she said.

'What, I'll just have to give in to you, will I?' he laughed.

She looked down at the streets and the view down the hill to the docks. 'I've never seen so many houses all crammed into one place,' she said.

'It's the Sixteen Streets,' he told her. 'It's always been the whole world to me, though a lot of people look down on this place. Everything goes on here. Everything that ever happens in life. And when you live here, you feel properly like you're a part of everything going on.'

She nodded firmly. 'That's what I want.'

'And, when the chimneys are blowing out fumes from the biscuit factory, you know, that's all you can smell for miles around. The gorgeous, melting smell of sweet biscuits. It's like magic, that.'

She smiled at him. His round face in the pale light looked like the moon itself. 'I think I'm going to like your family. They seem like a bunch of interesting characters.'

He chuckled at that. 'One way of putting it! That's definitely one way of putting it.' Then he looked at her seriously. 'We'd better get under that eiderdown, you know. It's a bit chilly in here. Come on, lass. I'll warm you up, if you like.'

She stifled her giggles. 'Shush! The others will hear you . . .'

'They can't hear anything if we're up in the attic,' he promised.

Irene's first night on Frederick Street had begun, and she was asleep as soon as her head touched the pillow.

Chapter Three

Irene was building up a picture in her head of this new town of hers by the coast. She wanted to see it as Tom saw it. She wanted to see it through his eyes when he was a kid. As he showed her around South Shields his eyes gleamed with teary nostalgia. It was a magical place to him.

Together they took long walks through the town: along the backs of the Sixteen Streets, and she heard a dozen people call out his name within twenty yards of leaving the house. Those steep streets seemed to go on forever and at first she thought they all looked rather shabby: all that dingy red brick and the chimneys smoking away all day. But on closer inspection she could see that the net curtains at the windows of all the houses they passed were immaculately white, and the front doorsteps had all been scrubbed until they shone. Though the air was smoggy and thick with dust and ash from the docks, she was aware from the start that there was an army of women who lived behind these doors, scrubbing and polishing and mopping like mad, and trying to keep everything decent and clean.

At the end of the long streets, way down at the bottom of the hill, lay a complicated skyline composed of steel towers, cranes and brick chimneys. The vast hulks of incredible ships could be seen lying in dock, or passing by, sliding without seeming effort through the deep waters. It was amazing to Irene, to see ships gliding by the end of the street, as if between the houses: it brought home to her just how close they all were to the open sea, and how close the great engines of war came to the homes where they lived.

Despite all the dingy smoke and fumes emanating from the factories and work yards, the air smelt delicious almost constantly. The rich, malty, sugary aroma came rolling up from Wight's biscuit factory, the tall chimneys belonging to which could be seen from Irene's bedroom window. The people here were quite used to the warm scent of baking biscuits wafting through their homes like a lovely, almost edible sirocco. It made already-hungry stomachs curdle and groan with frustration.

On their walks that week, Irene was introduced to beaming strangers again and again, and she did her best to seem not too shy and self-conscious. They gabbled away at her, these South Shields people, and everyone seemed glad to welcome her. Every now and then, though, there would be a dreadful encounter with someone Tom knew and they would be looking haunted and wrung out, and they'd tell a tale of a recent, terrible event; a shelled-out home; a loss of hope.

Tom would say words of comfort and hug these friends of his. He was warm and consoling, and not afraid to show his feelings, and this was something else Irene loved about him, of course. His round face would glow ruddily with the chilly breeze from the sea and high emotion, and he'd put his arm around his new wife, and squeeze her shoulder. He seemed proud to introduce her to his people.

They walked through the busy streets of the town centre. The old Victorian and Edwardian shop fronts seemed very grand to Irene. It seemed so much bigger than Holt, or even Norwich, to her. The awnings on the shop windows were huge, flapping in the sea breezes. They created shaded caverns that sheltered shop window displays, which were fancier than any Irene had ever seen at home in Norfolk. Tom, though, shook his head and tutted when he saw the shops of South Shields, and how their stocks and supplies seemed sparse compared with what they were usually like. He took her round his favourite stores, the ones he had known all his life, and bemoaned the emptied shelves and the general air of depression that hung around the aisles.

Some places were still jolly, however. There were queues at the butchers, where Tom was familiar with the old man and his son who'd managed the place for years. He knew women in the market and the greengrocer's. In the pubs he knew men by name, and Irene was introduced all over again to a blur of smiling, nodding faces. She sipped a bitter lemon in the snug of a pub in the town centre, warming herself by the fire, and a gang of old fellas fussed around Tom, admired his uniform and insisted on buying him a pint.

They ate hot sausage sandwiches in the street: soft buns that had been dipped in pork fat, the whole thing slathered in some kind of queer savoury substance Irene didn't like at all. 'It's called pease pudding!' Tom laughed at her. 'It's like one of our national dishes up here. It's traditional!'

Irene wasn't sure she liked the buttery, mashed up stuff at all, or the pale sausages, but she smiled and didn't complain.

This busy, long main road was called Fowler Street, and it swarmed with shoppers, vans and trams. Until this trip north Irene had never actually seen a tram before! Tom could hardly believe it when she told him, and when she gazed in wonder at the high-sided vehicle shunting along proudly down the main thoroughfare, with all the faces looking out at the windows. It seemed somehow magical to her, tooting out warnings at stray passers-by. She wanted to sit on the top deck, and Tom promised her they would; he'd take her on a trip along the seafront. It was a good hour's ride along the coast, and she'd get a lovely sense of her bearings that way.

Every little stage of their trips out together during this leave were like adventures to her. She was encountering something brand new each time, and they were all things she knew she must get used to, since this was to be her new town.

When they took the tram along the seafront they went to the end of the line and then walked back, breathing in the salty air and getting soaked with sea spray. Irene gazed out at the flat expanse of sea going far into the horizon. To the ends of the earth, probably. Worse than endless horizons: the feeling that over there, not so far away, beyond this chilling, metallic sea, the enemy lay in waiting. The enemy who would rather Irene and Tom and everyone they loved were dead.

She walked with Tom along cliff-top paths. The wind was fierce and she felt like she was going to go over the edge. The beach seemed so far below, at the bottom of the huge, jagged sandstone cliffs.

Tom showed her Marsden Bay, where the vast edifice of Marsden Rock was as big as the town hall itself, rising out of the foaming surf, high as the surrounding cliffs and covered with screaming sea birds.

The sea was a lot wilder than she was used to seeing down in Norfolk: the coastline was craggier and everywhere seemed much noisier than she was used to.

When they gazed down upon the beaches Tom told her that the barbed wire wasn't always there. The sands of South Shields hadn't looked as bleak and tangled and forbidding as this before the war. Those boarded-up shacks had been ice cream kiosks and amusement arcades in happier times. Once, there used to be a fairground here. Everyone had once been allowed to flock to the beach. It was all wonderful, golden, sandy coves. A northern paradise. Maybe one day it would be again, and then he could share it properly with her.

As teenagers he and his friends had actually slept on the beach during summer nights. They had lit small fires and dropped asleep on the sand. They'd had wonderful adventures and knew the habits of the tide and the safest parts of the beaches to play.

He made it all sound so wonderful. Irene pulled up the collar of her good woollen coat, trying to see Shields as he saw it. Trying really hard. The smile was frozen on her face as they spent these few days of his leave together. She really didn't want to say anything that sounded like she was complaining, or to give away her feeling of disappointment, but really, she'd never been so cold in all her life. It was like living at the North Pole and all these relatives of his seemed hardier than she would ever be.

Oh, all his relatives! That was another thing. Would she ever be able to keep track of them all? She was struggling with names and faces and she knew that she would be giving offence before long. The old ma was already exasperated with her new daughter-in-law. Irene could tell. She had caught Ma Ada rolling her eyes at things Irene had said. She had been a bit caustic once or twice in Irene's presence. Her words scoured at the girl's skin like baking soda scrubbed into the kitchen table.

'Oooh, haven't we dressed ourselves up for our tea tonight?'

Irene had blushed and stammered through a few of these familial encounters. Was she dressing up too fancy? She didn't know. She couldn't tell. She wanted to look her best, but she also wanted to blend in with everyone else. Also, the fact was, with only one suitcase of belongings to her name, she had only been able to bring relatively new clothes. She only had her very best blouses and sweaters and skirts to wear. They'll think I'm swanking about like Lady Muck, she thought desperately, as Tom led her through the beautifully autumnal civic park.

The bandstand he'd talked about had been dismantled and the paths were clogged with yellow, unswept leaves. She felt a fool for wearing her best coat and shoes. They'll think I'm trying to put on airs. To rub their faces in my difference to them. But it's really that I've got no choice. This is all I have to wear. Mum and Dad put everything they had into getting me a few new things for going away . . .

Tom put his arm around her as they strolled around the small lake. Somehow he had picked up on her mood. He knew how hard she had been trying this past couple of days, and how she was fretting over getting things right.

'Cheer up, hinny,' he grinned. 'You've only got me in your hair for another couple of days.'

She felt winded, like someone had punched her in the stomach. 'Ah, don't say that. I don't know what I'll do when you go back down south. What's it going to be like without you?'

'You won't ever be lonely,' he promised. 'Not with all my clan crowding round you. They still haven't all had a look at you yet. The town is full of my folk! The novelty won't wear off for a while.'

Irene tried to smile, but the truth was, she was already a bit tired of his family members coming up to her and peering right into her face. 'Let's have a good look at you, then!' They prodded and pinched at her like she was livestock. They called her 'hinny' and 'pet'. Everyone in his family had bright blue eyes and they stared at her with unnerving frankness. They asked her things right out, as if they had no shame or tact or embarrassment. 'Won't you be missing all your own family, then? Being so far away from home and all?' 'What is it your own people do, then? Tom tells us that you come from the back of beyond!' And, most mortifying of all: 'What's it like living with the old woman, eh? Is she making your life a misery yet?'

Irene nodded and smiled and said as little as she could in answer to all these questions. She wanted – she was desperate – to make a good impression, but it wasn't easy when all her insides went cold and her smile curdled on her face.

'It'll all get much easier,' her beloved Tom reassured her. 'You'll settle in. They'll soon all love you as much as I do.'

'Hey, look! Franchino's is still open!' He burst out with this joyously, gripping her hand and tugging her along. The wind was picking up, blowing wet leaves around them as they exited the park onto a long street. Across the road there were the welcoming, golden lights of an ice cream parlour. It looked incredibly inviting, with its art deco paintwork of pink and mint-green stripes.

'Ah, this was the place, Irene! When we were kids we'd save up our pennies for a little smidge of ice cream from Franchino's. Me and my brothers would share an ice cream sandwich wrapped in fancy, lacy paper and we'd sit there in one of their booths. I can't believe it's still open! Old Tonio's managed to keep going even with the war on! Let's go and see. I'll buy you something special! An ice cream sandwich!'

'A what?' Irene laughed, letting herself be pulled along, towards the glowing parlour. It was like they were running after a mirage.

'It's a block of the most wonderful Italian ice cream wedged between wafers. I used to share one with my three brothers and it was the best treat we could imagine . . .'

She thought Franchino's was magical inside.

'I've never seen anywhere like it,' she breathed, as Tom led her into the spacious, pastel-coloured parlour. They sat themselves across from each other in a little booth. There weren't many customers at this time of day. Outside it was too blustery and nippy and town was quiet.

Tom was telling her further tales about how he used to come here with his brothers. They would while away whole Saturday afternoons sitting in these booths, hunched over dishes of ice cream and hot frothy coffee. He described in detail the way that the wafers in an ice cream sandwich were dipped in glossy chocolate and then covered in chopped nuts. 'It was just like heaven,' he grinned. 'We had to share between four of us boys – can you imagine how fierce that got? But we never had enough money for a whole dish each. The old fella who runs this place – Tonio – he would be pulling out his hair because we would spin out a cup of coffee and an ice cream sandwich and make it last all afternoon. We'd have all our friends come by and we'd gather here before going down to the beach . . .'

Irene listened, marvelling at his words and trying to picture it all. Tom as a cocky little kid, one of the middle brothers in the family. She tried to picture them in this fancy place: scruffy kids messing everything up. Now that she looked closer, the violet and green woodwork and the frosted glass panels and the angular furniture all seemed a bit faded and chipped. They hadn't been able to keep the place in tip-top condition, with the war going on and everything.

When she came over to tell them what was and wasn't on the menu, the waitress had looked exhausted and pale. It was like she was only half there. Her paper hat was crumpled, Irene noted. Curls of raven black hair were escaping from her hairnet. Then Irene saw how Tom was looking at the new arrival.

'Bella?' he gasped, like he wasn't sure he'd recognised her.

The tired girl blinked at him and then gave a brilliant smile. 'Oh, Tom!'

Next thing he was up on his feet, embracing her where she stood. The elderly couple enjoying their tea at the next table was watching with great interest. Irene flushed and didn't know what to say, or where to look. All at once she realised who this must be. This slightly slipshod waitress – she must be one of Tom's earlier girlfriends. She was darkly glamorous.

'Irene, this is Bella – I've known her all my life. We were at Bessy Street Infants together from the very first day . . .'

Now the waitress was laughing, and looking brighter with a bit of colour in her cheeks. She was clearly delighted to see Tom. 'I'd heard that you'd been seen in town,' she said. Her accent was exactly the same as Tom's. 'Your Aunty Madge was bragging all about you in the butcher's queue on Fowler Street. She said you came back just after the bombs fell on the town. She said you were back with a bonny wife . . . Oh! This must be her! Are you her?' Bella held out her hand for Irene to shake.

Irene put her hand over her mouth as she always did when she felt self-conscious, as if to hide her slightly crooked teeth. 'Pleased to meet you, I'm sure,' she said. Oh, why do I sound so stiff and unfriendly? She cursed herself. All of Tom's family and friends must think I'm stand-offish and peculiar. Why can't I sound as warm and spontaneous as this girl, Bella?

Tom sat himself back down, straightening his dark blue tunic. 'This young lady,' he told Irene, 'is one of the heirs of Franchino's amazing Ice Cream Empire.'

Bella pulled a face and wafted the menus at him, letting herself complain for a few moments about how the business would be lucky to last out the year. 'All the shortages and that. It's hopeless. Sugar and cream. That's what we've built this so-called empire on. What are we gonna do when the supplies dry up, eh? Me dad's going crackers, man. He says it'll kill him if this place goes under. He built it up out of nothing, twenty-odd years ago . . .'

Bella spoke quickly and ferociously. Her accent was so thick Irene had trouble keeping up with the sense of what she was saying. Unlike Tom, she didn't slow down for Irene's sake. The girl's glamorous Italian features were accented beautifully by skilfully applied make-up, Irene noticed. Looking up at her, Irene felt like a little girl only pretending to be a grown-up woman.

'Is it that bad?' Tom asked, real concern showing in his voice.

'Aye,' said Bella. 'We're serving Camp Coffee, condensed milk, tinned fruit and powdered custard most of the time, but we have to keep going, don't we? And we've got to thank our lucky stars, haven't we? We could have been flattened like all those other poor buggers – pardon me, poor souls – the other night. Any of us could be gone in a flash, any time of day or night . . .' Bella shook her head, deciding to put a stop to all the gloomy talk. 'Listen – this is my treat. For the newlyweds. Don't tell anyone.' Suddenly she was darting off down the aisle, clip-clopping over the lino and through the swing doors into the kitchens.

'She's a live wire,' said Irene.

'Bella's a good lass,' Tom told her.

Irene was dying to ask him whether this ice cream person had once been one of his old girlfriends. There was an obvious, easy rapport between them. Did they have a history of some kind? And if so, how much of one?

Irene sighed. She knew she wasn't the first girl Tom had been serious about. He was a man of the world, as the saying had it.

When they had made love on their wedding night he'd been only slightly less nervous than she had, wanting everything to be just right. But he'd been tender and slow. To Irene he had seemed like an expert. Surely he must have had girlfriends . . . lovers . . . before? She had asked him this, aloud, as she lay bewildered and smarting in their rumpled bed.

'Why, aye,' he had laughed, smoking in the dark. She watched the orange cinder of his tab weaving like a firefly. She thought it was dreadfully common but somehow very thrilling that he smoked in bed. What if the good sheets got burnt? 'I'm a man of the world,' he had chuckled. 'I know what's what.'

She lay there, suddenly bashful, and was desperate to ask him more about these other women he had lain down with. What kind of people were they, to do this with him? It all seemed so surprising and intimate. More intimate than she had expected, somehow. The whole making love thing had taken Irene rather by surprise: the way it had blotted out everything else in the world for the time that they spent together in this bed . . .

She was avid to know who else he had shared this experience with and how long he had been doing things like this, but at the same time she didn't feel she could ask too many questions. It seemed too bold, too pushy.

But this Bella person. She seemed to Irene to be a likely contender. There was just something telling about the way she looked at Tom and how he talked to her. The way she pushed out her hip when she stood there, towering over them at their table.

All of a sudden the waitress was back. She had a small glass dish and two long-handled spoons with her. She placed this on a paper doily between the newly-weds with a great air of ceremony. 'There you go, hinnies. Now don't say I never give you nowt.'

Tom beamed at her, looking really touched by her generosity. 'An ice cream sandwich!'

Bella shushed him, clouting his shoulder. 'Don't shout it out loud, or they'll all be wanting one. This is just the last scrap of ice cream we've got left.' Her face softened as she smiled at him. 'But I wanted to give it to you and your nice new wife. I wanted to give you something good, to say congratulations, and welcome you home, bonny lad. Eeeh, it is good to see your face.'

Chapter Four

All the ceilings were so low. Tom and his brothers were tall men. They crouched everywhere they went in their ma's house, as if they were continually bowing their heads in deference.

There was no doubt that the old lady ruled the roost. She sat in that parlour and when the boys came in with their pay packets on Friday night they would line up to hand them over, one at a time. Ma Ada would unfold the notes and tot up the pennies. She would put everything in a tin box in the top drawer of her dresser, right beside her chair. Then she would hand each lad a small proportion of their earnings back, and that was their allowance for the week. Beer and fag money. What else did they need?

Irene was amused and appalled by all of this carry-on. They were no longer boys. Tom was thirty-two and his three brothers – Sam, Tony and Robert ranged in age from twenty to thirty-four. How could they bring themselves to submit to the old lady's rules? Three of the four were married men – how come their wives didn't intercede? Only Tom, because he lived away, was spared a part in this humiliating weekend ritual. Irene watched them with astonishment as they stood before She Who Must Be Obeyed with their wage packets.

Up in the attic, the night before Tom's leave was up, Irene said: 'I hope your ma doesn't expect me to treat her like the Queen of the house. I can't carry on like all the others do.'

Tom found the whole thing very funny. He was chuckling as he folded up his freshly pressed clothes and fastened up his battered suitcase. 'Ah, you'll be all right here. I promise. She's a good woman. She's looked after us all for so long, just her on her own. No one to help her. We'd all do anything for her. She's getting on a bit now and she can't get out to work.' He smiled shakily and suddenly Irene saw how worried Tom really was about them all; about leaving them all up here in Tynemouth while he fought the war elsewhere.

'She's not as robust as she makes out. Ma Ada will need your care and help and companionship, too. The other wives – Megan, Beryl – they're all right, I suppose, but they're flighty and daft. I don't think Mam quite approves of my brothers' choice of wives. But I think that she likes you. I could tell that she liked the look of you, pet, as soon as she clapped eyes on you.'

Irene pursed her lips. She looked at herself in the mirror. She paused in the middle of putting her rollers in before bed. 'Do you really think so?'

'Aye, I can read my mam's expressions as clearly as I can the headlines in the *Shields Gazette*. She thinks you're a canny lass.'

Irene turned to him. 'Is that good?'

'Aye! It means you're a good 'un, but it also means that you're clever and practical, too. You're nobody's fool. You'll be a big help to her, but you'll stand up to her, as well. You won't let yourself be walked all over.'

She nodded. That was quite true. Irene was used to sticking up for herself and, when the occasion called for it, speaking her mind. Still, there was something about that cross-looking, tiny old lady that made her feel nervous, though she strove to hide that reaction.

Tom came to stand behind her and stared into the reflection of her eyes. 'Now you've made me leave you here to look after them all, Irene,' he said. 'You will do that, won't you?'

She stared back at him and nodded slowly, promising. She loved the way he saw this strong person inside of her. To him, she was someone who could do anything: who had infinite reserves of strength and tough willpower to draw upon. Tom had faith in her, and that felt good.

The next day she went with his brothers and saw him off at the station. It was very low key. They didn't make a big palaver out of it. That wasn't Tom's style. 'I don't want flags waving and a big band playing,' he smiled. 'If I got that, I'd start to suspect you weren't expecting me to come back.'

Irene frowned as she hugged him. 'Don't say that.'

He promised to write as soon as he could. Of course he couldn't tell her anything concrete or exact about what he'd be getting up to. She'd learn nothing about the missions he would fly or the dangers he'd been coming through unscathed. She was quite used to the secrecy of these things. 'Just write what you can,' she told him. 'Tell me trivial things. Tell me about the birds that you hear, and the plants and the flowers. I'll miss all the countryside, living up here.'

He would try to remember the names she'd started to teach him, for the wild flowers and the birds and everything. Maybe he could even remember which bird was which from the songs they sang. 'But I can't see me taking walks in the country by myself,' he said. 'What's the point of going, without you there?'

This was on the platform. They were shielded from the crowd around them by his brothers. They were like a wall of solid masculine flesh in that mass of humanity. Already Irene was used to going around her new town with all these great, galumphing grown-up boys as her protectors and she rather liked it. It was very different to being the eldest in a family of sisters. It was less fuss, with fewer words and niggling fights. In a way it was like having a bunch of great big dogs fussing round you, keen to keep up and going everywhere with you. Yes, all those brothers – though she was still getting used to them – made her feel secure.

Tom told her: 'Next time I'm home we'll maybe go out to the countryside here. Further up the coast, if we can get there. Where it's all wild and beautiful. There are castles and forests and mountains. I'll show you more of this land that I've brought you to. You will love it. I hope . . . you'll love living here.'

Now the train was eager for the off. Doors were smashing shut and whistles were blowing and the crowd was saying rowdy goodbyes. The hissing steam of the engine threatened to engulf their farewell moments. Irene tried to tell him: 'You don't have to do anything special. We don't have to go anywhere beautiful or amazing. I'll just be glad to see you home again. I want to see you safe home, that's all.'

Tom nodded and prepared to go. If he didn't move now he would miss his train and he couldn't afford to do that. 'I love . . .' he began, and grinned at her. 'I love the fact that you're calling this place home. That's what it is now, Irene. It's your home.'

The very night that Tom was gone and Irene was alone with his family for the first time, there was an air raid. The sirens went blaring as they sat drinking tea in the back parlour and the old ma's face went dark. 'They left us alone for a few days,' she growled. 'Is that all we get? Just a couple of days off?'

It was as if, magically, Tom's presence had kept the Nazis at bay.

At first Irene couldn't move. She couldn't think or do anything sensible. The rest of her new family were on their feet. Even the old ma, Ada. Irene realised that she had never seen her on her feet before, though she was hardly any taller when she was standing up. Irene sat there with all her thoughts deafened by the wail of sirens. How did they make them so loud? It was like that noise could be heard everywhere. It penetrated deep into your mind and wouldn't let you think about anything else.

It was Tom's youngest brother, Sam, who stopped what he was doing and came and talked kindly to Irene. He was the closest to her in age and, in the short time she'd been in South Shields, he'd been the nicest to her. 'We have to get moving, pet. That's the signal, you know. We have to get to the shelter.'

Irene didn't even know where the shelter was. She knew that they didn't have anything under the house, or in the tiny backyard. There was only a coal hole and that horrible, draughty privy. Hardly enough room for Lucky, let alone Tom's whole family. Irene stood up and wanted to fetch her bag and other things from her attic room.

'What things?' snapped old Ma Ada. 'You can't bring *things*. They tell you not to dither about grabbing things. You have to get yourself to safety.' The old lady looked exasperated with her, and there was a deliberately challenging look on her crumpled face. She pulled a black knitted shawl around her shoulders and filled a carpet bag with her needles, wool, several numbers of *Picturegoer* and a handful of her best silver from the top dresser drawer. 'Well, that's me ready to go now, lads.'

Irene wondered: What do I want to take with me? All she could think of was Tom's letters. She was already wearing his ring. Nothing else seemed that precious to her. She wasn't the sort to get attached to things. She'd learnt that lesson, even as a child. The things you valued could be taken off you, quite easily. They could be taken away and destroyed. It might be for your own good. It might be absolutely necessary, but it still hurt when it happened. But even so, she'd have liked to have

Tom's letters with her. They would have protected her. She could keep them pressed close to her heart. His words would be in there, rumbling along, like his voice did in the night.

Next thing she knew, they were out in the lane, bustling along Frederick Street where the noise was even fiercer, and all the other narrow houses were disgorging their tenants. The sirens were ear-splitting, but Irene was amazed at how calm everyone seemed. She thought about the last air raid – on the very night of her and Tom's arrival – and how many had been injured or killed? Scores of them. Whole households, whole shops and stores had been blown sky high. The paint shop had taken a direct hit and the flying debris and hot, noxious, soupy mess had proved deadly to anyone in the vicinity. That dreadful night was still fresh in everyone's memory, yet as another raucous, shrieking night grew darker around her, Irene was astonished they weren't all flying around in panic and hysterics.

The Farley family could only move as fast as the old lady, who shuffled along as well as she could. 'My bally feet are ruined,' she grumbled. 'And my knees. And my hips. It's cleaning what's done that. Skivvying for others. It's ruined me for good. My dancing days are over now!'

Irene stared at the tiny figure, lugging her carpet bag of goodies in her arms. She could never tell when the old woman was trying to be funny or not. She hardly ever cracked a smile.

Ma Ada was surrounded by three sons and her two other daughters-in-law, Megan and Beryl. Just then Beryl caught Irene's eye. 'What's wrong with you? You're not having a funny turn, are you?' She grabbed Irene's arm and linked with her. All at once Irene was glad of the human contact. Beryl was bustling, no-nonsense, and Irene was glad to be dragged along by the eldest sister-in-law. Right now she needed to be told what to do. 'Come on, pet. It isn't far. And it's quite nice, really, when you get there. Sometimes they have tea on, and sandwiches, too, if anyone's had time to be prepared. There's often a bit of a sing-song and you'll get to meet everyone from round our way.'

The old woman heard this and laughed mirthlessly. 'Aye, it's one way of getting to meet the whole neighbourhood, I suppose . . .'

The three lads were grim-faced, pushing along ahead and casting nervous glances at the sky. The family wasn't moving fast enough. Irene saw the looks they were giving each other. She thought: we're so close to the docks. At the end of some of these streets you can actually see the great ships wedged into the horizon. This must be one of the most dangerous spots to live in the whole of the country . . .

Beryl still had her arm crooked through hers and she was marching her firmly through the thronging streets of terraced houses. 'You'll be all right, hinny. There's nowt to this carry on.'

Presently they came to the shelter's entrance, at the back of the town hall. There was a jumble of sandbags, tangles of barbed wire and a door that seemed to open right into the hellish underworld. Everyone surged forward, as if they knew exactly where they were going.

'This is us,' Irene was told.

Before she knew it the earth had swallowed them up and they were sitting on benches in the near-dark, pressed together with their feet on damp concrete. Hundreds of others were down here, shifting and stirring and trying to get comfortable. Soon the sirens wound down and there was quiet. It seemed to last forever. Ominous, dark, endless silence. Even that piercing warning seemed preferable to this hateful quiet.

Irene sat there tensely, every muscle in her body frozen. How long must they sit like this? Hour after hour? She couldn't keep her teeth from chattering. Everyone was crammed together on the benches, but Irene had never felt so lonely in all her life.

Why wasn't Tom here with her? She needed him beside her right now more than she ever had.

She cursed herself for a fool. You've only known him a few months, Irene. And yet here you are, in a strange town, in the dark, with a whole lot of strangers. What the devil have you let yourself in for, you daft girl?

A baby was crying lustily. The noise set another one off. Their mas shushed them. In the dim, dusty light Irene saw old Ma Ada calmly take out her knitting and start clicking away. She looked quite at home, squashed there between Sam and Tony. 'Eeeh, poor old Lucky,' she sighed, whistling between her tiny brown teeth. 'Did you see the poor little mite on the front room windowsill? Watching us as we left? I should have gone back and popped him into my bag. I feel just awful for leaving him at home.'

'Lucky will be all right, Mam,' grinned Sam. 'Everything will be just where you left it. You'll see.'

The ma gave her youngest a dark and complicated look. 'You'll learn soon enough, lad. That's just not true. Not in this bally life. You leave stuff, you put it down and when you go back, it's hardly ever still there. Things get nicked or spoilt or taken away. Or like you bairns. You bairns go wandering off of your own accord . . .'

As far as Irene could tell, the old woman had done a pretty good job at keeping all her children close by her. Only Tony and her Tom had fled her cloistered coop so far.

Then came the dull crump and boom of bombs falling somewhere, not too far away. Somewhere on Tyneside. A tense, terrified silence fell on the family and everyone around them. It fell on the hundreds of bodies in the shelter by the town hall.

They listened and tried to calculate where that devastation was falling. How near or far away it was.

It was quite impossible to tell.

Chapter Five

She took a deep breath and joined the crowd.

It felt a bit like jumping into a river and being pulled along by the current. Irene had her two sisters-in-law either side of her as they marched along Frederick Street down to the docks, and she smiled as others called out greetings to them. It was Monday and everyone was still half asleep after the weekend and two air raids on the trot, but the crowds were still heading to work at the crack of dawn. Their shoes clopped noisily on the cobbles of the Sixteen Streets.

Irene had her hair tied up and a spare pinny and set of overalls on, all ready for her first day. She might not have a full-time job yet, but Beryl had helped her to look the part, and all set for work.

'Just you watch what we do and say,' Beryl told her. 'And who we talk to, as well. Not everyone's nice. Most of the lasses at Wight's are really lovely. Just ordinary girls. But there are some awful ones, too. People to avoid. Same as anywhere.'

Megan and Beryl linked arms with her as they went into the factory grounds through the tall iron gates. It reminded her of feeling flanked by her sisters, down in Norfolk, where she was the oldest and the one that everyone looked up to. Here she was the youngest sister and, if she was honest, she felt at something of a loss. It was tough, trying to learn everything new and unfamiliar. But at least she had these two new sisters either side of her, gripping her arms protectively like this as they surged along through the crowd. Mind, Megan was nipping her a bit as she grasped her.

All around them the tall chimneys and silos and three-storey buildings rose up, vaguely menacing and dark. She didn't know what lay inside each of those buildings yet. They seemed mysterious with their dark, dusty windows and the noise already blaring out of each one.

Beryl took charge, leading her to the office where she had been asked to report for duty. That morning Irene felt like she was being processed through the factory herself, and recreated into an employee. There were forms to fill in, and various people to be polite to, and questions to answer. Business about gas masks and shelters and other important information she had to absorb. She was met by stern-looking ladies in hairnets and a seemingly important gentleman in a tweed sports jacket. They each made notes about her and nodded solemnly and passed her on to the next room.

There was talk of a medical, which made Irene flinch and start to panic slightly. She didn't even admit to herself why that might be so. But, in the event, it merely involved a man in a white coat looking down her throat and into her ears. He glanced at her nails to see how clean they were. That appeared to be it. Nothing more intrusive than that. She felt obscurely relieved.

Then, some time around lunchtime, they announced that she could indeed have a job at Wight's biscuit factory, and that she should be very pleased and proud of herself for joining a work force that had been going strong for over a hundred years.

'As long as that!' Irene gasped.

The supervisor lady nodded, rather grandly. She was called Mrs Clarke, and took her position very seriously, it seemed.

45

'Oh, yes. We are a great institution, here on Tyneside. And at no time more than this present one have we been more essential. The sweet biscuits we manufacture here will be dunked into cups of tea the whole world over. Wherever our boys are fighting back the tide of wickedness and fascism, our biscuits will be helping to maintain their splendid morale.'

Irene smiled at her. 'I never realised biscuits could be so important!'

'Oh, but yes,' said the supervisor. What a huge bust she had, Irene thought. Crammed underneath that white coat. Mrs Clarke looked like she was about to topple over. 'Biscuits are a very serious business here at Wight's factory, Mrs Farley, and you'll soon come to share that view. Now, I suggest you begin work in the packaging department. They need someone on the Penny Packets today.'

It was a long, low-ceilinged room she was shown to, and Irene was pleased to see that she was being placed in the same section as Megan, who smiled at her stiffly when she arrived. There was no sign of Beryl, who seemed to be working in a different part of the factory altogether. There were at least a dozen other girls working on the Penny Packets, each with their hair up in nets with a little cap on top. Each of them nodded affably at the new arrival.

She had her own small workstation, and she stood there expectantly, looking at the various pieces of equipment laid out for her. She was working next to a small girl with pale hair and a raspy voice. 'I'm Mavis,' the girl said shyly.

Megan came over and demonstrated what they were supposed to be doing. It seemed fairly straightforward. 'It's the easiest job on the line, really,' Megan said. 'You just take four biscuits at a time, as they come down the conveyor, and put them into the paper packet, fold it round and crimp it using the crimper, like so.' Megan sounded very calm and professional, the way she demonstrated. She stood to watch as Irene took a turn, and nodded with satisfaction when her sister-in-law seemed to get the hang of it.

The Penny Packets then needed a colourful label pasting on and this was the best bit, painting on a dab of glue from a pot. Then they were all laid neatly in a box, twenty at a time, waiting in a perfect pile of boxes for the wheelbarrow girl to come and take them all away. The whole operation seemed to go like clockwork, and after a faltering little start, when she wasn't sure if she was crimping right, and her packets looked a little lopsided, Irene soon felt she had the knack of it.

As the day advanced she could smell the heady aroma of molten biscuit mix being cooked in the bake house. It came into their work room through the tall, dusty windows: a sweet, oaty smell that made her stomach rumble. All she'd had for lunch was a crust of bread and dripping, the same as all the other girls. They'd introduced themselves: Gladys, Effie, Edith, Mary and Mavis. All of them had shown her their own meagre lunches, supplemented with cigarettes and mugs of tea in the little yard tucked away in the factory grounds. The few scraggy trees were shedding their orange leaves and there was a proper nip in the air. Irene was shivering as she tried to keep up with her new colleagues' welcoming chatter. And then, after lunch, it was time to return to work, still hungry.

The tantalising smell of biscuits coming from the bake house was likely to drive her crazy. Her fingers fumbled with the Penny Packets and she thought: what if I were to eat a couple? What would anyone say? Would they even notice? Today it was ginger snaps, which she wasn't all that fond of anyway. She shook her head and berated herself: how would it look if she got chucked out on her ear, on her very first day at work, for nicking handfuls of biscuits? She'd be so ashamed!

Across the way from her, Megan seemed oblivious to the delicious aroma wafting into the room. She wasn't paying attention to anything at all, just the endless activity of putting biscuits into wrappers, labelling them and piling them up. Her fingers were a blur of constant motion. Already Irene had mucked up her paste pot a bit, and some of her packets were sort of glued together in their pile, but she was hoping no one would notice.

The other girls in the room were so accustomed to their repetitive tasks that they were able to talk loudly across the room to each other. They chatted happily about dances at somewhere called the Alhambra, and about films coming on at the picture house. This was the kind of thing that Irene loved to hear about, and she was keen to ask Gladys, Effie and Mary questions, but she was scared of losing her concentration and making a muck-up of her Penny Packets. She did, however, get to say a bit more about herself to the others as they worked, and explain that she hailed 'from Norfolk way. From a little village near Holt, which is twenty miles from the city of Norwich. All the way down south.'

The girls nodded and smiled, and one of them – a plump, confident girl called Mary – remarked on her accent, which she said sounded almost foreign to her. 'Foreign!' Irene gasped, thinking that this wasn't good news. She didn't want to be going round in wartime with everyone suspecting she was foreign. They might start thinking she was a spy. But really, who would she be spying for? It almost made her laugh. Then she reminded herself: she was the outsider here. It was her job to fit in and reassure these girls, and everyone else, that she was just the same as them. She just had an unfamiliar accent, that's all.

They were all friendly enough, anyhow. And she was glad that this first, long morning hadn't seen her working anywhere too noisy, with too many machines nearby, or somewhere too hot, like the bake house. At least here she felt she was being brought gently into the factory.

The oddest thing was that Megan was probably the most stand-offish of everyone she met on her first day. But maybe that was just how she was, and she didn't mean anything by it.

In some ways, the girls here were friendlier and more immediate than the girls she had got to know back in the Land Army. During those months away from home, living in those bare little barracks in the middle of the fields, cold and homesick and lonely as they all were, it had taken a few days for them to all thaw out and start to talk to each other and become friends. Here, though, all the girls were chattering away like mad and deliberately including her from the first.

Megan had sat further apart at break time, nibbling her home-baked bread and keeping quiet. She didn't quite seem to be part of the crowd, and Irene wondered if she herself was doing wrong by sitting between Mavis and Effie and the others. These girls were closer to Irene's own age, and perhaps they were as intimidated as she was by Megan's looks and her slight seniority?

Through the afternoon and into their later break they were gossiping about menfolk. Someone brought a tray of mugs of hot, sweet tea, and the girls smacked their lips with relish and got on with the serious business of discussing blokes.

Some of them, it seemed, had already waved their husbands and boyfriends off to war, and they were missing them terribly.

'I can't see how I'll cope,' sighed the one called Mary. 'It sounds awful, but I wish we'd never had our Ernie now. That's three bairns under five I've got and only his ma to help out at home. I'm that worried about them all day, because she's blind as a bat and half-daft . . .'

'Eeeh, you shouldn't wish your bairns away!' gasped Edith. 'You shouldn't regret them for a minute. They're a blessing from God, they are! You should know that.' Edith was known for being a bit Goddy. She was a staunch Catholic, like all her family, and all the girls groaned at her predictable comments.

'I'm not wishing I didn't have them, Edith,' sighed Mary. 'I'm just wishing we could have looked ahead a bit more, and seen what might have happened, with him being called away . . . and no one knowing what's gonna happen next . . .'

'It's all in God's plan,' said Edith smugly, and slurped her tea.

'Aye, well I wish he'd let us in on it a bit more!' laughed Chrissie. 'He's not doing that good a job of looking after us all lately, that old God of yours!'

Edith looked scandalised at this. 'If you went to church a bit more, the lot of you – maybe then you'd all know a bit more about the Almighty and his mysterious ways.'

'Ha! I couldn't give a bugger about his ways, mysterious or not,' Effie laughed. 'I just wish he wouldn't keep taking all the men away. What are we gonna do if they all get sent to war? What are we gonna do in a town without fellas in it?' She looked so comically bereft at the thought of it, she set all her friends off laughing at her. Effie was well known for being keen on the company of fellas.

Mavis was giggling next to Irene, and trying not to. 'Eeeh, I shouldn't laugh at them when they say rude things!' she told Irene. 'They can say some awful things, these lasses!'

Mary took notice of the new girl then, because she called across: 'And what about you, then, Irene? Are you fixed up with a fella then, or are you still looking?' She was a plump girl, mischievous-looking, and Irene liked the look of her, though she thought she was probably an awful gossip.

'Irene's already got a man,' Mavis piped up. 'A very handsome fella. She's married to one of the Farley boys from Frederick Street.'

There was a round of 'oohs' and some whistling at this. Apparently the Farley brothers were well known to the girls of Wight's.

'He's away being an airman,' Irene said, raising her voice, but putting a hand partly over her mouth as she often did when feeling unsure of herself. 'All the way down in Lincolnshire.'

'And you've come to live up here, have you, with his family?' asked Mary. 'He's gone and dumped you in the Sixteen Streets, has he? While he goes flying about like a fancy airman down south?'

Irene nodded. 'Aye, it was my idea. I told him I wanted to live with his people. This is where I belong now. I want to do my bit.'

'By packing biscuits with us lot?' asked Effie, mockingly.

Irene didn't know if she was laughing at her or not. 'It seemed like the best place to find work.'

'I'm going to train to work on the anti-aircraft guns!' Mary burst out. 'Can you imagine? I'll be out on the cliffs and I'll be scanning the skies for them Jerries coming over the horizon. And then it'll be: POW POW POW! I'll blast them all to buggery!'

Everyone was very impressed by Mary's plans. Mavis seemed particularly taken with the idea of manning those hefty guns. 'POW POW POW!' she repeated, eyes gleaming as the hooter sounded for the resumption of work.

'Don't you get carried away,' Megan called out to her, as they filtered back into the work room. 'They'd hardly let a girl like you loose on them anti-aircraft guns.'

'Why not?' Mavis gasped. 'I'm just as good as anyone, aren't I?'

Megan chortled at her and adjusted her headscarf as she prepared to start the final shift of the day. 'No, you're not, pet. You're useless. Has no one ever told you that?'

Irene's eyes widened at Megan's casual cruelty. Her heart went out to the pale, defeated Mavis as she replied: 'Oh, yes. Everyone's always told me I'm useless, my whole life long.'

Then the work started again, and Irene had to concentrate once more on her glue pot and her biscuits.

'You're doing quite well there,' Megan told her approvingly, towards the end of the day.

Irene smiled at her, and confided: 'Some of the packets got a bit of extra glue on, but I think they've dried OK.'

Megan nodded thoughtfully. She had wandered over to Irene's station and seemed to have something on her mind. 'Yes, I'd say that all in all, you're doing a good job, not just here. But at home, too.'

'What's that?' Irene smiled uncertainly. It sounded as if Megan was in a reflective mood, now that the two of them were separate from the rest of the family.

'You've made a fine impression on all of the Farley clan, I'd say,' Megan went on. 'And on the neighbours and the extended family, too, I believe. Almost everyone you've met here seems to think you'll fit in fine. They reckon you're a good match for their lovely Tom.'

There was something about her tone, though. Irene couldn't put her finger on it exactly. There was something challenging in Megan's bright green eyes as she looked at Irene. Suddenly Irene thought: she's not being as nice as I thought she was. Her words are friendly, but there's something underneath.

Megan leant forward fractionally and lowered her voice so that no one in the work room but Irene would hear what she said next: 'But just you watch out. You just watch yourself, Irene.'

Irene jolted with surprise. 'What? What do you mean?'

'I've seen your sort before. *I* don't think very much of you.'

Irene simply stared at her new sister-in-law. She couldn't believe what she was hearing. Megan was still smiling at her, but her voice was dripping with poison.

'I could make things very difficult for you, Irene Farley.'

Irene gulped. 'But I . . .'

Megan wasn't listening to her. She whirled away and there was a sudden crash.

Everyone looked up from their stations to see Megan apparently racing into action. 'Oh no! Oh, what a shame! All your work! And on your first day, as well!'

Irene stood there dumbstruck. She had seen, plain as day, Megan knock all of the Penny Packets onto the floor. All of the Penny Packets that Irene had spent all afternoon putting together. 'Oh dear! Oh no! What an awful waste, Irene! How clumsy of you!'

The other girls in the room must have seen what was going on. When Irene could breathe again she looked at them – Mary, Edith and Effie – but they just shrugged and went back to their work. There was a snort of laughter from one of the girls – perhaps Chrissie. Only one of them came to help her, the small, grey-faced girl with pale hair. Mavis said in her raspy voice: 'Here, look, I'll get the broom and the pan . . .'

Megan simply turned and walked away, her heels crunching on broken biscuits.

Irene stared in horror as Megan returned to her own workstation, and stood beside her own perfect pile of packets, stacked ready for the wheelbarrow girl. 'Oh dear, Irene. What an awful mess you've made,' she smiled sweetly. 'I'm sure the supervisor will put it all down to first day jitters and your hopeless butter fingers. I'm sure they won't punish you unduly. Not on your first day.'

Irene didn't say anything. She could feel a hot red flush rising up her cheeks and she had to button her lip to keep inside what she wanted to shout at Megan.

It wouldn't do to start fighting in here. Not in front of everyone. She glared at her sister-in-law in mute outrage, and Megan grinned back at her, looking very calm and pleased with herself.

At the end of that day Beryl caught up with them as they exited the factory gates. She looked breathless and excited.

'Where were you at dinner break?' Megan asked her.

'I snuck out,' Beryl grinned. 'And I got my name put down at the shipyard. I went over to the offices at John Redhead and Company and I told them. I want to work there.'

'You never did,' Megan gasped.

Beryl bustled along, looking very businesslike and determined. It was bitterly cold and already dark, and she buttoned up her coat over her pinny. 'I told you I would. And they listened, an' all. They listened to me when I said I wanted to do something proper. Like welding and riveting and everything that the men do. And they put my name down!'

Megan fetched out her cigarettes and tutted. 'They were just humouring you, I reckon.'

'But they *do* take women on to do those things,' Beryl snapped back. 'I could tell they were listening. They took me dead seriously. There's already women over there, doing proper hefty jobs. I knew there was. Our Sam told us so, remember.'

Megan rolled her eyes. 'Our Sam. What does he know about anything?'

Irene butted in, staring at Beryl. 'Are you leaving the biscuit factory then, Beryl?' Irene felt a bit selfish, because she felt like Beryl was abandoning her already, on her first day in a new job.

'I want to play a bigger part, Irene,' said Beryl. 'Bigger than just making a few flippin' biscuits.'

Megan snorted. 'I can't see Ma Ada being all that impressed with the thought of you welding. It's hardly very ladylike.' Both

Beryl and Irene completely ignored her. Irene was still cross and confounded by Megan's strange, nasty behaviour back in the work room.

Beryl was continuing: 'Look! Look at the funnels and the masts filling up all the docks. Look at them! We see them every day. Jerry's mad keen to blast them all to smithereens. They are the very reason that we all live here and why these streets we live in were built in the first place. They're the most important thing to come out of this whole town. More than bloomin' custard creams and ginger nuts! And I want to be involved in that. I want to do the proper, hefty jobs that they usually have the fellas doing. Welding and riveting and all the rest of it. I want to be part of these massive, beautiful ships going out into the world!'

Irene was impressed. The three of them were hurrying up the cobbled hill now, and the vista of the busy docks was growing grander. She turned round to take it all in and imagined working on those ships like Beryl was describing. Just imagine being responsible for the joints and the rivets and all the actual stuff that held the great hulks together. Imagine being one of the task force that kept the ships watertight and steaming through the oceans.

Suddenly it made her struggle to put biscuits into packets and to stick the labels on straight seem a bit soppy.

She felt even more pathetic when she thought about how she'd just stood there and let that Megan smash up her whole first day's work. That snide bloody cow! She darted a sideways look at the blonde bombshell as she smoked and sashayed her way up the lane. She hadn't even fastened up her coat against the cold. It was like ordinary things like the October chill didn't even affect Megan. She let her coat flare out and her golden hair shake free of her hairnet and, as she did so, Irene felt a quite unfamiliar emotion steal over her.

Resentment. Bridling fury at the injustice of it all. That little cow, she thought. Knocking over all my work like that. And she flushed with even greater anger when she thought of the look on the face of their supervisor when she saw that Irene's work lay ruined on the tiled floor. 'What's happened here, then?' Mrs Clarke the supervisor frowned.

'I . . . I . . . There was an accident,' was all Irene would say, tight-lipped. Across the way, Megan had smirked at her.

The supervisor wasn't impressed, noting the wastage down on her clipboard. 'Your wages will be docked, pet. That's not very good on your first day, is it?'

Those words were still ringing in Irene's head as she made her way to Frederick Street with her two sisters-in-law and all the other lasses finishing their shift in time for tea.

I'll get her on her own, Irene thought. I'll get Megan on her own at some point and have it out with her. That's what I'll do. With people being nasty bullies like that, it's the only thing to do. Then she thought: but maybe I've got it wrong. Maybe it really was an accident, and Megan was really horrified at what she'd done? Right now Megan was linking arms with her, like they were fond of each other. But this is all for show, Irene suddenly thought. Of course she smashed my bloody biscuits on purpose!

'Well, what about you, Irene?' Beryl suddenly asked. 'Come on, hinny. Tell us! What was your first day like in the factory? Did you manage all right?'

Before Irene could say a word, Megan broke in: 'Ah, she was smashing. She's got a real knack for it, I think. She looked happy as anything doing that same old repetitive thing all day long. I think being boring suits her down to the ground! I reckon our Irene will make an expert biscuit packer. Probably the best that Wight's has ever had!'

Beryl laughed at this, and squeezed Irene's hand. 'Don't mind Megan, pet. She always talks a load of rubbish. You must have noticed that about her already. She always likes to take the mick out of everyone.'

By now they were on Frederick Street, and doors were clattering as folk arrived home, and others headed out for their later shifts. Kids were playing out on the road and getting called in for their tea. Households were settling down for the night-time as the temperature dropped and everyone tried to forget about the possibility of another air raid tonight.

'It was a good day,' Irene said. 'As first days go, I think today was all right.'

Beryl smiled at her and she caught a fleeting glimpse of a scowl from Megan. Yes, that was the best way to deal with her. Pretend like she couldn't hurt you. Just smile and carry on like she's not upset you one bit. And then, when you get her alone for a moment, ask her straight out what her problem is.

Then they were home, and hurrying into the hallway of Number Thirteen, which was almost as chilly as the street outside. The parlour at the back was warmer, though, and that's where they gathered for a pot of tea with Ma Ada, who was keen to hear all their day's news.

Chapter Six

It was daft really, dwelling on the idea of Christmas this early. They were still getting through autumn yet Irene found herself thinking about it because it was going to be her first Christmas away from her family. Being the oldest sister, Christmas wasn't the same to her as it used to be, of course, but she used to love to be there watching the way the younger ones reacted to everything.

Not that any of them were given anything much. An apple, a satsuma, a handful of nuts. Perhaps a book or a small doll. That was usually the extent of it. But it was the special atmosphere that would descend upon their cottage and was felt throughout the village. Peace and goodwill. Even her ma would be less fractious than usual, putting aside her vendettas with various neighbours for the duration. Well, this year, they would just have to manage without Irene.

With a bit of luck Tom would get leave. If not Christmas itself, then some time around then would be just as good, she hoped. He would be back with her in South Shields and by then – a whole two months away – she intended to be fully settled in.

She would be used to her new routine at Wight's biscuit factory. She would be like an old hand on that conveyor belt. It would feel as if she truly belonged there, breathing in that sugar-sweet air and pasting on those labels. Hundreds and hundreds of labels. Her fingers were sore with scrubbing the glue off them and her legs and back ached terribly as she lay in bed at night after a whole day standing.

But it was work. It was good work. She felt like she was doing her bit. And so the days slipped by, bit by bit. Bringing her closer to Christmas and seeing her husband again.

Perhaps by the time she saw Tom again . . . she would have some news. She might have something special to tell him when he got home.

Also by then, she promised herself, she would know everyone who lived down Frederick Street and she'd even be talking in a Geordie accent like the rest of them. She'd be gabbling away, twenty to the dozen, like a real native. Well, perhaps not.

'Eeeh, that accent of yours!' said old Ma Ada as they stood in the scullery together late one afternoon. They were mixing up ingredients for fruit cake and it all felt deliciously moist and claggy in Irene's fingers. 'It's as thick as this mixture! What's it called, then? A Norfolk accent?'

Irene frowned. 'I hadn't realised I even had a local accent . . .'

'Eeeh, but you do, lass! Sometimes I have trouble making out what you're trying to say. It's like you're talking a whole other language.'

Irene blushed and pursed her lips, and concentrated on beating her bowlful of sticky dough as hard as she could.

The old woman went on, 'When our Tom first brung you into my parlour and you opened your mouth, I thought – help! He's gone and brought some foreign lass back to live amongst us! That's never supposed to be the King's English she's talking, is it?'

Then Ma Ada noticed the two spots of red on Irene's cheeks and relented. 'Hey, lass. I'm not being horrible to you. I'm just trying to put a smile on your face.'

A smile! Why would she smile about being mocked like that? Irene shook her head. There were certain things about these northerners that she'd never be able to understand. The rough way they sometimes talked to each other, bringing each other down and laughing in each other's faces. Mockery and embarrassment seemed like part of everyday life for them. Sometimes it seemed that the ruder they were to you, it showed the more you meant to them.

Another thing she would never get used to was the way they called each other 'man', regardless of whether they were male or female. They would use it in such an exasperated fashion. 'Oh, Irene man, howay! You have to be able to laugh at yourself, hinny. You have to be able to give as good as you get!'

But Irene didn't want to mock other people, or join in with all that jocular messing around. For the first weeks in that house she spent the time not knowing who all the others were laughing at. Their humour seemed as alien as their salty, vinegary accents. Yes, the accents sounded to her just like too much salt and vinegar on a fish supper, which was exactly the way the whole family liked their fish suppers. So salty they could sting your lips.

Sam, the youngest son, brought back everyone's supper from the chip shop on Friday nights and they'd all be seasoned liberally. Lucky would sit on the dresser waiting for the fish head they always brought him.

Despite everything and all the strangeness, Irene was slowly getting used to things.

Today in particular – a Saturday afternoon when the house was relatively quiet – she felt like she had passed some secret test. A strange initiation. Old Ma Ada had taken her aside and asked her to help with starting the Christmas cakes. It was a solemn undertaking, this annual ritual. It had gone on for many years and even wartime privations weren't going to get in the way of her baking her usual dozen fruit cakes.

'A dozen!' Irene couldn't believe it. Where on earth would she get all the ingredients?

It turned out that the close circle of family, friends and acquaintances was bigger than Irene had even imagined. And so here she was, ensconced in the chilly scullery, finding the job more arduous than she'd expected, kneading together endless claggy, doughy mounds of dried fruits and spices, fats and flour. Mysterious parcels of ingredients were brought out, one at a time, with great ceremony. The old woman thumped down bags of sugar, flour and all kinds of goodies. She'd had them secreted away in cupboards and under counters. Out they all came, these secret supplies. Evidently she had been squirreling stuff away for months.

'What do I call you?' Irene suddenly burst out.

The old woman was thumping away with gusto, covered in a dusting of flour, her hair scraped up in a bun. She looked absurdly short standing at the table. Suddenly she seemed less formidable and terrifying to Irene than she had during these past few weeks and this emboldened the girl to ask the question that had been niggling her for ages.

'Call me?' the old woman frowned.

'Everyone in this house calls you "Ma". Even Megan and Beryl.'

'You can call me that, too, if you like.' Tom's ma looked down at her hands as they worked at the podgy dough. Her hands were rough and almost purple in colour. Her manner in that moment seemed almost shy, which amazed Irene.

'No, I-I think . . . I think I'd rather call you by your name, Mrs Farley, or . . .'

'Oh no,' Tom's mam looked up. There was actual hurt in her pale blue eyes. 'Oh, that sounds much too proper and formal, pet . . .'

'Then I would like to use your given name. Your Christian name,' said Irene, who felt much better when this kind of thing was sorted out and she knew how the land lay.

'Well,' said the old woman. 'As you know, my name is Ada. But . . . no one has called me that straight out since my husband – who would have been your father-in-law – since he died. I haven't been just plain "Ada" to anyone at all since then. They call me "Mam" or "Old Ma Ada". Never just my name . . .'

'Is it all right if I call you that? Just "Ada"?' asked Irene.

Ada nodded quickly and stared at her new daughter-in-law. There was something about Irene. Something tough. Something forthright. Something that the old lady liked very much indeed.

There was Marine Park and Marsden Rock. There was the Chi and the Nook. There was Ocean Road and the Roman remains and Fowler Street, Binns department store and the market place. The butchers and the greengrocers and the town hall and the air raid shelter.

All these places were starting to become familiar to Irene, even the ones with the funny names. Her world was growing larger as she started to explore the new town.

She was taken under the wing of her sisters-in-law, Beryl and blonde Megan. Together they dragged her up and down every street of South Shields on any days they got free from the biscuit factory. Beryl and Megan tended to walk very quickly, gabbling away at top speed as they went. Between them they had a formidable amount of energy, and it seemed to sweep Irene along.

One Friday afternoon they took her shopping down Fowler Street. Decorations had been strung from the lamps for the festive season but they were meagre things that didn't look like very much at all.

'We'd be better off without them,' Megan sighed. 'They just remind us of what we're missing. It'll hardly seem like Christmas at all with the shortages. And all the changes . . .'

Beryl swiftly nudged her sister-in-law under the table. They were in Binns department store cafe, each with a cup of weak tea and a sticky bun shared between the three of them. 'Oh, come on, it's not that bad,' Beryl said with mock-heartiness. She was putting on a brave face for the sake of the new sister. It was no use if they all went sinking into despondency. What would Irene think of them all then?

But Irene wasn't even listening. She was off in a daydream of her own at that point, staring out of the rippled, leaded glass of the cafe's upstairs windows at the busy street below. She felt bad that she hadn't been paying attention to Megan and Beryl's chatter all afternoon, even when it was concerned with the important topic of their husbands and what the women thought about them going off to war. Irene still only listened vaguely as her new sisters discussed how they felt about their men going off to be soldiers and sailors and doing their bit.

Megan was all for it. 'What would happen if they didn't? What would everyone say? And how will we ever win the war unless blokes like ours show willing and make the necessary sacrifices, eh?'

Beryl wasn't quite so gung-ho about it all, nor so sanguine. Her own father had told her some horrible things about his involvement in the last war. If she thought about it for any length of time Beryl couldn't abide the idea of the boys going off to play at soldiers all over again. It all seemed foolhardy and wrong. She couldn't share Megan's feelings about it at all, but she couldn't find a way of voicing that. All she could do was think about her dad, who lived at the top of the town by the park, and who hadn't been properly right in the head for years. Nobody talked about it, not even her mam, but Beryl knew what was behind it all, and what had ruined her dad. It was going to the war and seeing the things that they were so happily sending their own men to face right now.

They're just lads, really, Beryl thought. All the Farley men – their mam has kept them as young lads all their lives. They're daft, and tied to her skirts. There's only Tom, who managed to get away and become a grown-up . . . Even her own Tony, who was the oldest brother, was a bit immature, now she came to think of it.

She glanced at Irene, who was picking at her third of the bun which Beryl had divided with a knife. Irene's thoughts were up in the clouds. Probably with her Tom, picturing him thundering through the skies in his Lancaster Bomber.

It was difficult to tune in to what Irene was thinking. Beryl usually thought of herself as someone quite good at guessing what was going on in people's minds. Irene was a bit of a closed book to her. It was like she was a foreigner with her funny accent and her dark eyes and the way she covered up her mouth when she talked sometimes. Megan said that it made her seem a bit sly, but Beryl didn't think so. She understood that Irene was shyer and more nervous than she pretended to be. She found it tougher than all the rest of them, living in that crowded little box of a house on Frederick Street.

Irene found certain things harder than the rest of them did, at least at first. Things like bath night and the way they were all quite used to queueing in the downstairs hall with the jugs of hot water getting passed back and forth. All the laughing and good-natured joking, all of them standing with their threadbare towels, waiting their turn. Then the tin bath in front of the black lead range in the back room. Everyone getting a fair twenty minutes behind the closed door. A scant twenty minutes to strip, dip, scrub and dry off and dress again while all the others cried out impatiently from the hall. Well, it was something the rest of the clan were quite used to by now.

Beryl could still see the scandalised look on the new girl's face as she stood in the hall with her dressing gown collar clutched about her neck.

'I didn't think we'd stand in an actual queue like this!'

'We can't waste hot water!' Megan sneered at her. 'You might be used to fancier ways down south, but we can't go refilling the bathtub with hot again and again.'

Irene shrugged. 'It isn't that. I grew up with six sisters . . . Of course I'm used to sharing everyone's bum water . . .'

Beryl shrieked with laughter, grabbing hold of Irene's arm. 'Eeeh! Bum water! Is that what you call it, hinny?' She bent over double, laughing. 'That's so funny!'

Irene was used to the phrase and she didn't see what was so funny about it. Megan curled her lip with disgust, and Sam wanted to know what they were saying. 'Never you mind!' Megan snapped at him.

'It's just the queueing outside the door puts me off,' Irene frowned. 'It's like . . . everyone can hear you taking your things off, and splashing around in the tub . . . It's a bit . . .' She shrugged, and glanced at Sam. 'I don't want to listen to others washing . . . themselves.'

Beryl had started laughing at this again. 'Eeeh, you're a funny 'un, Irene. I don't care who hears me washing! If you're that bothered, you should sing at the top of your voice while you're in there. We could all sing Gracie Fields!' Beryl started a lusty rendition of 'Sing as We Go', marching up and down the queue and swinging her towel like a flag.

Suddenly Ma Ada was out in the hall, with Lucky in her arms, asking what all the giggling was about on the Lord's day, while she was trying to say her prayers. Megan said, 'It's just Irene. She's fretting because of having to sit in everyone else's . . . *bum water*.'

'*What* . . .?' cried Ma Ada. 'What did you say? Don't you go saying "bum" in my good front hallway!'

Beryl told Irene, 'We just have to queue up so we can be quick, that's all, pet. Jumping in and out of the tub. Before the heat goes out of the water. That's why we stand here, like lemons in the hallway, clutching our towels. Just think of it as a relay race or something. We'll make it into a game!'

Beryl was being kind to her, Irene realised. She was making things into a joke, to ease over her various moments of awkwardness and misplaced modesty.

'*Bum* water, indeed!' Ma Ada had harrumphed, and returned to her prayers and her sherry in the parlour.

Irene was way down the pecking order when it came time to use the bath. The water was barely lukewarm and horribly grey-looking. She could hardly get a lather from the soap. Ah well, she thought. This was probably what they meant by mucking in.

Beryl felt sorry for the girl from Norfolk, those first few weeks and months of settling in. Getting someone else used to their foibles and routines drew attention to the way they all lived, and made Beryl feel self-conscious. Perhaps Irene thought they were strange, the way they all carried on? Maybe she was horrified at the way they had to live. Beryl had even said to her: 'You must be used to finer things down south? Better than the life we live here, eh, hinny?'

Irene laughed at this. It was a nice laugh. Her eyes twinkled greenish and gold when she hooted with laughter, so even if she covered her mouth, you could still see her eyes were amused. 'I'm not used to better at all! I'm really not. Honestly, you'd think the same as Tom did when he came home with me to my people. He thought we were living in the Dark Ages, in the time of Queen Victoria.'

Irene was laughing, but she felt a pang of loss for that dark little kitchen, busy with her sisters beetling about, and foggy with her da sat there, stinking them all out with his pipe and banging the dottle on the fire surround to shut them all up. Irene even missed her ma and her toweringly dark, awful moods and her need to pick fights with all and sundry just to pass the time.

Sitting in the cafe in Binns department store, Beryl shook her head and started laughing again. 'I'm still laughing about you saying "bum water" and making Ma Ada look so cross.'

Irene looked abashed and Megan frowned again. 'You two are so common.'

The sisters-in-law finished their tea and the stale, sticky bun they were sharing, and they marched out of the store together, three abreast with linked arms, through the aisles of ladieswear. Cursorily they cast their eyes over the depleted stocks.

'I would have loved a job here before the war, when they were doing well,' said Megan. 'It was so . . . sumptuous. All the fabric and finery. Sumptuous was the word, wasn't it, Beryl? It was like being in Paris or somewhere . . .'

Beryl smiled. 'Maybe not quite Paris, pet, but it was better than it is now, I agree. All these things they've put out since clothes coupons came in are like hessian sacks hanging up, aren't they? Even this time last year there was more of a selection than this.'

Megan said, 'I wish old Ma Ada would let us look through her wardrobes. All those things she got when her sister died, do you remember? She had them shipped over and we only got a glimpse before she stowed them all away. There were gowns and all sorts. Expensive stuff. Going back years, by the looks of it. Everything beautifully preserved. There was a right stink of mothballs. I saw fur stoles with heads and teeth and dainty paws and heavenly little evening bags.'

'Ugh, fur stoles,' Beryl shuddered. 'I wouldn't thank you for a fox head, or anything like that.'

Megan shrugged, as if glamour was something Beryl just didn't understand. They emerged from the store's revolving doors into the stinging breeze of Fowler Street. There was a spot of freezing rain coming on. 'But wouldn't you think the old woman would let us look in her closets, though? With three daughters-in-law living under her roof? You'd think she'd throw the doors open and let us have a rummage. It's not like she's ever going to wear those fancy things herself, is it?'

The girls wandered under the striped awnings of the shabby marketplace and perused a stall or two as the canvas flapped like sailcloth at sea. Irene was fretting about buying Christmas presents and what everyone might expect. Just some small, token thing for each member of the family. She couldn't afford much and there were just so many of them!

I'll have to buy something for Megan, too, she thought, even though her heart shrank from the idea. There had been no more overt bullying from the blonde girl – certainly nothing as bad as that queer moment when she'd smashed all the biscuits – but still Irene didn't trust her one bit.

At a haberdasher's stall she touched all the shiny, colourful ribbons just to feel the silk rushing through her fingers. Would the girls like hair ribbons? Her younger sisters at home, they'd be happy with small fripperies like that. But she doubted that such things would do for Beryl and Megan. She didn't know what they'd like or how she would ever stretch to buying presents for the whole family.

Irene was looking at boxes of bright buttons and it was only when they started to blur and glitter like fish scales that she realised she had tears brimming in her eyes. She rubbed them away quickly before the others could notice. She needn't start with the blubbing and feeling sorry for herself. She had to be practical. Cheap and cheerful. That would have to do for presents, and of course it would. They would all understand that. She would have to use her nous and think hard about what to give them all. She had to get it right.

Then Megan was saying, 'I'd love a little tippet actually, to drape around my neck. Little paws and glass eyes. It can set off any outfit, that kind of thing . . .'

Irene found herself replying, 'Well, maybe you could persuade Lucky to sit curled round your shoulders when you go out? He could lie very still and pretend. That would be a damned sight cheaper.'

Beryl cracked out laughing at this, glancing sideways at the nonplussed Megan. Irene was coming out of her shell, it seemed. She was even being a bit sarky. That was good to see, Beryl decided. She had something about her, that girl. Somehow Beryl knew that Irene was going to be good for this family.

Chapter Seven

There was something Irene was dying to ask her sister-in-law Beryl but she was too shy. It was too personal. She was worried that Beryl would simply tell her to mind her own business.

She watched both Beryl and Megan closely and tried to behave like they did, minding their manners and getting on with the routine of things at number thirteen Frederick Street and then down on the factory floor at Wight's. It was clear that Beryl and Megan both kept themselves crammed down and quiet when they were at home. You barely heard a squeak out of them and, for the sake of fitting in, Irene followed suit.

Ma Ada was watching them all keenly and Irene never forgot it. One time she told her new daughter-in-law: 'You're doing quite well, I'll give you that.' It seemed like the highest praise possible and Irene felt pleased with herself. I'm behaving like a prisoner, she thought. I'm glad of every crumb of praise and comfort.

After a full month of living there and only a couple of short, somewhat vague letters from Tom – both devoid of detail and real feeling – she felt that she had to have a proper conversation with someone or she would burst. Of course it was Beryl she confided in. Beryl who'd been nicest to her out of everyone she'd met, and a girl not too much older than she was herself.

It was towards the end of November, four weeks after Tom had returned south, that Irene went with Beryl to volunteer at the community hall, sorting through donations of old clothes to the local Women's Voluntary Service branch. It was a chance to spend some time with Beryl without Megan there. At work they were always in different departments, and Megan always seemed to be just a few yards away. Even though there was hardly an hour to spare in any of their busy days, Irene and Beryl found themselves pressurised by Mrs Clarke, their work supervisor, to do some voluntary work. It was all for a splendid cause, the large-busted woman told them. Megan shrugged and took no notice whatsoever, but Irene and Beryl went along happily to lend a hand.

As it turned out, the work wasn't too onerous. There was a lot of chatter, laughter and noise in the community hall all that late afternoon. The trestle tables were covered in emptied sackfuls of shapeless garments of all kinds. Some of them were none too fragrant and fresh-smelling. Beryl and Irene listened to the instructions for sorting them and made sure they stood together through the long hours of rummaging, sorting and folding. Despite the work, Irene felt glad to be doing something productive and helpful, even if her arms ached after a full day at the biscuit factory.

Beryl chatted away brightly most of the time, keeping up a flood of information about her own life in South Shields prior to her marriage to Tom's brother, Tony. She kept quizzing Irene about her family and life down in Norfolk. She thought the little village and the vast expanses of countryside that Irene described sounded wonderfully far away and exotic. Irene allowed herself the small indulgence of romanticising home a bit, especially when she described preparations for Christmas in Hunworth, the quaint ancient church, parties of carol singers traipsing between cottages and the simple pleasures of their rural traditions. Beryl lapped it all up.

'You'll find Christmas very different here,' she said. 'It's all down the Robin Hood pub for Christmas Eve, for brown ale and cherry brandies for the ladies, and a few games of darts and a sing-song. I daresay it'll be a bit rougher than you're used to. The old lady drags us out to church first thing in the morning, all with thick heads. Though she says now that she's less keen on all that devotional carry-on. She reckons she's not the believer that she used to be. The world's gone and disappointed her, she says. She told me: "The Almighty and I don't quite see eye to eye these days. Not since he started taking my boys off to war."'

Irene knew that this wasn't quite true. Ma Ada still believed. She sat there all day on a Sunday in her chair by the range, all dressed up and clutching a worn leather Bible thick as a brick. She never actually opened it or read any of the lessons – her eyes were too bad for that, and she reckoned she had them all by heart – but she wore her best hat and looked as if she was about to jump up and leave for church at any moment. She simply sat in her parlour all day long, radiating piety.

'Do you believe in God then, Irene?' Beryl asked.

'Oh, yes,' said Irene quickly, shocked that anyone would even doubt it. 'I believe there's a guiding hand, helping us along through our lives. Making sure that things work out in the way that they should.' She paused in her folding of a pile of old shirts as she thought this through. She had never quite put these thoughts into words before. She shrugged and blushed and carried on working.

'I think it must be nice to think like that, and to be that sure,' said Beryl. Irene glanced at her. Was she being a bit sneering in her tone? No, she really did look a touch envious of Irene. 'But I just can't set store in some old man in the sky above us. I mean, if he was there, I'd have to ask him – why make people suffer? Why put good people through hell like you do?'

Irene smiled, though she thought this was a bit blasphemous, especially saying it out loud in public. 'Maybe one day you'll get to ask him.'

Beryl pulled a face. 'Oh, this is getting too deep and morbid for me. Let's talk about something nicer. What about rude stuff? What about sex? Had you ever done it with anyone else before you did it with our Tom?'

The younger woman's mouth dropped open in horror and all the folds fell out of the vast summer frock she'd been folding. 'What?' she whispered, as if she thought she'd misheard.

Beryl waggled her painted-on eyebrows mischievously. 'Oh, come on! You can't be such an innocent, Irene. That husband of yours is a sexy fella. Almost as nice as my Tony. Tell me everything! You can, you know – we're sisters now!'

But right at that moment the looming shadow of Mrs Clarke fell over them. She glared at the pitiful progress they'd made in sifting through the jumble and said a few harsh words to that effect. Irene was transfixed by the shape and size of the woman's monumental bosom. Mrs Clarke presided over her own chest like it was a balcony and she was Mussolini.

The two girls were forced to stop talking until the job was done and they were free to escape into the street, where they found that the afternoon was over and the evening had begun.

'Well, that was boring. I'm not going back there,' Beryl laughed. 'It was stinky, too. Fancy donating stinky clothes to the cause! Don't some people make you sick? I bet those bloomers all belonged to old Mrs Clarke. My God, isn't she awful?' Beryl grabbed Irene by the crook of her arm. 'Look, I'll stand you a milk stout at the Robin Hood. We deserve a drink!'

'The pub?' Irene was scandalised. 'By ourselves?'

'We can go in the Ladies' Snug,' Beryl sang happily, dragging her over the street. 'There's nothing wrong with that. We've been working hard and I've got a dry throat from all the dust and fluff and muck in those old rags, haven't you?'

Irene had never been through the doors of the Robin Hood before and she was a bit nervous. She knew that it was supposed to be a good, respectable kind of place, though, because their Bob was the pot man there. It was his job to unload barrels on delivery day and to bring them up from the cellar and keep the ale running smoothly to the pumps. He worked for the widowed landlady, Cathy Sturrock, who was fifty and vivacious. Irene had glimpsed her in the street several times already and she could see why Bob talked about her in awed terms, as if she were the Queen of Sheba herself. She certainly carried herself with great aplomb, and this, too, made Irene feel somewhat nervy about venturing inside the public saloon.

Before she knew it, however, she and Beryl were sitting by the fire at a tiny ironwork table and sipping dainty glasses of thick black nectar. 'I've never drank this before,' Irene said.

Beryl laughed. 'It seems to be slipping down a treat.'

It was like liquid velvet, Irene was about to say, but then she remembered a particularly smelly black jacket they'd had to contend with in the community hall that afternoon. 'Urrgh – smell these pits!' Beryl had giggled, trying to shove the offending article in Irene's face.

They'd both been rewarded with a hard stare from stately Mrs Clarke. Irene realised that the two of them must have been the noisiest and least useful volunteers in the whole place. Mrs Clarke had clearly been vexed by them, the way she'd folded her arms under that massive bust of hers and glared.

As they sipped and giggled Irene felt herself growing braver. At last she was brave enough to ask: 'So . . . if you and Tony have been married for two years, and Megan and Bob even longer . . . how come there are no babies in the house? I've been meaning to ask. Why are there no children at Number Thirteen?' As soon as she asked this, Irene flushed red.

Beryl's face dropped. 'Well,' she said slowly. 'I can't speak for the other two. That's their business, but I suppose they're taking precautions. But Tony and I aren't taking any. We've been wanting kids. Oh, of course we have. Two years is a very long time when you're wanting and trying. It just hasn't happened for us yet.'

She stared thoughtfully at the leaping fire in the grate. The crackles sounded lovely and homely in the careful pause.

'I shouldn't be so nosey, I'm sorry,' said Irene.

'No! Hadaway, pet – of course, you can ask me what you want,' Beryl assured her. 'Please do. I'm not proud. I'm not secretive. Look, I'm your big sister now – or, as good as. And you can ask me anything you want. I hope you know that.'

Irene felt a warm glow of pleasure at this. Relief, too.

Then Beryl went on: 'Mind, I don't know what we're thinking of. Trying to bring a bairn into an unsettled and crazy world like this. With bombs and planes and anti-aircraft guns and ships and everything that's going on. We're mad, really. And in that house, too! There's not enough room for all the souls already under that little roof, is there? Imagine all that – and with a screaming baby on top!' She laughed and then looked thoughtfully at Irene. 'Why are you asking, then?'

'Oh,' said Irene. 'It's just that . . .' And she sipped her gorgeous, silky dark drink, biding her time.

'Eeeh, you're not up the duff, are you?' Beryl burst out. 'You've never gone and hit the jackpot, have you, pet?' The rising excitement in her sister-in-law was disconcerting. The Robin Hood's landlady Cathy Sturrock was shooting interested, intrigued glances their way as she dried up glasses at the bar.

Irene was alarmed by Beryl's noisy reaction. 'Shush! I . . . well, erm . . . I might be. I'm not sure . . . I can't really know for certain . . .'

Beryl thumped down her glass and cried out in triumph. 'You are! Why, I can tell! I just know it! Look at you, Irene Farley! You've got it written all over your face!'

Irene swore Beryl to secrecy, but a fat lot of good that did.

It was much too early to be saying anything. She was only a little bit late. Now she was wishing she hadn't said anything at all. 'I really don't want to jinx things. I'm gonna keep my trap shut for a while now.'

Beryl promised her: 'I won't tell a single soul what you told me. You can count on me.'

But Beryl did tell someone else. Less than a day later she let Irene's secret slip out to Megan, as the two more established women of the house were fetching groceries together at the market.

Megan went white.

Beryl could have bitten her own tongue off.

'Well, she really will be the favourite now, won't she?' said Megan bitterly, 'if she manages to give the old witch her first grandchild?'

Beryl frowned at her. 'I never realised it was a race.'

'You didn't? You really didn't?' Megan rolled her eyes. 'Then you're daft, Beryl Farley. You're even dafter than I thought.' Suddenly Megan had turned on her heel and was clipping away through the busy marketplace, clutching her basket to her side. She was stooped like she'd been wounded. She was clearly upset and now Beryl was consumed with remorse for letting Irene down.

It was the first real note of discord at number thirteen Frederick Street. Irene – counting the days, holding her breath – was quite unaware that the enmity that Megan clearly felt towards her had deepened that day.

Megan and Bob had the tiniest room in the house. They slept in what was essentially an alcove under the stairs. This

76

was because they were supposed to have moved out to a home of their own a couple of years ago. The staircase boudoir was a stopgap measure, and it was a kind of joke to everyone. Megan only pretended to laugh along at her own misfortune, however.

Something had gone wrong with a rental agreement. It was probably down to Bob doing something wrong, his wife suspected. Megan's dream of a little house on the estate by the cliff tops had frittered away. That hope had gone by the start of the hostilities.

Some nights she lay awake in that horrible cubbyhole, her bed sheets full of dust and grit from the wooden stairs and her eyes smarting with tears of frustration as she imagined herself living in that house by the White Leas. Having a little garden and plants to water. A clothesline to hang rugs from so she could beat them till they were immaculate.

And there'd be Bob, too. He'd be there. There would be room enough for both of them. They wouldn't be crammed into the dark hole under the stairs, like something out of an old ghost story.

They were getting on each other's nerves, more and more, the longer they lived in their straitened circumstances. It was two years since they were supposed to have moved out and now he showed no signs of wanting to budge at all. He was a pot man at the Robin Hood and he worked himself into a frazzle every shift, all for the sake of old Cathy Sturrock. He had no energy left after humping barrels to consider anything else.

They were going to be stuck here. No child, no real home. Living under the stairs like unwanted sticks of furniture. And it made Megan want to scream.

Now there was this new young girl. Wedded to the old ma's favourite son, she was already several stages up the pecking order, before she even started. This little bitch with her mealy-mouthed ways and her fancy new-bought clothes. Her bloody trousseau. The way she crept around and sucked up to Ma Ada made Megan want to be sick. Why had she been given the attic? Surely it was the best room in the whole house? Plus, there was only one of her up there now, with Tom away down south. It was just crackers.

It wasn't fair that Tom was always the favourite. His life had always been easier than everyone else's. He'd even been allowed to escape. Her Bob seemed to get short shrift from everyone. He was a bit slow, perhaps. They thought all his chances were gone. He was just the pot man at the Robin Hood and he was content enough to sleep under the stairs for the rest of his life.

Well, Megan certainly wasn't.

She lugged the vegetables home alone, yomping heavily up the hill, leaving Beryl far behind. She'd lost her patience with Beryl. She hated the sly way Beryl had brought up the baby gossip. Beryl acted like butter wouldn't melt in her mouth, but she was a mixer, Megan knew. She'd caused bother before with her telltale tattling and then feigning innocence.

By the time Megan arrived back in Frederick Street she was seething mad with the whole lot of them. The whole rotten clan in their overcrowded house could go to hell, as far as she was concerned.

She banged open the front door and hoped there was no one in.

'Hello?' she yelled into the dreary hall. How she hated that pale-yellow wallpaper and its primrose pattern. How she loathed the vast aspidistra with its dark leaves polished to a shine. She batted them away as she squeezed down the narrow hall, past heavy framed pictures of long-dead relations that were fading to brown smears on the walls. The whole house was steeped in the history of this family. It wasn't even her family, really. She'd just gone and married one of their less-promising members and now she was wishing she never had.

Oh, if only a German plane could fly over their street tonight and drop bombs and blow this whole dark house and everything in it sky high and into blazing bits. Wouldn't that make her happy? She'd be bloody cock-a-hoop.

Megan's heart raced. She was shocked and delighted by her own terrible fantasy. Oh, and if the old witch was still indoors when those bombs fell! That would be the icing on the mouldy old cake!

Just then the evil-looking bald cat came slinking down the stairs on arthritic legs and it glared balefully at Megan. She hated that thing, too, and wished that someone would put it out of its misery.

'Hello?' came a reply from the parlour. 'Is that you back in, Megan?'

It was the youngest brother, Sam. He was only twenty and really, he was the nicest of the bunch. Lanky and fair-haired and endlessly cheerful. There was just something about his good-natured silliness that usually cheered Megan up. She was glad that it was him here today.

He was sitting at the parlour table with Irene and Ma Ada. When Megan pushed round the door her heart sank at the sight of the women. They were all laughing together, like they had been caught doing something naughty and very amusing. Well, the old woman wasn't laughing, obviously. She would rather cut out her own heart with the bread knife than laugh out loud, but she was surveying the merriment of the two youngsters with a warm and indulgent eye.

'What's going on here, then?' Megan asked warily.

'Oh, Megan!' Irene laughed, through a mouthful of something she was chewing. Not very polite manners, Megan thought. 'We're having a feast!'

All three of them were chewing something. They were crunching and munching, looking furtive and very pleased with themselves. Then Megan could see. There was a plate heaped with broken bits of biscuit in the middle of the table. Custard creams, chocolate bourbons and ginger nuts. There was a huge sack of the things open on the table, too.

'Come and set the groceries down,' Ma Ada told Megan. 'And pour yourself a cuppa. We've got plenty of biscuits to share.'

'Megan!' Irene laughed. 'Our Sam says he nicked them! Can you believe it? He went over the back fence of the biscuit factory. And there were binfuls and buckets of them, apparently, weren't there, Sam? And they were all going to waste.'

Sam sat there looking like the hero of the hour. 'I'd heard the rumours that Wight's chucked out loads of perfectly good food. It's criminal, isn't it? I had to rescue the custard creams, didn't I?'

'And liberate the ginger nuts!' Irene chimed in.

Megan peered at the plateful of broken bits and crumbs. 'Do you not see enough of these things every day at work, Irene? Are you not sick of the sight of bloody biscuits by now?' She shook her head despairingly at the girl. 'Anyhow, they look stale and mouldy to me. You'll all give yourself the runs eating those. Or worse.'

Ma Ada narrowed her eyes at the mardy-looking Megan and snapped her ginger biscuit loudly with her tiny teeth. 'There's nowt wrong with these biccies, lady. Now, you say thank you to our Sam and get yourself a cup of tea and drink it with us and you can eat a bloody custard cream and be a bit more pleasant. And don't you ever, *ever* say "the runs" in my parlour again. Now, where's our Beryl got to?'

Chapter Eight

Mrs Clarke praised Irene for her competence.

'You're very dextrous, I've noticed that,' the full-busted supervisor told her. 'You're a very good worker, Irene Farley.'

Irene was aware of Megan glaring at her like daggers across the packaging room. But it was true that Irene found the work relatively easy to do, and even enjoyable, when she was in the swing of it. Her fingers could work away and she could let her thoughts drift to happier times and places. She often found herself dwelling on her spring and summer months of courting with Tom. It seemed a world away from these bitterly cold mornings by the docks.

'Eeeh, you were getting praised to the skies, hinny! I've never seen that old besom be as nice to anyone as she was to you! And did you see your bloody sister-in-law's face! She was spitting feathers, she was!'

This was whey-faced Mavis, with the skinny arms and the scraggy hair. She had latched onto Irene these past few weeks as they worked side by side in the factory. The small, rather sickly looking girl regarded Irene with something close to hero-worship.

As the weeks went by they were moved to other buildings in the factory, learning to work on new parts of the process. Irene found it easy to pick up new skills, and Mavis was glad of her help when she dithered and flummoxed and made a mess of things. At one point they worked side by side at the machine that rolled out the biscuit mix at the precise thickness for the cutters to stamp out the actual biscuits themselves. It was like being brought into the sacred heart of the whole operation; in the very deepest part of the factory, where the biscuits were actually born. Mavis and Irene had to inspect each one and make sure it was perfect before it was sent to be baked with all the rest.

Mavis took everything so seriously, and this made Irene laugh sometimes. She fretted quite a lot, and had to be reassured. She was forever getting into bother for having dirty fingernails, or her pale hair hanging down, coming untucked from her hairnet. 'Whatever shall we do with you, Mavis?' Mrs Clarke would boom. 'You're neither use nor ornament, girl!'

Irene thought that was rather harsh and hated to see the way the small girl flinched whenever anyone in authority came by. It made Irene wonder what kind of upbringing Mavis had had, that she seemed so defeated and meek. It was as if most of the spirit had been beaten out of her already, and she was only seventeen. Irene longed to ask her about her home life and her family but was wary of being intrusive.

Still the girl latched onto Irene and dogged her every footstep each day at Wight's factory. She sat with her at break and dinner hour, chewing on her bread and dripping. She was a hopeless chatterbox, and this only ever amused Irene, who was used to having six younger sisters, after all.

However, Mavis's verbal incontinence drove Megan crazy. The very day that Megan joined them by the stamping machine saw a flare-up in the first hour.

'For God's sake, girl! I'm trying to concentrate here!'

Mavis simply stared at the blonde bombshell. Megan's brusque annoyance seemed to suck all of the air out of Mavis's lungs. 'I-I'm sorry, M-Megan.'

'Just keep your trap shut, eh?' Megan snapped. 'Just keep it zipped for the rest of the day, will you? I've had it up to here with your blarney.'

Mavis instantly retreated into herself, staring down at her shaking hands as they tried to get on with their work.

Irene found herself staring at poor Mavis and then across at her own sister-in-law, who wore a gloating, triumphant look on her face. And all at once, something inside Irene snapped.

'I bet you're pleased with yourself, aren't you, Megan?'

Megan's eyes widened slightly as she stared at Irene. 'I beg your pardon, lady?'

'You! I said, I bet you're bloody well proud of yourself!' Irene felt her face growing hot as she shouted at Megan above the noise of the stamper machine. It felt rather good. As she raised her voice she felt like she was getting something out of her system at last.

'What's it got to do with you, Irene?' said Megan, in a warning sort of tone.

'I'll tell you what. I'll not have you putting down Mavis like that. Look at the state of her! She's only a bairn, and shouting like that at her, you've started her off bubbling!'

Mavis looked up tremulously. 'I'm not bubbling, Irene! I'm not!' But she had hot tears running down her face and there was no hiding them.

'Don't bother sticking up for her,' said Megan, jeeringly. 'She's just a gutter brat. She's just an urchin from the rough part of town. She's nowt. Her ma was a gypsy lass who was on the game, and her father! They reckon he was an Arab!'

Irene flinched then, as Mavis suddenly sprang into life and darted past her. She pushed past all the other women in the room to get round to the other side. Megan barely had time to draw breath before she found herself being pummelled in the stomach by the angry waif.

'Mavis, stop it . . .' Irene gasped, hurrying after her. 'Don't give her the satisfaction of seeing you upset!'

Megan grabbed her assailant's arms and pinioned her easily. There was no strength at all in the little girl. The force of her attack had been pathetic really, and only seconds later Megan was laughing at her again. 'What the hell was that supposed to be? You silly little bitch. Everyone saw you attack me. I've got a dozen witnesses. I could have you flung out of here in a second!'

Mavis was being restrained by her workmates now, and most of them were laughing at her. It had been a useless assault. 'I don't care! You can do what you want. You're not to say things about me ma and me da! They're nowt to do with you . . .'

'They're not even here!' Megan laughed. 'Why do you bother sticking up for them? When they both buggered off and left you and your soft brother to fend for yourselves? What do you care what I call them?'

Suddenly Irene found herself face to face with Megan. All she knew was that she was sick of hearing Megan doing her damndest to crush Mavis down. It was like she was taking huge pleasure in every word and the devastating effect each one was having upon the younger girl.

'Leave her alone, Megan. I'm telling you.'

Megan simply stared back at Irene. Very levelly. Very calmly. She looked like she hated her more than anyone else in the world. She looked like she hated her more than Hitler. 'Just you make me, Irene.'

Irene had large hands. They were hands that had worked in the fields and her father's garden from the earliest days. They'd been hardened by the tough work she'd been put to in the last few years. They were hands that were capable of packing a hefty wallop. And that's precisely what she did to her sister-in-law just then. She slapped her as hard as she could in the face.

Megan reeled backwards and almost fell. She staggered against the conveyor belt and screeched. She swore. She said words out loud that Irene had never actually heard another grown-up utter. 'I suppose you've just been dying to do that, haven't you, Irene?' Megan spat.

'What?'

'You've hated the sight of me ever since your very first day in Frederick Street. It's been plain from the start! You've resented me and you've felt jealous of me all along!'

'Jealous?' Irene frowned. Her face felt bright red from the embarrassment of everyone in the room staring at her. She saw a raised welt on Megan's face that was even redder, and that came as a shock. 'Why the devil would I be jealous of you?'

Megan's eyes blazed at her. 'No one likes you, you know. I'm the only one who's honest enough to tell you the truth. But everyone hates you at home. Everyone thinks you're a *cow*.'

Then: smack. Irene slapped her again. She hadn't even been conscious of the fact that she was going to. As she watched Megan drop to the floor she felt truly appalled at herself. She hated fighting or violence or anything like that. It was the kind of thing only the lowest of the low got into. But here she was. Slapping her sister-in-law silly, right in front of everyone at work.

Next thing, Megan's own temper broke and she was up on her feet and launching herself at Irene. She was scratching and kicking and spitting. The entire factory floor erupted into howls of mirth and shrieks of pleasure, and an even bigger crowd gathered around the catfight.

In the midst of all the noise, Irene distinctly heard Megan say: 'I don't care if you are up the stick! I'll bloody *punch* the bairn out of your belly!'

'STOP THIS AT ONCE!' roared a huge voice. It was the kind of voice that wasn't used to being ignored. Mrs Clarke had entered the fray at last, and she was livid.

85

All the women went scuttling back to their workstations. The supervisor came sailing grandly through the parting crowd. She was glaring at the combatants like she could hardly believe her eyes.

'What in heaven's name is going on here?'

Bravely Mavis tried to speak up. 'It's all my fault! It was me, Mrs Clarke! I'm responsible for this . . .'

The supervisor silenced her with a swift glance. She looked like she wanted to bang Irene and Megan's heads together. 'You silly little girls. Have you got nothing better to do than fight amongst yourselves? Have you got any idea what's going on in the world out there?'

Megan opened her mouth to protest, but stopped herself. She realised there was nothing she could say to assuage the situation.

Irene simply stood staring back at the woman who had given her a job. Her face was draining of all the angry scarlet and she was feeling numb.

Mrs Clarke dismissed them both with a wave of her hand. 'The two of you get yourselves home at once. I'll dock your day's wages. I can't stick the sight of you right now.' Then she drew herself up to her full height, turned and left them on the factory floor.

Well, now I've got myself a real enemy, Irene thought, as she watched Megan rush to grab her coat and hat from the cloakroom. And she knows I'm pregnant, too. She's got some kind of power over me.

Just as Irene was fetching her own coat and preparing to leave, Mavis said, 'Thank you for sticking up for me.'

Irene's heart went out to the waif-like girl. 'Aye, well. I shouldn't have slapped her, maybe.'

'Look, I've got a bit of money saved,' Mavis grinned. 'Not much. Just rainy-day money. I want to treat you, as a thank you. I'll buy you an ice cream later. At Franchino's.'

It almost seemed absurd. Irene was in disgrace and wondering if she might even get the sack because of this awful fracas. And here was this girl asking to reward her with ice cream. Beseeching her, really. But Irene didn't have the heart to pour scorn on the offer, or to turn it down. 'All right,' she said, and tied her headscarf on. As she hurried out with everyone's eyes on her, she felt ashamed all over again. Fancy having a scrap at work! Fancy slapping Megan in the face and everyone watching!

Fancy picking a fight with someone who lived in the same house as you!

One thing was certain, Irene was sure she hadn't heard the last of this.

'Haway, then! It's my treat, remember! I've brung all my pennies, Irene, and I'm gonna stand you a treat! What about a sundae, eh?'

There was nothing to do but submit to the younger girl's daft insistence. In fact, there was nothing Irene wanted less, that freezing November late afternoon, than an ice cream. But it was Mavis's way of thanking her, so she couldn't really complain.

'Eeeh, Irene. No one's ever stood up for me like that. Not in front of other people. Not even me own brother! I'm that chuffed!' The very pale-looking girl was beaming ear to ear as they bustled through the streets towards Ocean Road. 'Have you ever been to the ice cream parlour yet? I hope this is the first time for you. It's really special and grand!'

Mavis was eagerly squeezing her saved pennies inside her mitten, Irene realised. It was as if the coins were burning a hole in the wool and needed to be spent.

Indoors it was warm, smoky and welcoming. Just how Irene remembered it from her first visit. She wondered vaguely why she hadn't already come back here, since Tom had been gone. It was one of the nicest places he had showed her.

The elderly Italian man at the counter wore half-moon glasses and a spotless, perfectly creased white shirt with a black pinny. He waved at them genially and encouraged them to find a table. They had their pick, for the place was almost empty.

Great gouts of hissing steam came out of the frothy coffee machine, and Irene breathed in the gorgeous, roasted scent with great pleasure. 'You know, Mavis. If it's all the same to you, pet . . . what with it being so freezy out . . . I'd actually prefer a piping hot frothy coffee to an ice cream right now . . .'

Mavis sat across the melamine table and blinked her eyes earnestly. For the first time Irene saw how huge and grey they were. They were innocent and pale. 'Are you sure, Irene? I'd like to treat you to what you want. Money's no object, mind! I've got all my pennies with me!'

Irene couldn't help smiling at her serious tone. 'Aye, I'm dead sure, pet. A lovely frothy coffee, just like the one that old fella's whipping up on his machine . . .'

Mavis shrugged and went off to order at the counter, mumbling something about a cup of coffee not being much of a special thank you gesture. But it was, as far as Irene was concerned. If that coffee tasted half as nice as the aroma that filled all of Franchino's, it would wash away the muddy tang of the chicory they always drank at Number Thirteen . . .

'Hello there, stranger!'

It was a musical voice, only vaguely familiar. It took her a moment to peer round the frosted-glass partition between banquettes to link it to the curvaceous figure of the waitress coming up the aisle towards her. It was Tom's old friend, Bella, looking every drop as glamorous as on Irene's first visit here. She loomed over the table and gave it a brisk wipe with her cloth.

'How are you settling down, Irene? How's life with the Farley clan?'

'Ooh, it's all right,' said Irene, self-consciously touching her curls, which felt very drab and flattened by her hairnet from work. She stared up at Bella's lustrous dark locks and felt fleetingly envious.

'And I hear you've been working at the biscuit factory, eh? With your sisters-in-law?'

Irene frowned. News went round this town pretty quickly, she thought. Fancy this practical stranger knowing all about her business! But her vexation was soon quashed by the thought of how she'd slapped one of those sisters-in-law twice around the face this very afternoon. There'd be more gossip for all the tittle-tattlers, she thought. Wouldn't they love to hear about that! The catfights on the conveyor belt at the biscuit factory!

'Are you sure you're OK, hinny?' Bella asked kindly. 'You look a bit upset . . .'

Irene was horrified to find her eyes filling up with tears. 'They'll chuck me out! I'll be out on the streets!' The words were coming out of her own mouth, and she was appalled at herself and her own noisy wailing. Instinctively she started digging around in her coat pockets for a hanky.

'Eeeh, pet!' Bella cried out, worried at having started her off. 'Whatever's the matter? Who's gonna chuck you out on the streets?' She reached over to the napkin dispenser and offered a papery wad for Irene to blow her nose and wipe her eyes on. But the tears carried on falling for a few moments yet.

Mavis abandoned her coffee order and came bustling across. 'Irene, man! You're bubbling! What's the matter with you? Is it the fight?'

'Fight . . .?' gasped Bella. 'What fight?'

'Irene had a scrap at work today,' Mavis said, as Irene buried her face shamefully in her hands. 'She was coming to my rescue because that Megan was being such a cow. Irene stood up for me and smacked her one, right in the gob!'

Mavis beamed proudly. 'I reckon she's all upset out of delayed shock, though . . .'

Irene's shoulders were heaving as she sobbed into her winter gloves and the crumpled serviettes.

'Let it all out, hinny,' Bella advised her. Then she waved at her father at the coffee machine. 'Hurry up with the cappuccinos, Papa! This poor girl's had an awful shock! Her nerves are in tatters, over here!'

Papa Franchino leapt into action. He came toddling over with everything they needed on one tray. He put some special hard nutty biscuits out for dipping in their coffee, then he set it all down before them, looking concerned.

'What if they fling me out on the street for scrapping?' Irene cried. She might have lost her job and her home, all in one go. The enormity of it all had just occurred to her.

Chapter Nine

Sam was used to being the youngest in the house and everyone treating him like a bairn. When Irene came along she was even younger but because she was a married woman it wasn't the same. Sam was still the youngster and it was a position he was happy to keep. They all indulged him and he got away with murder, as Irene put it, later on, when they got to know each other better.

'You give them all that backchat and do as you please. No one ever really tells you off for anything.'

He shrugged happily. 'That's 'cause of my happy-go-lucky nature and my charm,' he said. 'They can't bring themselves to tell me no.'

He was Ma Ada's last child and he was her last remaining link to her husband and her youth, as she saw it. She had given birth to him impossibly late, as some of the women on Frederick Street liked to put it. When she was pregnant with him she had been huge, waddling up and down the Sixteen Streets, fearless and proud. A short, ancient woman with a bun in the oven. She glared at anyone who stared too long.

Within weeks, Sam and Irene were firm friends. Having only a year or so between them it was natural they would fall into an easy companionship.

She needed that uncomplicated ease right now. Especially after all the recent bother with Megan. There was a rift as wide as Tyne dock between Megan and Irene, and a silence as deep as the coalhole in the backyard. Neither girl would speak about why they weren't getting along, and a certain atmosphere hung over Number Thirteen for a week or two.

'Ah, it's just that Megan,' Ma Ada sighed grumpily. 'She can be bloody mardy sometimes.'

'I think Megan's just jealous of Irene having the top bedroom,' Beryl told her. 'She thinks Irene's had special treatment ever since she got here.'

Ma Ada harrumphed. 'My house, my decisions. My rules! If Megan's got any complaints, then she can come and spit them out directly to me.'

Beryl knew there was more to the spat between the two sisters-in-law. She had heard chapter and verse about the catfight from both combatants. But there was no way she was sharing an account of that shameful scene with old Ma Ada.

'You'll need to make peace with Megan quickly,' was all of Beryl's advice to Irene. 'She can be very difficult that one. You really don't want to be on the wrong side of her.'

Irene had a heavy heart about the whole thing. 'I already am on the wrong side of her. It's hopeless. The girl hates my guts.'

And so it came as a relief that she had this new friendship developing with Sam. She could disappear with him on evenings out, and any other time that she had spare. It felt good to be away from anywhere Megan might be.

Sam was a cheering personality to spend time with because he was, in a way, the most carefree person at Number Thirteen. Not that he was light-hearted, exactly. Not with air raids going on and disaster all around. It was more to do with the fact that he had fewer ties and responsibilities on him than anyone else.

Because, as he said, the Forces wouldn't take him, Sam was doing any bits of work he could find, casual labouring mostly, and he had lots of funny hours and free days. Irene didn't enquire further as to why the Forces wouldn't have him. She thought it might sound like she was asking him what was wrong with him. Probably he had some kind of medical impediment that meant he was exempt, but she didn't feel like she knew him quite well enough to ask him about it yet.

At this stage she was more concerned with what she was going to do if she was forced to leave the biscuit factory. So far there had been no actual reprisals following the fracas with Megan. But that wasn't to say there wouldn't be. For at least a fortnight Irene went around expecting to be chucked out on her ear at any moment. Her employment history there was a great deal shorter than Megan's, and if anyone was for the chop, surely it was Irene.

On her days and evenings with Sam she was dolefully mulling over alternative jobs she might do. She still needed to bring some money into the house, and she felt like she had already blown her first chance. No one said it outright, but there was no way their household could support someone not pulling their financial weight. She had to be out there, earning some cash!

'An usherette!' Sam kept saying, every time they went to the pictures together. 'Wouldn't that be the best job? You'd see every film for free . . .'

'Aye, again and again, until I was pig sick of them,' she mused. 'It wouldn't just be selling ice creams and watching the flicks, you know. It'd be dealing with the rough element in the audience, too. It would be picking up God knows what from underneath the seats when you have to tidy round at the end.'

Sam shrugged. It still seemed like a pretty good job to him. Better than lugging mucky and splintery crates around at the docks while fellas yelled at you.

The Savoy at the Nook was their favourite place for the movies. It was a good walking distance from home so it felt like you were getting away from the family and neighbours (though that was hardly ever true. You were always bumping into someone, it seemed, wherever you went in South Shields). The building was like a smooth white palace, all blocky and modern-looking. They would share a little tub of ersatz ice cream and soak up whatever was playing that week.

What they loved most of all were the melodramas. It was Sam who used this word about the films they enjoyed the best. Films in which someone did someone else wrong, someone lost all their money, murder was plotted, revenge was declared and there were denouements galore. Also, there was lots of shouting and guns getting waved about and folk driving away at top speed in glossy cars.

'Does our Tom ever take you to the pictures?' Sam asked her, lighting up his fourth fag since they'd sat down and they hadn't even got to the main feature yet.

'Yes, sometimes. We went in Lincoln and Norwich a couple of times. But he was on passes and sometimes they were just for a couple of hours. It seemed like a waste of time, he said – sitting in the dark and watching other people live their lives.'

'Ha! That sounds like our Tom,' Sam laughed. He smoked like a kid, Irene thought, sucking in greedy mouthfuls of smoke. 'What did he want to do then? Find somewhere private to go and get all lovey-dovey?'

Irene scowled at him and punched him playfully. 'No! Shut up, Sam. You shouldn't say things like that.'

He creased up laughing so loudly that the people in front started tutting pointedly. 'What's wrong with saying that? You must have been getting lovey-dovey and all that. It stands to reason!'

Irene turned prim, knowing that this would make him laugh even more. 'You shouldn't say it because it's rude.' She pronounced 'rude' in a funny way, like it had two syllables and this always made Sam laugh still more. His giggles brought even more shushing and tutting from the seats around them.

'But you're allowed to be rude,' he persisted. 'You're a respectable married couple! What did you do for fun, then? Did you go out into the countryside and roll around in the fields? Did you take all your clothes off and run around starkers?'

'Sam!' she hissed, appalled at him. 'Don't say things like that! And don't talk so loud!'

He loved to send her up and get her in a flap like this. She was dead easy to flummox and poke fun at. He never did it nastily, though, and Irene knew that. He was just delighted by this friendship with his new sister-in-law. He didn't think much of the other two. Beryl was soft and boring, he thought, and Megan was just a cow.

'Sam, you can't call ladies C-O-Ws,' Irene told him, spelling out the letters sotto voce. 'Not even Megan.'

'Is that rude, too?' he elbowed her. Soon, as the film was starting up and the titles flashing on, Irene was giggling too. She didn't even know what she was laughing about. It was all down to the daft way he was carrying on. It was infectious. Oh, but it felt good to laugh. She'd been wandering about in a state of high tension for days, it seemed like. Waiting to hear about her job and whether she still had one. Being wary and keeping out of Megan's way. And also, there was that other thing. That much more important thing. The thing that was a thousand times more important than a fight with a silly, selfish, vicious girl like Megan.

That other matter pressing on her thoughts was one which could change all their lives forever. And so Irene found herself waiting and worrying. She was waiting and watching and checking herself for blood. She was fretting and hoping all at the same time. She was dreading and dreaming. No wonder she was happy to be distracted from her endless churning thoughts.

A daft film about someone else's troubles, and a few hours of listening to Sam's cheery nonsense was doing her good.

'Hey, you two,' came a whining, nasal-sounding voice from the end of the row. 'Can you put a sock in it? Other folk want to listen to Joan Crawford, not you two.' A torch beam came shooting into their eyes, searing and blinding them for a moment. It was savage as the lights in the sky on bomb nights. 'Do you hear me, hinnies?' the voice demanded, its torch beam picking out Sam and then Irene, who shrank, horrified, into the worn velour plush of her seat.

'Y-yes,' she said, feeling like she was getting into bother in school assembly.

'I've got my eye on you two,' the usher said in a clipped tone and then moved on, getting murmurs of approval from other patrons.

'See? You always get us into trouble,' Irene whispered, pinching Sam's arm.

'What, with soft Arthur?' Sam laughed. 'I'm not scared of Arthur. We went to the same school together. Cleadon Park Infants. He was a snotty little bugger back then, too.' Sam didn't seem to give a hoot about being told off in public.

But what an extraordinary voice the young usher had, Irene thought. His words had flicked out along the row of fold-up seats like a whiplash.

As she sat there blushing in the dark with the film credits rolling Irene couldn't help smiling. That young man with the strange nasal voice was the only person who could silence Sam with just a few words. It made her chuckle to herself. What a funny character, she thought. He was like no one she had ever met.

It was Sam who tried to teach her a bit about history, and about how her new town had come to be the way it was. 'South Shields has been a port for about a thousand years, you know.

More, I reckon. These Nazis flying over and trying to put us out of action, they should know it's hopeless, really, because there's been ships here, landing here, getting built and being repaired here, since before the time of the Romans.'

'Fancy that,' Irene said. They were walking the long way back home after the cinema, so he could show her the Roman remains at the top of the hill. He reckoned it was an old fortress under the ground here and the end of Hadrian's Wall. Bits of it were still poking up through the earth and in between modern buildings, but you had to use your imagination.

Irene had a vague recollection of what Hadrian's Wall was all about. Something about keeping the Scots out? She could remember a few facts from doing it at school, but history wasn't something she'd enjoyed very much. It seemed to pass through her head and back out again as she listened. She couldn't seem to cling on to any of the dates or events. History felt like ghosts passing through her.

From up here they could see the great, dark sweep of the whole town. All the heaped rows of streets and steeples and chimneys and the jumbled shapes of the shipyards with their spindly filigree cranes and masts. Then there was the vast, sheeny swell of the tide pushing in and out of the harbour.

Tonight there was a good moon and even though the blackout was complete, they could see the whole of Shields quite clearly.

'It looks like a model made of boxes and folded paper,' Irene said. 'Something someone has spent years making, all delicately, folding and cutting round the edges.'

'Clear night,' Sam muttered. 'It's a bomber's moon. We should get home.'

From here it was easy to spot the dark patches and empty spaces where homes had been blasted into nothingness in recent months. It made Irene shiver, just looking from up here. 'I'd love to come back in the daytime and look at this view again in the light,' she said. What she really meant was that she'd have loved to have seen it before they started destroying it.

'It's one of my favourite places to come and sit and think things out,' he told her. 'Looking down at the whole town puts everything into perspective. When there's bother and rows at home and you hate everyone's guts or someone's been horrible to you, it's great to come up here and stare down at the whole lot and see all the little boxes, all set out in rows together. You can see how small we all are. And how many of us there are and how we're all having our dramas and upsets and we're all doing it at the same time. And no one's life is any more important or bigger or stranger than anyone else's.'

Irene turned to him, studying his face as he talked. 'Hey, you're a deep thinker, aren't you? All I meant was that it's a lovely view. Even in the dark and the bloomin' cold.'

Sam grinned at her. 'Ah, did you not know, pet? Had you not realised yet? I come from a family of philosophers and intellectuals.'

She laughed. 'No, I hadn't realised that . . .'

He started leading the way back from the top of the hill, jumping over chunks of rubble and stone, returning them to civilisation. 'Oh, aye,' he went on, 'they call me mam the Socrates of South Shields. And her little cat Lucky? He's gifted in that he can tell the future just by sticking his nose in your tea leaves. My Aunty Martha – three doors down – she's a mathematical genius, you know. And Great Uncle Derek – he's got loads of letters after his name. If you arrange them in the right order they spell out something mucky.'

Sam was messing on again and making Irene laugh, but she was glad that, just for a moment, he had let her see another side of him. He had been thoughtful and he'd shown her a place he thought of as special.

'Does my Tom ever go up there with you? Does he like looking at the town from the Roman remains?'

'Tom?' Sam smiled, shaking his head. 'He's not much like me in that regard. Tom's always been dead practical and sensible. He isn't daft like Bob, or really clever like Tony, or a dreamer like me. All four of us brothers – we're quite different really, for all we look a bit alike. Tom is the least like me of them all. Maybe we've just never had very much to talk about, I don't know. I mean, obviously, he's my brother and I love him and all that. But . . . I've probably talked more to you, Irene, than I've ever talked to him, in all my life.'

Irene felt flattered by that, but also vaguely saddened. She felt stirred to emotion by hearing a young man say that he loved his brother so openly, with so little embarrassment. It surprised her because the men she was used to at home and those that she had met so far in the north east, were all pretty tight-lipped when it came to talking about their feelings, or anything like that. They must feel somehow that it weakened them, even admitting that they had any.

They descended into the shrouded streets down by the docks. Everything was smudgy like charcoal, with that tang of soot everywhere. The stillness was such it seemed like there was a curfew on. A ragged, lolloping dog ran past them, barking madly. It looked lost and desperate to find its way back home.

'Ah, it's a shame,' Sam said quietly. 'There's homeless animals all over town. Some of them run away during the bombing or their houses and families are gone. I know some people who queued up at the vets to have theirs put down, to spare them the suffering when the bombs started to fall. The dogs can go out of their minds with terror, of course, because they don't understand what's going on.'

'How horrible,' said Irene, and all at once found herself thinking of Sally Ha-ha, her daft little terrier she'd had when she was just tiny. She hadn't thought of her for years, but suddenly she could feel that squirmy body sitting on her lap, and the coarse woolly fur. She could feel those dark tiny claws as they snagged her stockings.

'I don't see how they can do it,' Sam said. 'It's like destroying love, isn't it? They might say it's kinder, but I really don't know. It's love, and that's all that counts. The way dogs look at you. How could anyone be so cruel?'

'I don't know,' said Irene. 'I don't know how anyone can set out to be cruel. But I suppose . . . in some circumstances, people have to force themselves to be. Look at Tom. He'd never hurt anyone, would he? But right now . . . he'll be somewhere in the sky. Tonight, he'll be up there somewhere, and he'll be setting out to drop bombs on people he's never met and knows nothing about. That's his duty, and he's got to face up to that . . .' She shivered and wished she hadn't started on this train of thought.

'That's war, I reckon,' Sam said. 'That's what they have to do.'

Irene suddenly felt like she wanted to hold his hand, but resisted the impulse. She didn't want to give him the wrong idea. That could be disastrous.

They hurried along the final leg of the journey home, arriving at last at the corner of Frederick Street.

'I wasn't joking about me Aunty Martha being a mathematical genius, you know. Though it's mostly gambling that she uses it for, mind.' He looked at Irene and grinned. 'Really, I'm glad to be the skinny, useless runt of our family. I was all they had left over at the end of making everyone else. They'll never ask me to fight, you know. No matter how bad it gets, they'll never want me. I've got a heart murmur. It's like an echo of another heart grumbling inside my chest. Hopeless! Also, flat feet and rotten eyes. I'm pretty much rubbish. But I'm glad, really. I'd never say this to anyone else but you, pet. 'Cause if it came to it and they asked me to go and fight anyway, I don't think I could do it. I really don't.'

Chapter Ten

All the way to work that morning Irene listened to Beryl complain about being stuck at the biscuit factory, when the only thing she wanted to do was go and learn welding at the shipyard.

'I'm even having dreams about doing welding!' she laughed bitterly, and her breath came out in great white plumes as the two of them bustled along. 'Oh, why haven't they written to me, Irene? It's weeks since I applied. I feel like going straight to their head office and demanding to know why they think I'm not good enough for them.'

'I'm sure you're good enough,' Irene said. 'And I'm sure you'll hear from them soon. It's just everything is slower, with the war on, I expect . . .'

Beryl tossed her head. 'You'd think that'd make them even gladder of having willing volunteers like me, then! There's a state of emergency on!'

As they moved through the usual morning crowd surging through the iron gates of Wight's biscuit factory, Irene was picturing Beryl at work, wielding a blowtorch and shooting bright sparks everywhere. It must be quite a satisfying thing to do, mending and fixing and sealing things till they were airtight. She imagined seeing metal heating up till it became red hot and starting to bubble and melt. Surely it had to be a bit more satisfying than packing biscuits into boxes?

'You're back in the packaging room then, pet?' Beryl asked her, with a rueful smile.

'I think they're keeping me and Megan separate, in different buildings,' Irene admitted. 'She's still on the cutting and stamping machine, and I'm back in the shed with my paste pot and the girl coming round with the barrow.'

'Could be worse,' Beryl laughed. 'I've known lasses been given their cards for scrapping.'

Irene nodded. 'I've been going round in fear, expecting to be sacked any day.'

'Eeeh, lass. But you've got to get it sorted out with Megan. Ma Ada has started looking furious about the way the two of you don't even talk to each other at home. She's on the warpath about it, and she wants it sorting out by Christmas.'

'Is that what she's said to you?'

Beryl nodded solemnly. 'Ay, it was. She says that the two of you are like two bairns and she won't have tensions in the household, especially not at a holy time like Christmas. She says there are always two sides to every fight, and the two of you had better sort yourselves out.'

Irene felt sick with dread. Even sicker than she already did that morning. 'But there aren't two sides. Not really. Megan just hates me. It's as simple as that. She's been after me ever since I arrived. She doesn't want me to be happy here . . .'

But then it was time for the two of them to separate. Beryl was in the bake house now, and anticipating a day in the smoky hotness of hell, as she put it. 'But at least me bloody toes and fingers won't be cold.' She stared levelly at the unhappy Irene and said, 'I want you to make peace with Megan, too. We should all be walking into work together in the mornings. There shouldn't be any fall-outs between us. We're family, aren't we?'

Then Beryl was off to her biscuit ovens and Irene was left to traipse back to her shed, where her pot of glue and her endless cardboard packets were waiting.

Mavis was waiting for her, too, looking a little less grey and tired than usual. There was a touch of colour in her face, and it seemed as if she had washed her hair. 'I'm glad we're back on working together, Irene,' she said, at one point during her unbroken gabble of nonsense that morning.

Irene was trying to be charitable, and not to be irritated by the usual deluge of blether from her younger friend. She tuned out for a while as the girl described her weekend, shopping in the flea markets of North Shields with her brother. They both liked to buy bagfuls of old clothes and items that nobody wanted any more. 'And some of it's real treasure, like!' Mavis beamed. 'That's what our Arthur says. Hey!' Suddenly she burst out and waved her hand in Irene's face. 'Our Arthur reckons that he met you the other night, at the pictures where he works!'

It was hopeless trying to focus on work with Mavis rattling on like this. 'Hm? Oh, that was your brother, was it?' Irene's thoughts went back to that abrupt and peculiar person standing in the gangway with his torch. 'That's your Arthur?'

Mavis beamed proudly. 'Aye, it is. He's the best brother anyone could ever have.'

'I'll take your word for that,' Irene smiled.

'He reckons that you were there seeing the new Joan Crawford picture. Ah, I love her, but she scares me a bit, too.' Mavis lowered her voice. 'She reminds me a bit of our enemy. She's who Megan's like: a blonde Joan Crawford.'

Actually, that wasn't too far off the mark, Irene thought.

'Hey, Arthur reckons that you were laughing and carrying on with some young fella. Sam, he said. Your brother-in-law.'

'We weren't carrying on!' Irene protested. 'That sounds wrong! You shouldn't go round saying that. People will get the wrong idea . . .'

Mavis shrugged. 'That's what our Arthur said, anyhow.'

Irene pursed her lips crossly. 'Well, maybe your Arthur ought to shut his trap and stop gossiping about folk he doesn't really know.'

'Our Arthur just speaks as he finds,' Mavis said. 'It's one of his very best qualities, he reckons.'

Irene sighed heavily. 'Look, let's not fall out over this, Mavis . . .'

'Oh! No, we can't. I'd hate to fall out with you, Irene! I never would! I promise!'

'Well, then, let's have no more gossip then, eh? I go to the pictures with Sam because he's my brother-in-law and we enjoy each other's company, but that's all there is to it, right? There's nothing to gossip about.'

Mavis nodded very seriously, and suddenly Irene felt bad for ticking her off.

Then they had their supervisor, Mrs Clarke, sailing down the gangway towards them. 'Irene Farley! You are wanted!'

It felt like Irene's whole body suddenly went cold. It was a rush of icy water that went right through her. 'W-who wants me?'

Mrs Clarke folded her arms around her huge bosom and smirked at her. 'You are wanted upstairs. By Mr Wight himself.'

Up here the wood-panelled rooms smelt of wax polish and a ground-in, ancient biscuity smell that seemed to come out of the wood grain itself. Irene barely glanced at the portraits in oils that waited for her at the top of the stairs. They represented more than a century of Wight family factory owners and managers.

She was much too nervous to take in more than a scant appreciation of her surroundings.

A severe receptionist with iron-grey hair ushered her into the inner sanctum. Who'd have thought there'd be rooms as grand as these, deep within the docks at South Shields? Irene winced as her heavy shoes clopped on the shiny floor.

Soon she was standing in front of the old man's desk.

He was a funny-looking old thing, she thought. His ears stood out from his head like two floppy rashers of undercooked bacon. He peered at her through thick, smudgy lenses and he had bushels of thick hair protruding from both nostrils. Mind, his suit was beautifully cut. You could see it was real quality.

'Mrs Farley,' he frowned and studied her carefully. 'One of our very newest recruits.'

'That's right, sir,' she said, and was ashamed to hear her voice sounding so quavering and unsure.

'You've recently settled here from down south. From Norfolk. Hmm. I had an aunt in Norfolk. Strange woman.'

Irene felt herself shifting uncomfortably before him. She was longing to sit down, but he hadn't invited her to do so.

'Are you happy working here at Wight's biscuit factory, Mrs Farley?'

'Yes, sir.'

'Everyone has been kind and helpful, I hope?'

She nodded decisively.

'And you understand, of course, the vital work that we are doing here?'

She parroted what she had heard umpteen times over from her supervisor. 'We are sending out a patriotic taste of home comfort to our brave boys all over the world. Wherever they are drinking their cup of hot char, they can dip a Wight's biscuit into it and remember what this war is all about.'

The old man beamed and steepled his fingers. 'You are a very bright young woman, Mrs Farley.'

She nodded and hoped he'd simply let her return to her work now. But the interview wasn't over yet.

'Yes, you seem very bright, Mrs Farley, which makes it even harder for me to fathom why you'd then be found brawling on the factory floor with your sister-in-law. For that *is* what it was, wasn't it? A common brawl.'

Irene hung her head. She felt like she was seven years old again, and back at her old shack of a school in Hunworth. 'I suppose it was, sir.' She knew it was rarely worth arguing the finer points of fighting with figures in authority.

'Is there nothing you'd like to tell me about this unfortunate scene?'

She felt so miserable. This was the comeuppance she'd been fearing for days. Now she was going to be sacked from her brand-new job, and it was all that cow-bag's fault. It was all down to Megan. And where was Megan now? Why wasn't she being held to account for her behaviour?

'Mrs Farley?' the old man prompted her. 'I am a very important and busy man, as you must surely know. I don't have all day to cross-examine you about this, pleasant as your company may be.'

Irene felt her face grow hot and she knew it would be glowing red. Such a giveaway: she never could cover up her vexation and frustration. 'It's not fair!' she burst out all at once.

Mr Wight's lips flickered, as if he was allowing himself just a small smile at her. Irene didn't even notice his amusement. 'What's not fair, my dear?'

'She was picking on Mavis. That's what it was all about. That poor Mavis – you can tell, she's never had much luck in life. She's not got much going for her. I mean, it's one thing Megan picking on me and making my life a misery, but it's quite another having a go at poor Mavis . . . I couldn't stand by and let her do that.' Irene realised she was gabbling breathlessly in a manner reminiscent of the girl she'd been sticking up for. She broke off and winced. 'Sorry, sir.'

He stared at her and pulled absent-mindedly on one of his rasher-like lugs. 'I thought as much. When Mrs Clarke came rushing in to spread the tale, I had a feeling this was the case. You see, my dear, I like to keep my ear to the ground and my nose to the wheel . . .'

His curious turn of phrase forced her to stare at his strange ears and his bushy nose, and she almost burst out laughing, despite the seriousness of the scene.

'And I do understand that Megan Farley is something of a termagant.'

Irene stared at him. 'A what?'

'An overbearing bully,' he clarified.

She flushed. She had thought a 'termagant' was a kind of sea bird. 'So, you know what she can be like?'

He chuckled and wandered to his office window, which looked out over the many buildings of his factory and the various workers flitting busily between them. 'I pride myself on knowing who I employ, and what happens here in my premises. As much as I can, anyhow.' Irene watched him looking at his factory and he had a proprietorial, fatherly look on his face.

Imagine looking at something as grand as this factory, she thought, and knowing that you owned it, and that everyone in it was here because of you. Imagine having all that responsibility! All she had to do was get herself here in the morning and do back-breaking work till it was time to go home. She saw that she was just one tiny cog in the process. All at once she felt a small glow of satisfaction that Mr Wight was showing any interest at all in her welfare.

Now he turned to her and said, 'I know it was all down to your sister-in-law. I've had to reprimand her for her carrying on before. She's rather too fond of causing bother, that one. If she misbehaves again, you must tell me, Mrs Farley. Irene, if I may.'

Speechless, Irene nodded. 'So . . . I'm not in any trouble then, Mr Wight?'

He smiled at her genially. 'Not on this occasion, my dear. But now, perhaps, you'd best return to your work? I believe there must be biscuits that need packing. There always is, you know. That's the nature of our work! It's the way it's been for a hundred years of those ovens down there, baking away. There'll always be more biscuits that need packing and sending out! We are just the humble human beings doing our bit to send them on their way.'

Minutes later Irene was back down the stairs and heading towards the packaging department. It was just possible, she thought, that Mr Wight was rather eccentric.

'Is everything OK?' Mavis asked her worriedly, as she rejoined her at their workstation.

'Everything's fine,' Irene beamed.

'Have you still got a job?' Mavis asked in her raspy voice.

In fact, that very day Irene was about to be offered a second job.

Chapter Eleven

It was Bella at the ice cream parlour who offered Irene her second job in South Shields. This came as quite a surprise, because when Irene had first met her, she'd felt a bit suspicious of Bella. Surely this was one of Tom's old girlfriends? Maybe they should be feeling envious of each other?

But Bella wasn't like that at all. Irene had seen her a few more times at Franchino's since then, and the girl had been friendly and warm. She seemed genuinely to enjoy Irene's company when the Norfolk girl popped in for a frothy coffee and a brief chat.

Bella knew that Irene was working hard every day at the biscuit factory, but she knew that she still had evenings free, and one or two afternoons, too. When she realised that she needed some extra help at the ice cream parlour, it was Irene who she thought of first.

After Irene's curious interview with Mr Wight, the day ended with a coffee with Bella at Franchino's. By now the two of them talked to each other almost as if they were old friends.

Bella asked her straight out: 'Would you like to come here, and work at Franchino's, with me? Just a few hours each week? It wouldn't interfere with your hours at the biscuit factory, and it'd be a few extra shillings in your purse. And it might be fun, too, mightn't it?'

Irene came to realise pretty quickly that, really, Bella couldn't afford to take on another employee. Business wasn't great at Franchino's, especially as the weather had worsened, but it seemed that Bella wanted to help her friend's new wife. Perhaps Bella wanted the company, and saw in Irene a possible new friend? Her old dad Tonio was a nice enough old gent, but it was possible that Bella was seeking a colleague who she could talk to through the evening hours at work.

Either way, Bella had extended a very generous invitation to Irene, who vowed to never forget that kindness.

Irene was still somewhat nervous around Bella's beauty. The more she saw of the girl she wondered why Tom hadn't ended up choosing her for his love instead. In comparison with Bella, Irene felt like a dowdy hedge sparrow.

She liked the black and white uniform she got to wear for her evenings at work at the ice cream parlour. The last helper at Franchino's had been about the same size as Irene. 'She was a chunky girl as well,' Bella said, watching Irene tie the pinny round her waist.

Chunky? I've never been chunky, Irene thought.

Oh, hang on. Yes. She could suddenly see, now that she looked at herself in a full-length mirror. Her waist had thickened. Her body was changing.

Her period hadn't come.

She was still at the stage of not daring to hope.

She turned to Bella and all of this was plain in her expression.

'You aren't, are you?' Bella sighed. 'And this is what you tell me on the first week of working here?'

'It's still very early,' Irene said. 'I haven't told all the family yet.'

Bella tossed her dark, lustrous hair and gazed at her new employee appraisingly. 'What about the doctor? Have you had yourself looked at?'

Irene admitted that she hadn't even signed up with a doctor in her new town yet. There hadn't been time to think about it.

'Of course there has,' Bella snapped. 'And if you're thinking of having a bairn, you should have fixed yourself up with a doctor ages ago. You can't go skulking about, avoiding the issue and hoping for the best.' The older woman sounded quite severe and a part of Irene was on the point of rising up against such bossiness. As Bella went on and talked about her own family's doctor, whose practice was in one of the old, posh houses behind Ocean Road, Irene softened towards her. The Italian girl was only trying to be kind and caring, however brusque her manner.

I mustn't be so jumpy and defensive, Irene thought, watching as Bella wrote down the doctor's details for her.

The thing was, she hated doctors. She had a deep aversion to their manner and their probing questions and the way they looked at you. She hated the smell of the instruments and bottles they brought out of their bags. The coldness of their fingers when they touched your skin.

All of these things, if she thought about them, would make panic rise up inside her, along with a dreadful feeling of helplessness.

It all went back to the months she had spent recovering from diphtheria when she was a kid.

All the girls in her family had been ill, but she had been struck particularly badly. She was kept in quarantine in their attic all through the summer she was twelve. She could hear the others playing and squealing and enjoying themselves out on the village green and in the rooms downstairs. It had almost felt to Irene as if they were exaggerating their noise and their pleasure, just to rub her nose in it, as she lay there, aching, tired, disoriented and cross. It had been a dreadful few months.

Lonely and miserable, with only her book of fairy tales for comfort. Her *Great Golden Treasury of Tales*. The book that she could disappear into when she was in exile and when she was no longer wanted by the rest of the world . . .

These thoughts and memories came back to her that first evening working in Bella's family's ice cream parlour. She took her first lesson working the frothy coffee machine, yanking at levers and handles and getting it hopelessly wrong the first few goes. Steam shot out and she dropped a whole tin of gritty coffee grains on the counter. But it was OK. She wasn't completely clumsy and stupid. Actually, she was quite a quick student when it came to learning new skills and practical tasks. Bella praised her as she created her first, not-too-shabby cappuccino and held it up in its smoked-glass cup for everyone to admire.

The old man, Bella's father Tonio, was there and he applauded Irene's progress, too. They were all being very nice to her, and she blushed with pleasure.

It was so nice to be away from the other members of the Farley clan, even if it was for just the evening.

Even an evening spent scrubbing down melamine tables and mopping the lino. Even hours spent with her arms in soapy water washing up all the coffee cups and dainty ice cream dishes. She was out in the world and doing something for herself, earning a few extra pennies on top of her factory wage that she was going to keep to spend on herself alone.

There was no way she was queueing up with the others to hand over this wage packet to Ma Ada on Friday night. No way on this earth.

Even as she mulled all this over on her first evening of employment at Franchino's, she was still thinking about the months she had spent in solitary confinement as a girl. Had that done something to her personality? She wondered, as she had often wondered about this before. Had it made her shyer, made her find it harder for her to fit in?

It made her value things more, she knew that much. She clung to her few belongings in a way that was more fierce, perhaps, than it would otherwise have been.

This was because she was haunted by the smell of smoke from the bonfire outside their house. It was right at the end of her illness. She was well, but weak as a kitten, and she had watched in dismay and then mounting horror as her da and the doctor took away all her toys and clothes and bedding. She was like a prisoner up in that attic room, and she didn't understand. She had to have it all spelt out to her.

'We don't want you or the others to get germs,' her da said, trying to sound kindly. He was taking away her dollies, and Edward Bear, who she'd had for as long as she could remember.

Her sisters were standing in the garden, watching solemnly as her da heaped all these things onto the bonfire. Village kids were hanging over the back wall, laughing and pointing at her stuff as it was put to the flames.

Irene watched out of the attic window, bawling her eyes out. She felt exposed, betrayed and mortified, all at once. Her clothes were curling up and burning right in front of everyone. Her toys. Her bear. Everything. It was like she was dead and they were destroying the evidence that she had ever lived there amongst them. And all the kids were laughing at the sight of the black scrags of ash lifting out of the pyre and floating in the updraft. They thought it hilarious to see the bear in flames. Her sisters cried a little, too, of course, but they didn't feel it the same as Irene.

The Great Golden Treasury of Tales was burning as well. Her da practically had to twist her fingers off to pry it out of her grasp. Irene knew almost every word by heart, and she clung to the book, pressing it to her skinny chest. But they had taken it off her and tossed it into the flames.

It probably explained a great deal about her and how she was, with her belongings and her secret thoughts and the way she felt about other people. She readily acknowledged it herself: that illness had probably done her more damage than anyone had ever suspected.

Still, it wasn't good to dwell on such things. Specially not when she was supposed to be concentrating on her work.

That was the reason she hated going to the doctors, though. She didn't trust them and never would. They might cure you, and they might mean the best, but Irene would always be wary of the things they commanded you to do. Maybe she could just get through this whole having a baby thing without actually seeing a doctor or a nurse until the very end? Until the bit at the end when they actually brought the baby out? Was that possible?

'Hey, you! New girl!'

Suddenly there came a loud, pinched-sounding voice from across the other end of the counter.

Irene looked up in surprise, feeling dazed. Who was that?

She blinked and stared and thought: I don't know that person at all.

'Yes, you! *You!*' he added, and came striding towards her. A pale-faced boy, very thin, with dark, greasy hair and a long green mackintosh. 'You're one of the Farleys, aren't you? Yes, I've heard you giggling and sniggering and messing about at the Savoy. I'm Arthur Kendricks and I'll share a banana split with you if you've got one, and I'll tell you a tale or two about that family you've married into. Oh, hello there, Bella hinny – are you gonna join us?'

Amazingly, they managed to scrape together the makings of a banana split. 'With banana substitute,' Bella said, no trace of apology as she plonked the dish down between them on the table.

The three of them were crammed into a corner booth during Irene's half-hour break. It was to become their own particular corner for many free hours to come.

'What's the substitute?' asked Arthur haughtily.

'Promise you won't pull a face,' snapped Bella.

Arthur looked down his long nose at her. 'What is it?'

'Cold roast parsnip with a squirt of banana essence,' Bella said quickly. 'And a scoop of ice cream and some carnation milk and some chopped nuts and a cocktail cherry. Try it!'

'A parsnip!?' Arthur crowed. His laughter erupted out of him, too loudly, too outrageously. Irene couldn't help laughing along. There was just something about him and the way he talked that made her giggle. 'You've put ice cream on a parsnip? Bella, you are losing your mind, pet!'

'It's delicious. You'll see. You'll never look at another banana again, once you've had this.'

That made Arthur laugh even more. Irene took the spoon Bella offered and cautiously scooped up a mouthful of the strange dessert. It was . . . odd. But nice. She frowned. Maybe it wasn't as nice as she thought.

'What kind of world are we living in, eh?' Arthur sighed, with mock melodramatic heaviness. He's been watching all those films, Irene thought. Going round again and again in swift rotation. He's picked up all the gestures and intonations from the leading ladies. He's holding his head in just that way, with his chin jutting out. And the way he's lighting his cigarette. He's doing it like everyone in Franchino's ice cream parlour is staring at him. Which, to be fair, they are, she thought.

'My sister knows you,' he told Irene.

'I know,' said Irene.

'She says you've been very good to her. Sticking up for her, and so on. Thank you, Irene Farley. My sister's a bit soft in the head, but she's even softer in the heart.'

Irene nodded. She didn't know what to say to that. But she liked the fact that they had Mavis in common. Yes, Mavis was soft in the heart, and that was one of the things that drew Irene close to her, no matter how daft she sometimes went on.

There was something compelling about Arthur. A feeling that you never knew what outrageous thing he was going to say or do next. He smoked elegantly and refused to eat more than a single bite of Bella's ersatz banana, and studied Irene carefully. He had shucked his green mac and the suit he wore underneath was a beautiful blue one, rather old-fashioned, but immaculate.

'He takes lovely care of his clothes,' Bella told Irene. 'He goes shopping in all the junk shops, all over the town and finds the most amazing bargains. He's got a real eye.'

His eyes were hooded and wary as he looked Irene up and down. 'So how's your parsnip, hinny?'

Irene frowned and chewed and tried to smile. 'I think it . . . could do with some more caster sugar, maybe? If some was sprinkled on *before* it was roasted? It would bring the sweetness out.'

'Listen to her!' Arthur gasped. 'Telling our Bella her own business!' His eyes darted with mischief. He loved to stir things up.

'Maybe she's got a point,' Bella frowned. 'That's quite a good idea . . .'

'I don't mean to be rude . . .' Irene said.

'Oh, don't worry about being rude,' Arthur wafted his smoke away. 'We say just what we like to each other, don't we, Bella? We always have done, since the very first day at infants' school, when we became best friends. We've been a special little gang ever since. And you, lady,' he added, glaring at Irene. 'We might consider letting you join our little gang. If you prove interesting enough.'

Irene chuckled. 'I don't think I'm very interesting at all, I'm afraid.'

'We'll be the judges of that,' Arthur told her. 'Any girl chosen by the heroic and handsome Tommy Farley is worthy of anyone's attention, I should think. He must have seen something in you worth taking note of.'

She felt baffled and confused by his words. She blushed slightly at the mention of her Tom being heroic and handsome. Well, of course he was, but she didn't understand what Arthur meant by saying it in this way. Was he being snide and taking the mick out of her fella? She had never met anyone quite like Arthur before, so she couldn't quite tell.

'You'll get used to Arthur's silly ways,' Bella promised. 'Don't you worry.'

Arthur stubbed out his Woodbine and coughed unhappily. 'These filthy cigarettes. Do you remember the cocktail cigarettes we used to get, Bella? With the golden tips?'

'How could I forget? We used to sit here smoking them all afternoon, thinking we were *it*. Thinking we were Marlene Dietrich's two glamorous younger sisters. We used to get them off the market, at the old tobacconists.' They glanced at each other. 'That's gone now, hasn't it? Blown to bits.'

Arthur sighed. 'Fancy blowing up a tobacconists. Of all the places! Blow up the town hall. Blow up the big school! But give us our fancy cocktail cigarettes.'

He offered Irene one of his Woodbines and she politely declined. 'I can't stand smoke, I'm afraid.'

'How do you cope with Tom, then?' Bella asked. 'He smokes his head off! He's always got a tab on the go. Right from being a bairn, when we were hanging around the streets.'

'I can't abide it, actually,' Irene said. 'When they all start puffing away at Number Thirteen, it's like sitting in the clouds round there. You can't see a thing. I reckon it's why all the cat's hair fell out.'

This made them laugh. 'The cat's bald?!'

'The old ma calls it "Lucky", but I don't see what's so lucky about it. It's a miserable-looking thing.'

'I've only been round there once or twice, when I was a kid,' Bella said. 'But the old woman terrified me. Sitting in the corner in her chair, ordering everyone about. You're a braver woman than I am, Irene. I wouldn't go and live under her roof . . .'

'I was determined to,' said Irene. 'It just happened like that. We were married and next thing I knew, I'd decided to move here, with that lot, and I hadn't even met them before. I didn't know any of the Farleys except Tom. The thing was, I was sick of my own family in Norfolk. It sounds awful to say, but I was fed up with belonging to the same old place.' She toyed with the last smidgen of banana substitute and wondered vaguely whether, having met her new family and especially her oldest sister-in-law first, she still would have agreed so readily to move in? She shuddered as she mulled this over and swallowed the strange dessert.

But there was no use thinking about things like that, was there? Her decisions had been made and they could hardly be turned around. She was here now and she was probably pregnant and she was making the best of it all, and everything was going to be wonderful.

'I'd be fascinated to see inside the Farley place,' said Arthur, as if it was somewhere special or famous, like Buckingham Palace. 'I've seen the old woman, occasionally, galumphing up and down the terraces. But I wouldn't dare speak to her. She scares the Bejaysus out of me.'

'She's a funny old stick,' said Bella. 'But Tommy and the rest of them dote on her, don't they?'

Irene nodded. 'They certainly do.'

She realised Arthur was staring at her. 'You get on very well with the youngest one, don't you, Irene? That Sam?'

She nodded. 'He's a canny lad.'

'Aye, I saw you both, messing on at the flicks, a few times. I had to tell them off, Bella. I had to shine my torch on them and stop them giggling and carrying on too loudly.'

Irene protested, 'Not like that! We were just laughing. You make it sound like we were –' she lowered her voice – 'canoodling.'

Arthur burst out laughing. 'Oh, I've seen worse things than canoodling at the Savoy! Don't you worry, hinny!' Then, all of a sudden, he was up on his feet and dragging on his bright-green mac. 'Right, ladies, I will have to love you and leave you. I've an appointment at eight. I can't be late.'

'Oh, yes?' Bella gave him a sly wink.

'It's a dance. I'm a wonderful dancer, as you know. I go every week because I like to keep my practice up. There are lots of unaccompanied older ladies who need a partner and I'm happy to help out. I cut quite a dash on the floor. And, it's just like my old nanna used to say – it's what to do if you want to meet company. You always get a friend if you go dancing.'

With that, he was gone.

'He never pays a penny,' Bella sighed.

'He's quite something,' Irene said. 'He's like no one I've ever met before.'

Bella nodded. 'That's what everyone says. Come on, then, lady. Let's get back to work. There's only an hour till closing tonight.'

Trudging home from Ocean Road, through the rabbit warren of streets, Irene was amazed at herself for knowing her way around already. She was barely thinking about where she was going, but her feet seemed to find the right route.

She cut through the end of Fowler Street, where the shops were doing their best to look as festive as they could. The butchers had various fowl on display, hanging in their window.

There was a toyshop, too, with what seemed to her like an impossibly beautiful window, with dolls and wooden soldiers and a wooden gingerbread house. There was fake snow made from carefully crumpled tissue paper. She found herself staring at this for some time, standing in the cold as the rest of the evening crowd shuffled quickly by.

Again she was thinking about the toys and books and belongings that had been destroyed after her bout of childhood illness. Can't I leave those thoughts behind? She was cross at herself, turning and hurrying on, past the town hall, head down against the biting wind. I could have died of the fever. I was lucky to survive. My parents just did what they had to do when they burnt all my belongings. But still . . . she had nothing from her early life. She had hardly any belongings at all.

Now she lived in a street where people were so settled. Ma Ada's boys had lived in that little house on Frederick Street all their lives. They had roots and connections and a feeling of belonging that must make them feel very secure.

Irene didn't feel as secure as she would like to. She felt like she was busy living someone else's life.

But still . . . today had been good. Today she felt she had made new friends. Bella seemed like someone she had known forever, and Arthur was a revelation to her. She had loved sitting with the two of them in their alcove, feeling all cosy and like they were letting her into their gang. It was very generous of them, she could see that now.

Yes, they didn't have to be so welcoming, did they? Most people would freeze the stranger out. Irene wasn't so sure she herself would be as open and welcoming as that, if the tables were turned. But those two had been good to her tonight.

They had included her. Also, it really felt like Bella had taken her under her wing and tried to talk sense to her. She had scrawled down her family doctor's address on a napkin, and Irene had it in her bag. She would go there and submit to an examination. She knew she had to, now. There was no hiding from it, and Bella had helped her to see that.

Soon she was back in the part of town that the locals called the Sixteen Streets. Counting as she walked along, Irene mused that there were probably more than that number, if you added all the crossway streets to the total of long, terraced roads that ran down to the docks and the arches, but for some reason the name was one that everyone used, and she got the feeling that it was a name that went back a hundred years or more.

How many hundreds of thousands of lives had been lived here in these smoky little back-to-backs? There were far too many people crammed into each poky house, and she guessed in the olden days it had been even worse. There were lots of Catholic families round here, too. The Irish lot, as Ma Ada called them – with a curiously caustic tone in her voice – and they were known to breed like rabbits. Irene flinched and blushed when the old woman spoke like this. She could be quite coarse at times, and Irene had become adept at hiding her primness when such language came out. She couldn't afford to be seen to be prim. Not when she was living with the Farleys, right in the heart of the Sixteen Streets.

It was early evening and the households were settling down to their early-evening meals. What did they call it here? Dinner? Supper? Tea. They called it tea, even if it was a full meal. Irene was still trying to sort out all the differences in her head. Woe betide her if she came out with the wrong name for the wrong meal! They'd look at her like she was putting on airs. Once – once only – she had made the mistake of referring to a midday meal as 'lunch'. Oh, how they'd hooted.

Ma Ada, Megan and even Beryl, screeching with laughter at her red face. 'Lunch! Lunch! She sounds like Queen Mary! What would Her Majesty like for lunch? Bread and dripping like the rest of us?'

Sometimes their words were a bit abrasive. They loved to catch people out and mock them. You just had to get used to it, though. Irene was sure that they didn't mean any harm. They were just used to their own ways and the words they used for things. Anything else seemed strange and laughable to them.

She could smell dinner in a hundred different houses as she turned the corner into Frederick Street. The savoury aromas of stewed vegetables flavoured with scrag end and the bones of a Sunday joint. People were getting by on a lot less food than they ought to. Irene was learning, though, that the deprivations of the war were taking these people back to older habits. These were the old slums, really, going back years. The people here had a collective memory of getting by on a whole lot less than they were accustomed to even nowadays. They were a people used to bracing themselves for hardship.

She didn't have her own key. She stepped up to the well-scrubbed doorstep and took hold of the brightly polished brass knocker. It was humiliating, knocking on the front door and asking to be let in.

The lace of the net curtains in the front room window stirred. Out of the corner of her eye she caught sight of Megan's narrowed eyes and pale face, staring out at her. The Nottingham lace ruffled and fell back into place, and there were footsteps in the hall.

'How was your day?' Megan sneered and held open the door for her as she huddled in. Now she was indoors the warmth was very welcome. She pulled off her headscarf and realised her face was frozen from the breeze coming up the long street.

'Oh, it was fine,' she smiled. 'It was good fun, actually . . .'

Megan nodded patronisingly, and looked like she couldn't care less. She was wearing a red woollen dress that clung to her figure. She undulated down the hall, looking very sophisticated, Irene thought. She looked far more glamorous than a woman who slept under the stairs had any right to be. Anyway, why was she being so nice to Irene? Asking about her day, and so on? She was never usually interested.

Irene followed her sister-in-law into the parlour and there they saw Ma Ada, stooped over the big table, sorting through papers of all kinds. They looked like official letters and telegrams. Tattered envelopes and pages of splotchy handwriting. When she looked up at Irene she seemed oddly out of breath and distracted.

'Look who's home,' Megan said.

'Oh, Irene,' said Ma Ada. 'Go and put the kettle on, would you, girl? I'm parched for a cup of tea.'

Irene smiled and even made an effort to rub Lucky's ears as the bald, pink cat jumped up on the table for some attention.

'Gerroff of there,' Ma Ada snapped, and the cat slunk away.

In the scullery Irene removed her heavy coat and tied on a pinny and set about brewing some tea. There was definitely something queer in the air. She had the feeling she had walked into the middle of some kind of scene or discussion that she wasn't meant to be privy to. She set the kettle on the gas flame and sighed. Well, if it was anything important, they'd be bound to tell her, sure enough.

Minutes later she brought their tea into the parlour. Ma Ada slurped hers without much enthusiasm.

Megan stirred her spoon round and round. 'Eeeh, I dream about having sugar in my tea. Isn't that daft? I have dreams where I'm spooning sugar in, three, four, five spoonfuls. And I could just about die of the sweetness.'

'Don't go talking about dying,' Ma Ada reproached her. 'Brings bad luck, mentioning death like that.'

Megan rolled her eyes. 'Superstition. Old wives' tales. Talking like that belongs to the Dark Ages.'

'Mebbe it does,' grumbled the old woman. 'And mebbe I do, too. But I've lived longer than you, Megan Farley, so think on and shut up. It doesn't do to mention death so lightly. Especially when he's so busy and going about his business all around us all the time. When he could come landing on our house at any given moment. You go tempting fate with your loose talk, lady.'

Megan snorted and sipped her tea noisily. Irene was amazed that she managed to get away with twisting her face so scornfully as the old woman spoke to her.

Then Irene realised that Megan was looking at her. She wore a strange expression. 'Oh, Irene, you've had something nice come in the post.'

'I have?' Irene sat up straighter in the straight-backed chair. 'In the post?'

Megan laughed at her. 'It's only a letter. Don't get so worked up! What did you think it was – a Christmas hamper from Harrods?'

'Leave the lass alone,' Ma Ada growled, chinking her cup back in its saucer. She reached onto the dresser beside her and came up with a flimsy envelope. 'Here you are, Irene. You've had a letter.'

Irene's heart thumped hard when she recognised Tom's handwriting on the front. His lovely, loopy cursive lettering. His missives always made her think of a little schoolboy, trying his best to be neat and write clearly. The writing inside would be something he'd laboured over. It took him hours to inscribe just two sides of a letter, she knew. A letter from Tom was very precious to her. She would have clasped it to her chest, had the other two women not been sitting there, watching her every move.

Strange, how they were watching her so closely. She noticed them exchange a small, complicit glance.

Well, never mind. She had a letter from the airbase. From Tom.

'Maybe he'll say when he's got leave!' she burst out, turning it over and fiddling with the sealed-down flap. 'Maybe he'll be getting home for Christmas!'

She could hardly contain her eagerness and excitement. But then, something brought her up short.

The envelope was damp round the flap. It wasn't quite sealed properly. It felt exactly like it had been steamed open and then hastily sealed up again with the last bits of sticky left on the edges.

Irene frowned and looked at her ma-in-law and sister-in-law, who both returned her stare defiantly. Before she could stop herself, she burst out: 'Have one of you opened this already?'

Chapter Twelve

The two women were scandalised by the suggestion.

'What? Us? Are you joking?' Megan was overdoing it, jumping up in her chair and putting on a horrified expression. 'Why would we go opening your letters? Don't you think we've got enough to do, that we have to go snooping into your life? Ha!'

Irene clutched Tom's letter to her apron. It was wrinkled and damp. She recognised the signs of an envelope that had been opened by steam kettle and then inexpertly resealed. Her own ma was a dab hand at such tricks. 'Why would you open my post?' she asked, and she hated her voice for coming out in such a pathetic bleat.

Ma Ada was stroking Lucky and pursing her lips in a disapproving way. 'Get on with you, lass, and don't bad mouth your elders. Of course no one's touched your silly letter. Just go and read it in peace and thank goodness you've got one. There's lots of young wives who get a telegram, not a letter, as you know. And telegrams never have good news in them.'

Megan nodded firmly. 'Exactly! At least your Tom's alive and at least he's coming home on leave soon, and . . .' She stopped abruptly. She put a hand over her mouth.

'You *have* read it!' Irene burst out. She felt her face suddenly getting hot and tears rushing into her eyes. 'How could you do that? How could you pry into another person's private affairs?'

Megan turned swiftly from looking defensive to scornful. 'Oh, calm down, you silly girl. You're going on daft.'

Ma Ada growled. 'You should know that letters are read by lots of people, Irene. The MoD censors everything coming out of an airbase like where Tom is. You shouldn't leap to conclusions, girl. Nothing is private in this day and age.'

Irene glared at them both. 'Aye, it's not, is it? Nothing's bloody private. I've got nothing of my own. Nothing belongs to just me! Nowt at all!'

As she thundered off into the hall and up the stairs to her room in the attic all her thoughts were blotted out by anger. She knew she was overreacting, and that she was storing up trouble by going on the attack with her ma-in-law. And yet she couldn't help it. It was like she had a boiling lump of rage in her chest and she could hardly breathe past it. It was something about never having her own things, or her own privacy. They were luxuries she had never enjoyed in all her life and now it seemed like she never would.

Megan's mockery and Ma Ada's gruff complacency made everything worse. Irene felt like her own feelings were worthless.

She lay in the attic till late that night, ignoring everyone's calls to tea and late supper. There was some broth on the hob, she was told, and some fresh bread Beryl had baked.

Beryl came tapping at the attic door. She called to Irene, and her voice was so soft and kindly that Irene couldn't help reassuring her. 'I'm all right. I just have a headache.'

Beryl was in her dressing gown and curlers. She looked exhausted after her day working in the bake house and her evening with the WVS. She frowned at Irene, who lay curled under her pink candlewick bedspread. 'I heard what went on earlier.'

Irene propped herself up on one elbow. She was parched, and squinted at her alarm clock. Lord, she'd drowsed crossly for hours and it was nearly nine o'clock. They'd all think she was sulking up here. 'Are they all talking about me?'

Beryl shrugged. 'Bob and Tony are pie-eyed from the pub, and they couldn't care less. Megan is sat there like a boss-eyed cat, stewing in her fury. Eeeh, lass, she's not worth getting angry over. Megan's a funny girl. You just have to get used to her. She's all bitterness and disappointment because her life's not turned out how she thinks she deserves.'

'You should have seen the looks she was giving me,' Irene said. 'She was defiant-looking, like she didn't think I had any right to any privacy. She'd read my letter and found out all my news before I could. And she let it out with such pleasure . . . It was worse than having that fight with her.' Irene felt her body shiver and she started sobbing again. She couldn't stop herself. 'I-I'm sorry, Beryl. I shouldn't go weeping . . .'

Her kinder sister-in-law came to sit on the edge of the bed and put a comforting arm around her. 'I know. I understand. I heard what the letter said. They told me. He's not getting home for Christmas, is he?'

Irene shook her head and found she couldn't speak for a few moments. 'I shouldn't be so stupid and selfish. It's Tom who's got it worse. He has to carry on and work right through . . . But it's just . . . it would have been our first Christmas together, Beryl. It seems too awful, to be apart for the season. Especially when we already have to spend so much time apart . . .'

Beryl tried to make her see the bright side. She rubbed her back and made her sip the tea she'd brought her. 'Aye, pet, but look at it this way. He's coming home sooner than Christmas, isn't he? He's getting home at the start of December. Four whole days Ma Ada said! So, what you'll have is an early Christmas, won't you? You'll get to celebrate earlier than the rest of the world!'

Irene stared at her. 'I s-suppose so.'

'You have to make the best of everything, hinny,' Beryl said. 'All the moments you can find to treasure, all the good points you can salvage from the disaster all around us. Don't give in to the despair, Irene. You're the youngest of us here, with the most to look forward to. If you go under, then we all do. Now, come on. You get your face washed and come and sit in the parlour with the rest of us. Show Megan that you don't give a hoot for how sly and rotten she can be . . . Come on, love. You have to prove to the whole family, that you aren't some soft ninny. You can stand up to the lot of them! I know you can do it!'

This was why Beryl was one of her favourite people Irene had met so far in her new home. When everyone else was bustling along and keeping busy, fighting off despair and keeping their feelings locked tight inside, Beryl somehow seemed to know just how she was feeling. She took the time to be kind to her.

Irene blotted her eyes and combed her hair and straightened her clothes. Then she went downstairs and took a deep breath before opening the door and stepping into the parlour. She smiled brightly at the busy roomful of people and set about pretending the earlier fracas had never happened at all.

She found that the whole of Number Thirteen's inhabitants had assembled for the evening. There weren't enough chairs for them all, and Megan was perched on her husband Bob's knee as he sat at the table. How proud he looked, sitting there like Megan was some kind of prize. Well, she was bonny enough, and he must think well of her. But Irene didn't think Megan was nice enough for Bob, who would never hurt a fly, if he could help it.

As Irene passed through the room, asking who'd like some cocoa, if she were to put a pan on the heat, there was an air of jollity about the place. Sam was just finishing off telling some daft story about the docks that afternoon – something to do with the gaffer they had working there now. He was the one who picked out which men were to be given work each day, but he was blind and lame and didn't have a clue. Sam was always coming back with funny stories from the yard. He had all the others cracking up now with his impersonation of the blind gaffer, and he came to his punch line and basked in his family's laughter, just as Irene squeezed past him into the scullery.

'Hey, kidda,' he said, jumping up and giving her a hug. 'I heard the good news!'

She blinked at him, at first thinking Beryl had told him something she oughtn't. 'Oh . . .!' she said, realising he meant Tom's leave. 'Yes, well . . . I wish he was going to be here for Christmas, but . . .'

'Ah, Christmas doesn't matter all that much,' Sam smiled. 'There's plenty to distract you then, anyway. And this way, you'll be getting to see him much sooner, won't you?' The boy beamed at her in such an open way that her heart went out to him. He really cares for my happiness, Irene thought.

She spooned cocoa powder out of the tin into the enamel pan. She really had to scrape the spoon into the bottom corners of the tin, getting the last of it out. The drink would be mostly hot water, with only a splash of milk, and it would be dark and not really sweet enough, but it would be hot and wet and would have to do.

'Well!' said a voice at her back. 'I hear tell that both your jobs are going well and that you're settling in fine.'

Old Ma Ada had slipped into the scullery behind her. Sometimes the old lady could move as silently as a shadow.

She came closer to Irene, staring intently up into the girl's face. This close, Irene could see the slight milkiness in her eyes and the few dark bristles on her chin. Ma Ada said: 'You mustn't mind us, pet. You mustn't get upset. When we do things that rile you, or when things get on top of you. You know, the thing to do, always, is never let folk see that you're upset. If you do, they'll have your life. What you have to do, Irene hinny, is toughen yourself up.'

Irene nodded wordlessly. Aye, I'll toughen up, she thought. She felt a fool for bursting into tears in front of Ma Ada and Megan. It was only a letter that didn't even say very much at all. That's all it was. So they'd seen Tom's news before she had. So what? Their own lives must be bloody boring if they had to open other people's letters to get a thrill. If they were that bored, then good luck to them. Next time she hoped Tom would write something rude, something to give them a shock! That would serve them right.

Her eyes must have flashed just then, as she hatched her rebellious thoughts. Ma Ada seemed to notice, and nodded her approval. She'd seen the same greenish-gold spark in Irene's eyes that Tom knew and loved so well. 'I can see you'll be OK,' old Ma Ada said. 'You're a good lass, Irene. Just don't let anyone get the better of you.'

The cocoa was bubbling and frothing in the pan, and so she turned down the flame. Something in her longed, at that moment, to tell Ada that she thought she might be pregnant. She wanted to turn to her as if she was her own ma, and say that she was going to see a doctor and have an examination, and that she already knew in her own mind what the outcome would be. For a moment she bit her lip, hesitating over whether to say anything or not to Tom's mam.

The old woman seemed to notice that the girl wanted to say something and braced herself for it.

But then the moment passed and Irene simply poured out the cocoa. No, let them wait. Let her be sure first, before she told them anything. She wasn't ready yet to offer the old woman the fragile gift of her secret hopes.

Of all the people she had met so far in South Shields, it was Bella that Irene talked to most about Tom. This was probably because she knew that Bella had known Tom forever. She had known him from childhood and knew what he was like when he was away from his family. Her Tom was more like Irene's, in a way.

As Irene learnt the ropes of working in the evenings at Franchino's, the two young women shared stories about their families and their pasts, and Irene found that the things she most wanted to talk about related to Tom, and events of the past few months. It was as if she could conjure up her absent husband in words, as they whiled away the hours in the ice cream parlour, mopping and scrubbing and brewing up coffee.

'I can't really talk about him at Number Thirteen,' Irene sighed, 'because it upsets Ma Ada. She'd never say so, but I know it does.'

Bella shrugged. 'But if you want to talk about Tom, you should! He's your husband! You're the one who's missing him most!'

Not in Ma Ada's world. In her tight-knit world, she was suffering terribly from the absence of her son. There was no love like a ma's love and Irene just wouldn't understand . . .

'You know what she's like . . .' Irene quipped, and went to serve two old ladies who'd strayed in for a cuppa.

Bella said: 'Tell me about when he went to visit your family. You make your ma sound just as fierce as Ma Ada is. How did Tom get on with her?'

This made Irene smile. It was just a couple of months ago, but it already seemed like a different lifetime . . .

'My mum can be pretty fierce indeed,' said Irene. 'My da just sits there by the fireplace mostly, knocking his pipe out and stuffing new baccy in and trying to light it up again. When we visited, Tom soon won him over by handing him a packet of American cigarettes he'd got from his airbase. My da was delighted! It was like treasure! And the two of them sat puffing away by the fire, happy as anything. And I thought, maybe it'll be OK, and they'll all get on.'

Bella listened carefully, absent-mindedly nibbling an ice cream wafer. 'You always make your village sound like it's hundreds of miles from everywhere, and somewhere deep in the past! All the talk of donkeys on the village green and thatched cottages, and sitting on a horse-pulled carriage to get to the nearest town . . .'

'It's true! It's all like that!' Irene chuckled. 'Tom couldn't believe his eyes when he came out to meet them. He thought he was going back into the olden days with me, sitting on the back of that cart. He laughed at first, but then I think, really, he enjoyed every single moment of it.'

It was such a happy journey, the way she remembered it now. Something so simple, that she'd done a thousand times in her life: sitting on the back of old man Archer's cart as he got his horse ambling from Holt down the rutted country lanes to Hunworth. It was a perfect summer's day, and the hedgerows were overgrown and humming with insect life. Irene pointed out and named all the flowers for her young man: harebells, cowslips, wild poppies. There were swallows dipping through the warm air and Tom pretended that he'd never seen birds and flowers in such profusion before. 'All we have up north is seagulls! And no flowers can grow in such a cold and sooty place.'

She half-believed him when he made Tyneside sound so bleak and uninviting, but she was still building a romantic picture in her head of the frozen city in the north he belonged to.

'Were all your sisters there to meet him?' Bella asked, breaking into her reverie. Bella was intrigued by the fact that Irene had six younger sisters. To her it sounded lovely, because she'd always longed for a younger sister, for company. Irene had told her about reading them all fairy tales under the eaves of their attic bedroom in the cottage, and Bella loved the idea of that. She had only one, much younger, brother, and though her family was warm and loving as could be, she had still grown up feeling slightly lonely at home.

'Oh yes, they were all there to check up on him!' Irene rolled her eyes. 'The whole bally lot of them! Sitting on the stairs, heads poking through the banisters, watching him coming into the house, and ducking his head because he found our ceilings so low. And didn't they think he was so handsome and smart! It was all they could talk about for days!'

Bella wanted to know all about what they'd eaten and what they'd talked about, and Irene filled her in on the various details. There was Cromer crab, dressed fancily in their dainty shells for the grown-ups. Tom had gamely tasted his, and then looked queasy as Irene's ma told him to pick out the tastiest morsel: the dark little brain. All the kids were eating bloater paste sandwiches in stodgy home-baked bread, staring at the adults as they carried out their rather formal visit.

Irene's da had asked Tom questions about planes and armaments. He seemed to be far more clued up about that kind of thing than Irene or her ma might have expected. Tom answered readily and knowledgeably, and the old man had rewarded him with a trip out – just the two of them – to the Honeybell pub, across the green, for a pint of beer together.

'It must have been lovely for you,' Bella said, 'to see the visit going off so well, and to have your parents' blessing.'

'Oh, yes, it was,' Irene said. 'Though things are never as straightforward as that with my mum, of course. She's got to bring a bit of doom and gloom in somehow. When the fellas were off at the Honeybell she turned to me and said, "Well, he's like a movie star, coming in here with his hair slicked back and his fancy uniform. He's like someone famous, getting everyone's attention. But he'll take you away, our Irene. Fellas like that come into your life and your head gets turned and then you move away forever. Nothing about your life will ever be the same again. And we'll lose you forever, won't we? Everything is going to be different from now on.'"

Irene had looked at her ma as she stood there wringing her damp tea towel in her hands, and she looked rather vulnerable for once. Irene had not been able to lie to her: 'Yes, mum. Everything is going to be different. There's no easy way of telling you this, but I'm moving north with him. He doesn't want me to. He says it's too dangerous. But I want to move to the north and be with his family and see a different bit of life to what I'm used to.'

'Away from us . . .!' her ma had gasped, and looked upset for a moment, before her expression had hardened and closed up like a fist. 'Aye, well. I suppose it had to happen. I knew you'd leave us. I knew it was gonna happen, sooner or later . . .'

Back in the ice cream parlour, Bella laughed ruefully to hear this. 'Mas know how to make us feel guilty, don't they? They know just how to turn the screws. Here, let's have more coffee. The place is almost dead now. We'll shut up shop in a bit. Let's have a last cup together.'

Irene smiled at her, and felt her residual guilt draining away. Yes, I was right to come here, after all. No matter how guilty her mum had tried to make her feel for fleeing the nest, or however much Tom had warned her about the bombings and the craziness of his family.

Right now, as Bella poured out the last coffee of the evening and dolloped foamy milk on top of both cups, Irene really felt that she was living and working in just the right place for her. She felt right at home at last.

Which was just as well, considering the condition that she strongly suspected she might be in . . .

A couple of days later she was perched on the edge of a smooth leather armchair in an unfamiliar sitting room. It was the formal waiting room of the doctor that Bella had recommended. The place seemed far too fancy for Irene, and she dreaded what all this was going to cost. A beautiful clock on the mantle was ticking through expensive-seeming minutes as she waited. Even the magazines spread out in a fan on the coffee table were the glossier, pricier titles.

Bella's family are more well-to-do than us, she was thinking. It was daft of me not to seek Beryl's advice, say, about where to go.

But she wanted some privacy, didn't she? She didn't need everyone knowing all her business all the time.

The receptionist was cool and immaculate and blonde. She called Irene 'Mrs Farley' and took her through a corridor that smelt of beeswax polish, into the doctor's consulting room. She was asked to undress and to put on a paper gown. It all seemed a proper faff for something that, with increasing confidence and certainty, Irene already knew the answer to.

The doctor was a small man, rather old, with snowy whiskers and a perfectly smooth, bald head, rather like a pink billiard ball. Irene was fascinated with that perfectly round pate and it gave her something to concentrate on as he examined her and carried on speaking to her at the same time.

She found it bizarre that he could look down there and carry on talking to her. She stared at her own knees and the top of his head and tried not to want to drop dead on the spot.

He pressed her and prodded and looked at her for some time. It seemed like a hundred years before he straightened up and looked at her again. 'I am delighted to be able to tell you, Mrs Farley, that you are to be a ma.'

There was a rushing noise in both her ears. She could hardly hear what he was saying to her through the pounding of her blood. It was like the roar of the sea or the noise inside a seashell. She sat open-mouthed as he said a few more things that she paid no heed to whatsoever.

She went off to dress herself once more in a complete daze, said goodbye to the receptionist and stepped out of the hall and into the crisp twilight of the smart suburban street. I'm going to have a baby of my own, she thought, amazed at herself and setting her feet firmly back towards Ocean Road and her early-evening shift at Franchino's.

Chapter Thirteen

'I'm swearing you to secrecy,' she told Bella, and of course her new friend promised her she would never say a word.

When Arthur turned up an hour later for a frothy coffee and a gossip he glared at the two of them.

His eyebrows gathered and Irene stared at them. He must pluck them, to get them so neat! They were much nicer than Irene's own eyebrows. Eeeh, what kind of a bloke plucked his eyebrows into shape? One who fancied himself like a matinee idol, maybe.

'What's going on with you two?' he demanded, when they were all sitting in their usual booth in Franchino's.

Camp Coffee. Irene was almost getting a taste for it. It was quite palatable if you put a head of froth on it. 'There's nothing going on,' she demurred.

'Irene's had some news,' said Bella, and for a second Irene thought she was about to be dobbed in it. 'Her hubby's coming home next week from the airbase. Four whole days she's to have with him.'

'Ah, great, pet!' Arthur beamed. 'I'm chuffed as muck for you. That's great news.'

Irene smiled at him. For all his funny ways there was something so lovely about the way Arthur shared in your happiness when it came. He was never envious or begrudging of anyone, even though he was a gossip and liked a good tale to pass on. 'The thing is, it's instead of Christmas,' Irene said. 'We'll have to have a bit of Christmas early.'

'Any Christmas at all is a fine thing,' Arthur said. 'I certainly plan to ring them bells as soon as I can manage it.'

Irene wondered about Arthur. What kind of family he came from and where he lived. He was never very forthcoming about much at all. He said even less about his background than his sister Mavis did. Sometimes he made jokes about the dreadful, damp, buggy state of the place they were living in. Irene got the impression that Arthur regarded staying in South Shields as something of a penance and a pain. He'd rather be elsewhere, with a complete change of scene. Even though she felt she was getting used to him and his ways, and that they were even becoming friends, she still didn't feel confident enough to quiz him about his background and his past. She felt that some of it might be secret or dangerous somehow.

But then, perhaps she was romanticising him. She associated him with the Savoy cinema, of course, and all those dramatic movies. She had him all mixed up with the elaborate plots that unfolded in the dark where he stood sentinel most nights with his tray of ice creams and cigarettes.

'Right, you two,' he told them, suddenly, lighting up a Woodbine and picking errant bits of tobacco off his tongue. 'You're coming to the tea dance with me tonight. I've had it with sitting in there on my tod. Last time I was sat by the potted palms with a warm ginger ale all night. I want some company.'

'I thought you said you always get a friend when you go dancing?' Bella smiled and raised an eyebrow.

'I might have been exaggerating,' he said. 'All the single old ladies like to dance together, bust to bust. It's revolting.

I was looked at askance all evening, as if I was some kind of untrustworthy gigolo. Well, can you imagine? Me! A gigolo!' He shook his head fiercely. 'All I want to do is go dancing. I'm itching to be up on that shiny floor. You two have to come out with me!'

'When?' Irene asked. She wanted to ask, is it expensive? Will I have to dress up nice? Her mind went flicking through the few things she had in the great big sarcophagus-like wardrobe in her attic bedroom.

'It's tonight. You don't need to pay for a ticket,' Arthur said. 'And you've got about an hour and a half to nip home and tart yourself up.'

'Isn't he awful?' Bella said. 'Well, I'm game if you are, Irene.'

Out dancing! A slow grin spread over her face. It wasn't even the weekend. Why, it hardly seemed legal!

She thought about another evening sat round Number Thirteen with her in-laws, listening to the radio and all the gloomy war reports she only half understood and comedies where most of the jokes passed her by but made everyone else roar with laughter. And when the music came on it always made her feet jig about like they were trying to force her to dance there and then, even in the close confines of Ma Ada's sitting room.

Oh, now that she let herself consider it . . . Irene was longing to go out for a dance.

'Yes, please, Arthur . . . hinny,' she smiled. 'I'd love to come out tonight!'

'Eeeh, listen to her!' Arthur squealed. 'She's saying "hinny" like a native! She'll soon be fitting right in! And you'll love it tonight, pet. It's a special one. It'll be a lovely night, you'll see!'

After work Irene and Bella dashed off to Bella's house, off near Simonside way. Irene had thought she ought to go to her own home, but Bella wouldn't hear of it. 'You'll be able to fit into something of mine. You've an extra few pounds on you now, so you're more my size . . .'

Before Irene knew it, she was dashing up Bella's street and being dragged into a tall, red-bricked family home that took away her breath, it seemed so grand with its gabled attics and double garage.

Inside there was a flurry of early-evening activity going on and a gabble of beautiful-sounding Italian gossip as Bella breezed through the kitchen, introducing Irene to everyone. Irene caught an impression of a ma, an old aunty, a younger brother and the familiar figure of Bella's dad, Tonio. There were genial greetings in a tongue that sounded so lovely she wanted to sit and listen to them talking all night.

But there wasn't time. She was whisked upstairs to Bella's bedroom, where she gasped to see that her boss had a view of the sea from her bay window. 'Stop hanging out of the window and choose something to wear!' Bella yelled, and in the end picked out a dress for Irene herself: purple crêpe de Chine. It showed off how busty she was getting as a result of the pregnancy: something Irene had been careful to conceal in recent weeks.

'Show them off!' Bella laughed, as she hunted through the racks for something for herself. She seemed to have loads of clothes. Her closet was one of the kind that she could step right into, like another room. Irene peered over her naked shoulder at the rows of shoes, and hats and scarves that were heaped any old how in colourful profusion.

'You're so lucky,' Irene said. 'Look at all this!'

'It was me dad that did it all, really,' Bella said. 'He came from Naples with nowt. Literally nowt. He had to get out of the country because of family bother. I mean, nasty family bother. Gangster stuff. So he came here and started selling ices on the sea front. And look at what he did! He's got a little empire.'

'You must be proud of your family,' Irene smiled, watching her friend tugging on an emerald-green number, and pulling a face as she surveyed herself in the full-length mirror.

'Aye, I am, but when there's things like this war going on, it's hard. It's like we don't really belong here. Even after all these years. You still have people coming up and saying nasty stuff about Eyeties and wops and getting back to our own country. Me mam got spat at in the butchers, did I tell you? When she said her name as she handed over her ration book.'

Irene was shocked. 'You never told me that.'

'It's tough when people turn on you and tell you that you don't really belong. And yet we're in the same town, aren't we? We face the same dangers every day. We're all in the same boat.'

Irene shook her head. 'People are ignorant and frightened. But that's no excuse, really . . .'

Bella smiled at her. 'Zip me up at the back, will you? We'd best hurry up. We've got to get back across town in time to meet Arthur. He'll go crackers if we leave him standing on the steps of the Alhambra all by himself.'

And so they dressed up in a rush, leaving Bella's room all in a jumble. Before they ran back out into the night Bella insisted they swig a tiny glass of her aunty's home-made limoncello. Thinking it would be just like lemonade, Irene swigged too hard and choked, and had to have her back slapped.

Bella's father Tonio came out of his den to see what all the noise was about. When he saw them, he beamed. 'Oh, look at you! *Che bella!*' And then he added some admonitions about not staying out too late and making sure they had their gas masks with them, and checking they knew where the nearest shelter was in case of a raid.

'And you, too, Pop!' Bella warned. 'If those sirens go off tonight, get the whole family down the public shelter by Ocean Road.'

'Nah,' he shrugged and waved her worries away. 'Look at the wonderful huge cellar we have under this house! We're fine down there, with all the wine and everything. I'm not budging from this house, no matter what the bloody flamin' Nazis throw at us!'

Bella knew of old that her dad was intractable and hopeless. She shook her head and kissed him goodbye.

Then the two girls promised they'd be as good as they could possibly be and, giggling, they ran out of the house and all the way back into town.

It was much fancier than Irene had been expecting, and that was the truth.

On her way to the Alhambra with Bella that night she was picturing something a bit like the community hall by the docks, where she and Beryl had spent an exhausting afternoon sorting jumble and folding jumpers. Or like the barn in Norfolk where the Land Girls had attended dances and she had first met Tom. She expected everything to be basic and threadbare, and everyone making the best of it all.

Instead, when they met Arthur on the steps outside the Alhambra it was like they were going into a grand, oriental palace out of the fairy-tale treasury Irene had lost so long ago.

'Oh, my goodness . . .!' she gasped, as they stepped inside the brilliantly lit hall. All of the windows had been blacked out of course, and the effect of stepping indoors was blinding. There were wonderful Christmas trees garlanded with ribbons and chains of lights, and Union Jacks draped upon the balconies and banisters of the foyer. Music was already issuing brazenly from the main hall and, if her ears weren't mistaken, that was a live band playing.

The music tugged at her and teased her, drawing her into the ballroom. 'Oh, Arthur, I had no idea! It's so beautiful! No wonder you love coming here!'

'Well, it's a special one tonight,' he said. 'A proper band and there are sailors in town. And it's almost Christmas, too, so it's a bit of a fancy do!' He looked both Bella and Irene up and down. 'You two made the effort, I'm glad to see!'

The two girls grinned at him.

Maybe it was the lemony, alcoholic fumes of the liqueur she had downed, but Irene was feeling ever so light on her feet. Lighter than she had done for a long time. The dancing slippers that Bella had lent her were flimsy and delicate, and woefully inadequate for running on frozen pavements like the ones they had taken through town, and this added to her feeling of unreality. Charging through the night in an evening gown of a kind she'd never been lucky enough to possess for herself, and arriving at a gilded palace like this one, Irene felt like she was in a wonderful dream.

The whole dance hall was seething with dancing bodies. Green and blue and white uniforms, and girls in a multitude of patterns and colours. It was as if everyone had cast aside their cares and come out as their brightest, boldest selves. It was just like they were determined to pretend that the war was already over and this was their night to celebrate.

The music was insistent, booming, joyful. It made Irene feel buoyant and peculiar. She even felt . . . she had to admit it . . . a little bit alluring!

'Who's going to dance with me?' Arthur asked, with a grin.

He looked extremely dapper tonight. His hair was slicked back and, when Irene looked closely, was it even possible he'd painted his eyes, ever so subtly, with mascara? He looked like a screen idol. Like a Geordie Valentino! But maybe she shouldn't tell him, in case he got a swollen head? He was wearing a dark suit of impeccable cut. Like all his clothes it was woefully out of date. It came from the fashion plates of at least twenty years ago, but somehow the panache with which Arthur wore it made that seem irrelevant.

Irene pushed Bella forward to take the first dance with Arthur and waved them on their way. They swirled into the gorgeous crowd, looking so elegant and perfect on the floor together. All of Arthur's usual awkwardness dropped away as he started to move in time with the music, and Bella's body responded easily to him as he led them in the dance. She'd obviously had proper lessons at some point and found it easy to follow his steps.

But Arthur . . . he was something else. In a way he really became one with the music as the song developed. He swam into the middle of the room, not pushily, but as if both he and the dancers around him recognised his rightful place, on display at the centre. He grinned broadly as he cavorted, expertly, intently, in his very own element.

I can't dance with him! Irene thought, desperately, suddenly glad that she'd let Bella go first. He'll make a right show of me. I'll look like a galumphing carthorse next to him!

Others were watching and passing comment on Arthur and Bella's display. Irene smiled, feeling proud of her friends and the notice they were attracting.

'And now you, lady!' Arthur beamed at her, suddenly appearing at her side. Bella stepped back and Irene felt herself swept up into Arthur's arms.

The music shifted into something more up-tempo and jolly. She knew the tune, but the words eluded her as she was whisked around to the centre of the shining floor. Irene couldn't help throwing her head back and laughing with sheer exhilaration, feeling the eyes of her fellow revellers upon her and her elegant partner. The colourful spotlights shimmered all over her body and Irene suddenly felt lighter and more carefree than she had done for a very long time. It was as if her body itself was turning into dancing points of light. Her body, which often seem too heavy, or too cold, or too tired, or too hungry . . . now it was just a shimmer of light and air.

'You're good!' Arthur chuckled in her ear. 'Who'd have thought it, Irene Farley? You're a fancy little mover!'

She rolled her eyes at him and thought about the times she'd practiced with her Land Girl chums, and even with her sisters, at home with the wireless playing. Whirling around the room with the sound turned up too loud . . .

'This is just heaven,' she told Arthur, beaming at him. 'Thank you so much for asking us along.'

He twirled her around, perfectly in time with the tune. 'It's my absolute pleasure. I thought you could do with having a lovely time, my dear.'

After dancing with Arthur for three whole songs, and then passing him back to Bella, Irene found herself drifting further away from the dance floor. Perhaps she should sit out a couple of songs and get a sip of water or something. She was feeling rather hot. Of course, it was all the excitement. She should be more careful, really. A woman in her condition . . .

She took a paper cup of cordial and a seat by a table in the corner, beside some potted palms. Whew. Actually, she was whacked, what with one thing and another. It had been a long day. A full morning at the biscuit factory. The tension of the doctor's appointment in the late afternoon, and everything that had entailed. Followed by an evening stint at Franchino's, where there had been a rush on, and then dashing about tonight, all in a panic, to get here on time. Just as well to have a quiet little sit and gather her scattered wits after attempting to keep up with the brilliant steps of Arthur . . .

It was at this precise moment that she cast her eyes about the crowd, hoping to catch a glimpse of her friends and, in doing so, caught the eye of someone else. Someone she really wasn't expecting to see at that moment.

Perhaps, subconsciously, she had recognised the red dress first. It was the same woollen dress that she had seen Megan wearing just the other day. It had struck her then how well it clung to her sister-in-law's figure. Now Megan was wearing it to great advantage again, as she stood in the corner of the Alhambra dance hall. She was partly shaded by the rubber plants but she looked a million dollars. Also, around her neck, she was wearing an elegant fur tippet.

'Megan!' Irene started to call out in surprise. Why, she hadn't mentioned anything about coming here tonight! But then, Irene supposed, neither had she.

That was when she noticed that the older woman was kissing a man. At the sound of Irene's voice Megan stopped and glared across the room. There was a flash of genuine, horrible anger in those eyes. Megan's beautiful face hardened with loathing.

Suddenly Irene understood why.

Megan had been caught. She was out dancing with a fellow who wasn't her husband. That wasn't Bob's broad back and brilliantined hair. It wasn't his chunky arms that were holding Megan tonight.

Irene blinked and almost dropped her paper cup of pop as the man, sensing a change of mood, turned to look at Megan.

It was Sam.

He was brother-in-law to both of them. Lovely Sam. Irene's friend and ally at Number Thirteen.

And, judging by the way he was holding on to Megan, he was being rather more than a friend and ally to *her*.

Chapter Fourteen

Irene didn't say anything.

It was best, she decided, to say nothing at all. She would pretend she hadn't seen anything. She didn't know any secrets and, even if she did, she would never tell anyone a word.

She ducked away and went back to her friends. She tried to enjoy the rest of the evening at the Alhambra. It was heady and giddy and good fun. There was something potent lacing the fruit punch they all drank and the evening became even giddier. She tried to enjoy the company of her friends, and the dancing, and the fact that she was wearing the most beautiful garments she had ever worn, not including her wedding dress.

But she couldn't quite blank out the picture in her head of Megan staring back at her through those few feet of space. Megan with her arms around Sam. Kissing him.

Luckily, Sam hadn't clocked Irene standing there. He hadn't turned all the way round. Thank God. Oh, but she knew it was him. No doubting those jug ears standing out from his tidily shaven neck and his strawberry blond hair brushed so neatly for a night out. Eeeh, Sam – what was he playing at?

That look Megan had given her. It was sheer hatred.

What have I done to incur that from her? Irene wondered, as the night at the Alhambra drew to a close. Apart from smack her in the face at work, and then catch her up to no good at the dance hall. Well, if she didn't hate me enough before, she certainly will now. Now that I've clearly caught her out doing something she shouldn't.

But could Megan really be carrying on with her own brother-in-law? And him so young and callow? Could she really be doing anything so wicked, and right in front of all the young people at the dance? Surely the news of her carrying-on would be all around Shields the morrow?

As they left the noisy dance hall, issuing into the darkened streets, these thoughts went spiralling miserably in Irene's head. She felt way out of her depth and furious at herself for looking in the wrong direction at just the wrong time. At least she hadn't clapped eyes on them again. Well, didn't that just prove it? If Megan had scooted them both out of there? Why carry on so shocked and annoyed if there was nothing wicked going on? Why hadn't she just come over and greeted her sister-in-law? Surely she could have brazened it out?

No, Irene knew that it all portended something truly bad. There was going to be trouble in the family.

Oh, Sam, she thought. You idiot.

'Hey, lady!' Arthur nudged her in the ribs as they hurried along. 'You're a million miles away. Did you not enjoy our night out?'

He looked almost crestfallen that she hadn't seemed to share her friends' pleasure at the dance. 'Oh, sorry, yes! It was lovely, Arthur. Thank you for taking us out tonight. It was so kind of you.'

'Kindness, nothing!' he laughed. 'I just needed a dance, and you two were my willing victims. Hey, you're not a bad mover, Mrs Farley! I was quite impressed!'

'Yes, I was as well,' added Bella, as they hurried along, keeping huddled together against the suddenly freezing wind coming up from the sea. 'I wouldn't have had you down as a good mover, hinny! But you were grand.'

'And what about me?' laughed Arthur. 'You've never seen me move before, Irene. Aren't I amazing? Aren't I talented?'

She had to give it to him: he was a beautiful dancer. 'Where did you learn all that?'

'Well,' he said, and was about to leap delightedly into the long tale of himself and his talents, when a gruff ARP warden stepped out of the shadows with his torch and gave them a dressing down.

'Get yoursels home, you little gobshites!' he commanded them in a bellicose whisper.

'Ah, hadaway!' Arthur jeered, and ran quickly down the street, dragging the girls after him. 'Bloody little Hitler,' he cackled, as they eventually slowed. They had stitches and aching feet by the time they came level with the park. 'Eeeh, they give some of these blokes uniforms and they get above themselves. They turn funny.'

'*You'd* know all about funny blokes!' Bella laughed.

'Shurrup, you!' he shot back and the two of them were grappling with each other in the road, laughing like two kids as they did so. Irene didn't quite get what they were joshing each other about, but their daft wrestling and messing about brought her out of her funk and made her giggle.

Soon though, it was time to peel off in their separate directions. Bella wasn't sure they should separate. 'Why don't you both come to our house? Irene, you can crawl in with me and Arthur can have an armchair.'

'I'd best be home,' said Irene. 'It's after midnight. There'll be hell on if I'm not there soon. Ma Ada sits up in that chair of hers until everyone is back indoors. It's like she's on guard.'

They hugged each other goodnight under the beautiful clear moonlight. The wind was fierce now, rolling back all the clouds and making it feel like the dried sweat was freezing on their bodies.

Next thing, Irene was all alone and hurrying through the centre of town. She has heading back once again to the Sixteen Streets. She should have been there after work, or sent a message somehow, saying she was staying out to go to the dance. But she had neither gone home nor sent word and as a result she knew she'd be in trouble. Eeeh, tonight might cause all kinds of trouble, one way or another . . .

She hurried on, stumbling a bit in her borrowed shoes. My God, what am I thinking of? Dashing about tipsily in clothes as thin as these? I'll catch my death. And nowadays, there's more than just me to think about, isn't there? There isn't just my life at stake anymore.

Almost as if on cue, the air raid sirens started up at this moment.

Oh, no. Please, no. Not right now. Not just now.

But there was no mistaking that horrible droning whine. It filled up all her senses as she staggered along and brought streams of people out onto the streets. They came with their overcoats hastily dragged on over their nighties and pyjamas. Like hordes of disturbed sleepwalkers they spilled onto the pavement, whispering and trying to keep calm. The sirens blared and the somnambulant movement of the mass of townsfolk meant that Irene had to push and force herself through.

She was walking in the opposite direction to the masses of people moving past her. 'You're going the wrong way, hinny!' she was told. 'The shelter's this way!' And she knew they were right. She should just have gone along with the flow. She should have just tagged along and got to the closest shelter she could. That was what you were supposed to do in these circumstances. She should just find safety and sit tight there until the raid was over.

Yet she didn't do that. She couldn't do that.

She was almost home. The tall brick wall that abutted the docks was in sight and after that it was just a short dash across the Sixteen Streets to home. Here came the first rumbles and flashes of the bombs. Horrible fear gripped her insides. Her shoes slithered and slipped on the pavement. The flashes looked far away, didn't they? And she couldn't hear planes. Not yet . . .

Irene was within sight of Frederick Street. She just had to get there. Tonight something was telling her, insistently, that she had to get home to Number Thirteen . . .

There was no one at home but Ada and Lucky the cat.

'Everyone's left us here alone,' thundered the old woman. The siren was still going off in the streets when she opened the front door to Irene. 'What time do you call this, lass?'

She looked rattled, the old woman. She was in her hairnet, voluminous nightie and thick woollen dressing gown. Her face was craggy in the sulphurous light of the moon. 'I-I'm sorry,' Irene said, feeling horrible once again that she didn't have her own key to the door. 'Where are the others? I didn't think you'd be on your own.'

'I'm on me own and a raid's coming down over Shields!' wailed the old lady. 'I can't hardly believe that I've been abandoned at the end! And the bloody bairns I've skivvied for all me life; that I've skimped and saved for and made sacrifices for – they all bloody well abandon me when it comes down to it! And their bloody wives, too! You've all left me here all alone! There's only Lucky. Only Lucky who stays here and keeps loyal to his mam, don't you pet?'

She squeezed the cat to her bosom so hard it squirmed and wriggled to break free.

Now they were in the parlour and Irene decided they couldn't stand there debating the worthlessness of all the family members for hours on end. 'We had better get ourselves to the shelter,' she said.

Ada flashed her a grim look. 'I was ready to go as soon as the sirens sounded. But I couldn't get there by myself. My feet. My legs. I couldn't do it alone. I was here by myself. What was I to do?'

Irene saw that there was actual panic etched in her ma-in-law's face. She had been genuinely rattled by her plight tonight, and who could blame her? She must really have thought the whole family had run out on her, just when she needed them most. 'We must go now,' Irene said.

'Listen,' said Ada, in a low voice, staring up at the anaglypta ceiling with an intensity that made Irene think she could see straight through solid floorboards and tiles into the skies far above. 'The sirens have stopped. It's too late. We can't go out now. We'll have to sit this one out.'

A cold dread crept over Irene. It was too late. The old woman was right. They would just have to take their chances.

'I'm not clambering under the kitchen table,' Ada said. 'Not with my legs.'

'Maybe we should get under the stairs,' Irene said.

Ada pulled a face. 'I'm not getting into Bob and Megan's marital bed, even with the Luftwaffe breathing down our necks. No, I'll take my chances in my own parlour. If I have to go, I'll go with dignity, sitting in my own armchair, surrounded by all my nice and familiar things.'

Mention of Bob and Megan reminded Irene of that evil look she'd received from her sister-in-law at the Alhambra earlier that evening. There was definitely something too intimate in the way Sam had been holding her. The way they were kissing – that wasn't how a brother and sister-in-law kissed each other. It . . . it was like incest, wasn't it? Irene flushed at the taboo word and the images it conjured. Wasn't it incest, though,

153

what they were doing? She didn't even know. She didn't want to think about it anymore.

How distant that all seemed now, compared with the threat of sudden death in a bombing raid. Yet still she could see those flashing eyes and that crazy resentment in Megan's face. Oh, what a terrible night for them all to be out at the same time.

But Irene had been right, hadn't she? Her instinct to hurry home, pushing against the flow of the crowds as they sought safety: that impulse had been quite correct. Only she had made it safely home tonight to sit with Ada.

The old woman was trembling as she sat there. Irene had never seen her like this. The cat – growing sick of being mauled around – had jumped to freedom and was perched on top of the dresser, placidly licking himself and paying no heed to the human drama below.

The quiet in the room was almost more than Irene could bear. It was a waiting silence and both women knew what came at the end of it.

'We'll get through this,' Irene whispered to Ada. Why am I whispering? It's not as if the German pilots will hear . . .

Tom said that the noise in the cockpits was incredible, but you got used to it. You were in your own little bubble of deafening noise. He told her that the skins of the planes they flew were actually fabric stretched over metal frames. She had imagined that fighter planes would be more substantial than that. She had been horrified to hear that detail. It was like they were flying about on flimsy, home-made contraptions. Flying clothes horses or soap-box carts . . .

'Shall I put the kettle on?' she asked. She wasn't sure if they were even allowed to do something as banal as that during a raid.

Down in the shelters the rest of the local folk would be opening flasks and unwrapping snacks. They'd be leafing through newspapers and comics as they all sat hugger-mugger on the benches, trying to keep their feet dry.

To the people in the shelters it would be just another night-time of waiting for the all-clear. It was rather shocking how accustomed you became to the routine of it.

But being caught up here, above ground, brought it all back vividly to Irene. It brought back the intense and visceral reaction she'd had to the bombing on the first night she had arrived in South Shields with Tom, what felt like an absolute lifetime ago.

We cheated death then, she thought. We were fortunate. And we'll be so again. She tried to smile reassuringly at Ada. 'Tea?'

'Not yet, girl,' the old woman said. 'Come and sit by me for a moment . . .'

The neediness in her ma-in-law's voice caught her off guard. She drew up a dining chair and held out her hand. The hand that took hers was callused and hard. It hardly felt like a human hand at all, it was so work-worn and cracked. It must feel sore, she thought, to have hands like that. Ada squeezed her hand as if she was holding on for grim life.

Just at that moment they heard bombs dropping somewhere nearby. The dull explosion was several streets away, they hoped. Irene prayed that whoever had been hit had died instantly. You heard some terrible things about people caught in the blast or by debris. People who survived with the most hideous injuries and who had to linger and live on in awful pain. She thought it would be best to be caught smack dab in the centre with zero chance of survival. But she never mentioned this gloomy, morbid thought to anyone, of course.

More explosions. A horrible volley of cracks and booms. Closer, they seemed like. Or maybe the women were more attuned to listening for them.

Blood was pulsing in Irene's ears, almost blocking out the sound of anything else. She had to fight down the panic in her breast to hear what Ada was saying.

'They're after the dockyards again,' Ada said, gripping hard. 'They'll get them this time. Or next time. I'm sure of it. We're too close. It's too dangerous living here. But it's always the same for the poorest of the poor. Living right by the docks. Living in the worst places. It's always been true, that. Did you know my family's lived down here for over a hundred years?'

'Tom told me that,' Irene said. 'He was very proud . . .'

'Proud nothing,' the old woman chuckled bitterly. 'It just means we've always had nowt. None of us. We've lived down the Sixteen Streets all these years and none of us have ever had bugger all, or been able to change anything for the next generation coming up. Well, maybe it's best that the whole lot gets blown to buggery, eh? And then at least there'll be no chance of folk having to carry on living in these middens and slums . . . Maybe there'll be an end to it all . . .'

Irene didn't know what to say to that. Ada's house was immaculate inside, just like everyone else's down Frederick Street that they knew or were related to. These houses were little – if rather cramped – palaces inside. The windows and nets and doorsteps were scrubbed weekly. The walls were covered in beautifully framed pictures of olden-day scenes and photos of long-gone relations. Everything was scrubbed to within an inch of its life.

But dust lay thickly on every surface, even so, every day. The docks brought iron ore from abroad and the dust came out of the ships and the crates and up from the shipyards on the sea breeze and the boots and the clothes of the men who worked there. The dust came down every day and the women of these streets toiled endlessly, trying to keep everything clean. It was futile, of course. Ada's ruined hands and knees and craggy face were testament to a life spent toiling, trying to keep her little paradise clean.

Now men from abroad were raining death and destruction from the air. They brought with them more filth. Smashed masonry and sooty, choking fires all over town brought their own waves of muck each day.

I would just give up, thought Irene. I don't have the fortitude or the grit, do I? I couldn't live the life that Ada has done. Look at her! Even trembling and gripping my hand with fear, she still looks indomitable and dignified.

More bombs. Louder.

'They're coming closer,' said Ada.

She was right and Irene felt a dreadful ache grip her midriff. Her belly went cold inside. She suddenly wanted the loo, but there was no way she could get up and run outside to the yard and the outside privy. Her insides were churning.

She feared for the growing child inside her . . . How big was he or she? How much like an actual child would they be by now? She had no idea. She pictured it like a little mermaid, swimming about inside her. Hearing the muffled noise of destruction going on out here in the world she was waiting to be born into. What kind of world was this? Why was it so horrible and filled with hate?

What am I bringing her into, Irene thought?

Yes, it was a girl. All of a sudden, she knew the child was a girl.

Ada was watching her expressions changing and flickering. Ada was looking at her with a shrewd expression of her own. In the next silent lull she asked Irene: 'How come you haven't told me yet?'

'Told you w-what?' asked Irene, and averted her eyes guiltily.

'Ah, you know what I mean, lass. You should know that there's very little that can happen in this house without me knowing about it. I can read minds, you know. I can know everything if I put my mind to it. There's no one got any privacy around here!'

She was chuckling, trying to make light of it, but Irene felt discomfited by the old woman's words. As they sat there in the near-darkness she wondered if Ada had any inkling of the secrets that Megan and Sam seemingly shared? Surely she'd be less complacent and pleased with herself if she knew what Irene had learnt tonight?

'Tell me yourself, in your own words, lass,' said Ada patiently.

The explosions were growing fainter now. Muffled. Distant. Almost gentle-sounding, though Irene knew that thought was absurd.

'I w-went to see a doctor today,' Irene said.

'I see.' Ada nodded, and waited to hear the rest.

'I'm going to have a child, Ada. In the new year. Your grandchild. Your first grandchild.'

When the all-clear sounded it came almost like a fanfare to underline her good news.

'Eeeh, me first grandchild!' gasped the old woman. 'Me first! Me first grandchild! After all these years!' Her face lit up brilliantly and she seemed to shed about fifty years in a moment. 'This house has been filled with grown-ups for much too long. It's been crowded and noisy and far too serious. Now there's to be a bairn! A new bairn at last!'

Ada was up on her feet, rather unsteadily, and she was clasping Irene to her. 'And it's all because of you, lass! You've done this! You've brought us back to life! You'll bring this family together again. You'll give us all something wonderful to look forward to!'

Chapter Fifteen

It wasn't quite snowing when he came home, but snow was on its way. It was a sparkling, gloriously frosty night over Tyneside. It felt almost cold enough for the harbour to freeze across, just like some of the older souls said it used to in the days of yore. Irene shivered as she put on extra woollens, though it was as much from nervous anticipation as anything else.

Tom was making the journey north on those slow, dark trains by himself this time. Arriving late on Wednesday night he was bleary-eyed and just about falling asleep on his feet.

Of course Irene was at the station waiting for him, along with Beryl and Sam. She felt a bit daft, standing and trembling on the cold platform with a bushel of mistletoe in her arms. For a little while, anyway, until the excitement got to her and she realised: I'm really going to see him again. He's actually going to be here once more in the flesh. It seemed so long, it was like he had become a character she had made up in her head. Every other member of the family at Number Thirteen was more familiar to her nowadays than her own husband.

The mistletoe had been one of Sam's silly ideas. He'd picked it up from the greengrocers, he said – though Irene suspected he'd nicked it from somewhere. Everyone at home had laughed at the thought of Tom being grabbed as soon as he stepped off the train and getting lavished with kisses. It made Irene blush, and even more so when she looked at Sam and thought about how she'd seen him kissing in public, too, quite recently. Kissing someone he shouldn't have been kissing. But they hadn't talked about that. She wanted to confront him, or at least ask him about it, but she hadn't found the moment or the courage just yet.

Beryl touched her arm. 'You're looking nervous, love. Come on, buck up. He'll be wanting to see cheery faces to welcome him.'

Beryl was right. She was always right, but Irene's guts were churning around inside. It was like the little mermaid inside her was turning cartwheels and looping the loop with excitement.

When the train came shunting and steaming into the small station and the doors flew open there was a great surge of busy bodies moving to and fro. They brought with them the soot and dust and smells of the railways and all those other towns they had stopped at on the way. The travellers all looked worn out, but when Tom appeared at last, he looked the most exhausted of all. He had great big purple rings around his eyes, and grinning at his welcome committee when he clocked them seemed to take almost more energy than he possessed.

Irene simply hugged him, and the glossy mistletoe berries and leaves were crushed between their heavy winter coats.

'Hello, you,' he said.

'I can't believe you're actually here,' Irene said. When he looked at her she could smell the cigarette smoke on his breath, see all the little bristles in his five o'clock shadow on his chin. He was standing so close to her, it was all surprising. She hadn't been so close to anyone in weeks and it was like he was filling up all her horizons.

'Hey, let's get you home, man,' Sam grinned, taking hold of his brother's bags for him. 'You look dead on your feet.'

Beryl darted forward to kiss his cheek. 'Everyone's really excited to see you, Tom. Especially with the news and everything.'

They headed for the exit, pulled along in the wake of everyone hurrying home, keen to be out of the frosty evening. 'The news?' he asked, bemused.

'Why, the kidda!' Beryl laughed. 'The bairn on the way! Didn't you think everyone would be excited? Didn't you reckon on it being the biggest news this year? Your ma's going daft about it! I've never seen Ma Ada so happy!'

Tom's smile was frozen on his face. He stopped walking and turned to look at Irene. 'Erm . . . So, everyone knows? You've told them?'

Irene felt flummoxed. 'Well, yes . . .'

He winced. 'Didn't you think to wait? Until I was back? And we could tell them together?'

He looked almost hurt, the way he was looking at her. Suddenly Irene felt terrible. 'I . . .' She didn't know what to say. With all the crowd bustling around them still, she didn't even know how to start. What she wanted to do was leap back accusingly and say: 'You left me all alone with this. I was scared. How was I to know how to do anything at all?'

And besides, she thought, his wily old ma had figured the truth out for herself. During that air raid the other night, when the two of them were alone in the house, she had demanded to know outright whether a baby was on the way. Irene had found herself having to be honest and, once the truth was out, Ma Ada had had to tell everyone. When the family had crept back home after the all-clear, Ma Ada had started putting the flags out and shouting from the rooftops.

The news no longer belonged only to the prospective parents anymore. But how to explain this to Tom just now?

'Hey, Tom,' she snapped, going on the offensive, as she often did when she felt wrong-footed. 'Don't you be having a go at me. Have you forgotten what it's like living with your bloody family? You can't keep any kind of news secret!'

Tom glared back at her. 'Don't you tell me what me own family's like, Irene!'

'I probably know better than you do, these days. Who's been the one stuck with them all these weeks?'

'That was your idea! You were the one who wanted to live here!'

'Maybe, but I never really knew what it was going to be like, did I? You could have warned me more!'

Now they were standing at loggerheads on the platform. They were only five minutes into Tom's precious four days of pre-Christmas leave and already it had all gone wrong.

Beryl broke in and told him concisely what he needed to know: 'Your bloody ma got the truth out of her. You know what she's like. Also, Irene's showing early. Her belly's out to *here*. It's pretty obvious what's going on.'

Tom looked only partly mollified as they stepped out of the station onto the glistening, icy street. He took a deep breath and looked at the pointed rooftops of the orange-bricked buildings all around him, and the station clock telling him it was after six. He said: 'I'm sorry. Of course, I should have known. I'm really sorry for being snappy, Irene. I've had to stand up in the crowded corridor all the way since bloody Doncaster and I'm knackered. I just wanted to be there when they all heard the news. I wanted to see the looks on everyone's faces.'

She took his hand. 'You'll see them all now. They haven't changed. Everyone's delighted. They're all so happy about the baby, Tom. And they're gonna be so happy to see you tonight, too.'

She was smiling at him broadly, but she still felt miffed at him inside. Fancy starting a row as soon as he arrived home!

'I'm sorry, sweetheart,' he told her, and stared right into her eyes in the way that he did when he wanted to make her laugh. He'd defy her to be grumpy or cross or to blink. He held her close and made the others wait as he hugged her hard and crushed all of the annoyance out of her. 'I really, really don't mind who you've told,' he sighed. 'I'm just glad we've got happy news for once.'

There was a lot of noise at number thirteen Frederick Street that night, right from the first moment Tom came home. The radio went on full blast and his ears were besieged with chatter from members of his own family and all the neighbours who came tapping on the door to take a look at him.

He was leaner and somehow taller, Irene thought. Could that be true? Could he have changed in just a few weeks away from her? She had some trouble fitting this Tom to the one she thought she already knew so well. Perhaps it was something in his demeanour? She'd never seen him so loud and demonstrative before. Calling out to people and being so hearty. Grabbing them to hug them hard and looking almost tearful. Why, he even grabbed hold of his old ma and danced her around the cramped parlour, banging into the heavy chairs as they did so. The old woman had wheezed and gasped with laughing protests.

Irene watched it all. She felt a little bit separate from the celebrations, but not uncomfortably so. She basked in the raucous silliness and uninhibited shows of affection.

'Eee, you bugger!' one of the aunties shouted from the scullery door. Aunty Winnie, was it? She wasn't really an auntie, she just knew Ma Ada from way back. 'Eee, you're a sight for sore eyes, you bugger!' She had a lot of teeth and staring eyes, like she had something wrong with her. Suddenly this person turned on Irene, making her jump. 'And you're his young bride, aren't you, hinny? And you're gonna have a bairn, aren't you?'

The news had gone far and wide, Irene thought. She nodded, feeling abashed by the attention of this woman with her jet-black hair and all her tasselled shawls. She looked like a proper gypsy, like the kind you saw on the encampment at the White Leas.

'Let me see your hand, bairn,' Aunty Winnie said.

'Oh, Winnie man,' shouted Ma Ada. 'Let them get sat down to their tea before you start on with all your prognosticating.'

'Aye, let us get a cup of tea first,' Tom said. 'I've had nowt since Doncaster.'

Beryl and Megan were in the scullery, busy spreading precious butter on dainty slices of bread. While the tea brewed they were making up sandwiches very carefully, with great ceremony. A lot of the week's meat ration had gone on slices of best Yorkshire ham, which they were dividing up precisely into each sandwich. It was a great delicacy and rarely come by in recent times: best ham with a smear of pease pudding. Tom had already told them, back on his very first leave from the air force, that pease pudding was impossible to get hold of anywhere in the south. Everyone had been indignant at this. It was such a staple for every occasion!

'Come on, let's eat!' Beryl encouraged them all to gather.

Tom was staring at everyone, ticking them all off mentally. He'd been welcomed by his whole family: Bob mumbling and acting shy, Sam acting more like a grown-up than ever and taking charge of things, Megan rather quieter than usual, and Beryl simply beaming at them all. Tony was absent, of course, but he'd been called down south, suddenly, for training. Beryl was carrying on like everything was fine, but Tom knew how she must be feeling with her fella gone.

They sipped tea from the best china and set upon the special sandwiches with great gusto.

'Mam!' Tom suddenly gasped. 'You've put the decorations up already!'

Ma Ada's eyes were glittering softly with tears she was trying to hold in. She could barely choke down her ham and pease pudding. If only Tony was here as well, she thought, and I'd have all my chicks together again. Ah, well, it's not to be. Not this time. But at least I know they're all safe and well . . . She nodded sagely at her Tom and said, 'Aye, well, pet. It might just be the first week in December, but this year Christmas starts early, and that's because of you, our Tom.'

Irene had helped her disinter the faded boxes from the deepest recesses of the sideboard. Mostly her decorations were papery, fragile things. It was plain to see they had been taken down and folded away with great care year after year for decades. Chains and loops and home-made lanterns. Fairies and angels that had been tinted long ago with jewel-like colours.

There were Christmas cards that she had saved for many years, ones scrawled on by long-dead friends and relatives, and these she liked to put out on display, to remember those folk by. There were painted fir cones and one or two coloured glass ornaments that had to be treated as if they belonged with the Crown jewels in the Tower of London. There were iridescent bubbles of coloured light that Ma Ada tied with faded ribbon to the tiny, spindly tree top she'd blagged from the greengrocer, that sat proudly aslant, on a doily, on the dining room table.

'It looks lovely in here, Mam,' said Tom. 'It reminds me of all the Christmases when we were bairns and you had to do the whole thing by yourself for us four boys.'

Irene had been told the tales. When the two of them had traded memories of their most precious times, Christmas stories had come quite high up the list. Many of Tom's were to do with his good-for-nowt father, Billy, being down the pub much of the time, drinking himself into an early grave. Even before his death – somewhere around the time of Tom's eleventh birthday – Ada had been forced to create Christmas for her boys all alone, with very little money to spare. Yet somehow she had made every one of those years special for them. All four boys remembered each Christmas with great joy.

'She used to make us stand out in the hallway with our eyes closed,' Tom told Irene, and the whole room now, on the night of his return. 'It would be six o'clock in the morning, and still dark. If we weren't awake, she'd wake us up herself because she was just as excited as we were. And then she'd open the parlour door, leaving the lights off as we all shuffled in. We'd bash into the furniture and we'd be giggling, excited. And, even now, thinking of it, I can smell the fruit she'd had delivered. Satsumas in the bowl on the table in nests of tissue paper. Twists and garlands of holly gathered from the woods. The room smelt fresh and green . . . And then she'd put the lights on suddenly and we'd all look! She'd have decorated the room overnight and put out our stockings and it was so exciting! We'd be just about speechless with it all. I remember Sam getting so excited one year he just about widdled himself . . .'

Irene had heard all these memories before, but it was even nicer hearing Tom tell them again in front of his mam and the rest of the family. Ma and son looked at each other with fierce, fond, protective love. 'Welcome home, our kid,' she smiled.

'Come on then, come on,' urged Sam suddenly. 'Let Aunty Winnie do her fortune-telling! You can see she's mad keen to!'

Beryl touched his shoulder. 'I'm not sure that's such a good idea . . .'

'No, come on, Aunty Winnie,' Tom laughed. 'It's all just a bit of fun, isn't it? And it's like a tradition round here, isn't it? Get your crystal ball out, hinny.'

The travelling woman gave him a dark look. 'It doesn't do to mock, Tom. You need to respect the spirits of the season.'

He just smiled at her. He wasn't going to argue against her silly superstitions tonight. Not when they were all having fun. Let the old witch have her say.

'Eeeh, I wish I hadn't let her gab on like that now,' Tom smiled ruefully, once he and Irene were alone together in their attic room.

'Ah, it was just a lot of nonsense,' said Irene. 'It doesn't matter.' She was undressing hurriedly, as was her habit, in the chilly room. Snow was falling fast past the window now, landing heavily on the rooftops opposite and the street below.

'Me mam sets a lot of store by what Aunty Winnie foretells,' said Tom. He was watching Irene as she scooted about the room, folding up her clothes neatly and swiftly pulling on her cotton nightdress. She wriggled under the bedspread and lay there shivering.

'Quick, get in,' she told him.

He was watching the snow fall on the Sixteen Streets. 'It's so beautiful out there. These streets are the shabbiest and the poorest in the whole town. Probably in the whole of Tyneside. But look at it out there. It looks just like heaven.'

She smiled at him. She'd missed him so much. Just the solid, physical presence of him in their room at night. He seemed to take up so much space. His voice sounded so loud, roughened by cigarettes. He said things that she wasn't expecting. His thoughts ran in circles that hers didn't, and she loved being surprised by the things he came out with. Right now, though, she wished he'd just get into bed and stop wittering on. She could do with the warmth of him.

Soon they were snuggled in together. With the curtains half-drawn they could still see the snow falling. Maybe it would keep falling through the night and all tomorrow and all the next night and the day after. And perhaps it would freeze all of South Shields into a tight globe of ice and snow so that no one would be able to get in or out and Tom would be forced to stay here. He would never be able to go away again.

His feet were freezing. He was trying to warm them up on hers and she giggled, pushing him away.

'Aunty Winnie doesn't mean anything bad by the things she says,' Tom whispered. 'Don't let her worry you.'

Irene bit her lip. She had protested that she wasn't superstitious and that things like the tea leaves and the worn pack of cards and the lines in her hands . . . none of that meant anything to her. Yet that wasn't quite true. She wasn't as rational and non-believing as all that. Coming from the deepest, darkest corner of Norfolk she was steeped in country lore and inherited memories of the old ways. She knew you couldn't be unkind to a gypsy or they cursed you. You had to give them a welcome and a handful of coins and you had to listen respectfully to the things that they told you about your fortunes.

'She said that we were going to face hardships,' Irene said. 'The way she looked at me. It was like she felt sorry for me. Like she could see things in my future that she wasn't telling me about. Like she was sparing my feelings . . .'

He rolled closer to her. 'Hey, you're reading too much into it, pet. It was just the old blarney that Winnie always gives out. She looks at your hand and makes up all this old rubbish. She's always been like that. It's just hocus-pocus. Maybe me mam shouldn't encourage her.'

Irene wouldn't be mollified. 'She said that together, me and you . . . we'll have to face great sadness and loss. That's what she said. I think that's a horrible thing to tell someone.'

'But, look, love . . . everyone has to face great sadness or losses. That's no great bloody feat of fortune-telling, is it? It's just the way things are. It's a fact of life.'

She thought about that for a little while, lying there very still. He put his arms around her. He was right. And he'd thought about all this business a lot more than her, she was sure. He had faced life and death in the raw. He had flown in the face of danger and he had seen friends die. A part of her wanted to ask about these comrades of his, but another part shrank away from doing so. She wasn't sure whether he wanted to tell her about his everyday life at war, or whether he'd rather not. Maybe not tonight, anyway.

'I'll put it all out of my head,' she promised him. 'She was just a daft old woman, I know. She was just playing a part, being a gloomy old so-and-so.'

'She's always been the same,' Tom smiled. 'I remember her coming round when I was just a nipper. Mam would get the bottle of sherry out of the dresser and they'd have a few tots each and they'd get more and more pessimistic about the future. They'd sit there, getting slowly drunk, foretelling death and disaster on the heads of everyone we knew in the Sixteen Streets. Mam became quite addicted to it all. I'd sit there absolutely terrified, until I was old enough to see what it really was. And it was just two women thoroughly enjoying themselves.'

Irene laughed. 'Enjoying themselves? Making up death and disaster?'

'Warding it off,' he said. 'That's what it was. Like a magic spell. They were making up the worst scenarios they could imagine, and putting them into words, just in order to ward them off. Fires and floods, famine and curses and murders. They loved all that lurid stuff.'

Irene tutted. 'Your whole family is crazy.'

'I've been wondering whether you've figured them all out,' he said.

'Hardly. But I'm getting to know them. And I'm getting to know how much there is to know about them, under the surface.' Aye, and she thought: I'm getting to know some secrets, too. I'm getting to know of some things that Tom would surely rather not know . . .

'I'm glad they've taken you to their hearts,' he told her. 'They really have, you know?'

'Well, I'm not sure about that . . .' she said. 'It's still early days.'

'Nah, you belong here, true enough,' Tom told her. 'Walking into this house, and you being here with me. It's all meant to be, Irene. You've done a smashing job. You are a part of all of us now.'

'And the kidda,' Irene said, smiling as she used the word that Beryl used for the mermaid in her belly. 'The kidda, as well.'

'Aye, the bairn,' said Tom, sounding so pleased and satisfied with life. It made her heart glow just to hear him like that. 'Whatever that old Winnie says, I reckon we're very lucky, don't you?'

Chapter Sixteen

Of course their four days went by too fast. They kept busy the whole time in order to make every hour count, and in the process this seemed to urge time to go ever faster. But Irene and Tom were happy, nevertheless, as the snow continued falling on South Shields, almost without cease for the rest of the week and into the weekend. It lent a softness and a gentleness to everything. The ruins and rubble were smoothed away, almost erased from the town, blanketed under folds of pristine snow.

Even though Irene had been given four full days off work at the biscuit factory, and four evenings off from Franchino's, she still popped into the ice cream parlour to see Bella and her father, who both made a big fuss of the returning hero. As Tonio chattered with Tom at the counter, avid for all the details he could get of the airman's life, Bella took Irene aside.

'He was irked at first, that I'd told people the news,' Irene admitted. 'But he's OK. It was just his frustration that he wasn't here. He's dead happy, really.'

'I'm glad,' said Bella. 'You two are really meant to be happy. I look at the two of you together and I've never seen people more perfectly matched.'

Irene felt that too, more than she ever had before. When they walked, they walked in step. They loved just listening to the other one talk. They enjoyed doing the most dull and ordinary things together. Something as simple as a long walk along the White Leas was exciting because they were out together. They were free to say absolutely whatever came into their heads, without fear of boring or offending the other one. It felt as if they were more bonded now than they ever had been before.

They walked as close to the beach as the barbed wire and barricades would allow them. They strolled through deserted Marine Park just as a blizzard swept in across the sandy dunes. Irene screamed and clung to Tom's arm, feeling helpless and daft as she did so. The wind was too strong for both of them and they had to hide beside the boatman's hut until the storm died down. They kissed with cold faces, still laughing and catching their breath.

On Friday night they were invited to Bella's family home on Simonside for dinner with her whole family. The occasion was warm and wonderfully welcoming. Never having been a guest in such a grand house before, Irene felt a little out of her depth at first. It was plain to see that Tom didn't. He seemed to know the entire Franchino family very well.

He was greeted by Bella's ma and her nonna, who both pinched his cheek and told him how he'd been missed. Once again Irene found herself wondering what kind of past Bella and Tom might have shared. Surely they were more than just school friends, if the whole family seemed to be so familiar with him?

But it didn't matter really. None of that mattered. Whatever had gone on in the past, that was all over. In the present moment he belonged to Irene. And she loved and trusted Bella anyway. There was no need to be even the slightest bit insecure.

That night they sat by warm candlelight in a really fancy dining room and ate some wonderful kind of fish, all lemony and fragrant. Bella's nonna explained in halting English that it was a traditional family recipe for a Christmas meal. The family were having it earlier in Tom's honour, and hoped that he would enjoy it. Flushed with red wine the old man had brought out of his special store in the cellar, Tom had toasted the whole family and turned almost tearful with gratitude.

'You don't know what it means,' he said, looking at them all, 'to be back here and welcomed like this, to be among old friends. I can't believe my luck, really . . . at being home again . . . for a little while . . .'

They'd all cheered and clapped him, but Irene found his little speech made her feel sad. Her Tom was talking like he felt he was on borrowed time. He sounded like he thought his luck was bound to run out, sooner or later.

Later, as they walked back home through town, Tom told Irene tales of his connections over the years with Bella's family. How good they had been to him. How their place had been a refuge when his own busy, tiny, noisy home had become too much for him.

In turn, she described her recent night with Bella at the Alhambra, and how she had been urged into borrowing a frock. 'And I still haven't given it back,' she realised, with a jolt. 'I should have remembered and taken it back round tonight for her. Oh, it's a beautiful thing, Tom. I loved dancing in it.'

'Maybe we should have found a dance to go to together, while I'm here,' he said. 'I'm sure Bella wouldn't mind you borrowing her frock twice.'

His saying 'while I'm here' reminded them both that his scant few days in the north were slipping by. They clung to each other tipsily as they trudged through the deepening snow.

Saturday was bright and clear. The skies over Shields were a brilliant blue and, as soon as the Farley boys were awake and up and about, they all had the same thought.

'*Sledging!*'

Beryl rolled her eyes. 'Honestly, they'll never grow up, will they?'

Megan scowled, protesting that she had a bad head and awful nerves, and wouldn't be dragged out to play in the snow. Ma Ada, meanwhile, hooted her approval as Sam wrestled with all the accumulated junk in their tiny outhouse to find their old toboggan. How many years had it lain there with the paint tins and boxes, gently rusting away? At least six or seven. More than that, probably! It had been so long since there had been a proper snowfall, and since any of them had been as daft as boys.

Sam ran a tiny piece of sandpaper along the corroded runners and tested the wooden slats to check they hadn't rotted through. 'It's as good as new!' he said, grinning. 'So, who's coming out with me?'

Laughing, Beryl simply did as she was urged, donning her thickest jumper, gloves and hat and the sheepskin coat she was having to lay on her bed for extra warmth while Tony was away.

'We can't actually go sledging . . .' Irene said. 'That's just for kids, isn't it? Won't people think we're being silly?'

'Who cares?' Tom grinned. 'Who cares if people think we're being silly? It doesn't matter, does it?'

Sam also found some old hessian sacks at the back of the pantry. Ma Ada had been keeping them, sure they'd come in useful. 'We used to sit on one of these and go racing down the hill, as well,' he said. 'It was even better than the sledge sometimes.'

Irene vowed that she wasn't going racing about anywhere sitting on an old hessian sack.

'You won't have to,' Tom told her, as they all went hurrying out to the hills. 'You're just gonna watch us having fun. I'm not having the mother of my bairn doing anything dangerous while she's expecting.'

She wasn't sure how she felt about being told what she could and couldn't do. She was miffed and deeply pleased at the same time.

They crunched through the thickly laying snow down to the docks and then along, up the hill, and Irene realised they were taking the route of Sam's favourite walk. Up the hill to the Roman remains.

She watched the set of Sam's back as he hurried along, dragging the old toboggan after him, the rust of its runners leaving orange streaks in the snow. She hadn't had a proper talk with him in ages. She was acutely aware of what the problem was and he seemed to have intuited the fact that there was something on her mind. She felt awkward around Sam, and that was sad, since they'd been such good pals. Thank God Tom hadn't noticed any of this.

Beryl was in a loud, ebullient mood. She had a knitted hat like a tea cosy pulled right down over most of her head. Looking closer, Irene thought the hat might actually have *been* a tea cosy, once upon a time. There was a hole beside her ear, with a lock of her dark hair slipping out.

Tom clutched onto Irene's hand and he was excited, she could tell. The silliness of this whole trip out was making him happier than almost anything during this break of his. As they strode up the steep hill he was burbling away with Bob, who was red-faced and beaming, just because they were all together. 'Ah, our Tony should be here, though, man,' he said. Bob's accent was the broadest and thickest of all the Farleys. Sometimes Irene still had bother following what Bob was saying; he tended to mumble and gabble even faster than all the other fast-talking members of his family.

'Tony probably wouldn't do anything as childish as tobogganing, anyway,' Tom laughed. 'He's far too grand and intellectual, that one!'

Then, suddenly, with a whoop and a yell of delight, they were flinging themselves onto the sledge and those flimsy-looking hessian sacks. From up here, it all looked a bit steep and dangerous. Irene's heart leapt as she stood freezing at the top of the hill and watched them dive-bombing down the long, pristine slope.

It was perfect. No one had thought to come out yet and destroy this immaculate smooth slide. The Farley boys and Beryl were the first to carve long, erratic streaks into the snow. They flew down, one after the other, and hauled themselves back up, to set off again and again, gradually turning the powdery snow into polished white ice.

Irene puffed out huge clouds of frozen breath and gloried in the scene before her. The whole town was spread out, looking magnificent with chimneys issuing smoke that looked indigo against the pink-streaked skies.

She stood there, gazing at the expanse of her adopted town and watching her husband and her new brothers and sister playing together and being daft. She felt like she couldn't feel happier than she did right now. Tom had taught her right. She was in this moment and no other. She wasn't thinking about the future and anything it might bring them. She was here and now and it was wonderful.

'Hey, hey, man! Haway! Look at that lot! Eeeh, man! They've ruined all the new snow already! Whey, you bugger!'

There was loads of shouting suddenly, as others came to share the fun. Lads mostly, with the cracked and shrill voices of adolescent boys. They elbowed and shoved their way in, demanding their own access to the slopes. Good-naturedly, the adults let them join in and take their turn. Soon there was almost twenty of them shooting down the hill and labouring back up, dragging their sledges and coal sacks up the steep slope.

The snow was getting darker and slushier. Its pristine beauty was gone. The shouts were getting more raucous and rough, and Irene stamped her feet on the ground because they were going numb by now.

Tom dashed up to her, frowning. 'You're all right, aren't you?'

'Course I am! It's lovely watching you lot.'

'You just tell me if you're getting too cold. It's all right for us. We're red hot from rushing about.'

She promised that she would tell him.

Then the raucous voices were shouting out: 'Eeeh! Will you look at them! Just take a look at them two, will yer!' One of the lads was yelling, and another one picked up his theme. Their voices were incredulous and cruelly mocking.

Irene's first thought was: Are they saying that about us? Why would they shout about us two? But they weren't. Their attention was directed elsewhere.

Others picked up the hue and cry, and great bellows of laughter rang out on the hill.

'What's that all about?' Tom asked. He hated to see anyone getting picked on, and that's what this sounded like to him. 'Sam?' he called to his brother, who was tugging his sledge up the slope, completely out of puff. 'What's all that about?'

But Sam didn't know.

The younger lads had stopped sliding and messing about on the slope. They were hurrying down to the bottom of the hill, where they had intercepted two figures who were trying to walk past. Two figures in long coats, just minding their own business.

'I don't like the look of that,' Tom said tersely. 'What are those lads up to?'

As she looked down the hill, Irene felt something squirm in her gut. She had a vague premonition of something awful.

'Tom . . .' she started, but he was already off, running and slipping down the hill, to see what the matter was.

Irene locked eyes with Sam. He shrugged, and looked discomfited, and set off after his brother.

Beryl came alongside Irene, seeing if she might need a bit of help slithering down the hill. Her feet felt like blocks of ice.

'Eeeh! Who's this then? Who's your friend, eh? What are you two up to today, then?' The boys were hooting and screeching with laughter as they surrounded the two strangers at the bottom of the hill.

Irene couldn't understand it. Why were they being so loud and awful? Why did they sound so mocking and savage all of a sudden?

The two figures were dressed for the season, in long, shabby cloaks and hoods pulled round their faces. Were they both women? It was hard to tell, and Irene thought, that's what's got those boys all interested.

'Here, let us gerra look at yous!' someone shouted, honking with laughter. 'Let us see your faces, eh?' A hand reached out and grabbed at one of the hoods and the person underneath resisted, pulling away from him. A tussle was breaking out just at the moment that Tom came hurrying into their midst.

'Hey, lad! Here, you can't go grabbing a lady like that! What the hell do you think you're doing, man?' He shoved into the offending boy and made to grab him by the scruff of the neck. The young ragamuffin dodged him and sneered.

'She's no lady!' one of the other boys sniggered.

'What are you on about?' Tom demanded. He was joined by his two brothers at this point, and there was a tense stand-off with the young lads, who were all wiry energy and malice.

'Just look at them!' the boy Tom had tried to grab yelled out. 'That one's all right. She's just a scruffy young tart. But the other one! Just look, man! Can't you see?'

The two figures stood there, hanging their heads, terrified at all the unwanted attention from the gaggle of aggressive males standing around them.

Beryl and Irene were shuffling down the hill, panting heavily, as the scene unfolded. They arrived just in time to see one of the strangers snatch off their hood and glare furiously at the boys.

'You just leave us alone . . . you little buggers! Can't you just leave us alone for once?'

It was Mavis. Irene stopped dead in her tracks. Mavis was shouting and spitting at the boys like a cornered cat. 'Mavis, what's happening?' Irene called out.

The boys were still laughing at Mavis's defiant pleas.

'What's going on here, then?' Beryl asked. 'Haway, lads! What the hell do you think you're doing? These are just lasses you're picking on!'

The most outspoken of the lads, and the one who appeared to be their leader, reached out suddenly, once more, and grabbed the shoulder of the quieter of the two figures. Before Tom could stop him he shook Mavis's companion hard until the hood dropped away.

The face that looked back at all of them was pale with arched eyebrows and lustrous auburn hair.

'Just take a look at that, will yers!' the boy jeered.

The effect upon the assembled crowd was electrifying.

The person stared back defiantly at them all.

Irene's eyes were out on stalks.

It was like a star from one of the movies had stepped out into snowy South Shields. Or a creature out of an old fairy tale. A terrifying witch or an exotic princess, with high, silvery cheekbones and a steady blue gaze.

Before she could stop herself, Irene burst out: '*Arthur!*'

Chapter Seventeen

For a moment Irene felt disoriented, seeing both the pale, painted face before her and also Arthur's more familiar, everyday face underneath. It was like she was seeing two people at once, both in the same place. Arthur lowered his head and closed his eyes, as if drawing upon reserves of inner strength.

The lads were crowding around them and the cloaked couple couldn't pass by. 'Here, let them go through,' said Beryl. She hated any kind of scene and people being unkind.

'But that's a fella!' one of the rough young kids started shouting. 'Can ye not see? That one there's a gadgie! And he's got, like, lasses' make-up on!'

Arthur's sister Mavis glared at them all. 'What's it got to do with you lot? With any of you lot? Whey, you nosy buggers! You should keep your bloody nebs out of decent folks' business!'

One of the lads shot back: 'Decent folks? You lot? You're bloody gypsies, aren't yous? There's nowt decent about ye lot.'

Now it was time for Arthur to speak out. This last comment made him lose his temper, and when he spoke it was with the loud, querulous tones that Irene recognised. That voice seemed so bizarre and incongruous coming out of the theatrically painted face. 'Just leave us alone! What have we done to hurt you, eh? Why won't you just let us get on with our business?'

This brought a lot of laughter down on their heads, as the rowdy lads speculated about what kind of business the two so-called ladies might be pursuing.

Tom broke into all their hullaballoo. 'Now, look here,' he said, squaring his shoulders. He didn't like to see anyone getting picked on and bullied, whoever they were. 'I don't know what's going on here and, frankly, it's none of my business. But I'm not having any bother, all right? I'm not gonna let anyone be causing any aggravation here. We're all having a nice time in the snow, so don't spoil it, all right?'

But the lads were still sneering at Arthur and gathering round him. Irene didn't know what to do for the best. She still couldn't work out what he was doing there, all made up like that. Did he have women's clothes on underneath that long coat? Surely not . . .?

'We're going to a party,' Mavis said abruptly. 'That's what we're doing. It's fancy dress and we've gone to a lot of effort to make ourselves look this bonny.'

'Eeeh, bonny, eh?' laughed the boys. 'Aye, don't you both look bonny?'

'Arthur's gonna sing for everyone at the party,' the pale, plain girl announced. 'That's what he does. He dresses up like this only because he's, like, an entertainer. People pay him to get up like this and sing for them at their fancy do's . . .'

Arthur looked ashamed – not for how he was made up – but because his little sister was doing all his talking for him, and making excuses for why he was going about in broad daylight all done up.

'Gan on, then,' said the leader of the gaggle of boys. Still he had that nasty, jeering tone in his voice. 'Why don't you prove it, Arthur, man? Why don't you sing for the lot of us? Right now, eh?'

There was a pause and then all the others joined in, lustily chanting: 'Aye! Aye! Sing for us! Aye! Gan on!'

Tom didn't like any of this. There was an ugly edge to the whole scene. It was clear that these lads weren't going to let Arthur and the small girl go until they gave in and appeased them somehow. He shot Irene a look, telling her to get back to safety and away, out of this scene. Irene shook her head. She was staying right here.

To allay the chanting Arthur suddenly put up both hands, with a commanding gesture. It was so dramatic everyone found themselves obeying and silence fell on the afternoon scene.

It was a curious, muffled silence. A beautiful silence, Irene thought. They were all transfixed by Arthur's expression of concentration. Then he opened his mouth and sang, in the most wonderful contralto:

> *Lully, lulla, thow littell tyne child,*
> *By by lully, lullay thow littell tyne child,*
> *By by, lully, lullay!*

The song was slow and somehow ancient-sounding. Irene vaguely recognised the tune, knowing it was an old carol, but she wouldn't have been able to put a name to it. It was somehow very dark and melancholic. Its mood stole over the small crowd at the bottom of the slide.

Arthur stood more confidently and threw back his head as he continued:

> *O sisters too, how may we do*
> *For to preserve this day*
> *This pore yongling for whom we do singe*
> *By by, lully, lullay?*

The verses went on and Irene caught the name of King Herod and allusions to the slaughter of babies in the old Bible story. It seemed a very bloodthirsty and strange song to simply pluck out of the air. Yet it was striking and it had a curious effect on all of those gathered there, standing with their feet freezing in the snow. The discordant tune and Arthur's undeniably powerful voice distracted them all from their bullying and their jostling and contempt.

When he finished there was a great gap of silence that opened up between them all. It was like a chasm between the two gypsies in cloaks and the crowd around them. It was as if Arthur's song had pushed them all physically backwards. There was no applause. No one made a sound until Arthur said, 'May we go now?'

And those boys didn't say a single word. They simply stepped backwards. They were frowning and some muttered under their breath, but they were all abashed somehow. None of them would have been able to put their finger on why exactly, or how they had come to feel like that. They simply stepped aside to let Arthur and Mavis shuffle on through the snow.

Off they went to their party, wherever it was meant to be. Arthur didn't even look at Irene as he held his head up, with great pride, and moved on. Mavis gave her a quick smile as they swept past.

The small crowd quietly disbanded.

The lads went off to take over the sledging hill. For the Farley clan, all their relish had seemingly dissipated now. No one wanted to do any more tobogganing today. It was time to set off back home.

'Ah, I'm proper chilled through now anyway,' Beryl said, linking arms with Irene.

'What was all that about?' asked Bob, who'd been thoroughly confused by the scene that had unfolded before them.

'Ah, it was just daft lads, Bob,' said Sam. 'Don't worry about it.' Sam knew that if Bob couldn't follow what was going on, he generally got frustrated and cross with himself.

Irene wondered what Sam was thinking to himself about the whole thing. He knew Arthur even better than she did, and he hadn't stepped in or said anything to help or protect him. Like most of the others Sam had been rooted to the spot, gobsmacked and no use at all. What if there had been violence? Those lads looked like they'd have been happiest punching Arthur's lights out. It was lucky clever Arthur had been able to sing and stun them all into silence.

Tom was walking along beside Irene and was quiet most of the way back to the Sixteen Streets. 'So, you know that lad? That Arthur?'

She nodded. 'Aye, he's a friend. A good friend. One of the best I've made since I moved up here.'

Tom was scowling. 'I don't want you seeing him ever again. He's bad news, that one.'

'What?' She could hardly believe what she was hearing.

'Keep away from him, Irene. He's a funny sort.'

She shook her head firmly. 'Absolutely not. He's my friend. You're not telling me who I can be friends with, Tom Farley! You've got no right to do that. And I'll tell you that for nowt!'

She stomped on ahead, furiously, through the snow, leaving her husband and the others staring open-mouthed at her back.

Tom heard Beryl tutting. 'Did you try and be all commanding with her, Tom? Eeeh, lad.'

Tom was blushing. 'Not really . . .'

'If you did, our Tom, you don't know her half so well as you should do. You can't just assume Irene is like some kind of mouse, or a bairn you can just order about. She seems quiet and all that . . . but she really isn't like that, you know.'

Tom sighed and felt miserable. 'I know. You're right. We've just . . . been apart for so long, it seems like. Ah, man. I should have kept my mouth shut, shouldn't I? I can't go telling her who to be friendly with . . .'

'You certainly can't,' Beryl smiled, cheerily linking his arm with hers, and leading the Farley clan all the way home.

An hour later, after the light had drained out of the skies and a new snowfall was just starting, Irene managed to slip out of the back of the house and escape the rest of the family for a few moments. They had been having their tea and were gathered around the dining table. Somehow they had managed quite a lavish spread for Tom's last teatime at home, with cake and biscuits and even some sticky dates from Ma Ada's dresser drawer that went back to before the outbreak of war.

Irene just wanted a few moments in the still quiet of outside, to get her thoughts together. She was sick of smiling and being the dutiful wife. She was sick of the heavy feel of regret hanging about her neck. It seemed heavier whenever someone mentioned that Tom was leaving again tomorrow.

She went out into the yard and leant against the back wall. She felt the frozen, crumbling brick through the thin fabric of her blouse and it made her shiver and cooled the warmth in her cheeks. She had felt flushed and on the brink of tears all afternoon. It was moments like these when she wished she smoked. If she did she could have stood out here and watched the plumes of smoke spiralling upwards into the snowy skies and maybe she could have lost herself in a reverie. That was something Irene could never quite do. Perhaps I'm too practical-minded to have proper reveries, she mused.

She had only had a couple of minutes of peace before the scullery door popped open again. She cursed under her breath at the interruption, and then when she saw who it was her heart gave a pang of dismay. Sam. He was smiling at her uncertainly and asking, 'Can I join you out here, pet?'

Irene shrugged. Really, she didn't want to be alone with Sam. She hadn't had a quiet chat with him for weeks. If she were to have one now, she'd be forced to ask him all about the Alhambra and what she had witnessed that night. There was altogether too much on Irene's mind.

'Eeeh, what about that Arthur, then?' Sam said, shaking his head and smiling. 'What was all that about?'

Irene frowned. 'It was like his sister Mavis said. They were off to a party. I thought he was very brave, facing up to those ruffians.' She stared at Sam. Aye, and would you have stood up for him? she thought. What if those lads had got nasty? What would have happened then?

'Right enough, but he should have known better than parading about the town all dolled up like that,' Sam shook his head. 'He was always a funniosity, even when we were back at school. He'd rather be playing with all the lasses than the lads. He got a fair amount of mocking from everyone back then . . .'

Irene stared at him. 'You make it sound like that makes it all right. Like it's just a natural thing to bully him. That someone goes through life and it's OK that everyone mocks him and makes fun out of him.'

Sam said: 'Some people make targets out of themselves. They like the attention because they want to stand out. That's what I think.'

Irene was disappointed in her youngest brother-in-law. She was used to Sam having his own thoughts. Usually the things he said were things that he had figured out for himself. His mind was his own, unlike most people, who just went along with the crowd. Talking about Arthur, Sam was just coasting along and thinking the same kind of thing that anyone would. But Irene was different, and she wanted to understand.

She could still see those two figures in their cloaks, Arthur and Mavis. They had looked so vulnerable, swaddled up and hurrying away through the snow.

'You work at the biscuit factory with his sister, don't you?' Sam asked Irene.

'Aye, I do. She's a good little lass.'

Sam nodded. 'Aye, that's her. She was at school with us, too, same as Arthur was, but she was in a lower year. I remember that she was hardly ever there. She's supposed to have something wrong with her, I don't know what. They were a sickly kind of family, I seem to remember. Their mother was a gypsy, I think, and some said that their da was an Arab. There was talk that they got themselves a house and they settled near here . . . I can't recall the whole story.'

Irene stared at him. 'I thought you'd have more compassion in you than that, Sam. I credited you with more feelings.'

He looked away and fiddled with a soft pack of cigarettes – some of the American cigarettes that Tom had brought him from the airbase. He took a few delicious drags before answering Irene.

'Maybe you expect too much of me, bonny lass. Maybe your expectations are too high.'

'Aye, maybe they are,' she agreed, and the sharpness of her tone let him know that she had something else in her thoughts. She had something particular on her mind. As she spoke her fingers were prying absent-mindedly at the crumbling mortar of the garden wall, dislodging nuggets of frozen lichen and dirtying her hands. 'Maybe I thought you were a better man than you are, Sam Farley. And maybe I feel a bit disappointed by who you've turned out to be.'

He looked surprised. 'What do you mean by that, hinny?' Straight away he was on the defensive.

'Oh, look, I've got to tell you, Sam. I can't hold it in any longer. Look, man, I *know*, don't I? I saw you the other night at the dance hall. You and Megan. I saw the two of you together. You were over in the corner and you probably thought you were safe there by the potted palms and no one would ever see. In which case, you were both being bloody reckless fools, because you were out and kissing her in public. And I saw you and plenty of others must have seen you, as well. You were kissing her in a way that no brother-in-law has any right to do.'

Suddenly it was like all the blood had drained out of Sam's face. 'You never did.'

'Of course I did! How else would I know? I was there, Sam. It was an impulsive, unplanned thing and I was at the Alhambra with Bella and Arthur. And there you were. With her.'

He swore. She'd never heard him swear like that before and the rudeness of it shocked her.

'What the devil are the pair of you playing at, Sam? You must know it isn't right?'

He reeled and gave a bitter laugh. 'Of course I know it isn't right! Do you think I'm daft?' Suddenly he seemed to realise something and turned to her quickly. 'Did Megan see you that night? Did she notice that you'd spied us?'

'Yes, she did,' Irene said. 'Oh, didn't she just. She fixed me with the most evil stare. It was like I was the one doing something in the wrong!'

Sam dropped his tab end and stubbed it out furiously. 'Ah, bugger it. I should have known. There's been something the matter with her for days. She's been snappy and dead annoyed and she'll hardly speak to me. I just assumed it was something that I'd gone and done wrong. Ah, but now I know, don't I?'

Irene said, 'It's because the secret is out. She knows that I know what's going on.'

'You don't know anything, really,' Sam told her.

'I've got a fair idea! The two of you are carrying on, aren't you? Behind poor Bob's back. Behind everyone's back. It's a proper scandal. Eeeh, carrying on with your own sister-in-law! That's not right, Sam . . . And in public, too, where just anyone could see! Half the town could be gossiping and you two couldn't even care less!'

Sam looked very young and scared. He was almost as young as she was herself and suddenly he really seemed it. 'Ah, Irene pet, I just can't explain it. I wish I could. I just can't understand any of it.'

She relented. He looked like he was close to tears. The soft as clarts part of herself wanted to go to him and hug him and say it was all going to be all right. But she wasn't even sure that was correct.

'What is it, Sam? Does she . . . does Megan have some kind of . . . hold over you?' All at once this seemed the likeliest thing. The idea had popped into her head all at once. Yes, that was it. Megan was forcing this lad to do things that were out of his character. She was the older woman. She was the temptress who had led him into doing wicked things . . .

He was nodding miserably. 'Aye, you could call it that. I can't even say exactly what it's like. It's all very odd.'

Suddenly Irene knew she needed to hug him. He looked so pathetic standing there. She held out her arms and he went to her and shivered as she held him. There was something very strange about this whole business. He seemed like he was almost frightened.

'I'm . . . I'm not choosing this,' he said. 'I would never be doing anything like this . . . but . . .'

Irene just didn't understand any of it. How could he go round kissing someone and not mean to? How could he do it so brazenly in public and then claim that none of it was his choice? Surely he couldn't be saying that he had been acting against his will?

Now he was saying, 'You're not gonna tell anyone, are you, Irene? You won't, will you? It'll cause so much bother, if you do. People might get hurt . . .'

She didn't know what she was going to do. Really, she knew that none of it was really her business. And if others in town had recognised them, then she couldn't exactly stop them from spreading the tale, could she? The truth was, Megan and Sam had been much too careless and the damage was already done.

Then there came a cough from the scullery door. A pointed kind of noise. Irked-sounding. She looked over Sam's shoulder and let her arms drop.

'What's all this?'

It was Tom. He was staring at his brother and his wife sharing this quiet moment in the lee of the yard's brick wall. Irene knew how it must look and she was quick to allay his fears.

'It's nothing, Tom. Sam was just upset.'

Tom was already lighting his cigarette and frowning heavily as the two broke apart. 'Cuddles, is it? That's what you were having out here, were you?'

There was something in his tone. He was laughing at them, Irene realised. He wasn't really suspicious or annoyed. He realised how innocent they were.

'Ahh, it's just me, man,' said Sam, pushing his palms into his eyes and rubbing his tears away. 'I'm just being soft and crazy. Irene was consoling me.'

'She's good at that,' Tom said. 'But, you know, you probably shouldn't go round cuddling each other in backyards. Other folk may get the wrong idea about it.' He snapped the cigarette out of his mouth and blew the smoke up into the dark sky. 'It could upset a less secure fella than me, you know.'

'You don't mind, do you?' Irene frowned.

'Excuse me,' Sam was keen to absent himself from their scene. The relief was coming off him like a wave of heat. He was glad Tom's presence had prevented any more talk about the fuss with Megan. Swiftly he was back in the house and at his place at the tea table, and Irene was left with her husband, who looked cross and anxious.

'Of course I don't mind, it's just Sam,' said Tom. 'But you've got to think on, Irene. I'm apt to feeling left out of everything. I'm only here for four days every three or four months. I feel like I'm a visitor to what used to be my life. Or I've parachuted down into foreign territory . . . and it only has a vague resemblance to everything I used to know.'

He leant against the wall, wincing at the cold and trying to make sense of his words as he said them.

'Is that how you really feel?' she asked him. 'Like we're all foreigners and strangers to you?'

'Of course not,' he snapped. 'But . . . it's not the same as it should be. It can't be, can it? When we're apart, our separate lives move on so far and so fast.'

She knew exactly what he meant and she had had similar thoughts. It just made her sad to hear him come out with them, especially on the night before he returned down south. He sounded like he felt they were growing apart and it was all inevitable. Their very different experiences would drive them forever apart.

'Hey, look,' he smiled, seeing her face looking so downcast. 'I'm sorry. I'm talking rubbish. I shouldn't be saying things like that. Not after the Christmassy days we've been sharing. It's been a wonderful leave, hinny. At least it has for me. I hope it's been like that for you, as well?'

'Oh, yes, of course, Tom! I've loved every minute of it. It's been almost perfect . . .' She went to him and was glad to be held in his arms. His warmth felt incredible to her. It always amazed her, how much heat his strong body seemed to radiate. She drank it all in, through every pore. She was acutely aware of the skin of her arms touching the bare flesh revealed by his rolled-up shirtsleeves. It was almost like she could store up the warmth that came from the core of him and keep it inside her for as long as it lasted . . . perhaps as long as his next leave.

'It's just horrible that I have to go away again,' he said. 'But . . . we've had a Christmas, haven't we? We managed to get our own little bit of Christmas.'

She nodded and smiled. 'Oh yes, we did that. I've never had a better one.'

But she had. It was a lie, and he knew it. A white lie. A white, glittering, frosty lie that would melt like a single snow-flake if you breathed on it. Nevertheless it was a lie that they both needed to believe in right now.

'I've brought some little presents. Just trinkets and stuff that I picked up on my travels,' he told her. 'From Lincoln and Norwich. They're little gee-gaws I've wrapped up in tissue paper for me mam and the others. For the whole family. I thought it was something I could be doing while I was away. I didn't want to leave you here, thinking of what presents to get for everyone.'

She marvelled at him. 'You're the one at war! You don't have time or anything to go looking for presents!'

'I wanted to,' he said. 'When I was away, buying these things, it made me feel closer to everyone here. It really did. But they're only very little things. You'll hand them out on Christmas morning, won't you? You'll give them out and tell everyone that they come from the two of us?'

She burst into tears because of the sweet earnestness of his tone. She buried her face in his jacket and sobbed until it hurt her throat. 'Oh, Tom. Of course I will.'

She couldn't sleep that night, of course. She felt like the snowy silence outside was getting into her head and trying to blot out her happy memories. Also, she was haunted by a melody. She lay there listening to Tom breathing and it took a little while before she identified the tune as the carol they had heard Arthur singing that morning.

> *Herod the king, in his raging*
> *Chargid he hath this day*
> *His men of might in his owne sight*
> *All yonge children to slay.*

> *That wo is me, poor child, for thee,*
> *And ever morne and may*
> *For thi parting nether say nor singe,*
> *By by, lully, lullay.*

It was a strange and horrible song to have running through her head when she could feel the child growing inside her belly. That particular part of the Christmas story had always horrified her, even as a child herself. Back in their tiny parish church, their old vicar used to take a great relish in the more blood-thirsty aspects of the tales he told. He spoke of Herod's men rampaging about to find all the new-born sons and murdering them, and Irene had shrunk down in her pew. The pictures always came so vividly into her mind and she couldn't bear it.

Now it was the same, all these years later. Tom was no help. He was oblivious and snoring loudly. His lungs sounded tortured, labouring for breath, and she wondered how she had ever been able to sleep next to him. Just the other morning Bob and Sam had been taking the mickey out of him, reminding him that his snoring was the reason he had been banished into the remote attic bedroom in the first place. 'So that's why!' Irene thought.

'It's not just that,' Megan had piped up. 'It's because he's the favourite. That's it, isn't it, Ma Ada? Your perfect son, Tom. He's by far and away the favourite in your eyes, and nothing can ever be good enough for him.'

That was an awkward moment as they sipped their tea and everyone looked at the old ma. She had her teacup halfway up to her mouth and her cat dozing in her lap and the look she flashed at Megan was pure disdain. 'I look at all my bairns exactly the same. They're all perfect to me.' And then her face crinkled into a stiff smile.

Megan jeered at her. 'Perfect? I hardly think so. Bob's not perfect, are you, pet?'

Bob chuckled good-naturedly. 'Thick as mince, me,' he smiled foolishly, and Irene's heart had gone out to him.

'Aww, Bob, don't say that, hinny,' his ma said, looking heartsore hurt. 'There's nowt wrong with you.'

'Oh, but there is,' Megan shot back. 'There bloody well is.'

At that moment it had been Tom who had taken control of the conversation, making it swerve around the tricky corner. Bob carried on happily eating his sandwich, pulling all the luncheon meat out first, sucking up the jelly, and smacking his lips with relish. Irene was left wondering what they had all been alluding to. Nothing good, it seemed. To her it sounded like even more secrets that some members of this family knew and others had no clue about.

Queer that this memory should pop up for her now as she lay awake listening to Tom snore. She remembered the ice and fire in Megan's eyes and the very thought filled her with dread. There was someone determined to cause bother and upset at every turn. God forbid that she should ever depend on Megan for mercy or kindness . . . The girl seemed to be getting more bitter and dangerous by the day.

Dangerous, yes. That's what she was.

What time was it now? Surely Irene had lain awake most of the night and it must be dawn soon?

It was one way of making the most of every second with Tom: staying awake, keeping vigil. Counting every single moment . . .

But tomorrow she would be shattered and wrecked. She should really try to get some sleep.

Irene had always been hopeless at sleeping. Her mind whirled around like little coloured wheels inside an impossible machine. A machine that she didn't even know the purpose of.

Yet she must have slept a little, because the next thing she knew there was sudden brightness stinging her eyes and the mattress was moving as Tom rolled over and sat up. The room was filled with a milky light. He was gone for a few minutes during which she dozed, and then he was back. 'It's snowed again,' he told her, and pushed a mug of hot, black, sugary tea into her waiting hands.

'Oh, maybe there'll be no trains,' she dared to hope.

His smile was rueful as he dressed hurriedly in the cold attic. She watched his dear, bare body disappear bit by bit, back into his underclothes and his uniform. 'I still have to get there, Irene. I've got no choice. They're expecting me and there's work to do.'

What kind of work, she wondered? He would never be very specific about the missions he flew or the exact tasks he carried out. She knew he wasn't allowed to tell her, and accepted that of course, but in her mind she still worried about what precisely he was up to. He'd talked about lying down on a metal gantry, clinging on for dear life, with the whole plane shaking around him as they soared over enemy territory. The soft-bodied sides of the plane were rippling furiously and one of the engines was bursting into flames.

He had allowed her only a few moments of picturing this horror and then he stopped himself. He had already told her too much. As a result of this little nugget of information, whenever she pictured him flying, this was how it looked, and it was terrifying.

She sipped her tea, left it to cool on her nightstand, and braved the cold outside the warm bed. She dressed quickly and followed him downstairs, to find the whole house waking up.

Ma Ada was in her nightdress in the scullery, picking bones out of a mess of fish remains for the eager cat. She nodded at Irene and said grimly: 'You must be brave and not cry when he goes, pet. You've had your bit of Christmas with him and you must not spoil it now with tears.'

Irene shook her head grimly. She had no intention of spoiling anything with tears this morning. She was going to be brave, just like the old woman suggested. She was going to be tough and hard and not even think about the dangers he would be facing this time.

Ma Ada took her dish of fish guts and led the little cat back into the parlour, and Tom joined Irene by the kettle as she waited for it to boil. 'Another cup of tea?' she asked him, and he folded her wordlessly into his arms.

'What's the only thing better than a cup of tea?' he asked.

She stared up at him. 'I don't know. What?'

'Two cups of tea,' he told her, with a grin.

Chapter Eighteen

After Tom returned down south the days went back to their usual routines and Irene felt like she was out of synch with the rest of the world. For her, Christmas had come and gone, but for the rest of South Shields, they were still looking forward and hoping for a peaceful and joyous festive season.

In truth, she was left feeling quite bleak and hopeless in those middle days of December. She tried to pull herself out of it for the sake of the rest of the family, but it was hard. Days went by at the biscuit factory, and they were grindingly hard and dull. Her fingers were frozen as she set about packing endless custard creams and ginger nuts. Her feet felt like great big clods of ice.

Also, she was getting a bit of sickness in the mornings. It wasn't much fun crouching in that outdoors privy or the lav at work, chucking up everything she had managed to eat. Their outside toilet was spotless, of course, but it was still an awful place to spend a lot of time. The one at work was a bit less salubrious. Her guts churned up and she even feared that she was doing herself some damage.

'Eeeh, I used to get awful sickness with my bairns,' Ma Ada said. 'All apart from Tom. He never gave me a moment's bother! I hardly even knew he was there, until he was born!'

Megan rolled her eyes at this, hearing Tom's virtues extolled yet again. She still hadn't said a word to Irene for weeks, and Irene found this quite uncomfortable. She couldn't help trying to do something about it.

'If you've got something you want to say to me, you should just come out with it,' Irene found herself saying through gritted teeth, one day when the two of them were in the scullery washing pots together.

Megan slid her a nasty look and scrubbed even harder at a stubbornly sticky pot. 'I don't think I've got anything to say to you, thanks.'

Irene felt like she had been slapped. She had never been hated by anyone before, and that's how this really felt. Megan had dropped down the portcullis and pulled up the drawbridge and was glaring at her over the battlements, ready to pour boiling oil over Irene at the first sign of advance.

Irene made the mistake of trying again. 'Look, I'm not about to say anything to anyone. I'm not going to tell anyone about your secret . . .'

Irene had meant well, but to Megan these words came across as a threat. She couldn't hear the conciliatory sweetness in Irene's words, just a veiled warning that she could, if she chose to, cause complete and utter havoc.

'Don't you dare,' Megan hissed, spitting like a cornered cat. 'Just don't you dare, lady.'

That was the end of their talk that day, and Irene couldn't help feeling that she'd made things much worse.

The next day she shared a corner of the snug at the Robin Hood with Beryl and tried to talk about the whole business. The little pub had become a regular haunt for the two of them, and they loved to sit with a small glass of stout each, even if some of the old gadgies propping up the main bar muttered under their breath about women cluttering the place up. The funny thing was, Irene really did feel that the stout was doing her good.

'It's food, that's why,' Beryl told her. 'It's full of all the good stuff that your body and the bairn both need.'

If her mum and da could see her now, though! Drinking beer in a pub after a day down the factory and all her belly sticking out to here! They'd be scandalised.

'They've got some lovely decorations up in here,' Beryl said approvingly. Great big, glossy boughs of holly and fir adorned the smoke-seasoned rafters of the old place. The landlady – Cathy Sturrock – was said to have connections with a large, ancient estate out in Northumberland. That was the story, anyhow, and that was how she came by all her lavish greenery at Christmas. Irene thought that sounded a bit far-fetched.

'She was supposed to inherit this big house and all,' Beryl gossiped. 'But she fell in love with an Irish docker, didn't she? And she wound up here, behind the bar in a pub in the Sixteen Streets. They reckon she had the money to buy the pub outright, with the cash her father gave her. He said "Take this, and don't you ever bother coming back home again. You're doomed to live in the slums of South Shields with your fancy man forever, and you'll never see your family again." Anyway, that's how the story goes. She's a very nice woman, Cathy Sturrock, as it happens. This was all about thirty years ago, mind. Her fella's long gone. The drunken Irish fella she gave everything up for – he's not been heard of in ages – but Cathy's still got this pub to her name, so never feels that she's badly off.'

Beryl loved unpacking these bits of local lore for Irene. Everywhere they went there was a story or a legend or a bit of gossip. Irene found herself filing each little tale away, hoping they would help her get to grips with and understand this new place where she was having to settle.

'What can I do about Megan, though?' she asked, breaking into Beryl's stream of storytelling.

'I don't know, pet. But you're right, she really seems to have it in for you.'

Irene bit her lip and decided to tell Beryl a little bit of the truth. When she told her that she'd seen Megan at the dance she didn't say exactly who it was she'd seen holding Megan and kissing her.

'A man!' Beryl gasped. 'You saw her with another man!'

'Aye, I did,' Irene said. Despite the excitement, Beryl couldn't help smiling at the way Irene had started to pick up the local lingo. It did sound funny in her Norfolk accent. 'She was kissing him, like properly, right in front of everyone. I mean, they were by the potted palms but just anyone going by could see them.'

'And in a town like this, everyone knows everyone else, and Megan really stands out.'

'She was in her red dress,' Irene said. 'She looked really lovely. Also, she had a fur tippet round her shoulders. You know, one of Ma Ada's.'

This seemed almost more shocking to Beryl than anything else, that Megan would go rooting through the old lady's belongings for glad rags. 'She'll come to a bad end,' Beryl said. 'But what about you? Fancy going out dancing and not telling me, you devil!' Beryl grinned at Irene.

'Ah, it was a spur of the moment thing. It was Arthur, really. It was him and Bella, dragging me out, that night.'

Beryl looked at her curiously. 'The same Arthur we saw the other day, when we were sledging?'

'That's the one,' Irene said.

Beryl smiled and shook her head. 'Why, you know almost more people in this town than I do, hinny! More interesting ones, anyway! I do think you're settling in well!'

Irene felt a warm glow of satisfaction at this. Beryl had been a big part of her fitting in and feeling welcomed, and she would always be grateful to her.

As they drained the last of their stouts they were joined by the landlady, Cathy Sturrock. She was red-faced with shiny black hair all pulled up into an elaborate chignon.

'Compliments of the season, ladies,' she greeted them, gathering up their glasses. As she spent a few moments exchanging pleasantries with them, Irene studied the landlady, and thought about the tale she'd been told, of how Cathy had left behind a wholly different, much grander, life to come and settle here in streets that seemed no better to some folk than slums. According to Beryl, Cathy Sturrock had done it all for the love of a man, just like Irene herself had. Except her man had been hopeless and had eventually left her on her own. That would never happen to Irene, of course. She would always have her Tom, she prayed.

'Call me Cathy,' the landlady told them. 'And just remember, lady,' she added, looking earnestly into Irene's face, which was flushed from the fire and the half pint of stout. 'Anything I can do to help, just you bang on my door. I know what it's like to suddenly find yourself here in the middle of this lot. I know what the whole thing is like. So, you let me know if you need any kind of help, you hear me?'

It was Cathy Sturrock who recommended a doctor to Irene. One who was more local and less expensive than the one Bella had suggested. It was a small surgery that Irene reported to and it was a rather forbidding nurse with cold, fat fingers who she saw, every few weeks from mid-December onwards. The nurse was clean and efficient, and perhaps a little bit brusque, but Irene was relieved to hear that everything was going fine. She was in good fettle.

'You have absolutely nothing to worry about, Mrs Farley,' said the nurse, washing her hands briskly at the sink. 'A hundred million women have been through this before you. Women are giving birth all over the world, in paddy fields and deserts and war zones. There is nothing special about what is happening to you. As it happens, you're a splendid healthy specimen. You're as healthy as a horse.'

Irene dressed and thought about what the nurse had said. She wasn't sure how she felt about being compared with a horse. She was relieved, really, but it wasn't exactly flattering.

Later that evening at Franchino's she told Bella what the nurse had said and her friend laughed. 'Oh, you should have stuck with the surgery I recommended! They'd never say things like that there.'

Irene blushed, and didn't want to say that she couldn't afford to keep going where Bella had suggested.

The old father, Tonio Franchino, came bustling into the ice cream parlour and fussed over Irene, patting her belly and putting his ear to it, and making a big show of her in front of the coffee drinkers at the counter. 'You mustn't work too hard,' he admonished her. 'Don't let that slave driver my daughter keep you on your feet.'

There was little chance of that. While at work at the ice cream parlour these days Irene mostly found herself sitting in their usual booth, drinking frothy coffee and filling up on sugary wafer biscuits. It was Bella who scooted around the place doing all the work, seemingly without effort.

Arthur joined them when he could, looking more abashed than Irene had ever seen him, the first time he popped in after the scene on the hill. 'It was amazing, the way you sang,' she told him. 'It was like magic.'

He didn't seem to want to talk about that particular moment. The memory of the physical danger he and his sister had been in made him visibly uncomfortable and he squirmed on the leather banquette. However, he loved the praise his singing received from Irene.

'I've been performing at a few private functions and parties in the posh houses up and down the coast, and even been as far as Newcastle,' he confided to them. 'It's been lovely, seeing the insides of some of those grand houses. It makes me quite envious, seeing where these folk live. All that gracious living they do in their beautifully appointed homes. It makes me impatient for the day that I make my fortune and buy somewhere like that for me and Mavis.'

The two girls laughed obligingly at this, but Arthur was deadly serious. 'No, I mean it. I'm not living in that tumbledown midden for the rest of my life. I'm going to make something special of myself.'

Later, when he'd swanned off into the freshly falling snow, Bella commented: 'Sometimes I really think he will do what he promises, you know. I think there's something special about Arthur. There's something completely different about him. He has, like, a light shining inside of him and by rights he will be someone really special one day.'

Irene thought about this as she went about her lighter duties in the parlour. She knew just what Bella was talking about, but she wished that Arthur didn't make himself stand out so much. That day in the snow with those threatening boys, it had felt like everything was on a knife's edge. There had been real violence in the air.

'It's just the way he is,' Bella said, when Irene tried to voice her worries about him. 'He can't help drawing attention to himself. Why, remember him at the Alhambra that night. The way he danced and cleared that space in the middle so that everyone could watch him! It's all completely natural to him.'

Irene frowned. 'It's not good to stand out too much . . . if you're in any way . . . different . . .'

Bella looked her in the eye. 'Well, maybe. But I don't think Arthur minds about that much. Everyone can see he's different to anyone else round here. There's just no escaping that fact.'

Irene sighed. She didn't really understand any of this. Arthur was her friend and that would just have to do.

Irene came from a world in which no one was keen to draw attention to themselves. Everyone kept their heads down and felt ashamed if they had to stand up in public and do anything that people could hear or see. Her father had stood beside her in the church in Hunworth to give her away at her wedding and she had felt the tension building up in him as he stood there. He had been terrified of being in full view of everyone at the front, even though it was in the church he had known all his life; the church that lay twenty yards from his own front door.

Irene herself couldn't think of anything worse than getting up in front of a whole lot of people and having to sing or say something. She still did that thing where she covered up her mouth with her hand when she spoke. She did it quite unconsciously and annoyed herself when she realised what she was doing.

Beryl had quietly, gently asked her why she kept putting her hand to her mouth so much, and Irene had explained she was ashamed of her teeth. Beryl said she couldn't see what was wrong with them. This was a typical kindness from Beryl, but still Irene couldn't stop her feelings of self-consciousness. In some ways she longed to be more like Arthur. Maybe not even as confident as that. It would suit her fine to be as confident as Bella was. But if you were as beautiful as the Italian girl, it wouldn't be hard to be confident, turning heads wherever you went, like Bella always did. Strange that she wasn't boastful or horrible as a result. There was a warmth and generosity about Bella that made her even more lovely, Irene thought.

I'm lucky with the friends I've made since I've been here, she kept reminding herself. I've really landed on my feet. It helped, the fact that these friends were so good to her, in the times when she was missing Tom. And she was missing Tom something awful. That feeling was like a hunger that kept gnawing and wouldn't go away; or like frozen feet that would never thaw out.

'I'm like frozen feet?!' he'd laughed, when she tried to explain to him. 'Oh, hush,' she'd sighed. 'I can't explain it in words.'

She didn't have to. They both knew how much they missed each other when he was away.

At the end of that week something dreadful happened.

Irene took a tumble. She was getting larger and quite clumsy. She still wasn't used to where her centre of gravity lay. She still only had a tiny bump but her body was different and she was still getting used to that fact.

Also, someone had left something lying on the middle step of the staircase that led up to her attic. She had caught a glimpse of the dark mass at the very last moment and attempted to avoid stepping on it. Too late and too clumsily. She slid and stumbled and thudded heavily onto her bum and clattered down the remaining stairs. The noise was incredible and she wailed loud enough to raise the dead. To Irene it felt like she had fallen head over heels down the steps, the shock was that great.

At that time of day – late afternoon on a Friday – the house was empty apart from Ma Ada, who received the shock of her life as she sat knitting in her parlour.

'What is it? What's going on?' she cried, jumping up and dislodging her knitting and Lucky and all the shawls she had heaped over her shoulders. She thought the Jerries were getting into the house. The racket from above sounded like they'd landed one of their bombers on the rooftop. 'Eeeh, will someone tell us, what's going on, man?' she howled desperately, with panic clawing at her vitals.

It wasn't often that Ma Ada lost her composure, but this was definitely one of those times. She squinched her aching eyes and hauled her creaking body into the hallway and bundled herself up the stairs faster than she had in years. She wasn't used to moving as quickly as this, even during an air raid, where her philosophy was: they can bloomin' well wait for me before they start with all their carrying on. I'm not rushing for anyone.

But today it was different. Today the hullaballoo and the screaming was coming from indoors. From within her very own walls. Also, she recognised that voice as Irene's.

'Irene, hinny! Is that you? Are you all right, lass?'

Her accent became almost impenetrable to the girl from Norfolk. The old woman gabbled and keened in panic. Many years later Irene would still be able to hear that voice and she would be able to conjure up the picture of her old mother-in-law as she heaved herself up the first flight of stairs and onto the landing. She had never seen Ada looking so worried and dishevelled.

Irene was still shouting and moaning in pain. She was lying at full stretch on the bottom of the attic staircase. She was the right way up, but she had barely even realised that yet. She was feeling waves of hideous panicky pain rack through her whole body. They were centred around the back of her skull, which she'd banged hard against the banister, and her left knee, and also her belly. The sensations from her belly were strange and very worrying. A horrible fear gripped hold of her hard, and she was convinced she was going to lose her bairn.

Ma Ada came lumbering up and sank heavily to her knees. 'Eeeh, Irene man. What have you gone and done to yourself, pet?' She was shoving her face close to Irene's and the younger woman realised with a shock for the first time how bad Ada's eyesight had become. Her eyes looked opaque and milky and she was blinking hard, with tears streaming down her weathered face. Irene had never seen Ma Ada cry before.

'The b-baby . . .' Irene gasped, trying to sit upright, but getting beaten back by the waves of pain. 'I'm worried about the baby . . .'

'Don't move at all,' Ada snapped. 'Don't budge an inch. I'm going to go out and get the doctor. He'll want a look at you.' She cursed and swore. 'Why's there no one else in the house? Why's there no one who could go and run for him? Why do things always bloody happen when there's no one round to help?'

Irene was gripping her hand and still gasping. I don't want to lose the baby, she thought. I'm not going to. It's not going to happen. She's strong inside of me. She's not going to give up and die. She can't.

Already the mad panic ringing through her whole body was starting to slow and to ebb away. The pains were still there, but maybe the worst had passed?

'What happened, though, pet?' Ma Ada asked. 'Did you trip? Did you miss the step?'

Irene shook her head and tried to look back up the staircase, and to explain about the dark thing she'd seen lying there.

There it was. She'd brought it down with her. The rotten thing had slithered down to the landing with her. 'I stood and slipped . . . on this,' she said, and made a grab for the thing.

Ma Ada looked and made a funny noise when she saw what it was. Irene herself looked uncomprehendingly at the offending article at first. She wasn't able to make head nor tail of it. Two glassy brown eyes were staring back at her from the stairs. There was a frozen rictus of a snarl on the creature's face. Was it alive? Was it some kind of maleficent creature that had been lying in wait on the staircase, ready to spring out at her?

But no. An instant later and Irene knew exactly what she was looking at.

The fur tippet. It was the glossy pelt of Ma Ada's stole that had slithered all the way to the middle landing with her. The tippet that had been put away for safe-keeping in Ma Ada's wardrobe, and that Irene had last seen draped around the elegant shoulders of her sister-in-law Megan at the Alhambra dance night.

'What the bloody hell's that doing there?' Ma Ada cried.

But Irene couldn't answer her. She didn't have any kind of rational answer at all. The pains were coming back, and with them, a strange sensation of something quivering in her belly. A feeling that things weren't quite right inside.

And as she felt this, she stared back at those malevolent eyes of the marten or the mink or whatever it was the stole had once been. It really seemed like the nasty thing had intended her harm.

Just then the door downstairs was banging and someone was flying into a panic, alerted by all the cries from indoors. Beryl was back from the factory and hurtling into action. 'Who's hurt themselves? What's going on?'

It was Beryl who ran to fetch the doctor and had him back with her, upstairs at Number Thirteen, within the quarter hour.

Irene was helped into the nearest room, which happened to be Ma Ada's. She lay on the old Victorian bedspread and submitted meekly to a hasty examination. When the old family doctor declared that there was no real damage done as far as he could see, they all let out a huge breath of relief. By then, the others were coming back from their work, filling the house with anxious upheaval.

But it was all right. The doctor said that both Irene and the bairn were going to be fine. There was no reason to doubt him. The doctor was like the local vicar: someone whose word was beyond question. He wished them all well, conveyed the compliments of the season, and told Irene she had to take it easy for a week or two.

She was still biting back the panic and trying to calm down and not burst into tears.

'Just wait till that bloody Megan gets in,' Ma Ada growled. 'I'll give her what for. Leaving my things lying around. Taking them in the first place! She could have . . . she could have . . .' The old woman was just about crying again, but she marshalled her resources and hardened her expression. She held up the fur tippet as if she intended to wring its neck. 'I know what I'm going to do with this bloody awful thing.'

She took it downstairs and tossed it on the fire in the parlour. The hungry flames leapt up. Unfortunately, the burning fur sent a ghastly stench all through the house that made everyone feel queasy, if not sick to their stomachs. But the fur tippet was gone for good, at any rate. It was as if Ma Ada was trying to dispel some kind of evil influence from the house.

The next morning it was Sam's turn to rake dead ashes from the grate. As he was riddling them out he dragged from the clinker a white skull no bigger than his cupped palm. Its snarling teeth gave him the shivers. Hurriedly he tossed it in the bucket with the ashes and hurried with it outside to the yard.

Chapter Nineteen

Irene did as she was told and lay in her attic room, taking a rest. She was glad that Tom had given her that secret cache of presents for everyone at Number Thirteen, as it meant that she didn't have to go dashing out for last minute shopping like everyone else seemed to be doing. She stayed upstairs, keeping out of everyone's way.

There had been trouble at Number Thirteen, following Irene's fall. There was some kind of row down in the parlour, the very night of the accident. Even from upstairs Irene could hear raised voices floating up the staircases. They were more shrill and accusing than voices raised in argument in the Farley household tended to be. This seemed like a proper, serious row, and Irene wished she could hear what was being said. Naturally she asked Beryl about it, the first chance that she could.

Beryl sighed heavily over her knitting project. 'Oh, well, you know. Megan just played the completely innocent party. She acted horrified and then all shocked and really insulted that anyone could accuse her of any such thing.'

Irene groaned. She didn't want Megan accused of anything. It would only make things worse, wouldn't it? Megan would become an even bigger enemy.

Beryl continued: 'Old Ma Ada asked her right out. There's no messing about with Ma Ada. She can get straight to the point. Soon as Megan showed her face round here, she said to her: "Hey, you, lady. What were you doing with that old fur stole from my wardrobe? Leaving it lying around like that on the attic stairs. Our Irene nearly broke her neck and lost her babby today, all because of you, you thoughtless madam."'

'Oh, God,' Irene sighed. 'What did Megan say?'

'She's brazen and shameless. She tried to deny all knowledge. But who else would have the brass neck to nick stuff out of the old woman's room?'

Worse than the nicking though, was the deliberate leaving of the slinky, ratty thing on the staircase. It had been a deliberate trap, and one meant specifically for Irene and no one else, since she was the only dweller in the attic room. The thought made Irene sick to the stomach. Someone was living in that house who meant both her and her baby real harm. Irene didn't know what to do about it.

'She really hates me,' Irene said miserably.

'Because she knows you know that she's been carrying on,' said Beryl, almost too eagerly. She really did enjoy a gossip. 'So come on, spread the word. Tell me, Irene. Who was it she was with when you saw her?'

Irene shook her head. 'I really, really can't say. It would cause even more bother. Much more bother.'

The arguments had continued downstairs over the following nights. Megan's screeching voice was raised against her mother-in-law and Beryl reported back to the attic that it had been quite shocking. The young woman had sworn at Ma Ada. She had said something really awful. She had said words that Beryl had never even heard spoken aloud by anyone before.

'And guess what?' Beryl said, her eyes shining with suppressed glee.

Irene was just wishing the whole business would hurry up and pass over. She hated the family having rows because of her. The fur tippet business, though, came to feel like something of a pretext. It was the excuse for all kinds of tensions to come bursting out, just as the year entered the season of peace and goodwill.

'Screaming like banshees in the parlour, they were,' Beryl gabbled happily away, knitting with fast, expert fingers. 'And then, the next thing, our poor Bob is getting up on his feet and lumbering about. He'd been sat there eating his bread and dunking it in his tea, like he always does, even when it's got dripping on. And his face was suddenly black with fury, like I've never seen it.

'He gets up and he yells out loud. I couldn't even tell what words he was saying, if he was even saying actual words. It was just like a great big roar of pain, and it was all because he couldn't stand his ma and his wife fighting like that.'

Yes, Irene had heard that almost animal noise of agony and dismay from the parlour that evening. It had scared her more than the skriking and the shrieking of the women. She knew from experience that women were far more resilient than men and never really got hurt when they argued. A good row always let off steam. But when the men got involved, that was something different. That was when real violence erupted and things got said and done that couldn't be unsaid or undone.

'What happened?' Irene asked Beryl. 'I heard that shout and then there was some more noise, and a kind of kerfuffle, and then it all went very quiet for ages, until now . . .'

Beryl bit her bottom lip and looked scandalised. 'He hit her.'

'What? Bob? Hit Megan?'

'Right in front of the rest of the family. He gave that roar and he lumbered across the room and he raised his great big pan-shovel hand to her. Well, none of us could stop him. There was no time at all. And really, I'm not sure any of us would have wanted to. He was like a great big raging bull standing there. He'd knocked all the supper dishes over onto the carpet. Teapot and all. Megan took one look at his face and she stopped all her screeching and wailing and then – crack. He slapped her hard round the chops. He smacked her right in the cake hole.'

Irene's eyes bulged and she covered up her mouth in both horror and suppressed laughter. It wasn't that any of it was funny – it wasn't! It was horrible! – but the way Beryl had put it into words made her want to howl with laughter.

'Well, she just stood there,' Beryl finished up the tale. 'She glared back at Bob and at all the rest of us. That's Megan for you. She won't be defeated by anything. She stood there with her face all white and a big red mark coming up on her cheek. Man, you could see his fingerprints appearing on her face like it was a page in a magic colouring book. Then she turned on her heel and strode out of there. She kept her back straight and she marched right out into the hallway and then she was gone. She slammed the front door behind her. Didn't even take her bloomin' coat.'

'I heard the front door slam,' said Irene. 'So I knew someone had stormed out and I guessed it was her. Where do you think she's gone?'

Beryl raised her painted eyebrows. 'I reckon she's probably run off to this fancy man you saw her with. I bet he lives in a smashing big house in Sunderland, don't you? Somewhere on the coast. I bet she's decided to cut her losses with us lot and run to his arms at last, and that's the last we'll ever see of her! She'll be living the life of Lady Muck from now on, you'll see!'

Irene knew that Megan's fancy man wasn't some rich bloke with a big house in Sunderland. She knew he was much, much closer to home than that, and also – he had nowt to his name. He certainly wasn't someone she could go running to in her hour of need. Irene knew that Megan hadn't gone running to a fancy man at all. She had gone pelting into nothing, with nowhere to go . . .

'Eeeh, all this over a scrag of old fur!' Beryl chuckled darkly. 'Who'd have thought it? You know, there used to be nothing happening at all round here, before you came to live, Irene. It was quiet before you came to stay!'

'But I'm a quiet person!' Irene protested. 'I'm not the one who causes trouble!'

Beryl tossed her head and grinned at her and carried on knitting with a little flourish of her multi-coloured wool. It was some kind of matinee jacket, by the looks of it, Irene realised. Funny-looking article, really, but it was kind of Beryl to put the time and effort in.

'You don't have to go worrying about work, either,' Beryl told her. 'I've been in to see old Mr Wight himself, to explain about you.'

'You explained about me?'

'About you being up the duff, and all about you flinging yourself down the staircase and that.'

'Oh . . .'

'And he says not to worry about a thing, of course. He'll hold open your job at the biscuit factory for as long as it takes for you to get back on your feet. And when you do return, he says you'll have lighter work and fewer hours, while you're still up the duff.'

Irene rolled her eyes. 'He's very refined. He'd never say "up the duff".'

'Aye, you're right,' Beryl laughed. 'But you get my meaning. But, eeeh, he wasn't half concerned about you, pet. You should have seen his old face when I said you'd had an accident. He said, "Oh dear, she's such a very nice young girl. I do hope she's not hurt herself."'

Irene couldn't help herself smiling at the way Beryl told a story. She did all the voices and actions and threw herself into it. She went on, 'Do you know what it reminded me of? Going upstairs to his fancy old office to see him?'

Irene shook her head. 'Have you never been up there before?'

'It's not for the likes of me! Hobnobbing with the bosses! Ha! But really, what it put me in mind of was that bit in *The Wizard of Oz* . . . Do you remember? When Judy Garland and all her friends go into the palace to see the Great Wizard of Oz at last . . . and they're all dead scared. But then it turns out that he's just a little old fella sat there! And he turns out to be quite nice in the end!'

Irene couldn't help herself laughing at the idea of the biscuit factory owner being the Wizard of Oz. 'You're right! It was a bit like that for me too, going up there to his office at the top. Eeeh, and I thought I was the only one who thought of everything in terms of fairy tales.'

Beryl sighed. 'It's all a fairy tale, isn't it, really? Life and that? It's all like being in some crazy story that someone else is making up.'

Resting and recuperating, Irene thought this over, off and on. She liked to think of herself as being more in control of her own destiny than Beryl had suggested. She hated to think of someone else writing the fairy tale of her life and determining on a whim how it would all turn out. Why, she had made big changes of her own, hadn't she? She'd said yes to marrying Tom. She'd talked him into bringing her here, to Shields. If she wasn't in control of the changes in her life this year, then who was?

Irene lay there under the warm Victorian counterpane borrowed from her mother-in-law's bed, still feeling groggy and sore, and tried to feel like the mistress of her own fate.

It cheered her up when, after the factory hooter sounded at tea time, Mavis came over and sat and supped a pot of char with her. She brought some broken ginger snaps and told her all the gossip from the work room floor.

When they ran out of chatter about real people, Irene found herself sharing with her friend bits of fairy tales she remembered having told her sisters at home. That was who Mavis reminded her of now, she realised. That was probably why she felt so tender towards her. Talking to her was like talking to Irene's younger sisters, who – she suddenly realised – she was really missing.

Pale Mavis sat by the side of her bed in the attic with her mouth open, listening to stories about the Snow Queen and Rapunzel and Rumplestiltskin. The look on her face was strangely frozen, like a rictus of concentration. 'Where did you get all these stories from?' she asked Irene at last.

'Don't you know them already?'

Mavis shook her head, looking almost as if she was ashamed.

'Are you saying that no one ever told you stories when you were a little girl?'

That was clearly true, and not for the first time, Irene's heart went out to her.

Several days passed and she was soon back to feeling her usual vital, strong self. But Ma Ada insisted that she spend a little longer in bed. 'I'm not having anything happen to my grandbairn! Don't you hurry back to work too soon! Them biscuits can wait! And so can that ice cream parlour!' Her mother-in-law thought Irene was daft for having two jobs in the first place. She didn't understand that Irene enjoyed being in both places and was missing them both right now.

She forced herself to lie there and catch up with her correspondence. Irene wrote letters to her parents, her sisters and Tom. She didn't say anything about her fall to anyone, instead she wrote about Tyneside and tried to describe it all to them. For her sisters she concentrated on making it sound like a magical, exciting place. She told them about watching the sea from the cliff tops, and how wild it looked in the winter. She made the shops of Fowler Street seem sumptuous and far more luxurious than they had ever been, even before the war. In short, she made Shields sound like a place they might one day want to come and visit, once all the hostilities were over.

That seemed like the most magical and impossible idea of all. Much stranger than any fairy tale: the idea that one day this war would come to an end. And what would that ending be like? What would be left of them all? What would their world even look like?

Lying awake all day in bed trying to rest was sending her mind round and round with these thoughts, and it was probably no good for her at all. She was probably getting herself more agitated than she would have done by going to work.

The others came and sat with her, and tried to alleviate her boredom. Beryl sat there all the hours she could, when she was home from the factory. She was knitting busily with coloured wool garnered from old pullovers of her own which she was sacrificing for the cause. It was hard to make out what she was creating exactly, but Irene knew it was something for the bairn, because she was secretive and wouldn't let Irene get a good look at it.

Sam came to sit with her and made her laugh with his stories about the docks and the men and his usual chirping on about his everyday life. But there was a strange tension between them. They never followed on from their conversation in the yard about Megan. They never mentioned Megan at all.

Chapter Twenty

Cathy Sturrock came to see her, bringing three bottles of good, healing stout for the invalid to drink in bed.

'I'm not an invalid, really,' Irene said, trying to look bright and cheery as Cathy plumped up her pillows. It was strange, having someone she didn't know that well, suddenly turning up in her room. Cathy was vital and ruddy-faced, and her voice seemed to echo through the whole house.

'Take advantage of everyone thinking that you're not well!' the landlady laughed. 'And be glad of a few days off work and everything else. Because I'll tell you one thing, Irene Farley, and that's that, once your bairn's born, you'll not know a moment's peace. Not till it's fully-grown and off your hands, and that won't be for ages yet. So, just you rest up while you can, hinny!'

Cathy Sturrock produced a bottle opener from her pinny and with an expert flick, opened two bottles of beer and pulled a chair up beside the bed and ruminatively sipped while staring at Irene. 'Ah, you don't look too poorly to me. But I reckon you must have had a proper shock, falling arse over tit like that.'

Irene admitted it was horrible.

'Eeeh, there's always drama round here,' Cathy chuckled. 'Number Thirteen's never been starved of noisy goings-on. I've lived in these streets for twenty-four years come next spring,

218

and I've seen a few things. I could tell a tale or two about this family! Eeeh, I could!'

Irene tried to think of a polite way to prompt her to do just that.

'Not that I approve of gossip, mind,' Cathy added. 'But I do believe the old stories need passing down. We all need to learn from them, don't we? Otherwise each generation just goes on and on, repeating all the same mistakes, time and time again . . .'

Irene thought about what Beryl had told her, about Cathy's own past, and how she'd landed up living by the docks, ending up as a widow and a publican. It was on the tip of her tongue to ask her all about her own story, but Irene grew abashed.

Then the moment passed, and Cathy was opining loudly on the subject of Megan. 'That girl! She's always been a funny sort. I was gobsmacked when she first married Bob, I must admit. Him, the way he is. He's got the sweetest, kindest nature of all the Farley boys. Yes, he has – even sweeter than your Tom, though I know you'll say otherwise.'

'Actually,' Irene said. 'I do know what you mean. There's something very innocent about Bob. Something almost childlike.'

'Hmm,' said Cathy, knocking back another slug of beer. 'And there's good reason for that, an' all. Thereby hangs a tale, as they say.' She tutted and shook her head, and adjusted her headscarf with quick, nimble fingers. 'That poor, lovely bloke. He's been out every day and night after his shift's over at the pub, you know? It's the talk of the streets. He's been wandering about, looking for her. It's a horrible sound, like an animal in pain. The way he shouts her name. He's going about and begging her to come home to him. Begging her forgiveness for his having clouted her. It's pitiful to see. He adores her, despite everything. He really wants her back, even with all she gets up to.'

The way that Cathy said this made Irene think that she knew more about Megan and her activities than she was letting on. She might even know as much as Irene herself did.

'Someone needs to tell him,' Irene said. 'It'll do no good, wandering the streets and yelling her name. Wherever she's gone off to, that's not going to bring her back . . . She'll just say he's making a show of her.'

No one knew where Megan had slunk off to, after the drama of her causing Irene's fall down the stairs. Irene suspected that her sister-in-law was simply using the whole debacle as an excuse to run away for good. Clearly it was something that had already been on the cards. Sam wasn't saying anything about it. He had sat by Irene's bedside, but he wouldn't be drawn on the topic of Megan. He claimed he had no idea where she'd tootled off to.

Good riddance, was all Irene could think. She knew it was awful thinking this, but there it was. Megan's absence from the house was like a headache suddenly clearing up.

'You do know the story of why Bob is like he is, don't you?' Cathy Sturrock was frowning down at her, and Irene realised that her thoughts had been drifting for a moment or two. Probably the effects of the beer. Eeeh, fancy her, sitting up and drinking beer in bed!

'I don't know the story, no,' she said. 'I never knew there even was one. I just thought that was Bob, and that's how he is . . . naturally.'

Cathy shook her head and gave a low whistle. 'There's a reason for everything, Irene. There's always a story behind every single thing. And the thing with Bob is, you see, he's the real backbone of this family. He's the fighter. He's the one that would do anything to protect his mam and any of his brothers. Here, let me tell you . . .' Cathy flipped another bottle of beer open with her thumbnail, took a long draught, and started spinning her tale.

'You see, when he was just eight, it was him who came home after playing out one night round the doors and he found his dad Billy standing down there in the scullery, completely drunk out of his mind. He was screaming and yelling at Ma Ada, like he often did when there was no one else around.

'And young Bob came in, with his eyes wide and horrified, hearing all this language and all this palaver going on. Then, the next thing he knows, there's his dad suddenly setting about Ma Ada. He was battering her with his pan-shovel hands. He was a wiry little fella but he had these great strong arms and massive hands. He was thumping her hard, raining blows down on her head and shoulders.'

'No!' Irene gasped. 'I'd heard he was a drinker, the old man Billy, but I didn't know he did things like that.'

'Aye, that's how it was in lots of houses,' Cathy sighed. 'The frustrations come out, you see. It's the poverty and the drink and the desperation and the sheer bloody awful boredom of dragging yourself from one year-end to the next. It can turn man against wife and wife against man. That's a bit like it was with my own fella, the drunken sot. Luckily I could look after myself. But here at Number Thirteen, there's this poor little lad of eight years old, suddenly face to face with the true, brute reality of it all.'

'What happened?' Irene asked, with a feeling of creeping dread. These events were . . . what? Over twenty or more years ago, but she was experiencing them like they were happening at this very moment. There was something about the way Cathy was telling her that made her fear what was coming next.

'There's a couple of different accounts of it, of course,' said Cathy Sturrock sagely. She was thoroughly enjoying her tale-telling, Irene could tell. 'But everyone agrees that the father lashed out at the lad. When all the poor little mite was trying to do was protect his mammy. Well, any little lad would, wouldn't they? He went tearing in, grabbing hold of his dad's arm and trying to beg with him.'

'Oh, God . . .' Irene murmured. There was no relish for her in listening to this.

'Well, any normal man, he'd come to his senses when he sees he has his eight-year-old kid screaming at him, and he'd see what he'd done. But not Billy Farley. He was out of his gourd with drink. That's how he used to get. Did they not tell you that was how their old man Billy used to carry on?'

Irene nodded dumbly. Aye, Tom and the others had alluded to their father and his towering drunken rages. A little man, steeped in alcohol, fuming with colossal rage.

'And so he lashed out, that's what he did. He raised his fist to his lad and Bob didn't stand a chance. He went flying back across the room and it would have been all right. He'd have been knocked out of the scene and out of harm's way. Nothing worse would have happened to him, and old Ma Ada would have been glad. She'd have taken all the knocks and the beltings for herself. She didn't need anyone to come rescuing her. But . . . that poor little lad fell badly, didn't he?'

Another fall, thought Irene hollowly. Just like mine. Someone else went falling in this house, did they?

'He fell against the mantelpiece, did Bob. He smashed his skull on the stone fire surround. *Bang*. And he was out like a light. They don't even know how long he was asleep for. Minutes on end, perhaps, swimming in the darkness. He could have been dead, for all his beer-crazy dad knew.

'Billy kept on battering Ma Ada until her eyes and her ears were out like *that*, like big rotten black potatoes hanging off her head, and he'd worn himself daft with all the effort. Beating up his wife was the only thing that ever brung him out in a sweat, Ma Ada always said. Eeeh, by the end she hated his guts something rotten. And when he was finished, that's when he saw what he'd done to the lad.'

'Aww, no,' Irene whispered.

Cathy swigged down her beer and smacked her lips. 'I was one of those they called over to help, with the doctor, and everyone else they could find. They went crying in the streets for anyone to come and help them, 'cause they thought he was dead. We all went running round, of course, like people always did in those days. Everyone was always eager to help each other.

'And I'll tell you, Irene, what the funny thing was. Little Bob was lying there beside the tiled surround of the fireplace and he was perfect. There wasn't a single mark on him. The way Ma Ada was screaming out in the street, it had you expecting to find him lying there in all his blood and gore. You were expecting a scene of murder. But there he was. This lad lying there like an angel. A bit pale, mind. He'd gone completely white, even mucky as he always was.'

'Poor Bob . . .' Irene said. 'And what happened? He woke up and . . .?'

'And he could remember nowt,' said Cathy. 'He had to be reminded about it all. He was a bit dazed when they told him. He frowned when he heard that his dad had hit him and shoved him away. But there was no anger in him, no bitterness. That was the remarkable thing, you know. He just sat there blinking on the chair he'd been lifted onto. He looked pale and calm, and like he couldn't take it all in.'

'So what about the father?' Irene asked. 'Billy, did you say they called him?'

Cathy rolled her eyes. 'That one? Well, he ran off. As soon as he saw what he had done, with the lad lying there and not a mark on him. He thought he'd killed the boy stone dead, so, like the coward he always was, he turned and fled from the room, and from the house and from the street. He kept on running until the Sixteen Streets were well behind him. The story has it that he ran right to the beach and slept under the cliffs that night and for several nights afterwards. He wanted the sea to come crashing in and to carry him away. He wanted to die painlessly in the North Sea and never be seen again.

'Yet the drunken old sot couldn't even do that right. He stayed there, bone dry on the sands by Marsden Rock until all the fuss died down. He came slinking back to Frederick Street and connived his way back indoors. The boy was safe. He was alive, if a bit dazed. There were no recriminations and no one told the polis. No one said anything more at all. But, do you know what? No one ever said anything at all, ever again, to Billy Farley.'

Irene stared at her. 'They never spoke to him again?'

'Never. Not a single word. And three years later when his heart and his liver and everything else all burst inside of him and they nailed down his coffin lid at last, not a single person stood up and said a word for him at his funeral, either. And they barely ever mentioned him again.'

Cathy's tale was over then, and she finished off her beer with a noisy slurp. Irene had the idea that she'd told the story once or twice before and had finessed it through repetition.

Irene was dumbstruck by the whole thing. What a family! Tom had mentioned the fact that there'd once been bother with his dad, and his dad was long gone, but she'd had no idea it had all been so stark and brutal. Not for the first time Irene reflected that the Farleys made her own family seem like a rather sedate and refined lot.

'I'm glad you told me all that,' she said at last to Cathy.

'Well, now you see why Bob is the way he is,' said the landlady. 'When he hit his head, perhaps it should have killed him. It dulled and weakened his wits, maybe. But I think . . .

it also sweetened him. I sometimes think that man is too good for this world. He's too fine for this life that he's leading in the Sixteen Streets, anyhow.'

Irene studied her visitor and, with a dawning comprehension, heard a new note in the older woman's voice.

'It breaks my heart to hear him out in the road, walking the streets, bellowing after that hussy, Megan,' Cathy said. 'Begging her forgiveness, indeed. He deserves better than that.'

Cathy actually *loves* him, Irene realised. The landlady of our local is in love with her pot man, twenty years her junior and slightly daft, and she's just let me know that fact. He's her secret love, but does he even know? Would he ever realise?

'I'd best be off for opening the doors,' Cathy said at last, and took away their empties. She landed a light, beery kiss on Irene's forehead before she went.

As it turned out, Bob didn't spend many more evenings wandering the streets of South Shields shouting out the name of his lost beloved. A letter came addressed to him, and Ma Ada read it out to him the next morning. He was being called away to Durham and training, right before Christmas. It was Bob's turn to join the war.

'Maybe it's for the best,' his ma said fiercely to Irene, trying not to be upset about it. 'It'll take his mind off everything else. He doesn't like thinking about too much at once. It makes him too confused. He'll be happier away from here. Maybe.'

Chapter Twenty-One

She had never been so cold in all her life.

'Don't be nesh!' Albert laughed at her, and Irene decided she wasn't having that. She'd show him that she was just as tough as he and Bella were.

They were all three wrapped up against the biting December wind, though she might have put an extra jumper on, had she known it would be quite so cold as this.

They were braving the ferry that ploughed through the foaming, silver-grey waters between South and North Shields. The sea breeze blasted at them and took their breath away as they stood at the prow of the little ship. They were bathed in the most beautifully pearly light and clutched each other in order to stay upright.

'I can't believe you haven't already been across to the other side!' Arthur laughed. 'You've been living here for months!'

Irene didn't say that she had formed the crazy idea that North Shields must be like a mirror image of the town she already knew. It was a kind of Alice Through the Looking Glass idea she had daydreamed, and it had stuck. Across this coastal maw, across the other side of the Tyne, there was another town, in which everything was reversed and upside down. Perhaps all the people were very similar to the ones she knew, but important factors about them were very different and topsy-turvy. It was just the kind of fancy Irene enjoyed privately entertaining, though she'd never actually tell anyone about it, in case they thought she was daft.

The waters churned and rumbled beneath them and spatters of hard snow flew into their faces as the ship made the short crossing. There were only a few other passengers at this time in the afternoon, and Arthur took advantage of the relative quiet to fling back his head and burst into song.

The two women stood there breathless as he threw caution to the wind. He flung out his arms like he was on stage at the Sunderland Empire and performing for a full house. His eyes closed and his cheeks turned blue and he let fly with a zestful scrap of Puccini. It was an aria for Bella, from her dad's native land.

'Oh, Arthur, man,' was all Bella could say, when he had finished. Her eyes were misting up, and she had to blink the frosty tears away. A desultory round of applause came from the few other passengers, up on the deck above them. Everyone's attention had been drawn and they clapped his performance, though perhaps a little less enthusiastically than his two girlfriends.

Then the ferry docked and Arthur seized their arms to lead them ashore. This was his afternoon. He knew North Shields better than either of the girls did. He made some allusion to the fact that his mam had once worked as a herring gutter at the fish market. She had been lured by the promise of steady – if filthy – work, and that was how she had fetched up in the town in the first place.

'This part of town is where my earliest memories are set,' Arthur told them, leading them along the dark, slimy, cobbled quays. Bella and Irene both listened with great interest, because it was fairly rare that Arthur divulged personal details like this. 'When we were really little, me and our Mavis would even come and help our mam at work. They had us slicing open the fish's bellies with our little knives. Paying us a pittance to rip out guts and chuck them in a bucket. It was slave labour, man, but we didn't know any better. We were just glad to be with our mam all day.'

The real reason they had travelled on the ferry to North Shields was to visit the flea market, which was hidden away in a draughty hall not too far from the quay. As they entered the place Arthur became very intent and concentrated. He headed straight for the heaped piles of jumbled clothes and the endless racks of long coats and gowns.

Even in the cold atmosphere there was a musty, fusty smell. Irene pulled a face. Everything could do with a good cleaning, she thought. The piles of stuff that everyone – mostly older women, she noticed – was rummaging through reminded her of the donated clothes she'd spent a day folding up for the WVS. This scene, however, was a lot less genteel and ordered than the hall where the WVS had worked.

'Arthur loves a good bargain,' Bella smiled.

'What's he after?'

'Anything. Good quality rags of all kinds. What he doesn't keep for him and his sister, he sells round the doors. The two of them are good with repairs and alterations, you see. Very clever. They can take dowdy old rubbish from here and turn it into gorgeous stuff. You've seen some of the things I've got in my wardrobe at home. All the work of Arthur and his sister.'

Irene hadn't realised that her funny friend had yet another string to his bow, nor that Mavis had, either. She watched as he advanced ruthlessly along the messy trestle tables, diving between the grasping, darting hands of his rival rummagers. Soon he had a mound of items heaped over both his shoulders. He wore an almost comical expression of determination on his pale face.

Irene was thinking about that walk-in wardrobe of Bella's, and how amazed she had been by the racks of beautiful outfits the older girl possessed. It was strange, though: there was nothing snotty or pretentious about Bella. She would give you anything. Being well off and fortunate hadn't spoilt her nature one drop. She was one of the nicest girls Irene had ever met. Right now she was grinning indulgently at Arthur as he got carried away with his hunting.

'Look at all this lot!' he cried out, bustling over to them. To Irene's eyes it was just a lumpen mass of tatty fur, brocade and wrinkled cotton and silk.

'Where's it all come from?' Irene laughed.

He shrugged. 'Who cares? What matters now is that I rescue these lovely garments, so they don't end up on the backs of any of these dreadful old harridans.'

The girls laughed and shushed him, and made him go and pay for his choices. 'They're charging peanuts!' he sighed happily. 'Just peanuts!' Luckily he had brought enough string bags and paper sacks to stuff the garments into.

Bella helped him and muttered, 'I hope this stuff hasn't been looted out of bomb sites, Arthur.'

'What?' he frowned, scandalised. 'That's an awful thought! Don't say that! I'm sure that can't be true!'

The idea hadn't even occurred to Irene and, as they left the drab, freezing market hall and hurried back outside, she felt a little sickened. Just imagine if this booty really did come from the wreckage of destroyed homes? What kind of person would go dragging at rags and bones from amongst the debris and masonry and ruins of people's lives? Desperate people, she thought. Only the most desperate and hopeless of folk would go picking through the remains like that, if that is indeed where all this stuff came from.

She drove the awful thoughts from her mind. No, surely it was all more innocent than that. The material Arthur had bought reeked of mothballs and cobwebs. This was old rubbish that no one else had wanted. Fabric that had clogged up old shops and storerooms for many years. It was waiting for someone with talent and time on their hands to transform it into something magical.

'Come along, ladies!' Arthur was calling out. 'We'll get some chips in a minute, but first you have to meet Good Luck Dolly!'

'Who?' Irene frowned, and Bella laughed.

'He's right! You have to meet her! It's a tradition! You've got to greet old Dolly – it'll be good luck for the bairn!'

'She'll be good luck for the lot of us,' Arthur smiled.

The Dolly that the other two were so keen to introduce Irene to turned out to be a figure carved out of painted wood, standing alone on the quay. It looked something like a figurehead from the prow of an old ship: a very glamorous figure, despite the fact that it was weathered almost featureless by the sleet and wind. You could tell that her face had been painted time and again.

'This is Good Lucky Dolly,' Bella said, patting the figure on her shoulder. There was a great defiant energy about the strange figure, the way she squared her shoulders and thrust out her bust. Bella made Irene laugh by standing in just the same way, and staring at the far horizon, just as if she too was a sailing vessel's figurehead. 'She's been here for hundreds of years,' Bella explained. 'Well, this one is a bit more recent, but there's been a Dolly here for as long as anyone can remember. She gets worn and whittled away over the years, because sailors like to chip away a little piece of her, to take away with them to sea.'

Irene watched Arthur prising a small splinter of wood away from Dolly's arm and she felt horrified. The thought of that poor girl, standing there in all weathers, trying to bring everyone luck! And there she was, being picked apart and reduced every day by those she was trying to serve! It hardly seemed at all fair, and Irene said so. The others laughed at her.

'She's only a giant peg doll, Irene,' Bella chuckled.

Arthur passed her a small piece of wood. 'Here's a lucky spelk for you, hinny. Don't jab yourself with it. Put it away somewhere safe for all your future journeys.'

Irene stored it away in her penny purse, but she still felt unnerved by the painted effigy. She felt like its shining black eyes were staring right at her. 'But I'm not sailing anywhere.'

'It'll do for all kinds of journeys,' Arthur said wisely. 'And every journey through life can get pretty rocky.' He patted Dolly on the bosom and Irene giggled because she thought that looked rude.

As they wandered away from Dolly's quay, Arthur told them a bit more about things he knew about old sailors' lore from down here on the docks. 'They've always been a right superstitious lot,' he said, 'believing in luck and fortunes and magic.'

Irene found herself thinking back to the prognostications of old Aunty Winnie, and suddenly saw her, clear as day, sitting there sucking her tea out of the best china, at Ma Ada's table. She had said awful things about the hardships that both Irene and Tom would have to face in the future. It had seemed so unkind of her, not to paint everything to come as being rosy. Why cause unnecessary upset? Why not let people hope for the best?

Soon they were sharing a poke of chips together on a bench and watching the sea. The waves were getting rougher and the wind was getting icier, so they were glad of the shelter they'd found to sit in as they devoured their vinegary, golden chips.

'Imagine us as old fogies,' Bella laughed, poking her fingers into the scraps of batter at the bottom of her paper cone. 'We'll be sitting here, far in the future, when we're old and decrepit. Can't you see us sat here, just the three of us? Still friends and still doing just the same things?'

Really, Irene could see them being exactly like that, and the thought made her glow with warmth inside.

'No fear,' Arthur chuckled. 'I'll not be here when I'm old. Whatever happens, with the war and the future and whatever. I'm not going to be in North Shields or South Shields, nor anywhere near this place. I'm going to see the world and I should think I'll rarely come back.' He grinned at them with a smear of chip grease all down his chin. 'Oh, I'll send you two postcards and Christmas cards and all that, just to let you know how I'm getting on . . . but as soon as I get the chance . . . I'm off to see a bit more of the world.'

'If they'd let you join up, you'd be seeing the world with the army,' Bella said softly.

'Aye, I would, an' all,' he said. 'I'd have loved it, too. I know you think I'm soft as clarts and I'd be no good as a soldier. But that's not true. I'm as tough as nails, really, and I can fight my corner. I could be entertaining the troops somewhere. You know, they have whole . . . like, platoons, and that . . . of entertainers, and they go all over the world keeping morale up.'

'You'd be good at that,' Bella said.

He looked gloomy. 'Too much wrong with me. That's what they said.' He swung his feet heavily and sighed, and then crumpled up his chip cone and tossed it into the violent sea. Then he hugged his bags of fragrant purchases to his chest. 'And there was I always thinking I was perfect!'

Irene felt far too shy to ask him what was wrong with him, exactly, but she made a mental note to ask Bella later on.

Then it was time to run down the quay in order to catch the ferry back to their own side of the harbour. The snow was falling more thickly now, tumbling and twirling all around them as they stood in line waiting. When they travelled back across the water they found they had the little boat all to themselves and they took the top deck, where Arthur sang for them again. More operatic arias. Music that Irene had never actually heard before. She gasped at his ability to remember those strange, flowery, foreign words and the way he could get his tongue round them. Who was this strange young man, with his bagfuls of old, possibly stolen clothes, and his ability to move her so profoundly by singing words that none of them save Bella could even understand?

When they returned to the more familiar streets of South Shields Irene found herself saying she was worried about the bad luck that old Winnie had said she had coming to her.

'What did that old witch have to go and say that to you for?' Arthur tutted and shook his head. 'Well, you've got your bit of good old Dolly, to protect you against her silly words.'

Irene nodded fiercely. 'With the bairn coming and everything, I have to believe that everything's going to turn out all right.'

Arthur said, 'Well, don't get me wrong, pet. I think there's always going to be hardships and disaster, in your life, just as there is in everybody's life. That's just the way life always is. You can't hide yourself away and escape from death and disaster, you know.'

Irene smiled. 'I know that.'

'Aye, but do you? You've not seen much of life yet. Not really. You go along with everything and let other people shape your thoughts and opinions.'

She felt really stung by this. People only ever thought like that when they didn't know the real her, inside. When they hadn't bothered to find out what she was actually like. Most people didn't have a clue about how deeply and fiercely Irene really felt about things. In fact, it disappointed her that Arthur could dismiss her like this. 'I've got my own thoughts and opinions, thanks!' she said hotly.

He pulled a lop-sided face. 'I don't know. I see you with that Farley clan and I think – she's given herself up to them. She's been absorbed by them and soon there'll be nothing of Irene left at all . . . She'll be whittled away like old dockside Dolly back there.'

'Well, I'll just have to watch out and assert myself,' Irene said.

Bella laughed. 'Irene can be pretty tough and decisive, Arthur,' she said. 'You don't work with her! You'd know about it if you did!'

Arthur smiled. Irene had noticed that he would always listen to Bella and respect her opinions. In many ways Irene felt like the most junior member of their little group, and the one who had to do the most to prove herself.

'Everyone back to Franchino's for a frothy coffee?' Bella asked brightly.

'Oh, go on, I reckon there's time,' Arthur said. 'Then I have to run home with my bags of rags and be out at the Savoy in my uniform for two full houses till midnight. It's a Disney cartoon tonight and a new Bette Davis. I'll be in my element.'

Irene strode alongside the pair of them, up Ocean Road towards the familiar pastel glow of Franchino's ice cream parlour. Yes, she thought. You can't avoid sadness or disaster. You must open yourself out to life and take the risk of awful things happening. Otherwise nothing would ever happen at all and you'd never find any kind of happiness.

Irene knew she had to be strong and determined in order to get through all her tribulations to come in the company of those she had gathered around her. Like these two. The best friends she had ever known.

Chapter Twenty-Two

Christmas itself, when it eventually came, was here and gone in a flash.

'All my boys are away at the war!' Ma Ada grumped and wailed.

'What am I, Chopped Pork?' Sam shot back. He was laughing, but Irene could tell his feelings were hurt. It was as if, for a moment, his ma had forgotten he was still there.

'Ah, hinny, how could I forget you and your poor flat feet?' she laughed, and ruffled his hair. It weighed heavily on her that her other sons were away over all that festive period. There was nothing for it but to buckle down and have as nice a time as possible under the circumstances.

'Come on,' Beryl commanded Irene. 'It's all down to us, this.' The older girl turned into a whirlwind of activity and Irene was pulled along in her wake. They cut up coloured paper for paper chains, painted bits of cardboard and made table decorations and miniature Christmas trees.

'All right, girls, you can stop now,' Ma Ada growled. 'We've got enough decorations. It's like a fire hazard in here . . .'

Christmas Eve saw them down the market and queueing with all their tokens at the greengrocers. They already knew the butcher's on Fowler Street was hopeless. He'd had a meagre number of fowl for the orders that had been placed there for months. It was like a lottery, even for rabbits. The girls tramped home with vegetables and Beryl was talking about how she was planning to mix a bit of bread and chopped pork with onions and some herbs and mould a kind of ersatz joint, which they could roast in the oven and maybe it would do. Some of the women at the WVS had been explaining how it could be quite tasty as an alternative, but Irene didn't feel convinced.

Sam had worked a miracle, though, which they found out when they got home.

'A chicken!' Irene gasped, whipping her headscarf off and clutching it to her chest.

'Eeeh, you're not daft, are you?' Sam laughed.

It was a huge thing. Its feathers looked bright and extravagant as it lay there on the kitchen table. Its golden eyes gazed sightlessly at the ceiling and its scarlet coxcomb was strangely obscene-looking. The clawed feet were savage, nasty-looking things, all curled up and grabby.

'Oh, how brilliant!' Beryl grinned. 'We'll get about four meals out of that lot and soup for the last day. You're a genius, man! How did you get it?'

Sam tapped his nose. 'There's a swift trade in all sorts going on at the docks. No one needs to know where anything's come from. We're just saying that Santa's come earlier than usual.' Sam had had to pay a pretty penny for his contraband chicken, but there was no way he was going to tell his sisters-in-law exactly how much.

'Well, you've saved our Christmas,' Irene grinned, and hugged him. She could already taste roast chicken and its savoury gravy, flavoured with sage. It made her stomach rumble so loudly they all laughed.

'I'm not chopping its head off and pulling out all its doings, mind,' Beryl said, looking alarmed.

'I can do all of that,' Irene smiled. It was nothing to her. The others' squeamishness amused her. For once, coming from the country and the back of beyond, she felt like the more sophisticated one.

'Let's go and tell ma,' Sam said, grinning. He looked like a proud little lad, Irene thought. He couldn't wait to tell his mam what he'd done for them all.

Before they could tell Ma Ada anything, though, the old woman was up out of her chair and responding to a loud banging at the front door. 'Who's this on Christmas Eve?' she cawed, as Lucky followed her down the hall.

'Carol singers?' Irene asked.

'We don't really get them,' Beryl said. 'Not round here. All the kids round here would come out with rude words if you let them sing on your doorstep. They're proper heathens round here, man.'

The banging was quite insistent and it was taking a while for Ma Ada to draw back the heavy curtain she had over the door for the draught. 'Hold on! Hold on!' she bellowed.

For just a few seconds a daring hope was leaping up in Irene's chest. Could it be possible? Could it be, like, a wonderful secret, a last-minute surprise? But no, surely not. There was just no way. It was too soon since Tom was last here. And the other two had hardly been away any time at all, especially Bob. It was impossible that they'd been given leave for Christmas. There was just no way.

The same fleeting hope seemed to be energising Ma Ada, though, as she wrestled with the door. 'Eeeh, it's dark and late on Christmas Eve! Who are you to come knocking at this hour?'

Beryl, next to Irene, pulled a face. 'It's not that bloomin' priest is it? He'll be pie-eyed and after the sherry, if it is.' Irene had heard about Father Michael, the 'old get', as Ma Ada called him. He was forever trying to get Ma Ada to return to the church of her late husband. But his begging and blandishments never worked on her.

Ma Ada felt very ambivalent about the church that she had married into all those years ago. She'd much rather sit at home in her best hat with her Bible and worship in her own way. Maybe on Christmas morning she'd go to Mass and enjoy the singing and the prayers, but she didn't like to feel that the Catholics were reaching out to claim her or any of her bairns. She didn't think much of Father Michael, either, the miserable old soak. What she tended to do on Christmas Eve and other festive occasions was feed him some sherry and send him off again, blearily blessing everyone and moving on to his next victim.

But this wasn't Father Michael.

And it wasn't any of the boys.

Ma Ada flung the door open and let the frigid breeze into the hallway. 'By, it's bloody freezing and pitch black!' she cried. 'What are you doing calling on decent folk at this time of night?'

There was a shabby, rather pathetic figure in the doorway. A dark silhouette in the sodium streetlight. The snow had settled on her shoulders and in her hair. When she looked at them all she had tears coursing down her face and she seemed close to collapse.

Ma Ada reacted more swiftly than the younger members of her family. She held out her hefty arms to take hold of the woman before she dropped onto the doorstep in front of them.

'Megan Farley!' Ma Ada gasped. 'Look at the state of you, girl! Where the devil have you been? What have you done to yourself?'

Megan looked pinched, starving and ill. Irene had to blink several times and stare before she could even recognise this wretched creature as her glamorous blonde sister-in-law.

Suddenly they were all gathered around her, drawing her into the house and down the hall. The door slammed and Beryl pulled the curtain tight against the cold, dark night. The women fussed and filled the air with their tutting and cooing and whispered words of comfort.

Megan was shivering, her teeth were chattering and she seemed to be in some kind of shock. She inched along towards the parlour with them, and every step seemed to be painful.

Sam, Irene noticed, had suddenly made himself scarce. He was in the kitchen, putting the kettle on the hob to boil, making himself useful.

Megan was placed in the comfiest chair in the house: Ma Ada's armchair. She'd be dripping melted snow all over the cushions and antimacassars and the good woollen blankets and shawls, but the old mother hardly seemed to care. Her face was squinched up with concern. 'Now, you just take your time, pet. You get your breath back and warm up. Then you can tell us where you've been hiding out.'

Megan's hands and feet were like blocks of ice. Her lips looked like they had turned blue.

'I'm s-sorry,' she said. 'I'm s-sorry I've c-caused bother . . .' She looked up at her rescuers and tried hard to smile.

They clustered round her and reassured her. 'Eeeh, the important thing is that you're home, pet,' Ma Ada said, rubbing her hands between her own gnarled claws. 'You're back in the fold and you're safe.'

For a moment Irene felt her heart going out to the frozen girl. But then, as Ma Ada turned away to shout at Sam, to get him to hurry up with that tea, Irene caught a glimmer of something in Megan's clever eye. It was a glint of something shrewish and bright. A triumphant look that flitted across her expression and then was gone, as the girl started coughing and shaking all over again, and sobbing with relief that she was home.

Irene wasn't exactly miffed, but she wasn't far off.

Beryl put it into words for her. 'Megan's managed to get all of the attention onto her, hasn't she, and everything's forgiven?'

Ma Ada had made them all tend to the returning daughter-in-law, filling kettles and pouring steaming hot water into the tin bath. Megan sat there preening herself and combing out her hair in front of the stove.

'Prodigal daughter, isn't it?' hissed Irene.

She knew, though, that it was all about Ma Ada looking after her son's wife. It had cut Ma Ada to the quick, having to send Bob away to join the army. When he went he had just about been crying on the doorstep. He was confused and worried, and knew he had no choice. But he really hadn't wanted to go. Ma Ada had tried to comfort him, but she had to take control of the situation, too. 'Now, no more blubbing, Robert Farley! Don't you go disgracing the good name of our family!'

And so she had sent her sweetest and simplest boy off to war.

That was just last week and it still upset Ma Ada to even mention it. Perhaps she saw looking after the prodigal Megan as a kind of reparation? She knew how much Bob loved her, how he had torn out his heart when she vanished and he'd traipsed the streets calling her name. All of that was the reason for the special treatment the spiteful hussy was getting tonight.

Well, perhaps no one else thought of Megan as a 'spiteful hussy' in quite the same way that Irene did. But that was because she had seen through her and been witness to the worst side of her.

But it was Christmas Eve, suddenly, and that meant good will to all men and women. Even a nasty sister-in-law who seemed to have it in for her.

The radio was on, playing holy music and a peaceful hush fell over Number Thirteen. Irene repaired to the scullery, where she cleaned up the chicken Sam had brought home. Lucky sat patiently begging for scraps of the innards and was rewarded with the few bits Irene didn't boil up for stock.

It was noticeable that Sam had taken himself upstairs out of the way, now that Megan was home. Eeeh, what was the real story there? When Irene had asked him to explain he seemed to deny his own responsibility. He had made it sound like the woman had forced him into kissing her and doing things he shouldn't have been doing. Was that even possible? Irene was sure she didn't know. In the ways of the world, and of men and women, she sometimes felt rather innocent.

The evening whiled itself away pleasantly and the house filled up with the smell of slowly roasting chicken juices. Though they asked her where she had been, Megan avoided answering their questions. Irene's thoughts turned to the small cache of presents and trinkets that her Tom had brought back for her to dispense to his family. It was so thoughtful and lovely of him, to spare her the worry.

She wondered what he was doing tonight, and how he'd spend his Christmas Day tomorrow. He had mentioned a handful of names of men he was friends with. She had vague impressions of faces she had invented for them, but they were no more real to her than the names of characters in a story. Tom had said that it was hard becoming friends with people, because you never knew what was going to happen to them. You never knew who was going to come back from flying missions and who would never come back home again . . .

She wished, in some ways, that he hadn't told her anything at all about what went on. Other times, she wanted to know everything. She wanted to share in all of it with him. But really, she knew that she wasn't brave enough to hear everything that he had to endure.

Ma Ada appeared in the kitchen, sniffing appreciatively at the bubbling stock and bending to pet Lucky on his hairless head. She was stiff as she straightened up, Irene noticed, and out of puff from bustling around the house, bringing towels and clothes for Megan.

'Season of goodwill and all that,' she reminded Irene, with a stern expression.

Irene nodded, feeling flummoxed that she was the one getting a lecture, but she didn't say anything.

'I know there's a bit of bad blood between you and Megan,' Ma Ada went on, heavily. 'Well, not everyone can get along swimmingly. It's a bit of a difference in your natures, isn't it? But you have to try, hinny, to get along, for the sake of peace and quiet in the house? Now, do you understand?'

Irene felt herself blushing hard. She wanted to burst out suddenly with all the hurt she was keeping tamped down inside. She wanted to tell old Ma Ada a few home truths about what Megan was really like.

Instead she nodded and bit down hard on the inside of her cheek.

'You're a good lass, Irene,' said Ma Ada. 'But I have to look after all of you, and be fair to you all, don't I?'

Irene nodded again and longed to change the subject. 'I'll make a chicken broth with the bits and put it in the cooker tonight, while we're out at Midnight Mass. There's some celery and carrots and a swede. It'll be lovely to come back to some broth to warm us.'

'Eeeh, that's a champion idea, lass,' Ma Ada said. 'And I'm glad you want to come to Mass, too. I used to make all the others come along with me, but you can't force people can you?' She sighed wheezily as Irene started chopping celery and withered, twisted carrots. 'But I know that you and your family were keen on your church.'

'I'd feel like it wasn't Christmas without going at least once,' Irene smiled, but in truth she found the local parish church here rather draughty and impersonal. It wasn't massive and it wasn't exactly overrun with worshippers, but it was a world apart from the tiny, ancient Norman church she was used to in Hunworth.

Just thinking the name of her native village inside her head gave her a terrible pang of homesickness just then. It almost knocked her sideways. Her stomach churned and the mermaid in her belly seemed to quail and turn over in response, as if her unhappiness had woken her up.

'Your family will all be thinking of you tonight, lass,' Ma Ada told her softly. 'All those sisters of yours and your mam and dad.' She lumbered over to put her arm awkwardly around Irene's shoulders. It was rare that she cuddled anyone and Irene was amazed. 'Maybe one day,' she promised, 'when the war and everything's over, your people will make the trek up north to see us all? And we can have a proper meeting of the clans? Wouldn't that be marvellous, eh? That would be a fine thing to do. I'd love to meet your people, Irene. Especially if they're anything like you, pet.'

Chapter Twenty-Three

If she thought it had been cold before Christmas, January took Irene's breath away. That wind from the North Sea cut right into her as she shuffled along the frozen pavements on the way to work. Everyone walked with their heads down, careful not to slip, the women in headscarves, the men with caps pulled down over their ears.

A headscarf: that had been Ma Ada's gift to her. A beautiful one in heather-coloured wool, from a nice shop, but all the same, it was a present that brought Irene's spirits down somewhat in January. She felt like a proper Mrs Woman tying the knot under her chin and bustling through the town, same as all the other Mrs Women she saw beetling about the streets. I feel properly middle-aged wearing this! she thought, hurrying along.

But she had to count her blessings, of course. It was a new year, and there was a new bairn to look forward to. The actual business of giving birth still frightened her. She had heard some awful stories. Horrible stories, all blood and guts. Her sisters-in-law had passed on some choice tales of terror about childbirth as they all sat in the Robin Hood's public bar on New Year's Eve.

'Ah, what would you two know about any of it?' Ma Ada had gibed them, raucous after a couple of sweet sherries. She had allowed herself a little extra tipple to celebrate the coming of what they hoped would be a better year for them all. She cackled and nudged Beryl and Megan. 'You two know nothing!'

Megan's expression could have curdled milk. For a second she looked as if she was about to react and get all cross that her childlessness had been brought up, but she took a sip of eggnog instead and simmered furiously. Perhaps it had been because her Bob had a few days home over the new year, and he was sitting, beaming, protectively beside her. Maybe that's why Megan had been a bit better behaved?

Anyhow, New Year's had passed without a hitch. The Robin Hood had rung with the merry sound of a dozen favourite tunes, some of which Irene didn't recognise at all. They were local songs, she realised. Geordie tunes and sailor songs. The men in the bar who usually looked too decrepit to even stand up straight were suddenly belting out choruses lustily and trying to get the lasses up to dance. Cathy Sturrock held sway from behind her bar and brought out secret supplies she'd had squirrelled away in the cellar. Port and whisky and a huge jar of pickled eggs.

Bella came across for the evening, bringing with her a bottle of her nonna's home made limoncello, and everyone gasped at its tart strength. 'Crikey!' laughed Sam. 'That's like bloody lighter fluid!'

The smoke in the public bar made Irene's eyes sting. It was like sitting in a thick, noxious fog, or like travelling through some misty ocean aboard a creaking vessel sailing blindly at night. She thought about the baby in her womb and felt her turn over in her sleep, quite unalarmed by all the noise and hullaballoo of her relations celebrating the arrival of 1942.

This year we'll meet you, Irene promised her daughter. Why, this time next year you will be with us all. Perhaps not here in the pub, but you'll be part of our family. We'll all know your dear little face, and maybe all these voices and faces will be familiar to you by then, too. Of course, you already know the sound of my voice. You've heard it quite often inside your head, just like I make believe I can hear yours, too.

Her secret, ecstatic thoughts were all about having this daughter. A part of her, but not her. Separate from her, but part of the same living stuff. It was exciting and strange and yet . . . she knew already what it was like to be around babies and bairns. With so many younger sisters there was nothing new to her that babies could go through. None of that stuff – mess and colic and tish and sick – none of it daunted her in the slightest. And yet . . . the hugeness and the momentousness of what was going to happen between now and, say, next new year sometimes overwhelmed her.

Beryl was nudging her elbow and laughing. Her hair was hanging in damp tendrils round her face. She'd been dancing with some of the chaps who were on leave. 'Hey, hinny! You've been miles away!' she laughed, and drew Irene back into the bosom of her new family.

And so they had seen the new year in very happily, all together, mostly. Pledging solemn, tipsy toasts to those who couldn't be home with them. All feuds and tensions were forgotten for now, and all worries set aside. It had been a very pleasant finish to the annual festivities, all in all. Even Ma Ada had kicked up her heels and lifted her long skirts above her ankles to do a little jig on the sawdust floor as an old gadgie played the accordion and Aunty Madge from three doors down bashed away at the out-of-tune piano.

A good night. Irene would describe every bit of it in one of her letters to Tom. She would write it on her afternoon break during her first day back at work at the biscuit factory.

She hastened her pace, trip-trapping on the frosty path towards the factory gates, thinking of how she'd tell the tale of New Year's Eve to her beloved man. She'd tell him that she had learnt the hard way that pickled eggs and limoncello do not mix. The only let-down of the whole night was being a little bit sick in the ladies' toilets and trying not to look too green when she returned to the snug.

The thought of those eggs still made her feel queasy as she hurried to work down the docks, three days later.

She was used to the endless repetitive tasks in the work room now. She could have packaged up biscuits standing on her head. The highlight of this first day back in January was catching up with Mavis, who gabbled away happily about the few days' holiday she had spent with her brother.

Irene had invited the two of them over to the Sixteen Streets, to see the new year in at the Robin Hood. But Mavis and Arthur had demurred. 'I wish you had come over,' Irene told Mavis. 'It was a smashing night.'

Mavis smiled. 'I was dead keen, like. But Arthur said you'd only invited us in order to be nice. He said you hadn't really meant it.'

'But I did! Of course I did!'

Irene thought about it for the rest of that day and realised that Arthur didn't want to see the Farleys en masse again, not so soon after that curious scene at the sledging hill.

'He's made a few good bob, singing at posh people's parties!' Mavis was telling her. 'We were taken into quite a few grand houses. Eeeh, you want to see how some of those folk live, Irene. It was lovely! One place, they had this great big like, silver bucket thing on the table, and it was full of booze, and they ladelled it out into little silver mugs for you. They even gave me one, and I was just there to help Arthur out. Eeeh, and it was the loveliest, warmest thing I think I've ever drunk in all me life! I loved it!'

'And did they like Arthur singing to them?'

'He went down a storm! He was smashing! They were all saying "Eeeh, he could be a star on the stage or on screen, he could! Such a bonny lad! And what a voice!"'

It made Irene beam to hear the pride in Mavis's voice.

Then she pictured them, both wrapped up in their cloaks and hoods, clinging to each other in the wind and the snow, making their way to these posh houses to sing for the rich folk. They were like two orphans, Irene thought, singing for their supper.

'Mrs Farley,' came a boomingly familiar voice just then. 'Welcome back to the work force.'

'Good morning, Mrs Clarke,' Irene nodded at the supervisor.

'You seem to be showing a little!' said the older woman approvingly, staring straight at Irene's tummy.

Irene gasped. What a nerve the woman had with her personal remarks! And her with her gargantuan chest! How would she like it? Showing a little, indeed!

'How long do you intend to work here, Mrs Farley? Right up until baby is born?'

Irene hadn't thought about it very precisely. At the moment she was just glad to be back and out of the house after the enforced incarceration of her recuperation and then the festive season. 'As long as I possibly can,' she said.

'Very good,' Mrs Clarke nodded solemnly. 'I like good workers.'

Mavis was grinning at the supervisor. 'Am I a good worker, too, Mrs Clarke?'

'No, Mavis. You are what I like to call a hopeless case.'

Mavis pulled a face behind the large woman's back as she swept out of the room.

In their break the girls stood outside and Irene found herself making them all laugh: Mavis, Gladys, Mary, Edith and Effie. She'd begun quite seriously, describing how she'd had such a wrestle with making Christmas dinner for all the Farley clan, on a range that she still wasn't quite used to. 'And then I went and almost cooked that cat.'

'What?!' Mavis gasped, choking on her crust of bread.

'Well, there's a kind of warming drawer, near the floor on that old range, and I suppose when I was going to and fro with all the dishes, I must have left it open.'

The other girls were staring at her, listening with bated breath. 'Eeeh, tell me that the cat's not dead!' Mary cried.

'It must have been mooching about in the yard, looking for scraps and stuff, and then come into the scullery, looking for warmth. Anyhow, I didn't see any of this. It was only when we were all sat at the table and everything seemed to be going well, that Megan nips back to the kitchen for the bread sauce I'd missed and then, all of a sudden, she's screaming her head off.'

Mavis cried out, 'You'd cooked the cat!'

Irene rolled her eyes. 'Lucky was absolutely fine. But he was in Megan's arms and looking worried when she brought him through. She was trying to say that I'd shut him up in the oven and tried to cook him!'

The girls were laughing now and nudging each other. A great big whoop went up when they clapped eyes on Megan coming back from the lav. 'Hey, we heard you rescued the cat on Christmas Day!' cried Effie in her loudest voice.

Megan scowled. 'Yes! Can you believe it! That one,' she nodded at Irene. 'She'd only gone and trapped the cat in the oven!'

Irene was blushing fiercely. 'I still don't believe it,' she hissed to Mavis beside her. 'I wouldn't put it past Megan to have set that whole thing up, just to make it look like I wanted to murder the bally cat . . .'

Mavis tutted and shook her head. 'Eeeh, at Christmas as well. That poor cat has no luck, does it?'

It was a long day's work, going straight from the factory into an early-evening stint at Franchino's. At least work at the ice cream parlour wasn't too strenuous these days. The place was hardly ever that busy. And who'd be rushing there on one of the freezing days following the Christmas break? There was the usual gaggle of older folk, flocking in for their Camp Coffee and Woodbines in the very late afternoon, when the dark was settling down. Irene buttered some baps, cut some cake and wandered between the tables for a while. By about six o'clock her back was giving her gyp.

Still, she was so glad to be at work and away from the stuffy house where they'd all been cooped up for what seemed like about a month. She needed to be getting on with things and seeing other people now. It had been sweet chatting to Mavis today, and it was lovely to see Bella, spending time in their usual place. Maybe Arthur would pop in again, just before closing, and they could sit in their usual booth and hear direct from him what his Christmas had been like. She knew she'd heard a rather romanticised, glowing version from his sister.

Yes, all in all Irene was pleased to be getting back into a work routine at the start of this first week in January.

Tonio had welcomed her when she'd arrived, kissing his fingers and sending wishes her way, and bellowing about the new year. 'I can feel it will be wonderful for all of us!' he'd beamed. 'With an end to this war and all the suffering. And a beautiful baby for our beautiful Irene and her handsome husband back from the south! Come, have coffee with me. Is good for you. Look, I even have cocktail sugar for you. Rainbow colours!'

Irene wasn't sure too much coffee actually was all that good for her, or the bairn in her belly, but she always gave in to Tonio's sweeping, affectionate attentions. And sugar! Her mouth filled with a rush of saliva at the very sight of that treat. Cocktail sugar of pink and purple hues. How had he managed to come by such luxurious stuff?

Tonio meant well, and she would marvel at his ability to stay cheery, whatever else went on. He'd been given a bit of flak recently, she knew, from daft, ignorant people who were letting their prejudices get the better of them. He'd been jeered at in the street and people had yelled stuff at him – words that Irene hadn't heard spoken aloud, with such venom, before. And all because he was Italian. He had shrugged philosophically. 'My countrymen are a part of the enemy and a part of the problem,' he had said, very sadly, when they'd arrived one day to find horrible slogans painted on the ice cream parlour's windows. 'We shouldn't be surprised.'

Irene had helped him wash the nasty words off the windows, carrying buckets of hot, soapy water into the street to work alongside him. 'You don't need to help me,' he said.

'I do,' she told him. 'You've been good to me, you and Bella and all your family. Ever since I first arrived here. You know how to welcome someone.'

And he had smiled at her then, just as he smiled at her this evening. His leathery face crinkled up until his eyes were just like two dark currants in one of those spicy, glazed buns he liked to bake on Sundays. 'Eeeh, lass,' he grinned at her, full of pride at her blooming pregnancy and her fresh complexion. He was as proud of her as if she was his own. The curious Geordie lilt to his Italian accent always made her smile: it was such a funny sound.

Bella came and joined them for coffee and they laughed over the events of New Year's Eve, sharing with Tonio as much as they thought he would find amusing. He wouldn't like tales of how the women had got tipsy and sang along with the raucous songs. But he liked hearing that the Farley clan had all been together and were seemingly happy at this important turning point in the year.

'Is good for families to be happy together,' he nodded, stirring his frothy coffee with great deliberation. 'The Farleys have had their shares of terrible ups and downs in the past. I have known of them for many years and they had problems galore, at one time. With that old father and his drinking, and then his wicked old ma that used to live with them, making Ada's life hell. Yes, Ada has done herself proud, she is like a queen to those boys. She has seen them all grown up and settled. They are all responsible citizens, three out of four of them married and happy.' He glanced briefly at his daughter and Bella smiled ruefully at his next words. 'I should be so lucky to see all my children settled and married and off my hands.'

Bella clucked her tongue. 'I'll find him one day, father, don't you worry. But I won't go marrying just any old rotten bloke, you know. He has to live up to the image of my wonderful old dad, doesn't he?'

Tonio beamed and glowed at her flattery. Oh, he was easy to cajole and please. Irene thought it was delightful to see, the warm bond of love between father and daughter.

Then there was a small crowd shuffling in, bringing evening papers and fresh news of what was going on in the war, and who'd said what in the pub last night, and what was available in the market place for those up early enough to grab first dibs. The coffee machine steamed and snorted and Irene got to work serving everyone.

The evening passed in a seemingly normal blur. It was a reassuring feeling, that the days were soothingly dull in their rhythms. Nothing too strenuous or alarming. In some ways Irene wished more of life could be like this. Low key and somewhat quiet.

'Have you seen anything of Arthur?' she asked Bella.

Bella shook her head. 'Not since Christmas Eve. He came to our house, out of the blue. He brought little gifts for us all and he had a drink with me, to toast the season. There was something funny about him. Like he wanted to say something, to tell me something . . . but he didn't. And I couldn't winkle it out of him. Well, I've known Arthur for years. I know when he's up to something and when he's hiding something. I reckon that this is one of those times.'

Irene mulled this over. Now she wished that she had made more of an effort to drag him round to the Sixteen Streets on New Year's Eve. A simple invitation hadn't been enough to convince him he was really wanted. She could have gone and found him where he lived. She had seen him to talk to here in the ice cream parlour, and at the Savoy, but these were places that she always saw him. She felt like she needed to see her friend on his own home turf to gain a proper understanding of him.

There was something about her memory of the scene on that snowy day, when violence had been hanging in the air, and Arthur had assuaged them all with that incredible singing of his . . . it had made her want to reach out to him more, and to find out more about both him and his sister. There had been their day together in North Shields, of course, and she had heard a bit more then, about his mam's fish-gutting work at the docks, and Irene had gained a little more insight into what made Arthur tick. But she had to admit that mostly he was a huge mystery to her. An unknown quantity. And the fact that she hadn't seen him in a little while vaguely worried her, as if something awful might have happened to him quietly, off-stage, while she was busy concentrating on other things.

Her shift passed by and custom slowed down to virtually nothing. Tonio patted her shoulder as she stood slumped at the coffee machine. 'You can go home early, my lovely,' he told her. 'There's nothing more here today, I reckon.'

It was only seven o'clock. 'Do you mind?' she smiled grate-fully. Her back was really paining her today. She was starting to wonder whose advice to take about when to give up work for the sake of the bairn. Really, she felt like her ma was right, with the way she had behaved through all her many pregnancies: you just work through as late as you can. Her ma said she'd given birth in the middle of sowing a field, and kneading dough and getting water from the pump. It was just a part of a woman's everyday life and she had never needed cosseting. Ma Ada felt differently. More than once she had said: 'That's my first grandchild inside of you, hinny. You'd better look after yourself! I'm not having you going about looking knackered and making yourself ill!'

Irene said goodnight to Tonio and both he and Bella hugged her warmly goodnight, as was their way. Why, they hugged her more than her own family did, and certainly more than any of the Farleys.

The snow was fading at last, turning to brown, perilous slush on the pavements. It was worse than snow, as the temperature dropped. It made the going much more slippery.

Whose turn was it to cook tonight? She couldn't remember. It was a weekday supper. A quick, scratch meal, before most of them went out. Something light, she hoped.

Soon enough, she was back in the Sixteen Streets and the sodium lamps were glowing yellow and mothers were bringing their bairns in off the road.

She was glad to get in out of the cold and to close the front door behind her. If she could help it, she wouldn't be going out again that night. And maybe not all tomorrow, either. She'd wrap up warm and stay indoors and block the whole world out for a little while.

These were cosy thoughts, but Irene was to be thwarted that night.

Because that night the Luftwaffe came back to Tyneside.

It had been ages since there was a bombing raid, but now they were back with a vengeance, and all the folk of South Shields were to be dragged from their beds to seek shelter in the middle of the night.

That feeling of desperate panic in the freezing night air seized hold of them all once more – and the new year began with a tragedy.

*

The booming and crashing seemed louder than it ever had before. Closer and closer fell the bombs, and the Farley clan cowered with their neighbours in the damp, clammy shelter dug deep beneath the back of the town hall. 'This is worse, much worse . . .' Beryl couldn't help saying. It was an unspoken command from Ma Ada that no one mention what was going on above ground. While they sheltered here they were to pretend as best they could that they were doing it out of choice, and that nothing at all was going on above.

The whole place rocked and shuddered. Irene felt her ears pop as showers of filthy dust were dislodged and covered them with sandy grit. She felt like they were all rabbits, crouching down here, and that the Germans were predators hunting the country-side for them, prying into warrens, thirsty for their blood and flesh. Yet she knew at the same time that bombing was much less precise and coordinated than weasels or foxes or anything natural might be. They simply zoomed overhead and dropped their deadly loads where they thought they might cause the worst damage to the shipyards and the people who worked there.

For the first time, really, Irene came to realise what it would mean to be hit by one of those bombs and to suddenly expire in an instant. It would be like never having existed at all, in a way. She wasn't old enough to have left her mark on the world. Her baby wasn't born yet, and she would be erased along with her. And that would be it. The world would go on, grimy and dangerous, and there would be hardly any record at all that Irene Farley née Spencer had ever been here to experience it.

They've got no right to do that, she thought angrily, sitting there, gripping her knees and desperately wanting to wet. Those men homing in on us and trying to get to us. What gives them the right to finish us off in a flash? She didn't care what the wider story was, or what was at stake on the worldwide stage, or any of that stuff. That was for people much cleverer and more experienced than her to sort out. Surely their cleverness and experience ought to allow them to sort out the world without ordinary people like her having to skulk in underground basements like this?

More dust, more grit falling. More bone-shaking judders that seemed about to bring the makeshift rafters down. Surely there had to be a better way than this madness and slaughter?

Then she thought, very clearly and distinctly: my Tom is delivering this exact same misery and evil upon another city, across the water, at this very same moment. Perhaps even now. He's doing the same thing.

Tit-for-tat. Rat-a-tat-tat. Rats in the cellars. Tit-for-tat.

The clarity of the thought made her ears ring almost as much as the increasingly loud explosions from above.

Cries went up. Panic and alarm. The Farleys gripped on to each other as a wave of dismay travelled through the shelter. It's about to happen, Irene thought. We can all sense it. This is animal panic. This is us like beasts in the slaughterhouse, catching the scent of death and our fellows' blood. We know the end is coming for us soon.

'Our Father, who art in heaven . . .' Ma Ada's mumbled prayers reached Irene and she'd never heard the woman sounding so old and scared. She had left both her worn, shiny Bible and her cat in the parlour. Her two most precious items, after all her children.

Irene reached over and took the old lady's claw-like hand and held on to it hard, as if she was pacifying a kid with nightmares. The others didn't join her prayers, but Irene did, muttering the familiar lines along with her. She wasn't sure how she was feeling about God these days, and how shaken her previously sure sense of him was. Expecting like she was, she was hedging her bets. A miracle or two wouldn't come amiss, and so she was trying her hardest to believe in mercy and goodness and almighty power right now, and besides, it seemed to give comfort to Ma Ada.

There were Megan and Sam, sitting side by side. They were pressed comfortably close. They looked like they were used to sitting in such cosy proximity. Irene couldn't help keeping an eye on them. It was a Saturday night and they had clearly been out together. When the sirens sounded they came dashing in from the street and the panic of the moment had made them forget to pretend they were arriving home quite separately. So – it seemed they were still seeing each other clandestinely, Irene concluded. She couldn't help wondering what was going on between them and how it would all finish.

Maybe it wouldn't have to finish, she thought hysterically. Maybe a bomb's gonna bring that secret story to an end? Ah, who cares? She shook her head. If they're carrying on and they're having some fun out of life, and it isn't hurting anyone, and poor Bob is kept out of it . . . then who really cares?

No, no, it's wrong, another part of herself answered.

Megan looked bilious and green. They must have been out drinking and dancing again. Yet she was always good at holding her drink, when she could get hold of it in the first place. Yet Irene had never seen her oldest sister-in-law looking so queasy. It made Irene think of her own horrible morning sickness. That rolling, griping, cramping sensation and the blackness that seemed to roil through her head and down to the pit of her stomach, making it impossible for her to keep anything down. Why, Megan looked as if that's precisely how she was feeling right now.

Oh my God, Irene thought, with a bursting flash of inspiration. That's what she's gone and done. She's got herself pregnant, hasn't she? And it must be *Sam's* . . .

Then the bombing raids started up again, thundering through the thin crust of earth and stone above their heads and they all huddled together, moaning and chanting a ragged chorus, mustering all the hope they could . . . and the terrible night rolled on.

Chapter Twenty-Four

When they emerged in the early hours the town around them was changed. It always was, the morning after a raid. There was smoke and dullness and a gradual getting of your hearing back as the weak sunlight rippled through the fumes and dust. A terrible scorched smell of a dozen house fires, all at once. The whispers would go round town as the survivors bustled about, striving to return to their everyday lives: passing round the messages about who had gone, what was missing, who and what could never be brought back from the dead.

That morning Irene felt a gnawing sickness that pulled at her insides, making her throw up in the backyard privy as soon as they were back at Number Thirteen. She kneeled on the dank concrete floor and gripped on to the pan and everything was rocking like she was out at sea in a storm.

Lucky the cat was perfectly all right. He had been waiting for them when they came trooping back indoors, exhausted and covered in dust. 'That cat has more than nine lives!' Beryl had tried to make them laugh, but no one did.

Irene sat on her haunches and felt waves of nausea going through her and then gradually receding. She realised she could hear neighbours in the back alley. The women from a few doors down were hanging over their back walls, passing on the Chinese whispers, as ever. Jungle drums, Ma Ada always called it. Faster than the newsreels, faster than the *Evening Chronicle*. News went up and down these alley backs like a lightning flash.

'Simonside, Simonside . . .' they kept saying. A sibilant whisper. A name repeated again and again. 'Simonside bought it last night.'

Irene frowned. That was the far distant end of town. It was almost country. Views of the sea. A beautiful place, some of it. Less congested than here. 'Simonside. Simonside was hit.' But who did she know there? Did she know anyone who lived that way? Her mind was fuddled. She rubbed her eyes and smeared grit into them painfully. Who lived in Simonside? Why was she feeling so sick again?

She returned to the house, where Beryl was brewing up a big pot of tea. She was warming her hands on the woollen cosy as she placed it over the solid, reassuring shape of the Brown Betty pot. 'You look like you've seen a phantom out there on the netty,' she told Irene as she stepped back indoors.

'The women out there are saying Simonside was hit,' Irene said. Her thoughts had cleared of smoke and dust and now she had remembered who lived up that way. Bella and her family. That's who lived up Simonside way.

'Simonside?' Beryl was looking at her like the name meant nothing. She had a dull, numbed look about her that they all did this morning. There was also a horrible feeling that was familiar to Beryl. A secret, sneaking feeling of relief when you heard that somewhere else had been hit and devastated: thank God it was them and not us. Simonside sounded so distant and fancy and faraway. It might as well be on the moon.

Beryl started pouring big mugfuls of tea. 'We don't know anyone up that way, do we?'

Irene hurried from the kitchen.

In the parlour Ma Ada was petting Lucky and trying to reassure him. She looked up as Irene came thundering by. 'Hey, pet. What's up with thee, hinny?'

But Irene couldn't even answer. She squeezed through the overcrowded furniture of the room and headed to the hall, pulling her shawl back around her shoulders. Sam was standing there, talking in earnest whispers with Megan by the aspidistra. Irene barely noticed their hushed conference. Suddenly she didn't have time for all their clandestine nonsense. As she approached they sprang apart and the look on Megan's face was like a spitting cat's.

'Irene?' Sam asked, as she stormed past.

'I have to go,' she said, and the words came out thickly, choked-sounding, like she hadn't spoken out loud for years. Her throat was actually aching and hurting with dust and grime and a squeezing pressure that seemed to come from her heart and chest.

Irene ran out onto the street, which was quiet now. It was still only eight in the morning. Her heavy work shoes rang against the pavement and the sound was loud, staccato and somehow horrible. The whole street filled up with the noise of Dust Cart Harry coming round the corner with his shire horse and cart. Usually Irene would stop and talk and admire the huge, glossy, black beast. She loved being around horses again and went to talk to Harry and his ancient Hugo whenever she could. But not this morning. She went clattering past with her heart banging hard inside her chest.

She ran down the side lanes, cutting right through the middle of the Sixteen Streets. By now she knew her way through town. She could negotiate the quickest routes without much thought, which was just as well, because this morning her mind was all over the place. The streets swelled with all kinds of folk, struggling to go about their business. Not much bombing here in the centre of town. But the whispers still accompanied her. Simonside. Simonside. Eeeh, have you heard?

Irene caught the tram. Luckily she'd remembered to bring her little purse. She had only a handful of coins with her. She asked for her fare with a shaking voice. Then she sat there in agony, trying not to panic or cry or draw attention to herself. But everyone else on the tram was focused on their own private thoughts, caught up in their own personal dramas following a horrible night. No one even looked at her in her grimy shawl and her hair hanging down after a night sitting up awake underground.

She urged the tram to go faster, faster. But another part of herself was pulling back in resistance. I don't want to get there, she thought. I'd rather not know.

It was a horrible reversal of the route she had walked so contentedly, just a couple of weeks ago, with her Tom. They had left that gorgeous evening, just before Christmas, and a night of chatter and singing and everyone looking at them with such bright, welcoming faces. They had slogged through the snow in the shining darkness, back home from a very happy time. Now, in the drear dawn, not so long after, Irene was running back towards Bella's house with her heart thumping and bile rising up in her throat.

There was smoke and confusion and people milling round helplessly. Official bodies were there in their uniforms, issuing instructions and barking at people. It all looked quite chaotic to Irene. The noise was intense and blotted out her thoughts, which was a small mercy. For a while she was held up, roped into a chain gang passing buckets to a burning house. She stayed long enough to rub her hands red raw with the handles of the brimming pails, but then a warden noticed her and hoiked her out of the chain gang, reprimanding her severely:

'You can't go hefting bloody buckets, lass!' he growled, and sent her on her way.

She tottered through busy streets that had seemed so sedate and perfect, the first few times she had visited. These houses with their large gardens front and back and garages and bay windows had seemed the epitome of civilised living to her. They had seemed so untouchable. And yet they were so near to the coast. Bella had that wonderful view of the rolling silver sea, hadn't she? She had the perfect view of the wide open skies and the welcoming harbour: the huge, wide openness that the Luftwaffe had invaded last night.

Irene had the most hideous stitch. It was like a darning needle going right into her side, and the child was griping at her to stop. To stop dashing and haring about. She swung around one final corner, arriving at the cul de sac where Bella and her wonderful family lived.

All the houses here in this street . . . they were all right, it seemed. She had counted – how many? – three, four shelled-out ruins on the way through the estate. But here, the houses around Bella's seemed untouched. With her last few steps and her last few breaths before she turned the corner Irene even dared to hope that her friend and her family had escaped.

But, no. They were gone.

Their whole house was gone. It had been replaced by a litter of smouldering masonry and wood. It was hardly even recognisable as something that had once been a house. It was the only one in the little street to be destroyed.

The next-door neighbours had lost half their roof – but so what? A roof was just a roof. But this . . . this was utter destruction. There could be no hope whatsoever – Irene realised this at first glance – that anyone could have survived a direct hit like that. There was a crater at the heart of that house now and flames were belching out like they were coming straight out of hell.

The heart of that house was where she had sat with Tom, nonna, mamma, Tonio and the others, listening to them sing with their fine voices, their funny foreign-sounding carols. They'd all sounded like opera singers to Irene. They put her inept warblings to shame, but still she'd tried to sing 'The Holly and the Ivy' for them with Tom accompanying, picking out the tune one-fingered on their upright piano. The whole Franchino family had praised her rendition lavishly and she had basked foolishly in their pleasure and pride in their guests. She remembered the tart taste of the limoncello and that wonderful fish, stuffed with herbs from the old man's garden. It all seemed like about a hundred years ago, and now they were all gone. This heap of still-burning garbage was all that remained of them, down in the wine cellar that Tonio had thought so safe. This heap of smoking detritus was all that was left of their decades of living here at the very edge of their adopted town.

The firemen were there, and other grim-faced types in tin helmets with axes and buckets and business to be getting on with. To them she was just a gawker and a sightseer, like some of the others gathering at the end of the street. What were they all hoping to see? They weren't doing anything to help. Just staring. Gawping in slack-jawed dismay at the flames and the men getting to work. Maybe they were waiting for bodies to be brought out. Maybe they were ghoulish spectators. Or maybe they were looters.

That's what the wardens think we are, Irene thought wildly. She wanted to shout out: I was their friend! I was an invited guest inside the Franchino house! It was like a refuge to me, and a perfect, warm, luxurious home. I had never been anywhere more wonderful in my life . . . nor had I felt safer, and more like I was among loving friends . . .

A strange thought came out of the blue to her. I still have Bella's dress. The one she had borrowed, at first reluctantly, from Bella on the night they had their spontaneous dance at the Alhambra. That beautiful frock was still hanging in her wardrobe in the attic at Frederick Street. Purple crêpe de Chine. She had forgotten again and again to take it back, apologising each time she had seen Bella, and feeling embarrassed every time the girl laughed: 'You should keep it, Irene! That dress suits you like it never suited me.'

But it was expensive, you could see. All of Bella's clothes came from fancy shops up in Newcastle. She was only being polite, of course, and Irene could have kicked herself, each time she forgot to wrap the dress in tissue paper and return it to its owner.

Now it was too late. She would never be able to give it back. And all of Bella's other dresses would be cinders by now, lost somewhere inside that ragged inferno.

Along with Bella herself and all her family.

That was the moment that the shock took over Irene's body. She stiffened up for a moment and a great wracking sob came out of her throat, so loudly that the spectators around her turned to look. She heard a wailing that seemed as loud as a siren, and realised it was coming out of her mouth. Her emotions had caught up with her and now she was crying and heaving for breath, just standing there in the street among complete strangers. She had never been one to show her feelings and suppressed them when she could. But right now she had no choice in the matter. Wave after wave of misery and horror were going through her and she was being blown and buffeted about. She sank slowly to her knees and sat, panting on the verge. The grass was thick and oily.

I've got to stop, she thought. I've got to calm myself down. I'll have a miscarriage; I'll lose the bairn. I can't give in to this. I have to be stronger . . . And yet it was impossible. She groaned and wailed and her face was soaked with tears. She didn't care who saw her or what she even looked like, clawing up great clumps of grass and muck with her hands.

She made herself calm down. It took a lot of effort to drum down the panic in her mind. She shut her eyes and squashed her palms into the sockets until she saw stars. But still she could smell that horrible burning. She tried not to think what it was she could smell.

I have to get up and get away from here, she thought. The words were weirdly distinct against the backdrop of all the noise in her head. I can't do anything to help here. I can't get into that wreckage with the men and haul out bodies. It's too unstable and still in flames. All I can do is stand shivering in shock and the cold, and that isn't helping anyone.

Vaguely she wondered if she should stay and offer to identify bodies.

Forgive me, she offered up a quick prayer. I can't, though. I can't stand here and wait to look at remains. My heart would break. It's selfish of me: wicked, even. Shouldn't I do everything I can for the sake of those lovely people?

Irene turned away, pulling her shawl more tightly around her shoulders.

And she walked straight into a tall woman, who had just arrived in the street. A woman with raven black hair and a long woollen coat flaring open as she ran full pelt towards the disaster.

'Nooooo . . .!' screamed Bella, as she saw her home in flames.

Irene fell backwards, eyes out on stalks. She stood there with her mouth hanging open for a moment. Then she saw it was quite beyond doubt. This was her friend. It was her friend and she was alive and standing there with a face as white as the peaceful, milky clouds above South Shields. As white as the glorious ice cream that Tonio Franchino had created for all those years, from the recipe he had smuggled out of Naples.

Bella started screaming. She opened her mouth and one huge, single note came out. It was a horribly beautiful sound. She couldn't even howl in horror and pain without it sounding beautiful.

She stared past Irene and couldn't really comprehend the nightmarish sight of her ruined home. The only home she had ever known. Where she had always been safe under the protection of her beloved family.

'Are they all dead?' she asked Irene.

Irene opened her mouth to answer, and then realised she didn't know for sure. She didn't know anything for sure.

A warden came up and asked brusquely what their connection was with the family whose house it was. Irene answered quickly and explained about Bella. She realised as she did so that she didn't actually know how and why her dear friend had survived. Bella must have been out all night. She had been away, elsewhere during the night of the raid. She was coming back in the dawn in yesterday's clothes and encountering the worst news possible.

But she was alive! Irene wanted to scream it out loud and laugh and jump up and down, but she knew that she shouldn't, and that she couldn't. She was a mass of whirling confusion. Horror and joy were vying for supremacy in her breast.

'There's absolutely no chance,' the warden was telling her, keeping his voice low so that Bella wouldn't hear. 'It's obvious, isn't it, pet? Anyone can see.'

'But under the wreckage,' Irene tried to reason. 'They would have been in the cellar. They might be trapped there, safe and alive under all the timber and . . . and the . . .'

'We'll keep on digging and that,' said the oldish man. What use would he be? Irene found herself thinking nastily. He looked worn out and too weak. What good would he be to the firemen? He added: 'But it's burning down there. It's like a

266

furnace down in the cellar. You can't even see the worst, cause there's the house on top like a flattened pack of cards. But they reckon nowt could have survived down there. There's very little hope.' He glanced at Bella, who was frozen in shock, bracing herself as if she was preparing to run into the wreckage. 'Does she belong to the people who died in there?'

Irene nodded tersely.

'Whey, there's nowt you two lasses can do. She's off her head, you can tell, just looking at her. She'd be more hindrance than use. And you're expecting, aren't you?'

Irene frowned. She hated people seeing at one glance what was up with her, and then telling her, and deciding for her, what she could and couldn't do. 'Aye, I am.'

'Then the best thing you can do, hinny, is get that lass away from here. While they put out the fires and assess the situation and make everything safe again.' The old gent peered at Irene from under his hat and at first his expression was severe and commanding. Then his face softened and she knew that he was right, and that he meant well. What he means is that it's best if Bella's not here when they start bringing out what's left of her family. She really didn't need to be standing here and watching that. The warden was quite right.

'I'll take care of her,' Irene told him, and turned to take Bella in her arms. 'Hey, come on,' she told her softly.

Where can I take her? she fretted. Where can we go? The answer came to her at once. The ice cream parlour on Ocean Road. Franchino's. They could open up and make coffee and lock themselves in. It could be their refuge amid all this disaster.

And so that's what they did.

267

Chapter Twenty-Five

They sipped hot, frothy ersatz coffee all that morning and part of the afternoon. Irene kept going back repeatedly to the great big polished machine that Tonio had always tended so carefully, and worked its valves and various controls with an expertise she had honed over the past few weeks and months. The whooshing of the steam soothed her nerves and filled the air with busy noise.

Bella cried a little, noisily and passionately, as she sat in the booth at the back of the family cafe. She soaked through the hankies Irene passed her and didn't hold back. Irene was almost in awe of the loud, braying sobs and the wracking cries she let out. There was no embarrassment or crippling anguish to stymie her emotions. Most people Irene knew would do almost anything but let their true feelings out, even in front of their dearest friends.

But then, she had never seen anyone hit as hard as Bella had been. She'd never seen anyone suffer like she was suffering right now. Irene had never known anything as bad as this happen to anyone ever, she realised. Her friend had lost her entire family, in one fell swoop. They were all of them gone. Her whole home, her past, her belongings, everything. The faces that she had known all her life. It must be just like being killed yourself, Irene realised. Worse than that, in fact. It was like losing everything, and somehow having to find the strength to carry on in a world you felt you no longer belonged to.

Bella cried and raged and clung to her friend. Irene became alarmed and rather worried at being alone with her. What if she went hysterical and stayed that way forever? She sounded like she was losing her mind. What could Irene do about that? Was she going to be stuck here, behind locked doors, listening to this awful wailing for all time?

Gradually though, Bella grew exhausted and the first wave of violent grief subsided, like it had to. It went out like the tide, leaving her pale and wan. She sipped her coffee and grimaced and stared balefully at the shining zinc coffee counter. The two of them didn't say much for ages. What was there to say?

At last, in a voice that shocked Irene with its calmness and control, Bella started to talk. There was such a sweetness and richness to her voice as she talked about her father, her mamma, her nonna and her little brother. Irene had only been half aware before of the beauty of her friend's voice. She was musical in every fibre of her being.

She talked about her father coming to this country, so many years ago. All he had was a recipe that he wasn't even supposed to possess. It wasn't even an old family recipe, though in later years, when he was sentimental and romancing the story into a kind of legend, that's what he always claimed.

'No, it wasn't passed down through our family, that recipe. My father, he won it gambling,' Bella said. 'I forget the family that it belonged to, but they were the ones with the famous ice cream. Back in Naples. Up in the highest part of the town. The poorest, roughest, dirtiest quarter. The Grapellis! That's what they were called, I think. They were the ice cream kings, my father said, and it was this recipe that their old mamma had always protected with her life.

'Mamma Grapelli would sit on her doorstep on the steep cobbled lane with her dogs and brats playing in the street and she'd be mixing the ingredients in a china bowl, or she'd be polishing her revolver and spinning the chamber and filling it full of bullets. Then she'd be cracking eggs in the bowl and creaming sugar.

'Papa saw all of this going on . . . and he knew her boys. They grew up together, all together in that poor place, roaming the dusty streets. And it was one of those boys who gambled away the recipe in a game of cards with papa, and his mamma was furious. She was going to kill him, and she was serious. Then she sent the other boys after papa to get it back . . .'

Irene stared at her friend, gobsmacked by all of these details. This was like a movie. Like something she'd seen at the Savoy. She couldn't believe that Bella was talking about gangsters and revolvers and stuff like that, all taking place in real life. A proper, pistol-packing mamma in Naples, sending out ruffians to menace Bella's dad!

'He must have been spinning you a yarn,' Irene said. 'Surely . . .'

Bella shrugged tearfully and smiled for the first time that day. 'Papa always said he'd had to leave Italy in a hurry. He packed up everything overnight. He proposed to mamma very late on the Monday evening. They'd been courting for weeks. Suddenly he was in a rush. Nonna was sitting there with her needlepoint and she knew that something was up. The boy had got himself into trouble. She knew the signs. She had seen this kind of thing before. When you knew secrets, when someone needed to silence you, all that you could do was get out of town. She told her daughter to listen hard. If you want him, she said, you have to pack tonight. You have to flee.

'Well, mamma didn't want to leave Naples. Why should she? Just because this man said he loved her. Just because he had somehow got himself into trouble with his gambling. What was it, bad debt? Had he lost too much and couldn't pay? Papa shook his head: no, not at all. He had *won*. No one ever beat him at cards. Certainly not the Grapelli boys. No, he had triumphed and taken off them the thing that their family prized above all things: the source of their income and the few riches they had. The recipe. The legendary recipe that their mamma kept close to her heart quite literally, stuffed inside her whalebone corsets, scrawled in her own grandfather's hand on a scrap of old paper. Worn almost to nothing, but the most valuable thing their whole family possessed.

'My father would have given it back, gladly, for the sake of keeping the peace. But that wasn't good enough for the Grapellis. He had clapped eyes on the recipe and even that much had sealed his doom. He had to get out or they would garrotte him or shoot him or throw him into the sea weighted down with rocks. It was just as simple as that.

'"Oh, this is ridiculous," said my mamma. "Who could care so much about ice cream?"

'But her own mother knew, and she understood. She was already packing away her needles and wool and getting up to go and fetch her bags down from the top of her wardrobe. She understood the danger that my father was in. She had seen such things before. Yes, it was absurd and melodramatic. But families and the troubles they could stir up were absurd and melodramatic and extremely violent: that much she knew.

'My mamma kept saying how ludicrous it all was. All this over ice cream. "But just think of what ice cream it is," said Nonna. "Grapelli's. It is frozen nectar. It is like something from the gods. You know what people round here are like over that stuff. They go crazy for it."

'My mamma just shrugged at this. She'd never cared much for the stuff. Unlike everyone else in Naples at that time, she didn't have much of a sweet tooth. But that night she did as she was bade by the man who said he loved her, and packed her most precious belongings into two large cases.

'Then she noticed that her mother was doing the same. When Mamma asked her mother what she thought she was doing, Nonna shot back: "What, you think I'm going to stay here by myself and get bumped off by the Grapellis?"

'Legend has it that Nonna made my father stick a pin into an atlas, and that was how they settled on South Shields as their random, safe destination. So far in the north and over the frozen seas. The Grapellis would surely never find them there. Perhaps there was some truth in the story of the random pin: I never knew for sure.

'Now I'll never know,' she realised, with a jolt, sipping the cold dregs from her coffee cup. 'There are questions I never asked any of them. I thought we had all the time in the world. I took all their stories for granted. Me and my brother . . .' Her eyes went wide at the thought of her little brother, Ross. Perhaps for the first time it became clear to her that he was gone forever, too. That quiet little lad, Irene thought, feeling hollow with pain. That handsome boy. He was dead as well.

Bella carried on talking. 'We even got fed up and bored with their stories. We thought they were just fairy tales. We'd grown up hearing variations and exaggerations of these legends. We just thought it was the old folk being ridiculous. Old women with guns chasing them through the streets and down the hill as they raced for the midnight train to Rome. Vendettas over ice cream recipes. Fleeing the country and travelling under a cloak of darkness . . . We thought it was all such nonsense and we would laugh at them.

'It was a running joke in our family. Papa used to say: "Watch out for the man in the black hat and the white tie. That's the sign. One day they'll find us and come knocking at our door. They'll be after revenge for what they think I stole from them. They'll be angry that we have used their recipe, of course. But what else could we do? We had to live . . ."

'That was another family legend. Watching out for the man in the black fedora and the white silk tie. That's what all the Grapelli men had worn. "Watch out! One day they will come for us!" Papa had warned, and Grapelli had, down the years, become a bogie man to scare us kids with. Me and my brother would scream with terror when Papa told the old stories again. But as the years went by we found ourselves believing and listening less and less.

'And he really did come in the end, didn't he?' Bella said bitterly. 'The man in the black hat came calling eventually. He came knocking at their door last night . . .'

Irene didn't know what to say to that. She just hugged her friend as they sat in their booth.

Hours had passed by now and they had been left alone in peace. They were both startled by a loud banging at the front door. They jerked upright as if they had fallen asleep.

It was Arthur. His hands and face were pressed against the glass of the front door. The white flattened palms and the tip of his nose looked almost comical. Irene hurried over to let him in.

'I came as soon as I heard,' he gabbled. He was dressed in a weird assemblage of garments. He had an overcoat over a dressing gown and huge, baggy, black trousers. It was as if he was wearing half of that ragbag of second-hand clothes he had picked up at the rummage sale, all at the same time. He rushed to Bella's side.

'Have you been to the house?' she asked. 'Did you see?'

'Uh-hoh,' he nodded, and folded her into a firm embrace. His arms went around her and Irene could suddenly see how strong he was, and she thought about how warm that hug of his must be. 'I knew that you'd come here. I knew you'd hole up here.'

'W-where else could I go?' she asked, despairingly. 'There is nowhere else for me. At least we own this building. I'll have to live upstairs. I'll have to clear a space in the rooms he used for storage, all that old paperwork and junk. I'll have to make this place my home now . . .' Bella's mind was racing, blocking out the new parameters of her life. Her mind rebelled against the banality of such particulars.

How could she even think about things as mundane as where she was going to sleep at night and what she was going to do with the rest of her life? She was all alone on the face of the earth, as of today. What was the point in any of it, anymore? She might as well sit here in this booth with this empty cup of coffee forever. There really seemed like no point at all in going on.

Arthur looked at her, almost craftily. He looked as if he had suddenly thought of something he could say in order to coax her back into life. 'You do have the recipe, don't you?' he said.

Bella wore a faraway look. 'We were just talking about that. I was telling Irene the tale . . . all that nonsense that Papa used to come out with . . .'

'Aye, it's probably all just blarney and hogwash,' Arthur agreed. 'But you do have his recipe somewhere safe, don't you?'

She nodded heavily and a smile touched her beautiful, curving lips. 'Oh yes. He put it in the safe upstairs. With the deeds to this place, and the house, and his will and everything he deemed precious. He put the recipe somewhere safe . . . as insurance against the day the man came calling. The man in the black hat and the white silk tie . . .'

'Well, there you are, then,' Arthur said crisply. 'You have to carry on, Bella. You have to keep on doing your dad's work. This place is all yours now, and you just have to continue.'

Irene could have kissed him. He knew just the right thing to say. He had put determination and fire back into Bella's eyes. Then he turned to Irene: 'We'll all be needing some more of that coffee you brew so well, hinny. And maybe some grappa, eh? A nice little nip of grappa, as well.'

*

Later on it occurred to Irene to ask just how it was Bella had managed to survive the night her home had been bombed. Just where on earth had she been all night?

'She was at mine,' Arthur offered, relishing his grappa and staring defiantly at Irene. 'She was at my place last night. With me and my sister, Mavis. It was so late and so cold by the time we realised how late it was, we persuaded her to stay. And then the sirens went off . . .'

Bella looked abstracted and haunted then. It was as if she was just on the point of seeing how fortunate she had been. A fleeting shadow of relief went over her face, and then it crumpled again. She wept for a few silent moments and Arthur made her drink more of the potent spirit her father always kept under the counter.

Irene was still wondering what Arthur's home was like. She had never been invited, not even by Mavis. Story was, it was in the poorest and roughest corner of town. A row even shabbier than anywhere in the Sixteen Streets, with none of the inherent, brave dignity the folk of that quarter had.

'Eeeh, last night at yours seems like a hundred years ago,' Bella said in a hollow voice. 'It was such a happy evening. We had such a laugh.'

Irene hated herself for the swift, stabbing feeling of envy she got then. She felt left out of the gang. That was a shameful response, wasn't it? she thought. Fancy envying Bella! Even for a moment!

'Look here, pet,' Arthur said, taking hold of Bella's hand across the melamine table. 'You are very welcome to come to ours tonight. You know, you can call it your home as long as you need to, or want to. There's room enough for another, you know that. I mean, it's no palace. It's nowt like anything you're used to, but it's ours and you are welcome to share it with us.'

After this little speech of his Bella looked at her friend and tears fell silently down her face and she tried to smile her gratitude. 'Thank you, Arthur. I will take you up on that.

I-I've got nowhere else to go. I'm so lucky to have you and your sister to help me.' She hurriedly turned to Irene. 'And you, too, love. If it wasn't for you, I'd still be in that street, wailing and skriking and lying on the road by myself. You helped me right when I needed you most.'

Was it all that much, in the helping stakes? Irene thought probably not. Not like the help that Arthur was able to give her, offering her refuge and a new place to lay her head. That was the really important aid now. Irene should maybe offer refuge at Number Thirteen, where it was surely more comfortable than the rough place Arthur lived? And there was a bit more room now, with the men away at war. There was marginally more space for another woman. Especially one with no belongings to her name.

No belongings! No clothes! How on earth was Bella going to manage?

She imagined her having to wear the horrible, flea-ridden garments that Arthur salvaged from the markets and shops of North Shields. Poor Bella, who'd always been dressed so beautifully. She'd be going about in rags from now on, until she got settled. Eeeh, the poor lass. Irene had her evening dress she could return to her, but what good would that be for everyday use? It would be an insult, giving her that now. Irene tutted at herself. Why couldn't she come up with practical ideas, like Arthur did?

Now he was talking about how they'd have to contact official people and let them know where Bella was going to be staying. If they didn't tell the authorities where she was, they'd assume she had been lost in the same blast that had carried off her family.

The Italian girl gave a bitter little shrug. 'Perhaps that would be for the best. I mean, if everyone thought I was dead with them. I would be free then. I could simply wander away like a ghost. Because really, I should be dead. I should be with all of them. I don't deserve to be here on this earth by myself . . .'

Irene had never heard anyone sound both so lonely and guilty at the very same time.

'Now, look here, lady,' Arthur said angrily. 'Never let me hear you saying stuff like that again. You survived this terrible thing because you were meant to. You hear me?'

Bella stared at him. He was gripping her hands now, and the flesh was dimpling and going white.

'I don't believe in much,' said Arthur crisply. 'But I do believe that certain things are meant to be, and that we can't fight our destinies. And that also means that we have to grab our chances when we can. You are meant to survive this, Bella, and you can't just give up and give in to your sorrow. You have to flourish, for the sake of your mam and dad and your brother and your nonna. They'll be watching you and worrying over you. And what you've got to do, lady, is prove to them that you're gonna be all right. You're gonna be better than all right. You're going to live a happy life. For all of them.'

Irene gasped at his fierceness, and she realised that he was correct. Every word he had spoken was the exact right one. She could see the dawning realisation on Bella's face, and the determination creeping over her.

'I-I'll come to stay at yours, Arthur, if I may . . .' she said.

Outside it was dark already, and there was snow falling like it hadn't fell since Christmas. They drank some more grappa and Irene cleaned up the counter and the nozzles and pipes of the coffee machine. Then it was time to leave.

Arthur was in command. They would go by the police station and the town hall and tell all the relevant official bodies that Bella was alive and where she would be staying for the foreseeable future. Again, Irene was impressed by Arthur's firm good sense.

'And what about this place?' Irene asked, wringing out the dishcloths and hanging them to dry. Nothing worse than a foisty, damp dishcloth, she thought.

'This place?' Bella asked, glancing around at the immaculate tables and potted palms and pastel colours of the ice cream parlour's outdated art deco walls. 'Well, I'll open it up again when I'm ready to. This place will go on. I-It's mine now, and I need to keep it alive. I hope you'll be there to help me, Irene?'

'Of course!' Irene said.

'You need to get that old recipe out,' Arthur said. 'We have to see if you can mix up a batch of the special ice cream that your dad mastered so brilliantly . . .'

But all that was in the future, Irene thought, as they turned out the lights and locked up the parlour that belonged solely to Bella now. At the moment there weren't enough eggs in the whole of South Shields, and there certainly wasn't enough sugar. Right now there was nothing to make that magical ice cream out of . . . and maybe there would never be, for a very long time.

Suddenly it seemed like there would never be an end. To the war, to the sudden evil misery that could rain down out of the sky at any given moment. It was like there would never be a time that wasn't uncertain like this. No sugar for ice cream, and nothing to sweeten that feeling of terrible loss that hung constantly over their lives.

Arthur hooked his arm through Bella's, and Irene took the other side. She banished her private, gloomy thoughts, and became practical and cheerful and resolute for the sake of her friend. Bella had lost everything today. The things that everyone lived in dread of happening had happened to her today. Things could never get any worse.

They walked along through the quiet centre of the town as the snow swirled about them. It was like the whole place was in mourning, or had turned to their beds early, in order to catch up on last night's wrecked sleep.

And Arthur said it was all destiny. Everything was mapped out for you. That's what he firmly believed.

Did that mean he could get an inkling of what was coming for them all? Did he have some sort of magical foresight?

Irene wished that he would tell her more, about what was coming to her and what her own destiny might be.

Most of the pain of life was in the uncertainty about everything, she thought. We really don't know anything at all, do we? We're just left to scrabble around in the wreckage, trying to be as cheerful as we can.

'Won't there be gossip?' Irene asked suddenly. 'If an unattached woman moves in with you, Arthur? I mean, I know your sister Mavis lives there, too . . . but tongues might wag, you know.'

Arthur barked with laughter. 'Who cares? Let them wag!' He added, 'Where I live, it's not like the Sixteen Streets, where everyone's watching each other's comings and goings and there's gossip about everyone. Round our way . . . no one gives a hoot what goes on! No one will take a blind bit of notice.'

Irene wasn't convinced. She still thought people would think it was a funny business.

They walked together through the dark to Arthur's home. Irene found she was quite keen to see where Arthur and Mavis lived together.

'Let's sing, shall we?' Bella suddenly said. 'I want to sing.'

This startled her friends, who thought that singing would be the last thing she felt like doing.

Yet there was a song from the old country her dad used to sing to her. They had no clue what the words meant, but she taught them it as they made their way to Arthur's house, and all three of them sang it anyway.

Chapter Twenty-Six

Irene walked to work with Beryl, tucking her hair up into her new headscarf and preparing herself mentally for the day ahead as they joined the great crowd of women bustling towards the factory gates. The skies were pearly and dim at that time in the morning. The clouds were so dense it was like dawn had never happened and that dullness of the sky reflected her mood. But she refused to feel fed up.

'And so she's just handed her cards in? Are you sure?'

Beryl nodded. 'Megan's got rotten morning sickness. She says she can't stand the smell of the biscuits. She had no choice but to chuck work in and stay at home and put her feet up.'

Irene tutted. She didn't believe a word of it. 'Huh! You can't escape the smell of Wight's biscuits, wherever you go in the Sixteen Streets!'

'Exactly!' Beryl laughed. 'But you know her. She's a bolshy, lazy mare and she says she has no intention of going back to work at the factory.'

'We're best off without her,' said Irene, happy at the thought that Megan wouldn't be glaring at her across the conveyor belt anymore. She turned her attention to Beryl. 'What was your letter, anyhow, lady? You look like you're keeping a secret . . .'

Her sister-in-law was just about hugging herself with pleasure. 'Oh, Irene! I can hardly believe it! I've got news!'

Her enthusiasm was infectious. 'What is it?'

'They've asked to see me! At the shipyard! John Readhead and Company . . . They've called me in!'

Irene clapped a hand over her mouth. 'They're gonna train you to be a welder?'

'Now, I don't know that yet,' Beryl said, barely containing her excitement. 'But they've asked me in to see them! Next Monday! I shall have to ask for time off.'

Irene turned to her and hugged her hard. 'It's brilliant news, hinny.'

Beryl laughed. 'Listen to you! Saying "hinny" like the rest of us! Eeeh, Irene Farley! We'll soon have you talking like a native!'

That day Beryl was back in the packing room with Irene and Mavis, taking up Megan's abandoned place. Irene kept grinning at her sister-in-law, delighted by the glow of excitement that surrounded her at the idea of getting her hands on welding gear.

'I wouldn't like to use all that dangerous equipment,' Mavis said, when they explained it all to her. 'I'd probably burn my own face off.'

Irene chuckled. 'Perhaps you'd be best off not touching that sort of equipment, Mavis.'

'And working with all those men, as well! I'm not sure I'd fancy that. I bet they won't be too happy, with girls turning up to do their jobs . . .'

Irene shrugged. 'They'll just have to lump it, won't they?'

But Mavis was already on to another topic. 'Fancy Megan not coming back to work! Why, you're further on with your baby than she is, Irene. And you're still here! You're not going anywhere yet, are you?'

Irene smiled tightly. 'Not yet, I'm not!'

She was aware of Beryl's watchful eye on her. Yes, she was in some discomfort, standing up all this morning and getting on with the same back-breaking work. It was definitely harder to keep herself going now. She was gritting her teeth. She would have to think about giving up work eventually.

But did she really want to spend all her days at home at Number Thirteen under the same roof as her equally pregnant nemesis?

At break they all went outside into the cold yard to eat their usual bread and dripping, which they'd kept wrapped in grease-proof paper in their pinny pockets. They sat in the gap between the factory buildings with some of the other lasses – Mary, Effie, Edith and Glad – from their section and munched tiredly together. Irene could feel Beryl's beady, appraising eye on her the whole time.

'Are you sure you're feeling OK?'

'I'm fine. It's just a bit more . . . arduous than I thought it would be today.'

Beryl had warned her. She'd said, 'Look at my muscles! Look at how rock hard my arms have gone! I'm like bloody Popeye, working on that factory floor! Do you want arms like this?'

It was true that Beryl was good and strong from working at the factory, but there was no way she was looking like a fella, as she jokingly claimed. No, to Irene she looked strong and healthy, and that's precisely what Irene wanted to be. No way she wanted to loll about in the parlour drinking weak tea with Ma Ada, like Megan was content to do. She shuddered at the thought of that tea Ma Ada liked, made from three-times-used tea leaves. Pale and weak as nun's water. No, she wanted to feel strong. She wanted to stay at work for as long as she could.

But her head was pounding and she was aching from head to foot already. It had only been a couple of hours today and she couldn't imagine how she'd feel by five o'clock this evening. Then there was the next day to get through, and the next, then the next.

There were some new girls in the packaging department today. They had been newly transferred from the bake house and were glad of the respite from the heat.

'Hey, you're the lass in the ice cream parlour, aren't you?' one of them asked, as they sat there on their break.

Another one piped up: 'Aye, and I've seen you out with some young fella at the pictures.'

The girls introduced themselves and Irene reflected that it was true: South Shields was so small, there was always someone who knew what you were getting up to, and what your business was. Beryl was chattily describing how Irene fitted into the Farley clan, and the two young women in their headscarves – tied with ludicrously large bows – studied her carefully. 'Well, I wouldn't be working here if I was expecting like you are,' one of them told her firmly. 'I wouldn't take the risk.'

Irene hadn't thought of it as risky, just arduous. But as the rest of the day went by and she slogged through the hours, the girl's words played on her mind and she wondered whether she was putting her body under unnecessary strain.

When they walked home that evening through the dark, chilly streets, the sisters-in-law were unusually quiet.

'I'm sorry, Beryl, I must seem like I'm in a mood. But I'm not, I'm just feeling absolutely wrecked . . .'

Beryl glanced at her worriedly as they trogged up the cobbled hill to the Sixteen Streets. 'I reckon it's about time you started looking after yourself more.'

'You look very pale,' Sam told her on Saturday morning as she sat drinking her tea in the parlour. It was the first day in what seemed like a month that she hadn't been out the door while it was still dark. 'You don't look very well.'

His words set off alarm bells for Ma Ada, who peered into Irene's eyes and felt her forehead for fever. 'Hmm, I don't like the look of you, hinny. I reckon you've over-exerted yourself.'

Irene wasn't giving in that easily, though. She took one look at Megan, who sat curled on her own chair, sleek as a cat and well-rested. She thought: I have to keep on working. I don't want to be stuck at home with her any more than I have to. Megan narrowed her eyes and shot daggers at Irene, as if she knew she was thinking about her.

Later that day Irene was over at the Robin Hood, having a cup of tea poured by Cathy Sturrock. 'Are you sure I can't offer you a glass of stout?' Cathy asked. Irene shook her head at first. 'Ah, go on, then,' she smiled, giving in, and was amazed at how easily the velvety drink slipped down. She asked for a second, and started to feel a little swimmy and giddy. She sat there with Cathy, feeling more relaxed than she had in weeks.

'It's medicine! It's good for you, just like it says on the adverts,' Cathy smiled.

Irene hadn't been able to touch booze since New Year's Eve. Even the smell of hops when she stepped inside the public house had made her feel a little queasy but now she was beginning to feel marvellous. She basked in the glow of the fire and relished Cathy's gossipy company, and Irene found herself glad to be away from all the Farleys for a little while. Coming here was a safety valve for her. Cathy would listen while she got all her complaints out of her system.

'Is there any word of Bob?' Cathy asked, keen to hear about her sometime pot man. And there was more to it, too, Irene knew. She found it amazing, the way this clever, vital, amazing woman's face lit up when she mentioned Bob's name. To Irene, Bob was just Bob. A bit slow, a bit infuriating, but utterly kind and loyal. The way Cathy talked about him, it was like he was an Adonis. He was like something out of the old legends brought down to walk about on the earth. He wasn't just Bob, who slept under the stairs and about whom Megan was usually furious.

Irene told Cathy about the latest communications from Bob, who was expecting to go abroad any day. He was still away being trained in County Durham, and from the vague hints he'd been allowed to drop, it seemed that he was going to be shipped a very long way away.

Cathy looked dismayed. 'He'll not be around when his bairn is born,' she said. 'Not if they send him out to the East, or somewhere. Poor Bob. He's too good for Megan. I don't care who hears me say it. That wife of his is a bloody shrew.'

Irene wasn't going to argue with her about that. A shrew – that was exactly right. She sipped her tea and smiled. There was some devilment in Irene that afternoon. Something was loosening her tongue – rather unwisely. Perhaps it was her arduous week that made her careless, or her resentment of Megan sitting around so smugly on her arse all week. Either way, she said something to Cathy Sturrock just then, as they sat in the snug of the Robin Hood, that she really shouldn't have.

'Aye, she is a shrew. She's a proper bitch sometimes, as well. And you know something else, too, Cathy? I don't even think that the bairn in her belly really belongs to her Bob.'

As soon as the simple words were out, she knew she had done dead wrong. Cathy jolted and stared at her, white-faced. 'What do you mean?' she said, suddenly serious.

Oh God, why can't I just shut up? Irene thought. My bloody trap. I can't help opening it. And now the damage was done. Cathy's livid green eyes were turned on her like searchlights.

I'm turning out like my bloody ma, Irene despaired: her ma was known for causing trouble between all her neighbours in the village, just to keep herself entertained.

But that's not why I said it, Irene thought. I don't *really* want to cause trouble, do I? Do I?

But Cathy was grabbing hold of her arm. 'What are you saying, pet? How could you possibly know anything like that?'

It was like Cathy felt far more involved than she ought to. Of course, Irene thought: that's because she loves Bob. That's what it was. And Bob was being duped in the worst possible way by his wife.

Now Irene couldn't cover up what she knew. 'The bairn really isn't his own,' Irene repeated.

'What!? Irene, tell me everything you know. Right now.' Cathy was going to get it all out of her, by hook or by crook.

Irene took a deep breath and carried on. 'It stands to reason, doesn't it? They were trying for ages to have a bairn. That's what they always said, and it never took. They had given themselves up to the thought of never having one. Then all of a sudden – guess what? She's up the duff.'

Cathy waved this away. 'Oh, that's just how it happens sometimes.' Then she leant in closer to examine Irene's face. 'Unless . . . you know more about it, pet? Don't you? You live cheek by jowl with them. You know something, don't you, Irene? You're holding something back.'

There were no other drinkers in the snug this evening, just a few old men in the public bar. Even so, Cathy's voice was getting too loud for Irene's comfort.

'I just . . . I just don't know,' Irene said. Her heart was pounding, because she'd kept all this stuff pressed well down inside of her. She'd hardly said a word to anyone. Was she scared, or was she excited by the thought of letting out a little of what she knew? She didn't know. But it couldn't harm anyone, could it? Cathy Sturrock was in love with Bob – secretly, hopelessly. Surely she'd never do anything to harm him.

No, it was Megan – Bob's own spiteful wife – who was setting out to harm him.

'I think the baby she's going to have is . . . our Sam's,' Irene said, in a quiet voice.

Cathy Sturrock simply stared at her. She sank back onto her wooden chair, her face all creased up. 'Nay, lass,' she breathed sibilantly. 'That can't be. That can't be true. They'd never . . . surely, they'd never carry on . . . not under the same roof! How could they? How could you do so much as fart in that little house without the whole family finding out?'

Irene almost wanted to laugh at Cathy's vulgarity. The land-lady looked thunderstruck, and Irene was amazed and appalled at her own capacity to cause this reaction in her friend.

Quickly, without much embellishment, she told the tale of how she'd seen the two of them – Megan and Sam – at the Alhambra dance hall together. Looking shifty and strange. Looking hot and sticky and furtive as they embraced. And then she mentioned the brief couple of conversations she had managed to get with Sam, and the queer things he had said about Megan. About how it was like she was somehow coercing him into carrying on with her.

'Oh, my God, then it's true . . .' Cathy gasped, her hands covering her mouth.

And then, as if to clinch it, Irene told her how awful Megan had been to her for weeks and weeks. Megan had never been Irene's number one fan, of course. Looking back, she had seemingly resented her since the Norfolk girl had first moved in and taken up everyone's attention for a short while. And then there was the dust-up in the packaging room. But it was since the night at the Alhambra and Megan knowing that Irene safeguarded one of her secrets, that the older girl had been behaving quite appallingly. Irene was convinced that she had tried to make her fall on the stairs that time. And there were other things. Nasty remarks. Little jabs of her elbow. Hateful looks when no one else could observe.

'I feel like she's cursing me and my baby under her breath all the time,' Irene told Cathy. 'I've never really felt hated by someone before, and that's exactly how this feels. Megan absolutely hates my guts.'

'Oh, pet,' Cathy's natural protective instincts took over, and she came across to give Irene a hug as she started to bubble with tears.

'I keep crying about things all the time,' Irene said, once she'd settled down a bit. 'I don't mean to come over here and whinge all over you, and tell tales behind other folk's backs.'

The truth was, Irene was completely shattered with exhaustion, and a bit tiddly, and she hardly knew what she was saying anymore. She watched Cathy grow thoughtful and intent.

'What are we going to do about it, I wonder?' Cathy said. 'I mean . . . if they're lying and carrying on together. If poor Bob thinks that it's his bairn growing in that skinny cow's womb . . . I mean, that's not right, is it?'

'Does it matter?' asked Irene, who had thought this over a lot. 'Bob and Sam are brothers. Does it really count for all that much, the difference between them? Bob really wants a kid, and if it just wasn't happening for them before . . . So, all the lies apart, does this really matter, in the grand scheme of things?'

Cathy looked outraged. 'Why, Irene, pet! Of course it does! There's Bob – thinking he's on top of the world! Thinking everything's turned out right at last! And they are *betraying* him. That's what it is, hinny. It's bloody awful betrayal. There's no other word for it.'

An uneasy feeling was settling into Irene's belly now. She felt sick to her stomach suddenly. She had a feeling that she had unleashed something dreadful. Pandora's box had been opened and there was no way the lid was going to go back down.

'What are you planning to do, Cathy?' she asked, seeing that the landlady was thinking furiously and pacing about in the snug. She had placed all the cards in Cathy's hands . . .

The realisation came to Irene: Cathy could now see the wedge that she could successfully drive into the heart of Number Thirteen. She wanted Bob separated from his wife. That was her unspoken desire. Now, perhaps, she had the means to accomplish this. The crafty, calculating look on Cathy's florid face surprised Irene and she saw that she had perhaps gone and made a terrible mistake.

'There's only one thing I can do, in all good conscience,' said Cathy. 'I'm going to tell the old woman. I'm going to inform Ma Ada that she's harboured betrayers under her roof. They're like a nest of vipers, and they've played her best and most innocent son wrong. They've played him for the fool they think he is.'

Irene sat up sharply. 'Cathy . . . you can't go and tell her!'

Cathy Sturrock tossed her lustrous hair and downed the last of her stout. 'You just watch me, hinny. You just watch me!'

Irene opened her mouth to protest again. She had to try to stop her. 'Cathy, you'll ruin everything. This will cause chaos over the road!'

But Cathy was already gone. In seconds she was across Frederick Street and banging on the door of Number Thirteen.

Chapter Twenty-Seven

Early the next day, Irene knew just where to go to find Sam.

He had fled from the house and not come home all night, but Irene had a feeling she knew where to find him.

It was a bright, clear morning over South Shields. Beautiful, really. The days were starting to lengthen slightly, and it felt like they were emerging from those dark, wintry days at last. There hadn't been an air raid for several weeks and it even felt like there was a note of optimism in the air. Or maybe that was just the early morning breeze, fresh and salty, from the sea, as Irene hurried along Frederick Street, going about her business.

Last night, everyone had been in a flap. They were thinking he must have gone off on a bender, drinking himself sick. 'Just like his dad Billy used to do,' Ma Ada gloomed. 'That's his dad in him. That was always his response to any kind of trouble.'

But Irene knew that Sam wouldn't be out drinking himself stupid. For one thing, he didn't have the money. And it wasn't as if there was enough beer in the pubs for anyone to go on a really serious bender. Everything had to be shared out fairly.

Oh, Sam, Irene thought.

She crossed the quiet roads of the town centre, where life was only just starting up for the day. Market stallholders were arriving and beginning work. Shop workers were opening shutters and blinds. Irene bustled past all of them, making determinedly for that special part of town, where she knew Sam liked to sit and think.

Up the hill. Off the beaten track. A spot where he knew he could be quiet. A certain corner that was drenched in the silence of antiquity.

Sure enough, there he was. Perched on rubble that had been there almost two thousand years, and staring out at the sea. As Irene went across to him through the long, dewy grass, he didn't move an inch. It was like he was in a trance.

'I'm going to run off to sea,' he told her, without looking round. Without even turning to see who it was approaching, he seemed to know it was Irene, and this obscurely pleased her.

Oh, but he looked dreadful. The silly beggar was the white of curds and whey. His hair was plastered down to his forehead with the showers that had fallen in the night. All his clothes were sodden.

'Have you sat out here all night long?' she gasped.

'I wanted to see the dawn,' he said.

'Daft,' she tutted, and sat beside him. She had brought a flask of hot sweet tea in her shopping bag and set about unscrewing the lid and pouring him a small cup.

'Shouldn't you be at work at the biscuit factory?' he frowned.

'I've jacked it in,' she said, pressing the steaming cup of tea into his hands. 'I've told them at last, I want my cards. I worked for as long as I could, but I was a fool for thinking I could keep up with all the other lasses. I need to conserve my energy a bit more. For the bairn.'

'Aye, the bairn,' Sam nodded. Then his face crumpled up. 'The bairn.' He sipped his tea and she noticed that he was shaking. Something really bad was happening to Sam, she thought. Maybe he was having a complete nervous collapse.

And it's all my fault, she thought.

'W-what are they saying at home?' he asked, after a few grateful gulps of hot tea. Irene had taken a bit more of the weekly sugar ration than she ought to.

'No one's up yet,' she said. 'But last night they were going on and on.'

'About me?'

'About the whole thing. Your ma's going crackers, of course. But it'll all die down. She'll calm down in the end.'

'The gossip will spread round the doors, of course,' he said. 'The whole street, and then all the streets beyond. I'll lose my job, naturally. They won't want me when my shame comes out. When everyone knows.'

Was it really so bad? Irene wondered. She had been shocked to learn about what Sam and Megan had been up to, right enough. But her reaction had been nothing like Ma Ada's.

'It's forbidden!' the old mother had gasped, clutching her throat, as if unseen hands were trying to strangle her. 'This is wickedness! It's original sin! And under my roof!' The old woman collapsed into her chair and had to be revived by her daughters-in-law and a small nip of sherry from the sideboard. Her face was haggard and wan. 'This is *incest*,' she murmured, in a dreadful voice.

Irene didn't tell Sam exactly what his ma's reaction had been. She didn't tell him too much about the wailing and moaning and the somewhat Biblical language.

She had stood there, staring at Ma Ada, fearful that she was going to expire on the spot. Lucky clambered all over the old lady's lap, looking concerned, clicking at her tights with his claws. Ma Ada had kept raging on about incest and forbidden fruit and how Sam and Megan would drag the whole family into hell with them with this misbegotten bastard.

And Cathy Sturrock had stood there in the parlour in her hat and coat, pursing her lips in a strange expression of satisfaction.

She had come to impart the news, which had had even more of an impact than she was expecting. As the sobbing and lamenting became louder she even started to look alarmed. She had shot Irene a look that made Irene think she was having second thoughts about having let the cat out of the bag.

But it was too late now. Ma Ada knew the truth.

And she was ready to confront Sam with it when he came in from the docks that evening.

His fresh, bright-faced happiness. The Sam they all knew and loved. He came marching into the scullery at the end of his shift, mucky and shedding his boots and his donkey jacket before he set foot in the parlour. Grinning and glad to be home at the end of the day. That smile faded in an instant when he saw his ma's face.

Because she knew his terrible secret.

'Your nasty fancy woman is in her cupboard under the stairs,' his ma said, in a thunderous voice. 'We've shouted and shouted. We've told her we know the truth. But she won't come out. That idle trollop! That wicked little Jezebel. I've harboured a viper in my bosom!' Ma Ada's voice was starting to rise in pitch and volume. She was whipping herself back up into fury. 'And you! You, Samuel Farley! You've betrayed us all! With your base desires! With your wicked sinfulness!'

Sam had stood there with his boots in his hands and the laces dangling down, hardly able to comprehend what his ma was telling him.

'I know the truth, lad,' his mam had growled. 'And I know that the bairn is yours. The bairn growing in the belly of that harlot under the staircase – it's yours, isn't it?'

It was all Sam could do to nod, dumbly.

Then all hell had broken loose, for quite some time. He had women shouting at him, both Ma Ada and Beryl. Irene simply stood there dumbly. I did this. I did this. That was all she could think, as she watched his face drain of all colour and expression. It would all be a secret still if it wasn't for stupid me.

After a while Sam simply turned around, his boots still in his hands, and he walked out the way he had come. And he hadn't come back all night.

'Bad blood! It's bad blood!' Ma Ada had cried. 'It's his da! It's his bloody Da Billy coming back through him! I thought he was a good lad! I thought he was a kind, sweet lad . . . I've failed, Beryl. I thought I'd brought them up to know right from wrong . . . I thought I'd taught them to keep away from . . . from . . . wickedness . . . and trollops . . .'

So the night had gone on. Megan had not emerged from her tiny room under the staircase, and Ma Ada fulminated in colourful language, and moved on to the emergency brandy.

'I'll never recover from this,' she vowed, in an awful whisper.

Now, in the calm of daylight, Irene was staring at Sam's handsome profile as he watched the horizon and imagined himself running off to sea. Would they take him? With his heart and feet and eyesight as faulty as they were? And with his propensity for causing bother with his godless evil and his sleeping with harlots?

'I don't even know why I did it,' he said at last. 'It wasn't even like I made a choice to do it. I don't remember choosing . . . or even wanting her. It's not like I sat there, night after night for ages, lusting after my sister-in-law. You must believe me, Irene. It wasn't like that. Why, I don't even really *like* her all that much. She's a sly piece of work, I've always thought that. A muck-raker. A back-stabber.'

'Then . . .' Irene said, 'why, Sam? Why did you do it?'

She remembered how they'd talked a bit about it before. A little bit. She'd tried to get the truth out of him; she had tried to understand. He'd made it sound like Megan had controlled him. He had made it seem like he'd had no will of his own. But Irene knew that had to be nonsense. Men always put the blame on women. All that femme fatale stuff. It was just from the movies, wasn't it? Megan couldn't have put a spell on him like that. It just wasn't something that happened in real life, was it?

He sighed and hung his head. 'No one had ever talked to me the way she did. Everyone in our family, and the family round the doors . . . everyone always treated me like a little lad, all my life. I was the youngest. I was like a happy-go-lucky little daft lad. That's what they all expected me to be, all my life. Our Sam. Well, Megan wasn't like that. She noticed me. She treated me differently. And when I was with her . . . I felt like a man. An actual man.'

Irene thought about this for a few moments. 'I don't really understand any of this.' The way men talked, it was all so strange to her. Like being a man was something they had to prove, one way or another. They had to live up to it somehow, and show they were good enough. Really, it was all a lot of daftness, as far as she was concerned. She hated the way fellas would vie with each other and get into fights and show off and go strutting around like a bunch of fighting cocks.

It wasn't how women went on at all. Women were women, and they knew when they arrived at a grown-up state. There was a kind of hallowed ritual and sense of gradual becoming: there was a sureness about a girl's arrival at the state of mature womanhood. It was something Irene remembered well, and she remembered being glad, and proud of feeling grown-up.

Boys and men: it was all quite different. To her eyes, they seemed so hopeless and disorganised at becoming themselves. It seemed to involve a lot of violence and trouble, every time.

'You're a daft lad,' she told him.

'I know.' He smiled at her ruefully. Still the same Sam. Not the wicked demon his ma had spent the previous evening castigating.

'But I still love you,' Irene said, because she knew he really needed to hear that from someone this morning.

'Thanks, hinny,' he grinned. 'But what am I gonna do, though, eh? What can I do, to put all this right?'

Irene already knew the answer. She had lain awake all night, thinking it over. Now she just had to convince everyone in the know to adopt her plan, and then everything would be all right. She was sure of it.

'We lie about it,' she said, suddenly and decisively. 'We lie through our teeth about it. We keep the whole thing secret. For Bob's sake.'

Irene wasn't a sly or conniving kind of person. That just wasn't in her nature. She liked things to be straightforward, and for people to be honest. Really, she had surprised herself with this idea she suggested and the plan that she laid out to Sam and the others later that day.

'It's the best way,' she said. 'It's the only way of making it work. And of keeping the family together, and making sure that everyone is happy.'

Sam just stared at her. Lying about it? Covering it all up? Pretending that his brother Bob had really been given his heart's desire, and that the coming babby was his?

'That can't work,' he said flatly. 'Bob will smell a rat.' Even Bob. Even daft Bob who knew less about the workings of the world than a bairn.

Irene shook her head. 'No, it can work. I'm sure of it. We just need to talk with your ma and with Megan, and make them agree.'

Sam didn't dare look hopeful. He agreed to return to Frederick Street with Irene and weather the storm, and broach her idea.

Irene felt triumphant, leading him back home. She had found him and brought him back. She had done a good thing.

He stood shaking outside his own front door when they got there. The house he'd lived in all his life. The place that had always been a refuge to him. And now he was terrified of stepping foot indoors. He was covered in shame. All the dirty stuff he'd been tempted into doing. Stuff so rude and wonderful he could hardly believe it when it was happening. The thrill of mucking about in quiet moments and quiet corners with Megan. The family knew about it now. All his secret shame was out in the open. Worst of all, his ma knew about the pleasure he had taken, and she would be disgusted with him. Appalled by him. Surely he should have been different to the common ruck of men? Surely her Sam was better than the rest?

But he wasn't. He had known he wasn't. He was just a man. Just the same as the rest of them. And now it was time for him to face the consequences of that.

Having Irene with him – and Irene having a plan, no matter how crazy – made him feel braver, though.

They stepped into the dark hallway. It was just before dinner-time and the house was quiet. Lucky padded up to them and made a querulous mewing noise, turning round and leading them into the parlour.

Irene had to be the strong one, leading him indoors.

Ma Ada was waiting in her parlour, looking like Churchill in his war room, preparing to launch the offensive.

Megan sat at the table, her eyes cast down, tracing idle figures in the tablecloth's lace with her fingers.

'Can I make a pot of tea for everyone?' asked Beryl, hovering in the scullery doorway, looking worried.

'I'm pig sick of tea,' Ma Ada grumbled. 'I've been up all night drinking tea and I've had a bellyful.' She glared at her son as he took a seat at the table, and Irene sat beside him, looking supportive and brave. 'You found him, then. Well done, Irene.'

'He's frozen to the bone,' Irene said. 'He's been out all night, walking the streets.'

His ma shrugged, like she couldn't care less: like she was about to wash her hands of him.

'We need to talk this through,' Irene said, and took a deep breath.

'Oh, yes?' Ma Ada glared at her. 'What do we need to talk about exactly? That I've harboured evil under my roof all this time? That I thought I lived in a godly house, full of godly folk, and I was mistaken all along?' She put her hands up to her face to hide the tears that were starting to fall. 'I blame meself! This is all cause I got out of the habit of going to church! The Father was right! I should have been warding off the divil and his lascivious ways! He's got into my home and made a mockery of us!'

Sam couldn't stand seeing his ma upsetting herself. 'Nay, Ma. It's not like that. The devil's got nowt to do with it. This is just daft mistakes that people make. That anyone could make . . .'

He was on thin ice, even Irene could see that.

'Anyone could make that mistake?' Ma Ada's eyes flashed furiously. 'What are you saying? You took your sister-in-law to bed and it was an accident?'

He stared at his hands. 'I never took her to bed . . .' he mumbled.

'Pardon?' snapped his ma.

'I said, we never went to bed. It wasn't like that.'

Ma Ada looked disgusted. 'Then pray, tell me, what was it like?'

Megan laughed out loud then, making Irene almost jump out of her skin. Her laughter was piercing and nasty, like she had nothing but contempt for her whole step-family. 'We did it in your scullery, Old Ma Ada!' she jeered. 'That's what it was like! It was brutish and filthy and wicked and we loved every moment of it, didn't we, Sammy?'

Sam stared down at the table, refusing to meet her eye.

Ma Ada was aghast. Her voice came out very hollow as she repeated: '*In . . . my . . . scullery?*'

'Aye!' Megan laughed again. 'What do you think of that, then, eh? When we should have been doing our chores and running around doing your bloody bidding like we always do. Why, you deserve to have your scullery defiled, you old crow!'

Ma Ada gasped in horror, as if Satan himself had manifested in her parlour. Megan stood up and glared at them all, even Beryl, who was still trapped in the doorway of the scullery, holding the empty teapot.

'How dare you!' cried Ma Ada weakly.

'And how dare you, you old witch!' shouted Megan. 'You've got us all trapped in here, in your dark little house. We're like handmaidens to your oh-so-precious sons! The brave bloody Farley boys! They're like legends round here! And some bloody use they are! Especially Bob – especially the one I got myself lumbered with! The bloody duff one – that's who I got! Do you blame me for trying to take a bit of comfort? For trying to have a bit of fun?'

Ma Ada couldn't get her words out to reply. She was spitting feathers and looking so agitated Irene was worrying for her heart. 'Look out now, Megan,' Irene said, trying to calm things down. 'Stop shouting at her. She's had a shock, and you're making things much worse.'

Megan squawked with delight at Irene's intervention. 'Oh, you're speaking up now, are you, Irene? Good little Irene. Timid little Irene. Butter wouldn't melt in her bloody mouth, Irene!'

'Megan . . .' Sam said, in a low, warning voice, but she didn't take a blind bit of notice of him. As far as she was concerned, the youngest Farley boy had served his purpose and was of no interest to her whatsoever now.

'Don't, Megan . . .' Beryl tried to intercede. 'Don't you think you've done enough damage?'

'Hardly!' Megan jeered. 'My life's been wrecked! Look at me – living under the bloody stairs! Knocked up and married to that idle lump, Bob! Living in this flamin' shithole!' She rounded the dining table and towered over Irene. 'And you, Irene! You think you've got the right to meddle in my life and make it even worse. Dragging that old cow-bag Cathy Sturrock round here! Letting her ruin everyone's lives by telling the so-called truth. Oh, I bet she loved doing that, the bloated old bitch. She's been after my Bob for years and she's just been biding her time. You with your tittle-tattle, Irene, you let her swan in here and smash up everyone's lives!'

Irene gasped at this. 'But I never did . . . I never intended to smash up . . . anyone's lives.'

Sam jumped up to his feet. 'Megan, if anyone's ruined our lives, then it's you and me who's done it. We are all responsible for our own actions.'

'Oh, bugger off, you stupid sod and sit back down.' Megan snarled at him and prepared to launch one last potshot at Irene: 'You've made everything worse since you've been here, Irene Farley. You've spoilt everyone's lives, just by being here. You play the sweet and innocent, but I've always known, you're a conniving, sneaky little bitch, you are. You've been intent on causing bother round here since day one. And now you have. I hope you're happy with yourself!'

For a moment Irene thought the furious girl was going to slap her, but Megan obviously thought better of starting a physical fight. It probably wasn't the best idea for two pregnant women to start ripping each other's hair out, no matter how much they felt like doing so.

Instead, Megan managed to gather control of herself and stormed out of the room and into the hall. They heard the door of her tiny room under the stairs slam shut.

'We'll not see her for a while,' Beryl said quietly. 'She'll keep out of the way for a bit, knowing her.' Beryl turned into the scullery, deciding that she would make that tea after all. It was an excuse for her to duck out of the tension in the parlour.

Sam stood up. 'I'm going to bed. I'm dead on me feet.' He was swaying as he stood there, and Irene saw that he was trembling.

His ma didn't even bother answering him, or paying any attention as he left the room.

Irene was left with her own thoughts.

Megan was lying, wasn't she? She was just being as horrible as she possibly could. That's all her words added up to. Irene knew that she wasn't really as conniving and sly as Megan seemed to think. How had the girl ever got that impression?

Lucky jumped from Ma Ada's lap into Irene's own. He'd never been as friendly as that with her before. It was like he was trying to console her, by padding at her legs with his tiny paws and then settling down to doze on her lap.

Maybe I really am conniving and nasty? And I don't even realise it? Maybe Megan is even right about me? Maybe things were better here before I ever came to stay . . .

Later that day Irene bravely went to see Ma Ada in her room. The old woman had taken to her bed with a raging headache while Beryl and Irene tried to get on with the rest of their day. Irene popped out for a few errands and when she returned she took a drink up to her ma-in-law.

'She's gone,' was all Ma Ada would say. She had a hundred-weight of bedclothes over her shivering body and her hairnet on. She would hardly look at Irene when she spoke.

'Megan's gone?' Irene asked.

'Who'd you think I meant? The Queen of Sheba?' Ma Ada tutted. 'I heard the front door bang some time after you went

301

out for the shopping, Irene. She's cleared out her little room under the staircase and she's fled.'

Behind her Irene heard Sam's bedroom door creak open, and she was aware of him standing in the hall behind her, listening in.

'Where's the daft girl gone?' Irene was asking now, and Sam knew that her persistent questions would be bugging his mam. Irene was risking a full-scale eruption of volcanic temper.

'She left a note about going back to her people,' Ma Ada rumbled. 'They live on a farm near Hartlepool, or somewhere. She's gone back to beg them to take her in, I reckon. She always said they were as poor as dirt, so I can't see them being thrilled with her pitching up in that state.'

In that state, Irene thought. And yet Megan being in that state was everything Ma Ada had been wishing for.

'So, she isn't coming back?' Irene asked hopefully.

But the old woman didn't know. She shuddered and groaned and claimed that she couldn't care less either way. All these young people and their godless, nasty ways appalled her. She wanted to hide from the world forever and forget that the little angels she had brought into the world had grown up to be rapacious monsters and devils, just like all men.

'I'll leave you to your nap,' Irene said tactfully, and withdrew, with Sam.

Ma Ada stayed in bed for three full days and nights. It was Irene who braved her sepulchral den, bringing her beef tea and milk stout every now and then, and sitting by her quietly when the old lady seemed like she might want company. Irene understood that Ma Ada just needed to withdraw for a bit. Her faith in her son had been shaken and that had set her whole world rocking for a little while. She just had to lie still, to acclimatise and to let the nausea pass.

Meanwhile, everyone else in the house tiptoed around the question of Megan's baby's parentage. Beryl shrugged the scandal off with apparent equanimity. It was none of her business. And Megan wasn't even here. Why should they dwell on the matter?

Sam sat gloomily at the kitchen table. 'Oh, Sam, man,' Beryl burst out at last, sick to the eye-teeth of his moping around and endless contrition. 'You've not killed someone. What have you done, really, eh?'

He looked down at his hands as she harangued him, looking like a little boy at school. 'All you've done is succumbed to the wiles of a mucky woman, that's all. She seduced you, you dope. I bet you never went running after her, did you?'

He shook his head and almost started blubbing. 'I just don't know anymore. I feel such a fool. I'm such an idiot.'

He started going to church again, for the first time since he was a kid, when he used to troop out twice on Sundays with his mam. When he was nine he'd been a devout little thing, singing in a reedy, high-pitched voice, trying to please his ma.

Now he went back, comforted by the liturgy and the calm, quiet and cold of the church. He felt like he was doing penance for the hot desire Megan had provoked in him.

Also – drawn with the same atavistic need – the pub drew him in, too. He went to the bar of the Robin Hood, where he supped more than he should have, and fell under the scornful gaze of Cathy Sturrock, who knew more than she should.

'So, what's going on?' she asked him, challengingly, when the coast was clear and the bar mostly empty.

He had to admit he didn't know.

Cathy was soft-hearted, really. She listened to him and started to sympathise, even though this lad had pulled a filthy trick on his own brother – a man so full of goodness that it made Cathy's heart go sore at the thought of him. Eeeh, those Farley men, she thought. What a bunch. She was fond of them all in her own way.

Maybe she'd been wrong to go marching in there and setting off bombs? Maybe she'd made a huge mistake?

Irene, for her part, was glad that Megan was out of the house and back with her people in Hartlepool. It came as a huge relief not to have that catty piece hanging around.

But Megan's words still clung to her like burrs. Her spiteful words, castigating her and making her feel sick. Do they all think like that, deep down? Am I really not welcome here, among the Farleys?

Irene tried to bury these thoughts. They wouldn't do her any good at all. They were just twisted words from Megan when she'd been at her most spiteful and her most het up. They didn't mean anything really . . . did they?

Chapter Twenty-Eight

And so, for a while, things became relatively peaceful – or at least quiet – on Frederick Street. The war was changing daily, and this took up their attention, as news came over the wires and through the newsreels at the Savoy and they tried to keep up. Now the Yanks were actually in the war and fully committed, following the Japanese bombing of Pearl Harbor last December, everything had stepped up a notch. A new feeling of hopefulness and urgency was taking over everyone.

Ma Ada even let Beryl play American jazz records on the old gramophone and sat there tapping her foot grimly. She was in a sulk with the younger people still, as if she felt betrayed by them all.

Days went by and her feelings were gradually soothed and assuaged. 'Well, maybe we couldn't have coped anyway, with two new-born bairns in the same house, eh?'

Irene smiled, though she couldn't help thinking it might have been rather nice, with someone else going through the same things as her, and learning the same skills, and making the same mistakes. It would be company – even if that person was her sworn enemy Megan.

She knew that Megan would never be able to forgive the fact that all her secrets had been laid open for the family to see, and it was all down to Irene. That would be a schism through the family forever, Irene thought.

When Bob came back on leave he was upset and puzzled over his wife's absence. It broke their hearts to see him step over the threshold and have to be told that she wasn't there.

'What?' he blinked, and looked confused. 'You said she was gonna be here. You said she was back at home . . . waiting for me . . .'

'She's with her people . . .' Ma Ada started to explain, and Bob had hardly put his kit bag down in the corner for more than two minutes before he was fetching it up again and slinging it over his shoulder. 'Where are you going, lad?' his ma called, but Bob was already out the door.

'He'll be off to Hartlepool,' Beryl said, in a concerned voice, halfway through laying out the good china for his welcoming tea.

'Eeeh, and he's dead on his feet, you can see,' Ma Ada groaned. 'That poor lad. I didn't think he'd go straight out again, without a word. He must really love her, mustn't he?'

'Of course he does!' Beryl said. 'You know what he's like.'

Bob was gone for the rest of that day and night. There was no word from him until he got back to their house the next evening. By then he was even more hollow-eyed and exhausted.

'Eeeh, come in, lad. You look terrible,' his mother said. She was really worried about him. He looked like he'd been dragged through a ditch.

'She doesn't really want to see me,' Bob said, looking scared as he sat at the table and hungrily spooned up a hot broth thickened with pearl barley. 'I don't know why. I don't know what I've done to hurt her feelings.' He hunched over his bowl and tried not to cry. Fat tears were splashing into his soup, though.

'Ah, lad, nothing,' his ma said. 'She'll just be in a funny mood. Expecting can do all kinds of things to you. There's nowt wrong really . . .'

'I saw her mam and dad and they were nice,' he went on, stumblingly. 'I found where they lived in Hartlepool, by the sea. It was nice there. It was somewhere that'd be nice to visit. Anyway, they said she's been in a strange way ever since she came back to them. They were ashamed because she wouldn't even come down from her room to talk to me. They fed me, though, because they said that was only proper. I'm their son-in-law after all, and then they put me up in their barn for the night.'

Ma Ada was scandalised. 'In their barn?'

'There was no room indoors. And it was comfy and warm enough . . .'

Irene shook her head. Was there nothing that would ever make Bob lose his temper and spoil that sweetness to his nature?

She dreaded to think what it would do to him if he knew about Sam and his wife and all their carrying on. Irene bit her lip and wished and prayed hard, the whole time that Bob was there for his few days of leave. Her heart went out to him as he tried to fit back into place in their home.

Bob mumbled a few stories about his new life in the army. He tried to explain what it was all like, and Irene got the impression that he rather liked getting very straightforward orders that he could follow. In the army there was no room for mixed feelings or complications. He didn't have to think about anything very deeply: he just had to do what he was told, and this satisfied him. At last, it seemed, he was fitting in fine. It was easier than dealing with his wife and their married life, anyway.

Sam kept out of his brother's way for those few days. He used the excuse that he was getting terrible shifts at the docks these days, and that was true enough. But he was creeping around and keeping away, and this puzzled his older brother.

'I suppose I'll have to keep the dirty secret from my fella, too,' Beryl sighed in Irene's ear as they washed dishes one night. 'Tony would go mad if he knew all this stuff about Megan and Sam. He'd knock their bloody blocks off. Tony's cool and quiet, but when he loses his temper, all bets are off.' She sighed and tutted.

Keeping things quiet seemed all very well at first, but lies tended to grow and spread, until you were hiding a huge patch of growing concealment, like a patch of damp and mould on an old wall.

'It's women's work, this,' Beryl said. At first Irene thought she meant the washing up. She stared at the thin suds and the greasy greenish water in the Belfast sink. 'Keeping the peace, I mean,' Beryl added. 'Looking after the secrets and keeping a lid on it all. Seeing to it that war doesn't break out in the family. As far as I can make out, that's what the woman's role is like in most families.'

Irene thought this over and it was true: that's what it seemed like here, for the Farleys, and other families in the Sixteen Streets. Irene was still only just learning their ways. She herself had blurted out the truth and that had indirectly caused disaster. She had been behaving much more like her own mother, down in Norfolk, who was known for causing bother and telling home truths. Her ma couldn't sit on a secret, even if it was under pain of death.

'I don't think I'll ever fit in here,' Irene sighed.

Beryl was looking at her strangely and Irene thought she was about to reassure her, as usual. Eeeh, of course you will, pet. It's just a matter of time and learning our ways. But instead, Beryl said: 'Aye, maybe you won't, Irene. Maybe you'll never learn.'

This left Irene feeling stung.

The feeling stayed with her till the next day, when it was time for Bob to leave once more. Just before he left the post arrived, bringing a letter for Irene that knocked her sideways and almost distracted her from waving her brother-in-law goodbye. As she kissed him all she could think about was the contents of that crumpled letter in her hand. The scrawl was so bad it looked like a bairn had written it. At first she couldn't tell whose it was, or what they were trying to say.

Then she realised. It was her dad. Dated almost a full month ago. She had never seen a page written by him ever before.

It was about her ma.

Very ill. Come soon.

Chapter Twenty-Nine

'But, I can't! I can't just up and go! Not right down the length of the country.' Irene felt panic beating inside her chest as she said this, pacing around the living room at Arthur's house. The mermaid baby squirmed inside her belly, responding to her mother's agitated mood.

Arthur sat curled in his over-stuffed armchair, studying her carefully as she went on. There wasn't much room to pace about in this house, what with all the stacks of old junk in there. His and Mavis's home was filled with salvaged clothes and old magazines. Everything was in heaps and layered thickly with dust. The wintry light came shafting through the partially opened, tattered curtains, making the whole room look even more dreary than it already was.

'There's a war on!' Irene burst out. 'How do they expect me to go dashing about, willy-nilly, back down Norfolk way?'

Arthur frowned at her and took a long sip from the cracked china teacup he was holding. His tea was mostly brandy and already, by eleven in the morning, he was looking pretty stewed. But Irene found that he was a good person to sound off to. He listened in a way that no one round Number Thirteen really did – not even Sam.

'Sounds to me, dearie, like you just don't want to go home,' he opined eventually.

'No!' she protested. 'That's not true! They're my family. I'm longing to see them, of course I am! And Da says that mum is badly . . . my poor mum.' For a second she looked upset, as if the abstract knowledge contained in her father's badly spelled missive was hitting her for the first time.

'What's the matter with her?' Arthur asked. 'Did he say?'

'He wouldn't say in a letter,' Irene answered. 'He probably wouldn't even say at all, even in person. Woman's problems, I think. That's what I get, reading between the lines. But it's serious, I suppose, if it made him set pen to paper.'

Arthur nodded sagely. 'It means that she wasn't in a position to write to you herself.'

'Or she was too proud,' Irene said. 'That's more like my mum.' She stopped pacing round and gave out a small scream of dismay. Arthur's messy house was one where you could let out your feelings like that. 'Oh, why does it have to be right now?'

Arthur slurped his brandy and tea. 'It always has to be some-time, lovey. Something's always going on for some folk. We don't get to pick and choose our time of trials.' He shrugged. 'Plus, it isn't *now*. It was almost a month ago, according to the date on his letter, remember. It must have got lost on the way.'

'That only makes this worse!' she cried.

'I know, lovey,' he nodded. 'I know.'

She rolled her eyes at him. Sometimes – especially when he was pretending to talk like someone in a film – Arthur was no help at all.

Then, suddenly, Bella was with them. She entered the room quietly in her dressing gown and a silk turban that managed to hold in all her raven curls. She didn't have a scrap of make-up on but she looked stunning, Irene thought. She had the colouring of Snow White in the Walt Disney film. When she saw Irene standing there Bella gave a gentle smile. 'I thought I heard you down here. Arthur, is there tea in the pot?'

He jumped up. 'Just the dregs, hinny. I'll make a fresh one.'

'Thanks, love.' Bella shunted aside a huge, sliding heap of movie magazines and settled on the sofa. She lit herself a cigarette and didn't speak until she'd taken two huge drags and filled the room with indigo smoke. She was smoking like her life depended on it.

Irene determinedly put aside her own worries. 'How are you getting on, Bella?'

The older woman smiled at her again and wafted a hand vaguely, as if to indicate she was doing OK; she'd been better. *Comme ci, comme ça.* She had the most expressive hands Irene had ever seen. She could communicate so much with just a few precise gestures. Her bones were already fine and now they were even more delicate-looking. Bella had lost pounds, perhaps even stones, in weight. The dressing gown was hanging off her like it might a wooden hanger.

I've been selfish, Irene suddenly thought. I've not been over this way to see them for more than a week, she suddenly realised. I've been all caught up in my own cares and the dramas at Number Thirteen. Bella and the others were just carrying on alone in all this mess and a fug of smoke and morning brandy.

'Have you been out much?' she asked her friend.

'A little,' Bella said. 'Arthur's been trying to get me to come to the pictures with him. He says I could lose myself in the movies. Forget all my woes.'

'That sounds like it might be a good idea?' Irene thought it was sensible if Bella got into a routine of getting dressed and getting about, amongst other people. It wouldn't do slouching about here all day long in her borrowed dressing gown.

'I don't want to forget my woes,' Bella said. 'I want to remember everything. I'm terrified that I'll start forgetting things. And if I don't remember them . . . then it's like they were never alive, isn't it? I'm the only one left to keep my family's memory alive.'

Irene didn't know what to say to that. Suddenly she was aware of the huge weight of grief inside her friend. It was like sitting in front of the North Sea and being awed by that vast body of heaving, freezing water, and feeling helpless in the face of it.

This grief of Bella's stunned her into silence. Of course, of course all Bella wanted to do was sit and remember her folks.

Just then Arthur came crashing back into the room with an enamelled tea tray with elegant gilding and a picture of kittens on it. He had the best china service out, a huge teapot covered in painted roses, and a mostly-empty bottle of spirits. He set it all down between them and sighed melodramatically.

'Is she on the same old tune?' he asked, shaking his head. 'About remembering her people?'

Bella covered her face with her pale hands, and Irene was shocked at the abruptness of Arthur's tone. He almost sounded cruel as he went on: 'I've told her. I've said what I would do, if I was her. The best way to honour them and to keep their memory alive. It's quite obvious, if you think about it. She's got to get that ice cream parlour back up and running. She's got to get the Franchino show back on the road. She can't mope about round this dump all her life. She simply must get back to work and face the public! That's what I think, anyhow.'

Both women were staring at him, and Irene suddenly realised that she agreed with Arthur completely. What he said was exactly right. It was the only way.

But Bella was still sitting there with her hands covering her face, trying not to break down into tears. 'I just . . . can't . . . Not yet . . . Please . . . Just let me . . . do things in my own time . . .'

Suddenly there was another person in the room. Mavis. No one had noticed her stepping into the sepulchral gloom of the sitting room. She spoke up in her rasping, queer little voice and startled them all: 'It's a fantastic idea! And, do you know what? I'll help! I'd love it! I'd work for nothing! I'd love to work in an ice cream parlour and wear a little pinny! Especially Franchino's! Oh, let's do it! Can we do it? Can we go there today?'

Bella wouldn't leave the house, so in the event the other three made a little party and traipsed out to Ocean Road, where they pulled open the shutters that had been closed for several weeks, and entered the ice cream parlour like it was a tomb in the Valley of the Kings.

'Urgghh, everything in the fridges has gone off,' Mavis reported. 'What a bloody waste! Just a few weeks and the whole place has gone to rack and ruin.'

It certainly looked that way, Irene thought, surveying the bleak room and shaking her head. 'It's just as well Bella didn't come with us after all, and see the place in this state.'

'It's like it's just been abandoned,' said Arthur, and they realised that's exactly what had happened. No one had set foot in here since the very day Bella's poor family had perished.

There was only one thing for it.

'We've got to roll up our sleeves and get on with it!' Irene said.

It felt good to fill buckets with scalding hot water, and to smell carbolic and soap flakes. It was a good way of assuaging all her worries and stresses by scrubbing away at the floor tiles and the surfaces and bringing them up sparklingly clean. Mavis set to work beside her, happily taking orders and pitching in. She was a funny, daft-seeming girl in some ways, Irene thought, but she didn't mind a spot of hard work.

'This is endless!' Arthur moaned, clutching his back and going on about all his aches and pains yet again. 'Can't we get some more folk in to help?' He implored Irene with a tragic look. 'What about that handsome Sam of yours? And Beryl? Wouldn't they come to help out?'

Perhaps they might, Irene agreed, but she wasn't letting Arthur get away without putting in his fair share of graft. She almost laughed to see him mopping the floors with an expression of distaste on his face. It was almost like he'd never had to clean a floor or anything else in his life. Actually, judging by the state of his own home, perhaps he never had?

'Just think,' Irene exhorted them, 'imagine Bella's reaction when she comes here eventually and finds everything sparkling and as good as new! That would be the best tribute ever to her dad and everyone. She'll be so happy.'

Irene had her blouse sleeves rolled up and she was tackling the tricky task of cleaning the coffee machine inside and out. She had unscrewed too many of the parts in order to get all the grime out to her satisfaction and was having doubts about how they all fitted back together.

'Well,' Arthur announced at last, flinging down the mop he'd grown to despise in a few short hours. 'That's it for me, I'm afraid. I've got other work I've got to get to.'

He had a shift at the Savoy he had to do. He had to run now, to make it to the Nook on time. He told the girls he'd love them and leave them, and Irene smiled at him ruefully as he dashed off with relief.

'He's such a funniosity!' Irene chuckled, as they watched him race away down Ocean Road.

'He's all I've got,' said Mavis in a proud little voice. 'He's the best brother in the world.'

They carried on with their work, scrubbing and polishing and bringing Franchino's ice cream parlour back into pastel-coloured life. The whole place could do with a new lick of paint, Irene mused. But where would they lay their hands on enough paint to do this whole place up?

'I might be able to get my hands on some,' said Mavis, screwing her face up thoughtfully. 'I've got connections . . .'

She sounded so absurdly worldly-wise Irene almost laughed at her, but stopped herself, instinctively knowing this might hurt the younger girl's feelings. Instead she said, 'See what you can rummage up. Wouldn't it be splendid, to repaint the walls in here and surprise Bella with a whole new look?'

Only when Irene started to flag, and her limbs were quivering with tiredness, did they brew up a little shining pot of coffee and sit in their favourite booth. Mavis sat there sipping the boiling concoction loudly. She looked delighted to be included in Irene's gang at last.

'Here,' Irene had found a bottle of some kind of delicious syrup in the back of one of the cupboards. It was like a gorgeous elixir – just a few drops in their steaming cups – and the two of them sat together enjoying it hugely, like a just reward for all their hard work.

Then Mavis said, confidingly: 'I was hoping that they would fall in love.'

'Who?' Irene asked.

'My brother, Arthur, and Bella. I was hoping that it would happen, like, magically. When she moved in, and when she needed our help. I thought it would happen. You know, that's what happens in the movies, doesn't it? And I've seen plenty enough of those. Arthur smuggles me in for free at the Savoy.'

'They were never going to fall in love,' Irene smiled. 'They've been best friends for years. He's just helping her out and doing his best by her. Why would they suddenly decide to fall in love?' Irene felt fond of this little girl with the mucky face and the messy hair. She'd been nursing a futile hope for weeks, and there was something very touching about that.

'But wouldn't it be lovely?' Mavis sighed. 'Then she'd be like my big sister and a proper member of our family.'

'You've liked having her to stay, then?'

Mavis nodded. 'I love my brother, but it's the same old thing with him. All the same dramas and palaver. But having someone else living there with us, even though she's been so quiet and upset, eeeh, it's been lovely. Another woman in the house. Arthur lives like a pig in muck.'

They sipped their caramel-flavoured coffee together thoughtfully for a few moments. At last Irene said, 'Well, I don't think Arthur's going to fall in love with her, or vice versa, I'm afraid.'

Mavis smiled. 'I sleep in the room right above our front room. So when I go to bed I can hear them talking downstairs. And it's so lovely, having voices going on downstairs. I can't even hear what they're saying. Bella has the most beautiful voice. Warm and sweet, like honey. And the two of them talking together, I could listen to them for hours, quite happily, never having a clue what they're going on about. It's like . . . it's like . . .'

Mavis looked up at Irene smiling, and Irene was surprised to see tears misting up her blue eyes.

'It's like having a mam and dad,' Mavis said. 'It's like being a bairn, safely asleep upstairs, and there's a mam and dad downstairs, talking nicely to each other, and sitting watch over the house in the night. Eeeh, that's a lovely feeling.'

Irene smiled at her and felt her throat closing up with a suppressed sob. That poor little lass. She mustn't have had much in the way of security or love in her life, Irene realised. She didn't know what to say to her, at all. She just smiled and finished off the sweet dregs of her coffee. 'Come on then,' she said briskly. 'How's about we wash up and call it a day, eh? Then maybe you could come and visit home with me, and meet our little Lucky?'

The girl's eyes lit up. 'Ooh, is that the cat you were talking about? The bald little cat? Eeeh, I'd love to see him, Irene!'

'Come on then, hinny. Let's get a shift on.'

Mavis was all eyes when she was led by Irene into Number Thirteen. She seemed even smaller and skinnier than ever, like some waif and stray Irene had brought in off the street.

'Aww, it's lovely in here,' the girl said, in a quieter voice than usual. 'Your family's got nice things. Furniture, and that. Like it's been passed down. Everything we've got's been nicked or haggled for off the back of a totter's cart.' She gazed at the line of pot ornaments on top of Ma Ada's sideboard and nodded approvingly, and then started to examine the smudged and fading photographs on the walls.

'Maybe you can stay for your tea with us,' Irene said, nipping into the scullery to see what there was to cook up. There was a scrawled list of meals pinned to the pantry door, laying out the days and working out what food was left and what should be used and when. 'It's rissoles,' Irene said musingly. 'Beryl's speciality with what's left of the scrag end from Sunday. What do you think?'

Mavis beamed at her. 'I'd love to stay for me tea, Irene pet. If that's all right? If they'll let me?'

She was so nervy and grateful Irene's heart went out to her. 'Of course they will. Now, let me find that daft little cat for you. He's usually about at this time of day, expecting some kind of titbit.'

Sure enough, when she opened the door at the back of the scullery, in came Lucky, looking perishing cold and bright pink. Mavis fell in love with him at first sight. 'Aww, look at the little divil!' She swooped to gather him up in her arms.

'Eeeh, watch out!' Irene laughed. 'He doesn't like anyone else but Ma Ada to pick him up. He can bite and scratch a bit.'

'He's all right with me,' Mavis smiled, crushing the startled beast to her skinny chest. 'He loves his Aunty Maeve, don't you, Lucky?' The cat let out a strangled mewing noise and seemed content enough to be fussed by the strange girl.

Irene put the kettle on and yanked off her headscarf and coat. She lit the gas and started putting together the few ingredients needed for rissoles. She remembered what Beryl did, kneading all the bits of spare meat and suet and flour together. Anything else she could lay her hands on to pad them out and make them more substantial . . . She'd watched Beryl often enough, as they chatted in the kitchen. Irene's cooking repertoire had tripled since she'd moved here. She could make all kinds of things now, and she couldn't help reflecting how impressed her ma would be.

Oh, dear. Her ma. The guilty thought stabbed at her, making her wipe her floury, sticky hands on the tea cloth and retrieve the letter from her handbag. As Mavis dandled the curiously content Lucky, Irene scanned the page of her father's scrawl once again:

You know what she is like and that she is not one to complain, your mother. She says I am not to disturb you, with you settling into your new life and the baby coming and all. But she cannot do all the things she usually does, and she will not admit it. I think she is really ill this time and brushes me off when I try to bring it up with her. Please will you come home and help us out, our Irene? I think she needs your help and she's too proud to say, and also, with you being a grown woman now, you're more in a position to talk to her about what ails her. She will tell me nothing, as usual, what with me being just a man. I am still, though, your devoted,

Da. Etc.

It was dated almost a month ago. The letter had taken even longer than they usually did to wend its way up the country. A month later and how would her mum be by now? She could be ten times as bad in the time that had passed . . .

It was really hard to know what to do. Of course, it was perfectly possible that her da was overreacting. Any disturbance to the running of their household and her dad would start thinking the worst. He was spoilt, really, Irene suddenly realised. He'd had a lifetime of being tended to, with meals arriving bang on time, and the whole house being organised all around him and his whims and moods. Of course he was prone to fret, and to think that the sky was falling in, whenever his wife was poorly.

But how ill was she? The vagueness of his letter irked his daughter. It was either masculine squeamishness or simple ignorance, and probably a blend of both. Why couldn't her parents communicate properly with each other? It was like man and wife belonged to different species. That's what Irene had grown up believing: that men and women could never really communicate with each other or ever be truly honest, because they spoke different languages and had different priorities.

Now, as she found herself a bit older and more experienced, she realised that wasn't quite true. She and Tom met on a level of communication and reciprocity she would scarcely have believed possible, only a year before. The trouble lay with the peculiarities of her parents. And here was her dad, writing to her in so clandestine a fashion and she had no idea what state her ma was really in. Would she be annoyed that her husband had written like this? Above all, ma was fiercely proud and independent.

Irene sighed and folded the letter away. First things first. She had rissoles to roll out on the floury table and then she had to get them in the pan.

'Do you want to make that pot of tea?' she asked Mavis.

The girl was reluctant to put down her new, hairless pal, but before she could there was a kerfuffle in the front hall and the heavy noise of the door banging shut. Irene saw Mavis flinch and look worried. 'Hey, don't be nervous . . .' she started to say, but was interrupted by a thunderous cry from the parlour.

Lucky jerked in response and jumped from Mavis's arms, bolting across the kitchen. Even Irene was alarmed by the mournful cry of dismay that seemed to make the whole, quiet house quake.

'Ada?' she asked, dashing through with floury hands. Of course, that's who it was. The old woman was standing in the middle of the parlour, her grey shawl wrapped around her shoulders. She was wailing with her eyes squinched shut and her massive fists clenched in despair. 'Oh, my God! Ada, whatever's the matter, hinny?'

The old woman shrugged her off, as Irene tried to hug and console her. She roared and tore at her wispy hair through her hairnet. 'It's Bob!' she gasped. They were the first coherent words they could make out from all of her brouhaha.

Irene's stomach went icy cold. A dreadful feeling went right through her entrails. 'He's not been killed?' she asked, right out, boldly, urgently.

Ada froze in horror. She stared at her daughter-in-law with an appalled expression. 'No! No! Not killed . . . *Arrested!* They've gone and arrested the daft bugger!'

Lucky was sitting at Ada's feet, staring up in concern at his mistress. Irene was aware of young Mavis in the doorway of the scullery, just as confused and mute as the little cat. Ada seemed oblivious to both of them.

'Who's arrested him?' Irene asked, and gasped: 'The Germans? Is he a prisoner of war? Why, he only left South Shields yesterday!'

'No,' groaned Ada. 'It's our lot who've taken him. The military police. They came knocking here this afternoon. They say they picked him up in Hartlepool.'

'Hartlepool?' Irene chimed, stupidly. She couldn't quite figure out what must have happened.

'The bloody fool,' Ada said. 'The bloody idiot. He never went back. After he left here, he never reported back to his barracks. No, he went off on his own way, never telling anyone. He went after *her* again! That harlot, Megan! He went after her, to beg her . . . to come back to him! The bloody fool!'

Now Irene understood why he'd been found in Hartlepool. That was where Megan's people lived. He'd gone right out of his way to beg with strangers on a farm, somewhere east of Durham . . . The ones who'd let him sleep in their barn last time. It was shaming, Irene thought. Like he was the one in the wrong.

'Now the polis have taken him away,' Ada moaned. 'They said he went AWOL. They said he's no better than a bloody deserter!'

Chapter Thirty

They were left in some uncertainty for a few days about what was going to happen to Bob. A terrible sense of shame settled over the house. It turned out that the story had spread and other people in Frederick Street had heard whispers of what was going on.

'They're saying things like Bob has ran away from his duty,' Beryl told Irene. 'Like he's gone yeller and ran away. A yeller belly! Our Bob!'

'Don't say anything about it!' Ma Ada commanded them all. 'If anyone asks, don't say anything. It's none of their bloody business anyway.'

'Eeeh, our poor Bob,' said Beryl. 'He's so daft he probably didn't even realise what trouble he'd be getting himself into.'

'He was always prone to wandering off,' his ma growled, taking solace in a nip or two of sherry in her tea. 'I remember being in Marine Park when he was nowt but a tiddler and he went tootling off on his own way and we lost him for hours. It was a busy summer afternoon and I was bloody frantic.'

Irene kept picturing him sitting in prison and it was a picture comprised of scenes from films in which heroes were wrongly dumped in slimy, rat-infested dungeons and forgotten about.

This is all Megan's fault, was all she could think about, but lurking under that thought was the horrible feeling that it was her fault, too. She was the one who had let the secret out.

Cathy Sturrock was horrified to hear the news. 'Surely they'll see his side? Surely they'll be compassionate and see that he was in a state? What can they do to him for going after his estranged and crazy wife?'

Irene sat drinking a half of stout by the fire at the Robin Hood and between her and Cathy they were trying to imagine what must have been going on inside Bob's poor, befuddled mind.

'They say he went back to the barn where they had him sleeping on his first visit,' Irene said. 'Megan's family said there was no room in their house for him to stay. So he was sleeping in the hay with all the animals.'

'The buggers!' Cathy's eyes blazed. 'The bloody buggers! I bet that Megan loved that. Eeeh, and he'd traipsed all that way to see her. To reason with her. To beg her to come back to him. That poor, poor bloke. He's much too good for your lot. He's too good for the Farleys and he's too good for this whole world.'

If Irene was in any doubt about the fiercely protective love Cathy Sturrock felt for her pot man, she knew it for sure that night in the pub. Cathy looked ready to set off and find Bob and free him from prison with her own bare hands.

The person who was conspicuously quiet on the subject of Bob's shame was Sam, who kept out of everyone's way for a few days. It was just as well. The very sight of him made his ma remember that all this upheaval was down to him and his weakness in falling for Megan.

'But I never did fall for her,' he said gloomily, when he eventually talked to Irene about it all again. 'I don't even like her much, really. Not when I got to know what she was really like. But there's something magnetic about her, when she has you in her grip . . .'

Irene shuddered, trying hard not to imagine it.

Sam was trying to redeem himself with Irene. Somehow he had laid his hands on some surplus tins of paint from a warehouse by the docks. They were a bit rusty and battered and Irene had a suspicion that they were nicked, or they'd fallen off the back of a battleship, but she didn't ask too many questions. She helped Sam carry them in a wheelbarrow across town to Franchino's ice cream parlour on Ocean Road.

'I can't do too much pushing, though,' she warned him. She felt a bit wobbly with nausea that night. 'But I'll keep an eye out for wardens and police.'

The idea to give the ice cream parlour a new lick of paint was the best she'd had in ages. Cleaning the place was all very well, but it only revealed that it really was slightly shabby and needed a bit of a spruce. Irene decided it would be lovely to surprise Bella with a new look to her inherited kingdom, and this might be all the encouragement she needed to return to everyday life.

It took ages for Sam to push the barrow to Ocean Road.

Arthur and Mavis were waiting for them there, sipping Camp Coffee in a booth and smoking.

'It was tricky, sloping out of our house without letting on to Bella what we're up to,' said Mavis, looking excited. Her eyes glowed brightly. She addressed them all, but she stared only at Sam.

He was oblivious to the strange little creature's attention, laying out the rusty tins on the counter, but Irene had clocked it. It turned out that Mavis had a massive crush on the youngest Farley boy, no matter how terrible the gossip about him and Megan was. In fact, all that talk of forbidden fruit and secret lusts only seemed to spice things up, as far as the diminutive Mavis was concerned. The muttered gossip only inflamed her burgeoning feelings. She stared at Sam like she thought that he could never do any real wrong.

'It's the way his fair hair just flops over one way and then the other,' she sighed, telling Irene later that night. 'He's got a widow's peak either side of his forehead and his hair's always all over the place. I've noticed that. I think I'm falling for him, Irene. I think . . . no, it's more than that. It's more than what Bella says she feels for my brother.'

Irene frowned in puzzlement. 'What does Bella say about what she feels for your brother?'

The younger girl smiled. 'She says that they aren't in love with each other, because that's quite impossible. But they are in *like* with each other. And that that is quite enough.'

Irene smiled. The phrase made her laugh. 'And it's more than that for you and our Sam is it, then?'

Mavis nodded solemnly. 'I bloody *adore* him, Irene. Ever since I first saw him at Number Thirteen that day when your ma-in-law came in and said Bob had been taken away by the military police. Love came and hit me like a thunderbolt from heaven when Sam came shuffling into the scullery. We was rolling out the rissoles on the table, remember? And I was wondering whether I ought to be getting home, what with all the bother and the bad news? And in Sam walked and I just knew – there lies my future and all my hopes.'

Irene stared at her. 'Are you sure, pet?'

'Aye, I am. But he thinks I'm just nowt. He talks to me like I'm some scruffy little urchin. He talks to me like . . . well, like you talk to Lucky the cat.'

They were holding this hushed conference at the counter, as Irene brewed up some proper coffee on the gleaming machine that had once been Tonio Franchino's pride and joy. Across the room, Sam was in his shirtsleeves, energetically using an old screwdriver to lever off the lids of the purloined tins of paint. Arthur was watching him admiringly and waiting with scruffy-looking paintbrushes in hand.

'I'm going to have to tell him all about it,' Mavis sighed raspingly. 'It's no good holding it all in. There's nothing worse than letting love wither on the vine. It can send you bitter, that kind of thing. I have to let this out.'

'Uh-huh,' said Irene, dreading the worst. 'Well, maybe wait a bit. Wait till this bother about Bob has blown over a bit, eh, pet?'

The girl with the wispy hair nodded solemnly and pushed forward the cups for Irene to pour the coffee into.

'Hurray!' came a cry from the boys, as the tin lid came popping off at last, to reveal the thick, soupy contents within.

'What colour is it?' Irene asked, hurrying over.

The two boys squinted at it, frowning.

'It's reminiscent of our outhouse privy,' Sam said, in a disappointed tone.

'It's cappuccino!' Arthur corrected him. 'It's the colour of frothy coffee, that! It's absolutely *perfect* for in here! Bella's gonna love it!'

They made a little team, working in the evenings at the ice cream parlour, covering as much of the walls as they could with the pale-brown paint. When rust fell from the lips of the tins into the paint, they just stirred it in and it made the colour all the richer, Irene said.

She was their boss and their foreman, supervising their work, wincing as her belly twinged and her back ached.

Very gradually the place started looking fresher and, she prided herself, quite stylish.

Mavis spent most of her time hovering around Sam, staring at him and asking if he needed any more coffee.

'That ersatz coffee can make you feel a bit sickly, when you have too much,' Sam told Irene, as they walked home one night. The other two had peeled off in their own direction and the night breeze was cold off the sea, but there was a promise of spring in it, Irene thought. It even felt like they might soon be emerging from what had seemed like a very long, frozen winter.

'I think Mavis likes brewing it up and practising making it,' Irene laughed. 'She's hoping that Bella will give her a job there when she re-opens the place.'

'Her?' Sam laughed. 'Well, she'll have to smarten herself up a bit if she's going to work somewhere, serving people food and drinks. She looks like a mucky little urchin or something. She looks like she's crawled out of a hedge!' He chuckled at his own imagery.

'Oh, Sam, don't say that,' Irene gasped. 'She's a good lass. She's just not had the advantages that others have had. Them two – her and Arthur – they've had to drag themselves up by their bootstraps. They're like orphans living way across town in that midden of theirs.'

Sam nodded, trying to understand.

'Not every family is like you Farleys,' Irene went on. 'You lads have all been so lucky, growing up with your ma's protection. Ada's done absolutely everything for you lot. Taught you everything you need to know and kept you safe and well fed and warm all your lives.'

'Aye, that's true enough,' he nodded, equably, biting his lip. Irene seemed just a tad cross tonight and he was wary of her mood.

'You don't know how lucky you've been, you boys,' she said. 'Most people are just chucked out into the world and have to sink or swim. Your ma has stood by all of you and given you everything.'

He frowned. 'She can be a bit overbearing though, Irene. You must admit that. She wants to keep control of all of us all our lives. That's how it sometimes seems. And even when we get married, she wants to control the wives' lives as well! Like you! She's got you right under her thumb.'

'She certainly has not!' said Irene hotly.

'I reckon she has. She tells us all what to do and has us running round like mad things.'

They walked in silence then, for a while, as they came nearer to the Sixteen Streets. The lamps were on and the sky seemed gentler somehow. There were banners of pale pink – the pink of tinned salmon – on the horizon as dusk descended on the town.

Eeeh, lad, she wanted to tell Sam. Fancy picking fault with your wonderful old battleaxe of a mam. Even after she's forgiven you for going with your sister-in-law and giving her a bairn.

Sam didn't even realise how deep-down ashamed his ma was of him, and how much it was costing her to keep a lid on the whole sorry business and pretend as if nothing had changed. Irene could see it in the old mother's face: a kind of flinch whenever she looked at her youngest son and her erstwhile favourite. She tried to cover up her shame, but Irene saw it every time.

Sam, though, seemed oblivious. He seemed glad that he felt forgiven for his misdemeanour. Even the awful things that had happened to Bob hardly seemed to touch Sam's conscience. At least, that was how it seemed to Irene.

The last of the wintry days were fading. Hitler's planes didn't come again for a while and it seemed like that part of the war might even be over. The Farleys and their neighbours paid attention to the newsreels and followed the progress of the war with avid attention and heard tales of the Americans, now that they had joined the conflict. There was talk of the Yanks pitching up in towns in the south and the north-west. They were welcomed uneasily at first, and then with excitement. How long before they came here to the north-east, too?

Winter lost its terrible grip on the frozen town. It was like living on an iceberg as it slowly melted and returned to life.

Irene was glad of no longer having to muffle herself up in so many layers of coats and jumpers. For months she had felt like she was wearing her entire wardrobe all at once.

Her life took on a slower pace as she spent more time sitting with Ma Ada, helping her write letters to Bob and the relevant authorities. The old ma's eyes were bad with cataracts and her fingers hurt when she held the pen too long, so Irene ended up taking dictation and writing her windily-worded letters for her. It was a task she was glad to fulfil: she felt like she was helping out.

Bob wouldn't be spending very long in the military prison. Compassion and good sense had thankfully won the day and he was told he would soon be allowed to return to his barracks, to take up the duties he should have been doing in the first place. He felt chastened and confused, it seemed, from the tone of the pages of childish scrawl that he sent back to his ma and everyone else at Number Thirteen. He didn't understand at all why his wife didn't want him anymore and why his dashing off to see her had been such a crime.

'But there's only so much you can explain to Bob,' Ma Ada sighed. 'It's always been like that. Too much explaining and he gets upset. Perhaps it's best if he doesn't know too much. And he's left to get on and do his duty in peace.'

There was vague talk of Bob being sent abroad. Perhaps to North Africa, but he couldn't say, of course, and no one told them. His letters stopped coming for a while as he sat out his shortened sentence in solitary confinement and Ma Ada gave a sanguine nod. She held her breath and said a prayer for him, each morning and night, just as she prayed for her other two sons who were away, goodness knows where.

Irene thought the old woman was unimaginably brave in difficult circumstances. How must it feel to have given these boys life, and brought them up, and then to send them out into the greatest dangers possible? How could she look so calm and confident about it all?

'I have every faith in my boys,' Ma Ada said. And then she sighed. 'Well, most of them.'

Irene knew that she meant Sam. Deep down, the old woman would never feel the same about her youngest boy again.

Dear Tom,

I must say, your letters aren't as regular as they used to be! Why are you getting out of the habit of writing and telling me all your news? I know there's not much you can tell me about what you get up to, but you should still be writing and saying nice things about how you miss me and how you can't wait to get some leave again? It seems like a lifetime since I last saw you. So much has happened, it feels like, and I just keep getting bigger and bigger. This expectancy seems to have gone on longer than all of my previous life put together . . . how long is it elephants take when they have a bun in the oven? It's some monstrous amount of time, isn't it? Well, maybe that's it. I'm going to hatch out a bloomin' baby elephant for you.

Joking aside, I wish you would come back and see us soon. It seems so long since we had our early Christmas.

Things here are strange. Number Thirteen even feels a bit quiet and empty. Have I managed to scare everyone away, do you think? When I arrived it was a busy house, all bustling with life. Now it seems like there's so few of us, sitting quietly and creeping in and out . . . Sometimes I just want to scream with frustration.

At least the bombings have stopped for a while.

Arthur's coming over for tea on Saturday night. He's bringing his funny little sister, Mavis, who I know from the biscuit factory. She's a real card. You met them once, remember? She's got a proper crush on our Sam, who can't even see it. Ma Ada has heard so much about these two that she commanded me to ask them over for tea. I wonder what she'll make of Arthur? I know you weren't all that impressed, but he's been a good friend to me. As have Mavis and Bella.

Franchino's ice cream parlour is all but done. We're hoping to reopen soon. We're waiting for poor Bella to give the nod. We've managed to keep the extent of the refurbishments secret, as a surprise for her. Arthur says we should have a little afternoon party, to welcome her back and show her how we've turned it back into a little palace. All fresh and inviting. I wish you could be there for that, too.

But it's no use spending all your life wishing, is it? Life can vanish in a flash while you're busy waiting for it to improve. That's what I've learnt in this last year. It's no good biding your time and hoping against hope. Otherwise you might lose everything.

Did I tell you what Cathy Sturrock said? She told me — she's sick of sitting idly by and letting her happiness go to the wall. She's hankered after our Bob's company for all these years. She watched him being unhappy with Megan. Well, we all knew Megan wasn't right for him. She says she thought she was too old for him. An old widow woman in love with her pot man. She thought she was foolish. But now she says she owes it to both of them. When she gets the chance, she's going to tell him — he's hers. She won't take no for an answer, she says.

Can you imagine what your ma's reaction's gonna be?

But perhaps she'll be pleased about it. She might see that it's the right thing. I think Cathy really does love Bob and I think it would be wonderful. Don't you? I'd love to see that great daft lummox being happy for once. He deserves it. And so does Cathy. Who'd have thought, someone as loud and colourful as her, she could have kept a lid on her love like she has all this time?

Well, now she's decided it's time to let love out.

I loved the way she put that. 'I'm going to let love out,' she told me. And I thought: yes. What more can we do in this life? What more can we ask? We just have to find the right time and the right place and the right ones to be among, to feel safe at last. And then we have to let our love out. Because that's all there is.

Haha! Listen to me! I'm getting weepy writing this down. I'm at the kitchen table, Friday night. Scribbling by the lamplight and Ma Ada's knitting bootees like crazy. Beryl (our welder! Did I tell you she's actually got into the training to do welding?) well, she's also doing a smashing job of a matinee jacket. They unwound a huge sea-green jumper that used to belong to you, and they're ravelling it up into new shapes for the bairn, to keep her warm, when she comes to live with us at last. Our little mermaid.

All my love,
Irene

Chapter Thirty-One

Beryl was the first to come traipsing into Franchino's ice cream parlour to examine their handiwork. She exclaimed at all the right things and made a lot of fuss and noise about the muted, stylish colours and the gleam of the polished chrome. She groaned joyfully as she sipped the rare nectar of the espresso that Mavis brewed for her.

Mavis was in a smart, clean pinny, her hair denuded of frizz and kept under a little white cap. She was auditioning for her dream job and enjoying herself enormously as she watched Beryl smack her lips. When Sam joined them, moments later, her joy was complete as she set about making a cup for him, too. Her secret beloved.

'We found a special cache of espresso beans,' she told them. 'Bella's dad had squirrelled away some wonderful supplies for a rainy day.'

Irene went round checking that everything was just right. They had a bowl of beautifully multi-coloured cocktail sugar and freshly pressed napkins. They had brought out the best of everything to welcome Bella back to her family's emporium and she was due to arrive at three.

Irene had even roasted parsnips in honey, so they could all have fake Banana Surprise. It was a kind of joke, but she had set about creating the dish with absolute seriousness.

She hoped with every scrap of her soul that Bella was going to like what they had done with her place. More than that. She was desperate for her to love it. It felt as if there was quite a lot staked upon this refurbishment turning out right.

The minutes ticked by with agonising slowness.

Where was Arthur? He had agreed to fetch Bella and bring her here at the appointed time. The story was that he had made plans with her that they would visit and start taking an itinerary of stock. They would look at the place and decide what needed doing in terms of cleaning and repairs. Bella was dreading it, Arthur had thought, because so many weeks had gone by with the place lying empty. It would be a dark place, all dust and cobwebs and memories.

But all the work was done already. That was the secret Irene and her friends had so diligently kept. Without Bella having even the slightest idea, they had nipped in and done everything for her.

Now, at last, it was time to spring that surprise.

It was like setting a deadly trap for some rare and delicate woodland beast. They had left a crafty trail and covered up their traces. Now they were lying in wait.

The door went and everyone's head whirled round.

It wasn't Bella. Not yet.

'Ada!' Irene grinned. And here she came. Looking incongruous in her black lambswool coat and headscarf. She was being helped along by her friend and confidante, Aunty Winnie. Psychic Aunty Winnie with her shock of dyed hair and sticky-out eyes. For a moment Irene felt confused by seeing her mother-in-law in a completely new and different place. She seemed so much smaller and less forbidding when she was out in the real world, amongst other people.

Ada whipped off her headscarf, shrugged off her coat and glared around with great interest. 'I remember this place when Tonio Franchino first opened these doors! How many years ago was that? Donkey's years. Eeeh, but this is splendid. Is this what you bairns have been spending your time doing? Making it look as grand as this?' She nodded admiringly. 'Well, I'd say you've done a fine job. Well done you, Irene. You're not so daft, after all.'

High praise indeed, from Ma Ada.

Cathy Sturrock came careering in shortly afterwards, brisk and noisy in her purple coat with the dyed rabbit-fur trim. She lit up a cigarette and sat at a high stool at the coffee bar and toasted Irene and her friends in frothy coffee. 'Here's to happier days, kids,' she grinned.

Irene was anxiously glancing at the clock above the mirrored shelves. It was gone three o'clock already. Everyone they had invited was here and waiting.

But where was Arthur? And where was Bella?

'Oh God,' said Mavis in her strange, raspy voice. 'I think this is them now! *They're here!*'

Afterwards it would come to seem almost absurd, that Irene and her friends had been so nervous about what Bella would make of their handiwork. Given everything else that had gone on – the bombs and the bombshells of that year – a lick of paint hardly seemed important at all. And yet there was so much riding on Bella's reaction to the ice cream parlour's renovation. It was all about hoping that she would come to life again and shake off the terrible torpor that had taken her over since her family's deaths.

Easier said than done, of course. Irene had no idea what state she herself would be in if she'd had to face the things that Bella had. How could she function at all, knowing that she was the only one of her clan left on the earth?

But here she was. Looking elegant and beautiful, even with her hair tied up in a headscarf, and all bundled up inside a man's vast greatcoat. She wasn't dressed up, of course, since she was arriving at the ice cream parlour expecting to roll up her sleeves and get to work tidying and cleaning.

336

She looked startled when she came through the door, seeing them all standing there, waiting.

And seeing the whole of Franchino's gleaming, fresh and new.

They all burst out shouting at the same time. 'Surprise!' Irene cried out, and Arthur was already starting folk off giving three cheers, and Mavis was beginning a ragged chorus of 'For She's a Jolly Good Fellow'. Perhaps they could have coordinated their noisy welcome a little better, but their chaotic hullaballoo gave Bella time to absorb her shock and to take in exactly what had been done to her beloved emporium. She stood there with her mouth agape, simply staring.

The place did look rather smart, Irene had to admit. She wasn't one to brag or feel self-satisfied, but she knew that she and her friends had made a good job of doing the place up.

'This is . . . *amazing!*' Bella gasped out at last, and she sounded like all the wind had been taken out of her sails. Everyone cheered to see her so flabbergasted.

Mavis broke out a bottle of home-made limoncello that had been hidden away with the secret coffee beans, and after a sip of that – prepared so long ago by Bella's poor, dear nonna – she choked and spluttered her way back to being able to speak.

'Oh, you *lovely* people,' was all she could say at first, embracing them all as they laughed and cheered and hugged her back. Returning her embrace, Irene felt teary and shaky. She was feeling relieved by Bella's reaction, and was gratified that they had done the right thing.

'See?' Irene smiled gently. 'Everything is done. You can reopen right away, as soon as you like. Everything is back to how it was.'

Her words came out a little wrong, and Irene winced as she heard herself saying them. Of course things would never be the same again for Bella, and there was no use pretending that they ever could be. Her only hope – the only hope for everyone, in the end – was carrying on bravely, despite the circumstances.

You had to go on and do your best and hope that everything would be better soon. That was the only way to live.

Even Ma Ada was looking quite moved. Her eyes sparkled like frosted wine gums, though this might have been the effect of that delicious, tart limoncello. 'Eeeh, what about another song?' she burst out. She loved it when everyone sang together. Really, they didn't do it enough. She turned to Arthur, who looked startled by her attention. 'You, lad. I've heard you've got quite a set of pipes on you?'

'I beg your pardon?' he laughed and, with partly feigned reluctance, took up centre of attention in the ice cream parlour.

Arthur sang a song from just before the war. It was a song from a movie most of them had seen at the Savoy. A song that Arthur, in his capacity as torch-bearer and usher in the aisles, had stood and listened to perhaps a hundred times or more. And, just as Judy Garland had given herself to the song heart and soul, so Arthur did now, singing a capella in front of the frothy coffee machine. He sang 'Over the Rainbow' with great panache and had the whole lot of them in floods of tears.

'Thank you, my love,' Bella told him, enfolding him in a huge hug when he had finished and the rest of them hollered and cheered for more. 'And you,' she added, drawing Irene into their embrace. 'I know that this is all down to you, Irene Farley. Thank you. I'm so glad you came here, into all of our lives.'

It was all so wonderful. Everything from now on was going to be just fine, Irene realised.

And after the high spirits, the lemon liqueur, the ersatz banana splits and the strong, dark, roasted coffee, it was time to wander home again to the Sixteen Streets.

Bella, Arthur and Mavis went their own way, wending happily off to their own slightly rougher neck of town. The ARP warden shouted at them on Ocean Road for making such a boisterous racket and they jeered at him, laughing and bowling along in the brisk spring wind.

The Farleys ambled along together at Ma Ada's less energetic pace as twilight thickened and the stars came out over Tynemouth.

Sam linked arms with Irene on her left side, and Beryl crooked her arm through hers on the right, and Irene felt her heart rise up joyfully at this. Never had she felt this included and at home.

She had gone from being on the outside of this family, shy and young and a bit too soft, to feeling like she was right at the heart of the Farleys. She belonged, and she felt tougher and older and more ready for whatever life was going to bring her next.

This warm, confident feeling made her next decision much easier to make.

'Well done, you, missus,' Beryl said to her, as they went along the darkening streets. 'You did a good job there.'

Irene just smiled and squeezed her hand.

'So, what's next, eh?' Beryl laughed. 'Is there anything or anyone you want to sort out next? Or are you just going to take it easy until the bairn is born, hmm?'

She was only gently ribbing her, Irene knew. She was just gently mocking her, for the way she had quite forthrightly tried to help Bella. Irene would naturally think of herself as a less interfering body than that. She hardly knew how she'd had the nerve. But it was good, wasn't it? All these people, here in her new town. She had become a part of all of their lives, for both good and bad. Already she had come through quite a lot with them.

And now she knew what she must do next.

'I'm not going to take it easy or sit still,' Irene told Beryl. 'There's something I really have to do and I've only just made the decision.'

'Oh, yes?' Beryl smiled.

Irene nodded determinedly. 'I think . . . it's time for me to go home.'

Chapter Thirty-Two

Before she could set off down south and back to Norfolk, however, she had another journey to make, with Cathy Sturrock.

Irene had found herself promising the landlady of the Robin Hood she would go with her on what Cathy called a mercy mission.

'Bob's in a place called Sedgefield,' Cathy had explained. 'It isn't actually all that far away. It's in the countryside and we'll have to take all kinds of buses, through all these pit villages . . . I'd appreciate your company.'

Irene agreed readily. Anything for Bob. 'But I thought he'd been sent further away. I thought he was abroad already.'

'I've made a few enquiries,' Cathy said grimly.

Next thing, they were sitting at the back of a Shields bus together, waiting for it to leave the depot. 'I had to pretend I was his wife to get any proper information out of them, but they coughed up at last. He's in solitary confinement . . . It's what they call the glasshouse . . . Well, it's not as bad as that. They've just got him on his own for a while. They know he's not quite the same as everyone else . . . And even I don't know what you'd call it, exactly. I just know it's not fair to treat Bob the same as they would some deserter or traitor or whatever. He's not like that.'

As the bus trundled south, into the leafy hills of County Durham, Irene was wondering how wise they were to be interfering in Bob's life. It would be good to see him, though. She loved the idea of seeing his soft, dimpled, smiling face. She'd baked him a small portion of spicy parkin, using as much of the week's sugar ration as she dared. The small square of cake was wrapped in paper in her bag. It seemed a humble offering to take to a man who must be out of his mind with worry.

'They've still got him locked up in solitary?' Irene asked. 'Ada would go crazy if she knew that. She'd be down there, shouting all the odds.'

Cathy nodded. 'Then perhaps it's just as well that she doesn't know. We might be more effective.'

'I thought I was doing right. All I wanted was to see Megan. I didn't understand why she'd gone away. I wanted her to explain to me . . .'

The two women had been allowed to sit with Bob in his cell. It was a horrible, gloomy place. Irene thought it would be a shame to put cattle in a place like this, let alone a good man like Bob.

Cathy was even more formidable than Irene had thought. She'd managed to get them both in here for an unscheduled visit. It was as if people didn't dare say no to her.

'Bob, Bob man, you have to give up on Megan. She doesn't want you anymore, and I doubt that she ever did . . .'

Irene was alarmed to hear the landlady speaking so boldly. Bob stiffened and his face became even more hangdog. 'I know that now. I realise that now. She and her family . . . they didn't want to see me. They got the polis on to me, didn't they? They reported me, as soon as they could and got me taken away.'

Irene watched the two of them – the landlady and the pot man – and she felt a bit like a spare wheel as they huddled together. She felt like she was observing a very intimate scene. She let them murmur and chatter and she tuned out for a while, moving to the window and staring out at the empty hills receding into the distance. It was spring out there, and the air would be cool on her face if she was out in those fields. Suddenly she was longing to be out. This place was hideous and she didn't know how Bob could stand it at all.

She heard Cathy lulling him with her words: 'When all of this is over, and you get out of here, you must come to me. You must come to live with me at the Robin Hood. They'll say we're living in sin and I'm much too old for you, but really . . . I think it's about time we did, don't you? Come on, man. Life's too short to throw our time away on people who don't care about us.'

And Bob was allowing himself to be held and he was murmuring, but Irene couldn't quite make out his words. Would he give up on his wife Megan as easily as all that? Would he really go to Cathy Sturrock instead? Cathy was laying out her love so plainly and honestly and offering it all to him. It was actually quite hard to listen to. Could Bob even understand what his landlady was saying to him?

Irene didn't know. She just watched him being hugged by Cathy and felt her heart going out to them both.

Mostly they were quiet on the trek back home to South Shields on the little country bus. Quite content in each other's company and watching the sun playing over the fields of swaying grass. Less picturesque were the villages with their pit wheels and soot-darkened buildings, and the little huddles of pit ponies standing together with their blinkers on, looking lost in the sunlight.

'That's us, that is,' said Cathy Sturrock. 'The likes of us. We're just like them poor little horses they put down underground to pull the wagons full of coal. They live out their lives shunting back and forth and that's all they really see, the darkness of those hideous tunnels and endless work. That's the way life's meant to be for us, too.'

Irene listened and looked through the bus's smudgy back window at the receding sight of the ponies. She didn't think much of the comparison. It seemed a gloomy kind of thing to say.

'And sometimes we get out in the open air,' Cathy sighed. 'We get to glimpse a bit of sunlight and breathe some fresh air, and we can hardly bloody believe it. It makes us dizzy and sick because we're not used to it. And so we stick huddled together, trying to ignore the sunlight and freedom. We're happiest keeping our blinkers on. We're happiest sticking to the darkness we know.' Then she looked fiercely at Irene. 'But that's not good enough for us, hinny. We need to be happy and we need the sun and the air. It's no good just settling for misery in this life. You have to be brave and fight for your happiness.'

Irene thought about this. 'I hope . . . I hope that's what I do. I don't like being gloomy. I don't like to dwell on things.'

'Just you learn the value of everything you've got, lady,' Cathy Sturrock told her. 'That man of yours and your baby on the way. And the family that you have: the family that you love. You make the best of all of them.'

'I will,' Irene nodded at the landlady.

'I mean it, pet. Love is all that counts in the end. Love is the only thing that matters.'

Chapter Thirty-Three

It was several days before Irene could tell the story of how she travelled down to Norfolk on her own.

Dear Tom,

The journey wasn't easy!

I thought it was bad enough, when we travelled up the country together to the north-east. Do you remember? Last autumn? I'd never been so far in all my life and I couldn't believe that it just went on and on. And then we heard the whispers of the bombs and everything that was waiting for us. Tyneside was so dark when we arrived in Newcastle. I'll never forget that night. Dragging our belongings through the street as the night exploded. Then meeting your family for the first time!

At least I wasn't heavily expecting just then! I wasn't like this!

It wasn't spring, either. This time I was sweating cobs all the way in those stuffy carriages. It was a relief to change trains and I got a chance to sit on a platform at York or Peterborough for a little while in a cooling breeze, watching everyone else hurry by with their bags and loved ones. I felt like I didn't belong to anywhere, or to anyone. Is that how you feel too, when you travel alone from place to place? It's like disappearing between the cracks somehow.

I'd gathered together all the bits of money I'd saved to buy my tickets. Everything is dearer than I expected it to be. Your mam helped me out a bit, whispering that I should never tell the others I was getting a handout. She's soft-hearted, really, isn't she? No, that's not quite right. She isn't soft exactly. But she does care.

I felt like I'd disappointed Ada in a way, though, by going away by myself. Even though I said that it wasn't going to be for long.

'Where will you have the bairn, though?' she asked me, a few times. I realised that she wants me to get back north so I can have the baby there. She doesn't want to feel left out when it happens.

All I was thinking about was coming down here and seeing my own ma.

Ada made me sandwiches with a heel of bread and cheese and precious slices of tinned ham. She wrapped them in greaseproof paper and when she gave them to me, I felt all choked up. She called me 'hinny' for the last time and sent Sam with me to the station. He said, 'I don't know why we're letting you do this by yourself. Our Tom will go mad when he hears we've let you travel alone.'

But you won't, will you, Tom?

You'll understand, I know.

Sam waved me off with Mavis at Shields station and then they went off for coffee together, and once I was alone with my big and little bags and my huge bump I started to think: can I even manage this? Have I been a bit foolhardy?

Oddly enough, that was just what I was thinking when I made my journey up the country with you. Had I bitten off more than I could ever chew? Remember how I insisted on coming to live with your family? You thought I was crackers. We even argued on the train coming up. Our first proper argument!

But I think I managed OK.

And then . . . I was heading back to what you called the back of beyond.

All those stations: Darlington, York, Doncaster, Peterborough. Then the long stretches through the empty landscapes between King's Lynn and Norwich. By then it was late in the day and the moon was out and there were no lights. It was like travelling across the bloomin' moon. And the train was much emptier. It was rocking me to sleep. I woke up in Norwich, at the end of the line, and there I had to find the bus and the driver had to help me on with my bags. Telling me I was lucky. I'd only just made the last coach to Holt.

Winding and winding through those country roads outside the city. It went on and on. Trees loomed out of the flat fields. Those trees that you said looked like they were pulling on jumpers over their heads! Do you remember? Back when we were courting. Those lopped off trees with the ivy wrapped round them in thick swathes and their mantles of summer foliage: you said they were pulling on jumpers, that's how they looked to you. It was for saying things like that that I loved you, I realised.

Holt was always the big town to us. It was where we'd go for special things. Fancy clothes. Special supplies. We even went to a show there once. And now when I arrived, late on Saturday night, I saw how small it really was. I felt like I was seeing it all through your eyes, and how remote and tiny it all must have seemed, the first time you came here. But it's home to me, or near enough.

I was left in the main square with both my bags and I had no idea how I would get home from there. It was too late to catch a ride with anyone, of course.

346

There was only one thing for it.

All I could do was walk all the way home. All the way down the rutted dirt road, on and on past familiar fields. They're bursting into life with the spring, but everything's dark and asleep in the night. I saw little bright yellow eyes blinking at me from the hedgerows. All the creatures out and about doing their usual business. Seemed like everything has carried on here as normal, just as it has for hundreds and thousands of years. All the birds and the beasts chasing each other round endlessly. They don't care about wars or the comings and goings of people, or any of the things that we think are important.

It was quite tiring. All that way on foot. I had to keep stopping and changing hands with my bags, because one was much heavier than the other. I was worn out, but funny thing was: I never felt miserable. I never felt like lying down and giving up. I knew I was getting closer and closer to home. I knew every inch of this land like the lines on the palm of my hand. I knew just where I was heading to and that place was calling me on and on.

I got awful blisters.

And at last. The village. The muted golden lights of the windows under the thatches. The gently smoking chimney pots. The stirring of the sheep and goats tethered on the green. The snorting of horses. Every single one of them seemed familiar to me.

Eventually, home.

My sisters were all long abed in the attic. It was so late. I was dead on my feet. Crawling indoors. Falling into an uncomfortable chair by the dwindling fire. My ma was fast asleep in their room. 'She needs all the healing sleep she can get,' said my da gruffly. 'What kind of time do you call this?'

Like I'd been out having fun! Like I was late because I'd been out carousing! I turned on him to snap right back at him.

347

He wasn't getting away with that. I'm a grown woman now, and I don't have to put up with his nonsense anymore. But when I turned to bark at him he was pouring me tea from the battered old familiar pot and there was a look on his face so helpless and so full of gratitude for me being there that my heart just melted. He's glad, I thought. Da is glad I've come back here tonight, and he just can't find the words. He's one of those people who always puts things wrong, and never finds the right words. Well, we can all be like that, can't we?

I just took the tea off him and smiled. And I told him I was glad to be home.

And now I've been here for several days. I've been writing little dribs and drabs to you when I get a spare moment, when I haven't had the six kids hanging round me, wanting this or that, staring at my bump. Or up to my armpits in all the washing that's been building up.

I spent a whole afternoon running things through the mangle in the backyard and pegging out the line. And seeing to Da, and seeing to Ma. The good news is that she's on the mend. It's nowhere near as bad as Da made me think. She'll be back to full strength eventually, but not just yet. They still need me here, doing my bit, and I'm happy to. For now, anyway.

The whole village has been round to take a look at me and my swelling belly. They've all cooed and ahhed and patted me and asked me to tell tales about my travels in the north. At night my sisters gather round in the attic and I tell them stories like I'm reading them fabulous tales out of that wonderful old golden annual I used to have many moons ago. Remember me telling you all about that?

But now when I tell tales of Marine Park and the rocks of Marsden Bay, or the Roman remains or Franchino's ice cream parlour or the biscuit factory down by the docks that gives vent to that lovely sweet-smelling smoke . . . all of that sounds like some kind of fairy tale to me.

They hold their breath when I describe the bombs falling on streets and throwing up huge fires into the night. I tell them how we sat underground, singing songs together to drown out the noise. I describe everyone I met in the north and I make all the characters a bit larger than life, and I try to do the accents to make all my sisters laugh. Now they all go round calling each other 'hinny' and 'pet' and they laugh hysterically at the silly words.

Oh, this letter has gone on long enough! You won't be able to read a word! I've gone criss-crosswise and diagonally, up and down on every side in order to save paper, and it'll take you ages to untangle it all. I'd best finish up here, my love. And I hope that it won't be too long before I see your lovely face again.

Yours with love forever,
Irene x

Chapter Thirty-Four

Weeks slipped by and Irene was run off her feet, helping out at home and seeing to her mother. Her sisters surrounded her with their clamour, and her da asked her if she'd mind staying just a bit longer, and then just a bit longer again. Her ma was definitely getting better, but only slowly, and she still needed all the care she could get. Would Irene mind staying on to help out? 'Of course not, Da,' she answered readily.

Summer began and everything was mellow and ripening under the wide Norfolk skies. Irene almost lost count of the weeks she had been away from her new home in the north. It was like being lulled into forgetfulness. Whole months went by and while her mother got stronger Irene grew larger and slower until it was just about time for the baby to be born.

And then came something that woke Irene up with a shock.

It was a telegram, brought all the way out here, into the wilds, by a lad in a van. He drove all the way from Norwich, just to bring her the message. As soon as they saw the vehicle approaching the house, it was obvious that it wasn't bringing good news.

Irene stood shaking in the doorway. Her fingers trembled as she opened the flimsy envelope. Her da was standing just inside the dark interior of the house, watching her every move as she told the lad: 'There's no reply.'

The telegram boy nodded stiffly and hurried away, back to his van. What kind of reply could there have been? What was she supposed to say to the news she had just received?

'Lass?' her da asked, touching her shoulder. He was braced for the worst, she could tell. But it wasn't the worst. Not quite.

'H-he's missing, Da. That's what it's saying.'

Her dad's expression wavered and she watched his pale eyes trying to focus, as he worked out what she meant. 'Missing?'

'His plane w-went down . . . And they think he got out. He parachuted, they think. They think he might have been taken prisoner . . . maybe . . .'

Awkwardly the old man was trying to hug her, as they stood there in the doorway. Her huge belly was getting in the way, of course, and she felt suddenly self-conscious. The old woman in the next garden was having a nosey over the hedge to see what the news was. 'Let's get inside,' she told her dad.

All her sisters but one were out at school, and she was glad of the quiet in the house. Irene flopped down on the nearest chair and read through the telegram again. It was so short and opaque. She could barely make sense of it. 'But where did he parachute? Over Germany? France? Somewhere in the Channel? It doesn't give any kind of clue, Da . . . It hardly says anything at all . . .'

None of it seemed real. She was trying to conjure a sense of Tom in her mind. She was summoning up all her memories of him: the feel of him, the closeness of him. As if these sensations could summon him up like a ghostly presence, perhaps, and make him materialise in front of her. It was so hard, trying to imagine that great big solid bulk of her man simply vanishing. She couldn't imagine him being lost forever in some foreign land.

'They can't give you any proper details, girl,' her da said gruffly, fumbling with the copper kettle at the fire. 'It's all secrets that they gotta keep.'

'I know,' she nodded. She sat very still and wondered what was going to happen next. Did Tommy's own ma know about this yet? Would Ada have had her own telegram like this today? Was that how these things worked? There'd be wailing and moaning at Number Thirteen, when the impact of this news was felt. Suddenly Irene felt like she ought to be up there, in the north, waiting with them all – with all the Farleys – for further news of her Tom.

When she went up to her mum's room, moments later, she voiced this thought.

'How on earth are you going to make another journey north in the condition you're in, girl?' said her ma, caustically. Irene knew that when her ma sounded harshest, it was when she was feeling things most keenly. She might look furious, but inside she was heartsore for what Irene was going through. 'You can't go dashing about any more. You have to stay here with us. Have your bairn and sit it out. You just have to wait for news and look after yourself and your unborn baby.'

Irene knew that her mum was talking sense. She looked a little less peaky today, as if the flush of adrenalin that she'd got from the terrible news was actually doing her some good.

'You're right, of course,' said Irene. 'I can't go dashing anywhere just now.'

'Look after yourself, Irene,' said her mum. 'You're the one who comes first just now.' She took hold of her daughter's hands and squeezed them. It was the closest to giving an actual hug that she ever really came. 'Listen to me, will you? I'm sure your Tom will be fine. He's a strong, strapping lad. Even if he's been taken prisoner, or been injured . . . I'm sure he'll be fine. You two are meant to be together. I felt that, the first time I met him, when you brung him in here to meet your old da and me. I thought – them two, they're gonna last forever, they are!'

Irene chuckled at this, despite herself. Her ma hadn't looked like she was thinking anything of the sort! That first time she'd brought Tom to visit – all the way out here to what he called the back of beyond – her ma had looked frankly sceptical at the dapper young airman. She had frowned at his accent and pulled faces at his easy affability.

'Everything will be absolutely fine, our Irene. I'm telling you that – and, as you know, I've got gypsy blood on your grandma's side, so I know all about seeing into the future. So, just you harken to what I say! You just carry on and have your baby in peace, and stop worrying. You have to keep on hoping. You just keep writing your letters to that lovely young man of yours . . . and don't you ever dare give up hope! Do you hear me? Don't you ever dare!'

Perhaps it was the shock of receiving the news, or the worry that followed it. Or maybe it was Irene's moment for having the baby anyway. Either way, it wasn't long after the telegram came that she started having excruciating pains and sensations that she had never felt before.

That afternoon she stopped what she was doing and it seemed that time itself suddenly slowed down. She thought she heard a roaring noise in her ears that blotted out all the usual hullaballoo of her sisters and everything else in their home. It was a long, dragging sound like surf up the shingle of the beach. It was the roar of pain approaching and blocking out everything else.

She sat down on the settee in their living room and said in a very clear, decisive voice: 'I think my baby's coming.'

And then the pains began in earnest. There was no mistaking what they meant. It was her time. Right now, this very moment.

This was her time and her baby was about to appear. Her mermaid was swimming to the shore.

It was a very warm day and there was only the slightest breeze ruffling through the opened windows. Irene's mum was up and about again, feeling better than she had in a number of weeks. Almost at full strength, in fact. Which was good, because she was going to need every iota of her strength to help deliver her first granddaughter that evening.

Irene went into labour before her da could even get the kettle onto the hob to boil or fetch clean towels from the cupboard. The old man was last seen scuttling off in the direction of the Honeybell pub to sit with his cronies. His idea was to sit the whole messy business out, just as he had done with the birth of all his own babies. Let the women deal with it all, he thought, stopping briefly on his way across the village green to knock on old Ma Parkin's door. 'Baby's coming,' he told her, briefly, and then considered that his grandfatherly part in the process was over and done with. He could hear the screams coming across the green and he couldn't stand it.

This was woman's work, and he'd gladly step out of the way until it was time to come and inspect the new arrival. Till it was time to toast it with a nip of whisky.

The old man shook his head as he scurried to the pub. That young lad, where was he? It was just too awful, the thought of where he might have ended up.

He should be here, right now, waiting on news of his first born. It wasn't fair on their Irene that her man was God knows where.

Just as her ma had suggested, Irene carried on writing to Tom, just as if she expected he could read her letters, same as always. Best to carry on in hope.

She had news to tell him. The best possible news, and she just had to hope that he was going to be able to hear it.

Dear Tom,

We are both fine. That's the first thing.

Marlene was born in the early hours of this morning at my parents' house. Mum's usual midwife came all the way from Holt and she was just in time.

She's eight pounds and seven ounces – the baby, that is, not the midwife. She's a whopper. And she's perfect, Tom. She's absolutely perfect. Our little mermaid, with a scrap of gold blonde hair and the bluest eyes. But she hasn't shut up screaming all day long. I can tell that she's going to be a handful in the future.

The midwife said it was a rare, easy birth. I was no bother at all. I felt proud of that, which is silly, really, I know. But everything was bang on time and with a minimum of fuss. Not even that many stitches afterwards.

I won't go into details. I know men don't want to hear all that.

I'm not having another one, though, I'll tell you that right now. Even though you've made it plain you want two, three, four kids. You can have them yourself if you're all that bothered!

But maybe that's just how I feel today.

Oh, but if you could see her, hinny.

There's nothing – just nothing – like lying here with her in my arms.

Marlene. I don't know where the name came from. Well, I do. The films. It's a name straight out of the Savoy cinema at the Nook, but we can say it the English way if you like. I think it sounds lovely, exotic. I hope you don't mind that I've chosen already, without you. I had to call her something.

It's strange being here, with my parents and my sisters and not you. They're all going round quietly like I've suddenly

*changed. They approach the bairn like they're in awe, though
goodness knows, there's been enough childbirth around this
place over the years. It's hardly a novelty . . .*

*She's something special, though. And it's not just because
she's our very own. She's really something very special on her
own account.*

Our Marlene.

*All our love to you, Tom,
Irene and Marlene*

Chapter Thirty-Five

How much time had passed exactly? She couldn't be sure. Time seemed to move differently here, to how it did in the north. In South Shields everyone kept moving quickly and life went by at quite a clip. Everyone was in and out of each other's doors, and they kept moving and bustling about, as if there were never enough hours in the day.

Here, in the wilds, out in the sticks, it was just how Irene remembered. And that felt like moving through a different kind of element; it was like wading through a different thickness of time. She found it hard to explain. There was no urgency here. No feeling that someone was going to come bursting in to interrupt your routine.

The days were as long as they needed to be, even when you were busy with all the chores, like Irene suddenly found herself. The sun set in just the same way, with long shadows slanting across the village green, the same as they always had.

There were no bombs, no gunfire, no burning. No sudden death.

She had spent time looking after her mum and nursing her back to health. And in turn, following the birth, her mum had looked after her. Together they had come through some of the biggest moments that a mother and daughter could come through, and it changed things between them. They looked at each other differently, with a new closeness. There was a new light in her mum's eyes when she looked at both Irene and her new baby.

I've changed so much, Irene thought. When I left here last year I was still just a girl. I thought I knew everything. I thought I was a married woman with everything before me. All the future ahead of both me and Tom. I thought I could boss him into taking me north, and that I'd find my place among his folk. I thought I knew everything, but I knew nothing really. I see that now.

I was just what Ada thought she saw, the first time she looked at me. Just a slip of a girl from the middle of nowhere. A girl from the back of beyond who knew nowt at all.

But I've learnt a whole hell of a lot. And I've changed so much. I've had to change. I'm tougher and I know more and that knowledge has come at a cost. And I've got to carry on being strong now, haven't I? For the sake of my bairn and me. Because . . . maybe . . . it's gonna be just us on our own from now on.

It was best not to think too much about the future, and how life was going to be. In the meantime it was best to focus on practical things, simple things, and to ease through the days concentrating on cooking and feeding and washing and healing. The small, practical, comforting things were best.

In the time she had been in the north Irene had improved her repertoire of things she could cook in order to tempt her ma's appetite, and it worked. She used the plentiful vegetables and grains and the few scraps of meat she could get hold of, and stewed up wonderful savoury dishes and she watched her ma getting back to normal again, looking pleased and proud and hungry again. Irene, too, felt better following the birth than she had in recent months.

'Soon be time for you to get back up to your new family,' said her ma once or twice, testing her out. She was wanting to eke her plans out of her. 'You'll take that babby away to show them.'

'Aye, maybe,' said Irene, lifting up the tray of used dishes, hefting the basket of washing that needed to be done. She wouldn't commit herself to saying how soon it would be before she and Marlene left.

The truth was, she didn't really know.

It felt like sinking into quicksand. The old sweet molasses of the past was sucking her down, she could feel it every day. How easy it would be to simply stay here, and pretend that nothing had changed, that Tom had never gone missing, that no one at all was waiting for her elsewhere.

How easy just to sit here feeding baby Marlene and forget that she had ever lived anywhere else.

The child was contented. Her endless cries had settled down. She studied the world through bright blue eyes and seemed to be forming very definite, secret opinions about everything she saw.

Then letters and cards started to arrive. Funny, chatty ones. Pink ones with ribbons and funny animals and cartoons on. Sentimental ones. Beryl and Sam both sent lovely things. A card filled with indecipherable squiggles and rude drawings that seemed to be from Arthur.

The letters of congratulation arrived all mixed up with those expressing consolation and condolences on the news about Tom. No one knew quite what to say for the best. The only thing everyone's notes had in common was that no one was prepared to give up hope for him just yet. Some cards and letters from family and friends expressed this hope more eloquently than others.

Ada wrote very short notes. She always cut straight to the point. 'Welcome to the world, Marlene.' And: 'Your daddy will come home again. You'll see.'

Irene's post – which arrived almost daily – had her in a tumult of emotions. Hope and joy. Those had to be the main things she felt. That's what she decided, in order to cope. She would feel hopeful and joyful above all.

She received a letter in beautiful handwriting that she recognised at once as being Bella's. Bella had taken her time and written her a letter that Irene would treasure all her life. It was filled with congratulations about Marlene, but it was also a heartfelt thank you letter, and it was very elegantly put. In essence it said: 'Thank you for letting me allow myself to live again. Thank you for bringing me back into the world.'

Yes, Irene thought. That's what Bella had needed. That's what we tried to do for her.

We all need help moving into the wider world. We have to take that big step ourselves, into living. But we also need those who can help us on our way.

She worked and thought and mulled it all over, and she enjoyed sitting in the backyard of her parents' old shack at the edge of Hunworth village. The year was warming up and the sun felt wonderful as she sat there. The baby lay in a basket beside her, swaddled up in blankets, kicking her legs against the covers and quietly studying the clouds scudding overhead.

Simple things, like the smell of the yellow grass and the sweat of the horses as they ambled past. The clattering noise of them. And all that wonderful silence and those huge open skies. She had missed all of this in the months she had been away.

For the past week or so there had been no post at all. Not a scrap from anyone. As she sat there, shelling garden peas into an old tin basin she counted up and realised it was four days since she had replied to Ada's last missive. Everything had gone quiet in recent days, as everyone adjusted to the newness of things.

She was sitting on an old chair she'd had as a child. It was very low and had been handmade by her dad. She had sat in this chair reading her books when she was tiny. Even before she could read the words. She sat there very seriously turning the pages and looking so solemn her parents would laugh at her.

The little chair was on the back doorstep of the kitchen, and the warmth of the sun felt wonderful on her face. Marlene was kicking and gurgling happily in the old basket Irene herself and all her sisters had once lain in, and it was almost time for a feed.

It was very still in the early afternoon, when Mealy the cart-horse came pulling his cart, as he did most days, having traipsed all the way from Holt. Irene listened to the gentle clopping and glanced over to watch the massive old creature pass by.

Fresh deliveries from the nearest town. Sacks of flour and bags of tea, this and that. A bundle of post. Maybe she'd have word from her other family: her family in the north.

She blinked.

There was someone sitting on the back of that cart. A figure slouched there, looking quite comfortable. His eyes were squinched up against the brightness of the sun.

Irene dropped a handful of peas into the basin, and the empty pods she'd been shelling. She forgot she was holding anything at all, and the tin bucket hit the brick path with a clang and rolled away, but she paid it no heed.

She was up on her feet all of a sudden.

He, meanwhile, was standing up in the rickety cart as it drew to a halt and he was laughing joyfully.

It was him!

It really was him!

She bent down and picked up her baby in one swift, sure movement. She tugged Marlene free of the blankets and clutched her to her chest and the child didn't even make the slightest sound of surprise.

Then Irene was running down the red bricks of the garden path, her long apron swishing round her legs and the baby hugged in her arms.

'*Tom!*' she yelled out, and ran to him.

He'd come all this way and he'd never even warned her.

'I've come for you. For both of you.' He laughed, jumping down onto the grass. 'I've come to take you both home.'

'But how?' she gasped. 'How are you even here? They said you were missing! They said you might have been captured! Was it a mistake? Did you get rescued . . . Or . . . what?'

He tried to laugh, and ended sobbing low in his throat as he twirled them about gently. He felt thinner in her arms, and when she looked at him closely he was pale and drawn. He buried his face in his wife's shoulder for a moment. Then he chuckled and sighed.

'It doesn't matter. All that matters is seeing you again. And this one. All that matters is that I'm back with you now. I'm back with you both.'

'I'm so glad,' she said, and held the baby between them as he stared in amazement and joy. She felt tears glistening in her eyes. 'I'm so very glad, Tom.'

'Let's go home,' he said, and Irene knew in her heart that home to her meant South Shields now.

Tom took both his wife and his baby in his arms and held them as tightly as he could. It felt like he would never let go of them again.

Acknowledgements

Thank you to my agent Piers and my editor Victoria, and to Olivia, Amber and the team at Orion.

Thanks to Stuart, Jon, Nick, Georgie, Patricia, Steve, Jamie, Johnny, Rylan, Stephen, Matt, Jim, Sue, Anthony, George. Thanks to all the Fambles gang.

And thanks to my Mam, my Big Nanna, and all the women of my family for being inspirational.

Thank you to Jeremy and to Bernard Socks.

If you loved *The Biscuit Factory Girls*, make sure to follow
the saga of the Farley family in Elsie Mason's next
heartwarming novel

THE BISCUIT
FACTORY GIRLS
AT WAR

Home is where the heart is . . .

Beryl was the first bride of the Farley clan, finding a home
in the welcoming arms of eldest son Tony. His charming
voice, kind eyes and the way he truly listened made Beryl
feel valued in a world in which she had always been rejected.

Yet even now, wrapped in Tony's embrace, Beryl has never
quite been able to forget the past she decided to run from, nor
the devastating secret about her family's past she tried to bury.

With Tony away fighting the Jerries alongside his brothers,
it's up to Beryl and her sisters-in-law to keep the family
afloat. Beryl has never been afraid of hard work and the
sweat and toil of a second job working as a welder on
the docks doesn't faze her. But the sudden arrival of a
devastating letter does . . .

Will Beryl be able to hold her family together and face up
to her past? Or will the war take away the one thing she
holds dear – the person she never thought she deserved?

Available in April 2021 in hardback and eBook